THIS
BLOOD
THAT BINDS
US

S. L. COKELEY

THIS BLOOD THAT BINDS US

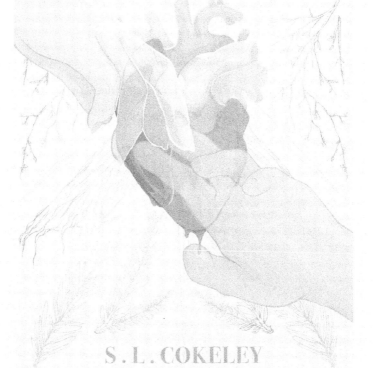

S. L. COKELEY

Cover and Interior Illustrations by Myriam Strasbourg.

Line and Copy Editing/Proofreading by Samantha Pico, Miss Eloquent Edits.

Updated proofreading by Dee Houpt, Dee's Notes Editing Services. October 2023.

Character Art by @Epsilynn

ISBN 979-8-9867119-0-4 (Paperback)

ISBN 979-8-9867119-1-1 (Hardcover)

ISBN 979-8-9867119-2-8 (Ebook)

Original publication October 11th, 2022.

Third edition. October 2023.

Slcokeleybooks.com

Oceanside, CA

Playlist

I Found by Amber Run

Cosmic Love by Florence + The Machine

Little Dark Age by MGMT

My Blood by Twenty One Pilots

You've Got The Love by Florence + The Machine

This Side of Paradise by Coyote Theory

Ship To Wreck by Florence+ The Machine

Paradise by George Ezra

All I Wanted by Paramore

How Big, How Blue, How Beautiful by
Florence+ The Machine

 Scan for more!

*All song recommendations are solely for inspiring readers'
imaginations when reading and sharing the love of music.*

Author's Note

This book and series contains content that may be triggering for some audiences. Please refer to the updated Content Warnings page on my website.

That can be found by scanning here or visiting *slcokeleybooks.com* :

For my dad, the original dreamer, who taught me how to always shoot for the stars and to never give up, my husband, who held my hand every step of the way, and my grandparents, who are, arguably, my biggest fans. I love you all.

One

AARON

T hat was my new life. Prowling through stupid trees in some stupid forest. I could have said stalking, but I hated that word. The night was stagnant as I waded through swarms of gnats and prickly cedar branches. It was like a scary movie—only I wasn't the idiot who decided it would be a good idea to investigate the noise coming from the basement. I was the bad guy. Next, I'd be a cameo in someone's shower.

My legs propelled me farther into the thicket. Twigs snapped with each step, sending a satisfying crunch into my ears. I wished nothing bad had ever happened. I wanted to be a typical college guy, playing shitty video games and getting too drunk on a Friday night, with my only real worries being money or failing all my classes. I wanted to be myself again, but as I walked and reflected, it was apparent my freedom would never come. I couldn't go back.

Up ahead, flickering fire illuminated the trees. Its shadows bounced and danced along the tree trunks. The fire whispered through incoherent crackling and popping. A pine scent hit me first followed by a strong aroma of burning wood. It was a surprise when I could pinpoint the smell of the dirt and decay orbiting my feet. I wasn't used to my stronger senses then.

My body moved forward despite my screaming heart. I was almost close enough to see the source. Warmth pooled in my palms, and I wiped my hands on my pants, anticipating sweat I no longer produced. Butterflies circled in my stomach as I bent over and crouched on my knees. A girl sat on a rock overlooking the cliff in the distance. The blinding, flickering fire highlighted her auburn hair, igniting the long strands that framed her porcelain face.

My stomach sank. It just had to be a girl. I cursed under my breath, wondering why anyone would even consider camping alone. I was the perfect example of what could go wrong. Though, I couldn't blame her for not anticipating a vampire stalking her in the woods. My shaky hands brushed against the rough bark on the tree beside me, my gaze unbroken as I inched closer.

Kill her.

The nagging voice was back. *It* popped into my head after the change, as if It had always been there. A part of me was glad I wasn't alone in my head anymore, but It only came out to antagonize me when I hadn't fed. Whatever It was.

The twigs crunched underneath my boots, breaking my focus. I wrapped myself behind the tree to hide from the warmth of the light. My fingernails dug into my palms, and I tried to get my hands to stop shaking. As I peeked from behind the tree, another branch cracked under my feet. I was really great at being stealthy.

She turned toward the tree line. The fire's reflection glistened in her soulful blue eyes, while her breath caught in her throat. Her heartbeat. It was fast, and growing louder by the second.

Get closer. We need her.

Fear struck deep in my chest. I took a step back, forfeiting a breath. My jaw tensed, and I moved my hands to my face, trying to regain focus. Pushing past everything physical, I walked into the open.

With eyes narrowed, she examined the tree line. "Hey. Private camp-site, and I don't feel like sharing, so . . ."

Her voice was liquid nitrogen injecting into my veins. I was frozen. If I had contemplated it for more than one second, I would have run back through the trees.

You want to kill her. You need to kill her.

It took every bit of strength I had to shut out the voice and drag my heavy body forward. Not only was the voice annoying, but It lied. I kept my eyes glued to her shoes. She'd have a hard time running in those. More pain inflamed my chest as my beating heart hammered against my ribs. *Blood.* I had to stop thinking and think only about blood.

"Stay away from me."

The conviction in her voice made me trip over my feet.

I had to stop thinking.

That's right. Stop thinking. Let me take over.

I wanted to listen, but letting *It* take over wouldn't help me. It hadn't before.

Tracking her feet as she backed farther toward the cliff's edge, I took another step. Her heartbeat was loud in my ears. I studied the way it fluttered in a consistent rhythm. Darkness of the night overtook the warmth in her eyes, her terror tearing my chest open.

Something deep inside me lit on fire, igniting my body from head to toe. My brain shutdown, instinct took over. Her heartbeat. Her skin. Her blood. They called to me. I lunged, grabbed her shoulders, and pulled her closer. I needed her closer.

Before I went for her neck, she twisted my arm and pinned me into the dirt. I wasn't ready for her to fight back. I hadn't even thought of the possibility. One part of me wanted to tackle her, the other part wanted her to run. Her yellow coat flashed in my periphery before disappearing into the dense brush behind me.

Instinctively, I followed her reverberating footsteps. It took no effort to catch up with her. Everything was easy in my new body. I wanted her to run faster, to disappear into the trees where I could never find her. She should have pushed me off the cliff when she had the chance.

That was the last thing I remember thinking for a while.

The other part of me took over—the dark, scary, ominous part I liked to pretend wasn't there. The Thing I was sharing a body with begged me to feed *It*.

In seconds, our chase was over. Our bodies collided onto a rugged patch of dry leaves and dirt. I pinned her arms beside her as she thrashed for leverage. Her fingernails dug into the soil. I went for her neck. My body moved as if it was an instinct. An instinct born of something foreign. It took over every thought. Every nerve. Blood was all that was left.

The taste rocked me momentarily. It was everywhere at once. Everything I could ever want but better. The numbness took over. Her cries were silent in that weird in-between place. Dull was the pain and any physical senses. It felt good in a strange way, like I could get lost there if I stayed too long. The voice won, consuming me with its carnal desire for destruction and death.

Her heartbeat reverberated in my veins. Electricity shocked my body in the form of fear. The numbness subsided, and the feeling returned to my hands. Like being chiseled from stone, one by one, I could feel my limbs again. As I thawed from that dark place, fear and horror filled my stomach. With every second, I regained my sense of reality.

Her heartbeat caught my attention again. The rapid beating echoed in my eardrums. It was so loud it hurt. Cupping my ears, I stumbled to my feet, then wiped the remnants of blood from my lips. It smelled sweet but tasted bitter.

The forest was quiet, other than bugs buzzing in cadence with my victim's heartbeat. The voice was gone, thrust back into my head somewhere. My feet were moving without my permission. I backed away until a tree branch jabbed me. Only then did I take in the scene fully.

Her body was a few feet away. Her skin was pale, her warmth fading into the damp forest floor. Her bright hair dulled as she lay on the ground.

Instinct told me to run, but my feet were glued to that spot. She was dying. I couldn't leave her there.

Fear and guilt swallowed me whole. My stomach rumbled in pain. Nausea traveled up my throat, and I retched out loud, covering my mouth. Even as a vampire, my body reacted to stress.

I dry heaved until I willed my wobbly legs to move. I wouldn't let her die. She had to live. After rushing to her side, I leaned down to search her bright fleece-lined rain jacket. Carefully, I rummaged in her jacket pockets, praying to myself.

I grabbed her cellphone with shaking hands and pulled it in front of my face. Squinting from the light, I fumbled past the lock screen. The call wouldn't connect. I jumped up, holding the phone in the air until it rang.

Softly, I laid it back in her hand, making sure the connection remained. It was the best chance I could give her. I wanted to stay with her and hold her hand and see life return to her face until help came, but footsteps echoed from behind me.

I left my heart on the ground and disappeared into the forest. My mind still raced, looking for a better solution. I slipped between the trees, hiding just outside of the fire's glow.

An unrecognizable male voice rebounded through the thick tree trunks. "Honey, she's fine. She said she does this thing all the time."

A glimmer of hope sparked a tingling in my hands that traveled to my throat. I thrust a hand over my mouth to stifle the desperate pleas hanging onto my lips.

A woman whispered, "I have a bad feeling. She's out here all alone. I just want to check on her."

A bickering husband and wife, no doubt. I walked closer to them, staying just out of sight.

The man spoke again. "Louise, we can't just have a fun camping trip, can we? You always have to be worrying about something."

"Shut it, Ron."

They were close, heading toward where I had left the girl. The smell of her blood caught in the breeze, swirling around us, the light of the girl's fire still burning.

It was the best gift of fate I'd ever been given. In just a few steps, they'd find her.

Another set of footsteps tore through the forest floor in the distance.

Two more people came running, leaving a path of destruction in their wake. That's when I knew exactly whose footsteps they were.

I ran as fast as I could toward the melody, and a strong set of hands cut off my momentum. They would have sent me flying if not for the firm grip on the back of my shirt, pulling me onto my heels.

My two older brothers stared back at me. Their protective shadow engulfed me, making me feel small. They were still in their sweats and baggy shirts. They must have gone after me right after I had left the house.

"W-What are you doing here?"

"We couldn't let it go. We followed you," Luke said as he towered over me, much like he would when we were kids. His eyes searched me up and down with worry.

"Yeah, fuck this 'on your own' shit," Zach said.

His shoulders fell away from his ears, and he stuffed his hands into his pockets, waiting for me to speak.

Luke said, "Are you okay?"

I was surprised he couldn't smell the blood, but I couldn't either. I had run farther than I thought.

"I think so. I'm all right." I lowered my gaze.

"Did you do it?" Zach's eyes darted to Luke. "You know, drink blood?"

Two months into being a vampire, and that sentence still sounded wrong in my ears.

"Yeah, I did . . . and it was fine. It's all fine."

I couldn't tell them about the girl. What would they think if I told them I had called 911? Would they be mad? We had to keep a low profile, and that was the exact opposite of a low profile. Soon, rescue crews would scour the grounds—hell, maybe even news crews.

"Can we go?" I blurted. "Please?"

They exchanged another twin telepathy moment, and I sighed.

I turned to Luke, knowing his vote was the only one I needed.

"Please. I-I just wanna go home."

Luke's eyes bore into mine. "Yeah, all right. Let's go."

With one final turn, I gazed through the trees to where the campfire's flickering light was, praying her light wouldn't fade.

Two

Everything was too bright. Too cold. Too loud. Nurses chattering accompanied the heart monitor's soft drum. It took me a few minutes to realize it was my heartbeat.

I opened my eyes. A large poster stared at me from across the room. The hospital. My brain rebooted like a 1990s computer. Pain shot through my arms and into my fingertips as I sat up. My fingers lingered on bandages that clung to my sore shoulder.

It all came back. The adrenaline. The black eyes . . . the fangs. It couldn't possibly be what I was thinking. There had to be another explanation. My thoughts betrayed my own resolve. What else could a man with fangs mean? Could there be another logical explanation? In a loop, I ran breathlessly through the trees until a man—who didn't look exactly human—pinned me down. That couldn't be possible. There was absolutely no way.

The heart monitor's rapid beating echoed as the nurse walked in. I wiped the sweat from the nape of my neck.

"Hello. It's nice to see that you're up. Kimberly Burns?"

She was fluorescent in her pink scrubs with her hair pulled into a clean ponytail.

"Uh, yes." I pulled my shoulders back, feigning a positive mental state. "I feel fine."

"Good, I just need to get some good information from you. Your belongings are right in that bag on the table. We don't have any emergency contacts on file for you in our hospital. Is there anyone you want us to call?"

"Oh, no, actually. I'm okay."

Her gaze lifted from my chart. "Are you sure, hun? We recommend at least a friend be here for emotional support and to pick you up from the hospital."

"I don't have anyone . . ." I shifted in my gown. The only person I could call lived more than two thousand miles away in New York. That disastrous phone call could wait until I had some idea of what had just happened to me. "Really, it's fine. Can you just update me on what happened?"

"You don't remember?" she said, a sharp line denting her forehead.

"I do. I'm just wondering when I'll get to talk to the police."

"The police—honey, you were attacked by an animal."

"No, I wasn't. Someone bit me. A man chased me through the woods and bit me."

She averted her eyes, her lips twisting into a grimace. "Let me go talk with your doctor for a moment. Hold on a second."

Her fluffy pink pen jangled as she left the room, leaving me with the television's low hum. I peeled the bandage from my shoulder and peeked at the jagged bite mark on my skin, a clear indentation of teeth. Oddly perfect.

Drawing in a quick breath, I closed my eyes. My body rejected the thought of it all. The black eyes, the teeth. The face of a man. The feeling of blood draining from my body. I had been awake for all of it. Up until the point my heartbeat pounded in my ears and everything went black for a while.

"Help is coming, sweetie."

I remembered the sound of that sweet lady's voice as she held my hand. She made me feel safe. I was incredibly grateful I had seen her and her husband earlier that day on the trail. She had

even offered me some of their packed food. Despite the sickness settling in the pit of my stomach, the kindness of strangers made me feel secure, even while being alone in that hospital bed.

My eyes opened to the empty room, the walls too close. The four white walls felt like a prison. There had to be another explanation, but an animal attack wasn't one of them. I'd just need to tell them. They'd have to believe me.

With the crack of the door, I pulled my blankets to my chest, savoring the little warmth they held. Every soft breeze of the air conditioner only exposed the rigid vulnerability shaking my entire body.

"Kimberly, I'm Dr. Hendrix. It's a pleasure to meet you." A large man walked through the door.

His muscles pulled at the edge of his doctor's coat awkwardly as he swung the door shut with unnecessary force. His dark umber skin complemented his tight black curls.

I shifted under the force of his gaze. "Nice to meet you."

"How are you feeling? You're a very lucky young lady. You lost a lot of blood."

"That's what they tell me. I feel fine. But my shoulder is a little sore when I move it back and forth."

He offered a small accepting smile. "That's normal. It will feel sore for a week or two. There's some pain medication I'm going to send you home with, as well as some antibiotics. Infection can accompany these types of attacks."

"What do you mean by 'these types of attacks'?"

"Oh, yes, sorry. The nurse told me you were having some memory troubles. That is to be expected after experiencing a traumatic event. Animal attacks are quite common in the area where you were found."

I sucked in a breath. I hadn't anticipated that answer. The word I was looking for was a little more taboo, and I didn't dare say it aloud.

"Memory trouble? No, I was camping in the woods, and a man attacked me. He bit me. I remember it. I even remember what he looked like," I said, finding my voice despite my dry throat.

His hazel eyes panned over me one moment before he took a seat in the chair next to my bed. "Kimberly, you were attacked by an animal. The level of blood loss when they found you at the scene . . . there's no way a human could have caused that. Not with the wound you have."

The lump in my throat went down slowly. My life was disintegrating right before my eyes. One moment, I was doing everything to graduate college, and suddenly, a huge vampire-shaped truck wrecked my life. Was it possible I could have hallucinated the whole thing? Was I the crazy one?

"We didn't find any drugs in your system. Do you have any preexisting conditions? Any history of mental illness?"

"I'm sorry?" I choked.

"Is there anything else that could have caused your lapse in memory?"

His gaze pierced mine. We held a look long enough for me to recognize the emerald flecks in his eyes.

I steadied my voice, trying to quell my heavy breathing. "No, I'm just a little groggy, I think. I don't think I'm remembering everything correctly."

His shoulders dropped from his ears. "Don't worry about that. It's normal."

"Was there anyone else with me? I remember this older woman. She was really nice."

"Yes. This older couple was actually there with you when the paramedics arrived. They said they had seen you on the trail earlier and came to check on you"—the soft morning sun's beams shone through the window and warmed up his features—"and they've already called to check on you, actually."

"That's how I survived the . . . animal attack, then? Because they found me and called for help?"

"We have already spoken to the police about this. Apparently, you were able to call 911 before losing consciousness."

"I-I was?"

I shuffled through the events again. My attacker's black eyes and the extended canine teeth were all that came to mind.

"Yes, you already had the paramedics on the phone when they found you."

I wished that were true. I wanted it to be. I single-handedly fended off my attacker and found the strength to dial the number. But it wasn't true. Everything after the attack was blurry, but everything leading up to the attack was plain as day.

My camping trip began like any other. A five-mile hike in the nature reserve located just a few miles out of town, a tradition I had started in the fall after I found out how truly abysmal finals could be. I prepared for every contingency: bears, unexpected rain, an assault of mosquitos. No bit of my fifty-point checklist could have prepared me for that night.

Once I heard the crackling of branches, I moved toward my tent to get my bear spray from my bag. Fear took over once I saw my attacker. The look in his eyes held me in place, infusing the darkest feeling of despair into me. Once my feet were moving, I hadn't even considered reaching for the phone in my pocket, since I thought I had left it in my bag at the campsite. I didn't call 911. "Right. I think I remember."

I forced out my best smile, pulling the blankets closer to my chest. Chills ran up my spine. I was thankful to be in the safety of the hospital.

"Well, I'm glad that's all cleared up. Your shoulder will be sore for a few weeks. We want to keep you for a few more days for observation, just to monitor for any lingering symptoms of shock or infection."

His words had me sitting at attention. The fear in my bones dissipated as quickly as it had come. "Is there any way I can be discharged sooner? I don't exactly have insurance, so if I'm doing well . . . I'd like to go home."

The corners of his mouth twitched. He wasn't going to find that an attractive option. I didn't either, considering a vampire could have been on the loose somewhere—or maybe I needed psychiatric help—but my brain flipped in cartwheels thinking of the hospital bill. A couple more days was going to set me back until I was at least thirty—and that was a generous estimate.

After some back-and-forth, he eventually agreed, though he had empathy in his eyes and a strong dad aura as he lectured me about the importance of taking care of my wound and looking out for any serious symptoms.

"Do you have any more questions?"

Those words snapped me back into reality. I had nothing but questions that begged to be answered. They danced on my tongue, pushing for my attention. But I wouldn't find them in that hospital bed, racking up a lifetime worth of debt.

I cleared my throat. "Uh, no thank you."

"The nurse will be back in shortly to discuss some follow-up care and instructions for your medication. You get some rest. No more hiking trips for a while—and bring a buddy next time." His voice echoed through the crisp white walls, leaving a deafening silence in his absence.

I was unbelievably confused. The urge to pull the covers over my head and hide expanded by the second, but I had an even greater urge to do that under my own cute strawberry-covered duvet. All I wanted was to nestle into my fluffiest pink socks and wrap my aching shoulder in my heated blanket. My first step was to get out of the hospital.

When the nurse came to talk to me, I sat up straight and softened my voice. I complimented the fluffy pen with the little silver balls. I put on my best fake smile, but I made sure to let some pain through, being a recovering patient, after all. The world was crumbling around me, but I needed to keep my feet steady, putting one very dirty hiking boot in front of the other.

My foot slumped into my thick-soled boot. Normally, I'd cherish strapping them on, but it was different. The usual strength and confidence they lent me was nonexistent as I struggled to pull my laces taut. Everything was sore, and my eyes were heavy. With no one to drop off some clothes, I had to wear out my hiking clothes. A few spots of blood lingered on my flannel, and my shorts weren't covering up my scratched-up knees. My hair smelled of bonfire as I pulled my yellow coat over my shoulders, little clumps of soil littered the floor around my feet. Jaw clenching with the movement, I let out a low groan. I needed more meds to survive the day. The only reflective surface in the room was an empty bedpan, and if I looked anything like I felt, it wasn't worth an attempted look.

The nurse led me out into the hallway, where I glimpsed my neighbors across the hall. Some were my age, asleep with a parent in the chair, their eyelids full with sleep, their arms draped across the armchairs. Others were older, with drooping faces and wrinkles settling into their frowns. I didn't know their stories. I wasn't sure I wanted to.

An older couple caught my attention, who reminded me of the couple I had encountered on the trail before my attack. Hair speckled with gray, wrinkled smiles. Love wafted off them in a way I could feel in the air. A tickle on my skin raised the hairs on my arm. The man lay in the hospital bed, his wife glued to his side. Children sprang from one side of the room to the next until they piled on to the hospital bed. Laughter reverberated through the walls. Their parents ushered them in for a picture, celebrating. Instinctively, I looked away, shielding myself from their light. Their love. My shoelaces snapped against the tile floor, and I stopped.

"Hold on a sec." I called the nurse, who was already a few feet ahead of me.

"Do you want me to take the picture so you can all be in it?" I said, pointing to their phone.

I knew I looked like I had been run over by a truck, but their moment was too special to pass up. The laughter's magnetism forced me to linger in the doorway. I almost hoped they'd say no, but the bigger part of me felt like a small child begging to be included in some way.

"Yes!" The woman's eyes lit up with excitement. "That's so kind."

Her warmth caught me off guard. The room radiated a euphoric energy of happiness and love. I swallowed the lump in my throat and took the phone. The kids clung to their elders, cheek to cheek. Their arms interlocked. Teeth flashed. The room erupted into a cadence of thank yous, laughter, and footsteps.

My nurse greeted me at the door, and we walked in silence down the hall. A hole had formed in my chest, and every time I inhaled, the hole expanded. I counted our footsteps as they echoed along the softer patterns of heart monitors and beeping machines. My phone was lead in my pocket. No one called. No one texted. After a deep, calming breath, I refocused. I wouldn't allow myself to think about it anymore, or I would explode.

Maybe the doctor was right. My memory loss caused some kind of wild hallucination. Meaning it would be safe for me to go back to my dorm without a care in the world. I could just go back to the way things were before. I could continue to work my butt off to get a good job. I could graduate college. It could work. If only my shoulder would stop throbbing.

Three

KIMBERLY

All my life, I've never really been afraid of anything. I suppose when I was a kid I had fears but not the ones most kids do. I feared for my safety. Growing up in foster care was scary at times. Not all foster parents were created equal, and sometimes, just for a season or two, I'd keep my mouth shut to survive. But those times passed quickly in a child's mind. I always had something to occupy myself with. Things I could throw myself into that made unpleasant times pass quicker. But when I grew older, the fear that seemed to hold most others from achieving their dreams never frightened me. Most students fresh out of high school feared the world. It was different for me. I had already seen the world. Seen the dark. For the most part, I had come out unscathed. When I aged out of foster care, I wasn't afraid. When I became part of an annoying statistic and lived in my car, I wasn't afraid. When I got down to my last dime, I wasn't afraid. I wasn't ashamed of being a foster kid. I was proud I could get to where I was on my own.

So, it was no surprise I wasn't afraid of returning to a world where vampires might have existed. If it weren't for my wounded shoulder, I might have let my brain believe I'd imagined it.

Hallucination still seemed like the most likely option of all.

But the bite stared me in the face every time I looked in the mirror. Throbbing. Festering. Not in the normal way wounds would. Tiny blue and red veins bloomed, along with a bruising that grew with time.

I sighed and rubbed the bite's indentation. I had done an extensive Google search on the subject, but I was smart enough to identify humanlike teeth marks when I saw them. I had given up on the thought of it going away. I ruffled my hands through my messy mop of hair and went straight for my closet.

I liked to describe my dorm room as cozy. I used the word as an excuse to splurge for an extra fluffy comforter and twinkle lighting that wrapped around the bed frame, but it was just to atone for my lack of space. A few steps led me right in front of two warm wooden sliding doors I had decorated with Polaroids and book pages.

My heart sank as I looked at the little green plaid dress I had picked up at the thrift store just days before the accident. I had been so excited to wear it to school, pair it with some platforms and maybe a cute hat. That was out the window. The delicate fabric brought the gentle scent of wool and too much fabric softener embedded in the fibers to my nose. I loved that weird smell. Thrift stores were good for much more than finding old books, like furnishing the majority of my wardrobe and my dorm. I grabbed an oversized sweatshirt, denim jeans, and fluffy pink socks to wear with my Docs.

My phone vibrated on my desk across the room, which was only two steps away. My loft bed took up most of the space, leaving minimal room for my desk underneath and a small bookshelf. The plants on my windowsill cascaded down to a mini fridge and covered the tiny cat magnets holding up my reminder notes.

Excitement hummed in my chest as I unlocked my phone. Just a spam email. No new messages. Not even from Chris.

Chris was my suit-wearing best friend, whose dream led him away from the lush mountains to a concrete jungle. The only relationship that had truly stuck after aging out of foster care. I pulled the phone up to my ear, trying to call again. After a few seconds of ringing, I placed my phone into my pocket. Oh well. It didn't matter.

The clock on my desk caught my attention. I shoved my bag onto my good shoulder and left for class. The bag crackled with the new additions I added over the weekend. Taking my only known information about vampires, demons, and general bad guys, I prepped for two approaches. One practical: pepper spray and emergency key chain alarm. And the nonpractical: a wooden cross from the craft section and a wooden stake from the home improvement store. I was grateful *Buffy the Vampire Slayer* had taught me a few things, but I still wasn't completely convinced I was sane. Either way, the additions wouldn't hurt.

My hospital discharge landed on a Friday, a day when I had one class—luckily, it was Public Speaking. I had no issues with missing any curriculum in that class. My professors were more than understanding when I emailed over my doctor's note. I used the weekend to recover. Frantically calling Chris—with no luck—I did whatever I possibly could to convince myself I wasn't losing my mind. I scoured the internet for every animal attack forum and recovery page I could find, a disgusting chore. I did it to find some peace of mind, but there was nothing. No Google images of a bite mark with bruising and little blue veins.

My calves ached in sync with my throbbing shoulder. Every step hurt as I sped down the busy hallway of Johnson Hall, a long corridor with high arches and light peeking through the windowsill at the end. It was the longest hallway our college had, and the end of that hallway just happened to be my writing class. I glanced at my phone. I'd make it just in time. My body was still sore, and I cursed myself for not accounting for my slowness.

As I reached the end, dirty-blond disheveled hair caught my attention. A vague sense of familiarity set my nerves on edge. My feet stopped before I knew what was happening. Standing twenty feet away from me was the monster that had haunted my dreams since Thursday. He

18

strolled with a group, two other guys at his side. One of them had to have made a joke because they were all laughing. His white teeth glistened in the morning light, and my stomach sank. Their laughter carried up the walls and up to the ceiling. His eyes . . . just brown. No hint of darkness from before.

It was him. That vampire was at my school. In my hallway. My heart kicked my ribs, and I ducked behind the person in front of me. My jagged breaths were getting me weird looks as I clawed my way against the flow of traffic. I wanted to run back to my dorm. But my class door was open, and I had already used up all my sick days when I got the flu that winter. Missing meant dropping a letter grade. That wasn't an option for me.

I spun, just in time to watch him disappear in the room two doors down from mine. He hadn't seen me. Just as the clock hit nine o'clock, I reached my classroom door and funneled inside. In a haze of exhaustion and wind-blown hair, I found my usual seat next to Mikayla. She wasn't someone I had considered a friend because we never hung out outside of class. I'd tried to invite her for coffee a few times, but it never amounted to anything. She always bailed at the last minute. But she was nice and praised me on my class presentations. Plus, small talk was her specialty.

"You look like you've had a rough day." A pointed smile played on her lips.

I ignored her, my eyes glued to the door. Every muscle in my body was on high alert, waiting to sprint out the door. I thought about saying something, but what would I say? He didn't look the same as he had in the forest. His cheeks were rosy, his eyes bright and full of life. Could I have been hallucinating again? Was I absolutely sure it was the same guy? I wasn't even one hundred percent sure there was a guy.

"Are you okay?" Mikayla watched me with a crooked thick brow.

I loved her Lily Collin-esque brows, and constantly gave her tips on how to enhance them.

"What gave it away?" I forced a smile, still short of breath. Blood pumped in my ears, and my hands shook. I willed my feet to walk to my chair and take a seat.

Our classroom was one of the least memorable on the campus. While some had stadium seating, wooden arched ceilings, and thick-framed paintings, this one must have been a broom closet at one time. It was smaller than my other classrooms, and the desks were old. Mikayla smiled. "Definitely the hair."

I chuckled. "Thanks. I woke up late this morning."

"Oh, I've been there. There's no shame in that. It's just unlike you. You're usually so polished," she said, reaching for her binder from her purple school bag hanging on her chair.

Mikayla eyed my university sweatshirt in her peripheral. She wasn't wrong. I loved dressing up for class and feeling confident. But confidence was miles away, floating down the river in the nature reserve.

Forcing my brain to focus on the present, I mirrored her movements. My fingers pulled the binder from my backpack and plopped my pencil bag on our table, the sound inaudible under the noise of the classroom.

Our professor had yet to arrive. I scanned the door. My forearms ached with tension, and I used my palms to try to get them to loosen.

"So, how was your weekend?" Mikayla said.

"My weekend?" My heart jumped into my throat.

"Jeez, too much coffee this morning?" Her voice was perky, but her eyes held no emotion as she flicked through each page in her binder. She stopped to point at the whiteboard.

In bold black letters, the board read, "Write a single page, front and back, explaining what you did this weekend."

I choked on the irony, covering my mouth for a cough.

"Didn't you say you were going camping or something?" She pulled her mechanical pencil out, clicking it a few times to move up the lead. "How did that go?"

"Oh, yeah. It was . . . great. Pretty uneventful. I read a lot. So, that was good."

My stomach twisted. At least it wasn't a complete lie. I pulled a piece of paper from my book bag, eyes still trained on the door, my only escape route.

"Well, that's way easier to write about than mine. I spent the entire weekend helping my boyfriend move into his new place. He was too cheap to pay for a moving truck, so we made, like, fifty thousand trips in my Fiat. Apparently, his brother stole his car, and his landlord wouldn't let him have an extension on the move-out date. It was so annoying." Mikayla groaned, resting her head on her hand. I was thankful for her long, detailed stories and lack of attention.

"Wow, that sucks. At least you guys can enjoy your weekend this week, right?" I gripped my pencil and concentrated on writing my name and the date in the left-hand corner.

She sighed, her brows pinching. "Maybe. I told him I wanted to go on an actual date. No more bars. He gets way too drunk, and I have to drive him home."

Our professor walked through the door and unloaded her materials from her rolling briefcase. "Good morning, class."

"Good morning," we both grumbled, along with just a few others in class.

I dug my pencil into the lines of my paper, leaving a little pile of lead. I could just jot down a quick lie for my warm-up, but my eyes kept floating to the door.

Out of all the places, the guy went to my school. What kind of hideous trick of fate was that? It was possible he wasn't a vampire at all. If it weren't a hallucination, he could be some kind of lunatic. For all I knew, there could be a cannibal cult running around, drinking blood. Somehow, that was the more likely scenario.

But something was still wrong with my shoulder. No amount of hiding could change that. It had no pus, no redness. Just these weird little veins that kept growing.

Before I knew it, the professor was doing her rounds, grabbing up our warm-up assignments. My page was still blank as I reluctantly passed it to her. The professor eyed me with disapproval. Warm-ups were meant to be an easy grade.

Not one word could I memorize or write during the class. I pretended to write most of the time, while violently scratching up my paper and glancing at the door every five seconds. The feeling rolling around in my stomach was confusing. On one hand, I was terrified. Obviously. A potential psycho was walking around my campus, and I still wasn't sure of how dangerous he could be. But another small part of me was relieved. If he was a vampire, then that meant I hadn't hallucinated, and maybe—just maybe—I could get a real answer about my shoulder.

My head hurt as much as my bite. That was the problem with fiction propelling itself into reality. Possibilities were quite literally endless. No matter which way I turned, I didn't have a good answer of what I should do, and I had no one to ask. No mentor. No parents. My only friend was still ignoring my phone calls. I could go to the police, but what good would that do? I'd be safe, but would I just be putting a bigger target on my back? Was my shoulder problem even something a doctor could fix?

I counted the tiles on the ceiling. One by one, I counted them until my shoulders dropped from my ears and I could take another breath. I glanced over at Mikayla, who was oblivious to my inner turmoil and picking dirt from under her nails.

The clock signaled five minutes till the end of class, and I prepared myself to go for the door. The only way I could make sure he wasn't some weird mirage or a figment of my imagination was to find him. I was already standing when the professor signaled the end of class. I shoved my notebook in my bag quicker than I thought humanly possible. My heart responded to another troubling thought. Could something be happening to me? Could I be turning into a vampire?

That thought was enough to set my feet on fire. I had to get answers. I had to know one way or another if I had actually seen him.

"I'll see you Thursday?" Mikayla looked up at me through her lashes, her eyes troubled.

"Yeah. See you then." I slung the bag over my shoulder and dashed to the door.

I was close. High on adrenaline, I crashed into a man who came out of nowhere. Stumbling back in pain, I clenched my jaw, my entire arm throbbing from the impact.

"I am such an idiot. Did I hurt you?" A smooth voice cut through the static of chattering students.

A man with dark-brown hair stood in front of me. His dark-green Black Forest University T-shirt stuck out to me. I focused on two little words under the bold black lettering. Swim Team.

"I'm fine." The words came out in one breath. My backpack had been unzipped, leaving my items scattered across the tile floor. Thankfully, the wooden stake hadn't found its way out, but everything else had. Pepper spray? Check. Small wood cross? Check. Taser? Definitely check.

"Here, let me help you." A broad smile danced on his lips before he hid it. With my only good arm, I shoved the scattered pieces of my disastrous life back into my school bag. "No, I got it, really."

He held up my pepper spray with two fingers. "You do not want to forget this."

His overall demeanor was calm, collected. Pieces of his brown hair cast a shadow over his dark eyes. The sides of his head were cropped but still had some length. He watched me with a worried expression, feet shifting in his high-top sneakers.

My focus moved to the door. The pain in my shoulder was so intense it made me forget about my vampire problem for a second. I feared I had let too much time pass. Tracking him would be impossible without catching him in the hallway.

"Are you sure you are all right?" he said, brows furrowing.

"Yes. Sorry, I'm really distracted today. Thanks for helping me with my stuff. I'm pretty sure I'm the one who ran into you."

"It's no problem. It's Kimberly, right?"

"Y-Yeah. Do I know you from somewhere?" I was taken aback, having no idea how he would know my name.

He was unfazed. "I sit right over there." He pointed to the chair in the far left of the room. "Don't worry. No one pays attention to who they go to class with. Well, usually. I'm William."

"Nice to meet you." I smiled, trying to mask the embarrassing arsenal he witnessed in my backpack. I didn't remember seeing his face, but I had never focused on memorizing my classmates' faces.

"I was actually coming to ask you if you had the notes on the final assignment. I was gone that day, and you are one of the only people I ever see taking notes."

"Oh, sure." I turned my bag around and dug for my binder.

My attention wandered back toward the door, where I caught a brief glance of the same tousled blond hair. The vampire was on the move. I dug faster, my sweaty hands struggling to grip the binder in one pull.

"I swear I'm not usually this . . . flustered." I yanked the paper from my binder and handed it to him.

"Flustered? You? I don't know what you're talking about." A toothy smile sprang on his face.

"Thank you. I promise to be more normal. Next time we talk, let's just pretend it's the first time we've met, okay?" I stumbled toward the door, dragging my still-open backpack behind me.

"Next time? Sounds like a plan." He brought two fingers to his brow, saluting me as I left.

I didn't give it another thought as I fought my way into the crowded hallway. I lifted on tiptoes to see ahead. It couldn't have been more than thirty seconds. He was gone, and I was lost in the bustle of backpacks and tired faces, breathless.

Sparing only a moment for the frustration, I went to work on how to find him again. I could wait till next week to find him outside the classroom, but that was days away.

I made my way to the large window at the end of the hall that overlooked the courtyard. Thick walls of black-and-white stone stood like mountains, contrasting with the bright-green grass below. It was more populated than usual. Finals were coming up, with the end of the spring semester drawing near. Everything was lush green, and the campus bloomed with vibrance.

Black Forest University was an old college, which meant a lot of money went into preserving its rich history that was embedded in the gray stone and large windowpanes. Students ducked in and out of the stone archways at the edge of the garden, their books pressed firmly to their chests. Jaws clenched and heads down. The campus's undeniable warmth made me want to spend hours outside watching the breeze blow through the trees.

I contemplated where my vampire would go. Our campus was moderately big. Lots of common areas. Plenty of different classes he could be in. How could I ever find him? The clock tower above chimed, and I looked at the ceiling. It was muffled, but my fingertips vibrated standing directly under it.

I strained my eyes toward the common area across the yard that led to the cafeteria, and with sheer luck or fate, I saw him. He was still walking with the same group as before. Even with just a peripheral view, I was positive it was him from the shiver that ran up my spine. He was real. I wasn't crazy.

Every movement looked so normal. The way his backpack slung across his shoulder, the way he had a skip in his step to his walk. He looked like a regular college boy. Soon, he disappeared around a corner but not before I caught a glimpse of his smile. A smile like that was going to haunt me for more than one reason.

I had to get away. I wanted to run. To do something about the utterly disastrous and dangerous path my life had taken. But I had Biology labs at four. So, I'd need to reschedule my mental collapse until after finals.

Instead, I opted for the next best thing, running on the treadmill. It gave my fight-or-flight response the sedation it needed to get me through the day. Doctor's orders were for me to take it easy, but walking just wasn't cutting it. Within the following days, I'd done nothing but go to class, then run right back to my room. I spent hours and hours combing the internet for anything I could find concerning vampires or strange sightings, and the closest thing I found were online forums where people pretended to be vampires. Cool but not what I was looking for.

I hadn't seen the guy, a.k.a. the Maybe Vampire Psychopath, since that time in the hallway, but it was all I could think about. I couldn't get through the day without ibuprofen and noting all the emergency exits.

It was taking over my life. Every waking moment, I wondered and waited. Any second, he could show up again, and what would I do?

My mind went wild with different scenarios. I could turn him into the police. That option seemed like the safest, but it left me with one problem. What the heck was I going to do about my shoulder? The antibiotics weren't working. I could try to confront him, but that was the most dangerous option of all. Whoever he was, he attacked me. I couldn't trust him to tell me any form of the truth. There were too many variables, and even after writing every way it could play out in my notepad, I couldn't reach a decision.

My calves ached, and I glanced at the little dashboard displaying my run time. Three miles in thirty minutes. Crap. I did the same in twenty-four last week. I smacked the big red button, and my wobbly legs came tumbling to a halt. Still drawing in short breaths, I grabbed my water bottle and brought it to my lips. Empty. Strange. I thought I filled it back up after my warm-up earlier. I added that to the list of the things I wasn't doing at my usual rate of perfection.

I left the long aisles of treadmills and headed for the water fountain. A largely built man dripping in sweat blocked my path, and I stopped just short of ramming into him and falling into a rack of dumbbells. I expected him to say sorry—or anything—but he didn't. He stared at me with lifeless eyes, the muscles in his face completely relaxed. With annoyance and a strange sense of bubbling anxiety, I went to wait in the short line for the fountain, where only one guy stood ahead of me.

"Kimberly?"

My eyes shot up, and I was met by a nonstranger. "William?"

William's cologne hit me first. It was a soft punch that reminded me of rich men golfing at the country club. One of my foster dads loved golfing, and I'd tag along. He didn't look fancy, though. Standard board shorts and a tight-fitting Black Forest University swim shirt that looked one size too small. With his light complexion, he didn't look like he got much sun. If ever.

"You were supposed to act like this was the first time we met, remember?" He was all smiles as he eyed me up and down. "Here, let me get that for you."

He held his hand out for my bottled water, and I obliged despite my sweaty hands.

"Thanks. Did you just get here?"

Not an ounce of sweat gleamed on him.

I tried to wipe mine from my forehead casually.

"Yeah, I'm about to head to practice." He motioned toward the big glass doors that led to the campus pools. Our gym was the most modern-looking building on my campus, equipped with skylights, a new indoor track, and a swimming pool. My guess was that it was a recent build. How the alumni were ever able to survive college without a gym, I couldn't comprehend.

"I'm training for a marathon," I admitted. "It's over in Big Sur."

"Damn. That's impressive." His dark irises dug into mine, pools of dark ink and chocolate.

"It's just running." I grabbed my water bottle, breaking eye contact. "Just something I like to do in my free time."

"It's definitely an accomplishment, considering most college students won't even get up to get the remote to change the channel." He smirked.

I shrugged. "Eh, I do that too. But thank you."

"You seem to be in a much better mood today," he said, moving our conversation from the water fountain. The gym was surprisingly busy for the early morning.

"I am." I lied. My line of sight went toward the front doors. Thankfully, they were sparkly clean and clear, so you could see someone coming from down the street. "You caught me on a strange day."

"Strange?" His jaw clenched, highlighting the strong bone structure along his face. "Well, I hope things are better for you now. Your notes helped, by the way. You're very thorough. Mrs. Castilla talks fast. I have a hard time keeping up."

"That's what I like about her. She is extremely smart, and I love listening to her talk," I said.

The smile on his lips grew. "Listen, would you want to go get some coffee with me after practice? I can bring you back your notes." He propped himself up against the wall with one arm overhead. "I promise fun, interesting conversation."

I snorted. The nineteen-year-old girl in me couldn't help but be a little excited. Mr. Tall, Dark, and Handsome, with the infamous chiseled jaw, was essentially asking me out, but boys were the last thing on my mind. Well, other than one in particular, who, thankfully, I'd managed to stay clear of.

"I can't. I've got to study, so . . ."

He was unbothered, as if he was expecting that answer. "If you change your mind, you know where to find me."

William leaned down, lifting his bag easily with one arm, the trim of his shirt hugging his biceps. He waved before walking toward the pool.

My phone vibrated in my hand and kick-started my heart. I quickly checked for messages. Chris had managed to dodge my calls but sent a text message to me at three in the morning, stating he'd give me a call that day. I could finally tell him about everything that happened. I could let go of everything I'd been holding in and have someone help me decipher my mess. I had it all planned out. I'd start with small talk, a little back-and-forth to catch up, then I'd deliver the news and show him the bite on my shoulder.

I would be lying if I said I wasn't worried. Chris was a practical person. He never believed in things like Santa Claus or the Easter Bunny, even as kids. Once, when I had lost a tooth and did my usual ritual for the tooth fairy, he devised a plan to keep me awake all night so I could see that our guardian, whose name I'd long forgotten, was putting the change under my pillow.

But this would be different. What I was going to show him was actually real.

My heart sank into the pit of my stomach. The text was a coupon for five percent off at my local grocery store. It was helpful but not what I had hoped. The anxiety was getting to me. How much longer could I stand hiding in my room?

The walls of the gym were starting to close in around me. The weight of my secret threatened to pull me onto the sweaty mat flooring. I stopped just short of the front desk, looking back at the pool. William had just left the locker room—shirtless, with compression briefs. Maybe a coffee wouldn't kill me. It might actually be nice to get my mind off things for a minute.

I walked up to the glass doors and waved him over before chickening out. He left his huddle and waddled over to the doorway.

"Yes, madam?" His eyes glowed with expectation.

"Want to meet at Roomies later? Maybe three o'clock?"

He smiled from ear to ear. "I thought you'd never ask."

Four

Aaron

The morning sun made me want to puke. Vampires couldn't get hangovers, but I swear my biological clock was still ticking somewhere inside my undead body, telling me it was morning and I needed to be in bed.

"Look, Aaron, these are handmade banana muffins!" Luke, the eldest by two whole minutes, thrust a fat, fluffy muffin right on my empty plate. "You used to love those, remember?"

I did remember. How could I forget when he dragged me and the rest of my brothers into the cafeteria every single morning to keep up with appearances? We'd walk through the same double doors, bicker, note the menu on the smudged whiteboard against the podium, bicker some more, then scan our school IDs to get a mostly empty plate.

Luke towered over everyone else in line. Not only was he the tallest of our group, but he was the bulkiest. His arms were the size of my head. I knew that because he loved flexing them in my face.

"Hey, Peggy. How are the kids?" Luke said, stopping at the end of the line to talk to one of the cafeteria workers. The edges of the hairs on his neck curled into a mullet, a ridiculous hairstyle he'd started growing since we left home, along with his beard.

Presley, the youngest, grinned and waved a pancake in my face.

"Dude, pass me the syrup."

"No, you're just going to waste it." I sighed and took another step forward, still waiting for Luke to stop holding up the line.

Presley leaned around me. He forced me into the bar, and his curly blond hair grazed my shoulder. "S'cuse me. Don't need that type of negativity in my life."

He proceeded to pour three different syrups all over his plate.

Zach groaned behind me and bounced on each foot, an empty cafeteria tray in one hand and the other shoved into the pocket of his sweatpants. He was wearing his black sunglasses inside, which told me he was still a little drunk. It didn't matter. Vampire or not, Zach and I were dead men walking when it came to mornings.

Growing up, our mornings were chaotic. Lots of cereal and lots of arguing. Once Zach and Luke had graduated high school and moved out, I missed our mornings together. But under the circumstances, it wasn't exactly feeling like the good ol' days.

Zach pinched the bridge of his nose, speaking in a whisper only we could hear. "Luke, please, for the love of God. Can we go sit?"

"I second that notion," I whispered, grabbing a few pieces of bacon and moving them to my tray. I'd been sneaking them to the campus mascot—a big fluffy Great Pyrenees named Pretzel.

Luke said his spirited goodbyes, and we searched for an empty table. The lunchroom was on the second floor, with wide windows spanning the entire dining hall. Beige. Everything except the warm wood around the windows was beige—at least that's what it looked like to me. The sun made it hard to see across the room, but a small table next to the window was open.

Once we sat, my brothers broke into conversation, but my mind wandered. That girl was all I could think about. I'd been constantly checking the local news station but no mention of an attack. More importantly, no deaths.

I had to picture the girl alive. It was the only way I could get through every day. I imagined her as a traveler. A young backpacker, just passing through the area on a soul-searching voyage. She had a large loving family and definitely a protective dad who was worried sick when she turned up at the hospital, but they'd flown out to be with her and took her back home. The memory of what happened would be a distant one, maybe an interesting story she'd tell her kids. She wasn't dead. She couldn't be.

We'd only been in Blackheart for two months, and things were calming down. My brothers seemed happier—relaxed, even. Somehow, I'd ruined everything in the span of a couple of minutes just a few days beforehand. I expected the cops to come through the doors at any minute and arrest me.

Maybe that was why I looked over my shoulder. A strange sensation tickled my spine. Someone was watching me. I scanned the room with no luck. No one was looking at us, and no cops were around.

"Aaron, how are your classes?" Luke's voice snapped me out of my inner turmoil.

"Fine." I shrugged. I moved around the pieces of bacon on my plate, breaking them off into little pieces.

Luke sighed, and guilt bubbled in my stomach like old soda. Luke was trying his best to keep us all together—and happy. But it didn't change anything that had happened.

We weren't some normal, lucky group of brothers who'd decided it would be a great idea to go to college together. Back in Brooklyn, my older brothers never planned on going to college. But they spent all their time trying to ensure Presley and I did. From a young age, they "worked" and helped my mom stay afloat. They never explained what they were actually doing. I wasn't the only one who had a secret. My older brothers had kept the biggest one of all that led to my current plight. A vampire who couldn't eat food, sitting in the cafeteria thousands of miles away from a home I could never return to. We were on the run, and I didn't even fully understand why.

I had no idea how they dealt with the guilt or if they even had any. Judging by the smiles on Zach's and Luke's faces, I assumed everything was easier for them. I was just too soft.

A flash of red caught my attention in my peripheral vision, and I looked toward the line of students walking in and going toward the food bar. I don't know what I'd expected to see, but I never expected to see her.

Cascading red hair fell from her shoulders. Her cheeks were full of life again, and I identified the sound of her heartbeat. Loud and strong in her chest. With my mouth agape, she scanned her card, grabbed a tray, and walked toward the cafeteria line. She looked healthy—happy, even—in her workout attire. A black two-piece gym set, and earphones draped across her neck.

My chest expanded with relief. She was alive. I drew a small quiet breath to expel the erratic excitement that had bottled itself in my chest.

"What's up with you?" Zach said, his dark hair falling into his face. He pulled it behind his ears.

"Nothing. Nothing," I said quickly, stealing another glance in her direction. "I think I just need to go get Presley some more napkins."

She was almost done and heading toward the silverware area in the middle of the room. My body moved before my brain, and I snapped up and out of my chair. I had to talk to her. Just for a minute, to make sure she really was okay.

"Thanks, brother!" Presley chimed.

But I was already halfway to the center island. The girl and I reached it at the same time. She hadn't seen me at first. Her attention was on the silverware.

My heart was in my throat as I struggled to keep my voice calm and soft. "Hi."

She turned to me, and her eyes grew wide. Her heart stuttered, and she lost her grip on her food tray. It clattered to the floor in a mess of scrambled eggs and hash browns.

We both went for her tray at the same time.

"Hey, let me help you." I grabbed napkins and furiously wiped the floor.

"Come closer to me, and I'll scream." Her hands were shaking, her blue eyes filled with determination. "I know who you are, and I know what you are."

She picked up pieces of egg from the floor, and the cafeteria went back to its usual dull roar.

"I'm not going to hurt you! I-I'm so happy you're alive. Are you okay? Like, really okay?"

By talking to her, I knew what danger I was putting myself and my family in. She could belt out my identity at any time and have a mob full of people come to her aid. But at that moment, I didn't care. I had to know she was going to be okay and I hadn't completely ruined her life like mine.

"What kind of question is that?" She stared at me for a moment, looking me up and down. "I'm sure this is a surprise to you, considering you tried to kill me."

"No. No, I wasn't trying to kill you. I can see why you would think that. But that's why I called 911, to save you." Smearing mashed hash browns all over the floor, I attempted to clean up. "I didn't want you to die."

She dropped her fork onto her tray. "You called 911? That was you?"

"Yes! It was an accident. This is all a big misunderstanding."

Her eyes lit with rage. "Misunderstanding? You attacked me."

"You're right. I'm sorry. This is all my fault, and I'd love to explain everything to you if you would give me a chance to."

What was I doing? Explanation was the last thing I should have been doing. But real fear flared in her eyes as she spoke. I wanted to let her know she didn't have to worry. I wasn't going to hurt her again.

"Start explaining," she grumbled, snatching more napkins to wipe the food off her finger.

"This might not be the best place for me to talk about it," I said slowly.

She scoffed. "Why? Afraid someone might find out you're a vampi—"

"Don't say that word! Not here." I prayed my brothers weren't listening to me. We had a strict no-eavesdropping rule, but I wasn't going to take their word for it.

"Why?" she said, her eyes darting around. A small crease settled between her brows.

"Because my brothers are over there, and I don't want them to know about this."

My brothers could never find out what I was doing. Ever. We'd be packed up in thirty minutes flat and headed out of state to God knows where. I didn't want to run anymore. More importantly, I didn't want to run from her. If my older brothers had no problem keeping their secrets, neither would I.

"Are they dangerous?" She looked behind me, as if they were going to pop up any second.

"Protective is the word I'd use." I stood and grabbed her dirty tray for her.

She snatched it from my hand and headed to the trash can. I kept in step with her effortlessly. "Fine. But I have questions for you that need answered. If you try to bring anyone or warn anyone, I'm going straight to the police." She motioned to her shoulder. "I have proof."

"You name it. Place. Time. I'm there."

Her eyes narrowed. "Ten minutes. Courtyard by the fountain."

"Ten minutes?" I shifted, stealing a glance at my brothers. "Uh, yeah, I'll make it work."

"Good." She flung her food into the trash can before pulling her shoulders back and readying herself to go for the door.

"I'm Aaron, by the way." I smiled nervously. "I promise I'm much less of an asshole in normal circumstances."

A slow breath left her lips. "Nothing is normal anymore."

"You won't believe me, but I know how that feels," I said, soft and sincere.

I thought her being alive would rid me of my guilt, but it was the opposite. It grew every second we were together. I dragged a complete stranger into my mess of a life. "Ten minutes."

I was fucked. I glanced at my phone. Five minutes to ditch my little brother. I did have one thing going for me. Zach and Luke had already left for their classes. Luke was notoriously a master at detecting my bullshit. He said I have an obvious tell when I lie. I was inclined to believe him, since he and Zach were the best liars I'd ever known.

"I think I'm gonna skip Chem and go to the library to study." I kept my eyes forward as we treaded the sidewalk, a row of oak trees on either side. The fountain was just up ahead, passing the community vegetable garden on our way. A gated area where students could learn to grow their own produce. I'd never seen anything like it.

"Since when do you study?" Presley elbowed my ribs.

"Since I'm already failing Applied Algebra, I need to get my grade up before Luke ropes me into an hour-long lecture about responsibility."

"I don't know why you care. This whole college thing is a sham anyway." Presley walked on my other side, his hands behind his head.

"Well, it's the only thing I have going for me at the moment, so—"

"Ouch. Now you've hurt my feelings," Presley joked. "You spend too much time moping. Live a little. We literally have eternity to do whatever we want."

It didn't surprise me when we woke up after Zach and Luke changed us and Presley didn't have one bad thing to say about it. He made the vampire life look easy and fun. An exclusive thing only the cool kids got to do.

I sighed, bringing my attention back to the only important thing I needed to worry about. "I don't need your permission to go."

"It's your funeral." He smiled with a carefree chuckle.

"I won't be alone. I'll be in a public place in the middle of the day. Who is going to take me in broad daylight?"

"The big, bad, scary vampire mob. Oooo." Presley laughed.

"Yeah, and I doubt they'll even think to look for me in a library on a random college campus in California. I think we have some time."

The Family. My brothers' secret had a name but no explanation. Some kind of gang or cult they were a part of. Presley liked to joke it was like the Mafia. They were the ones hunting us, but I didn't know why. I also had no idea what they looked like or how many of them there were, but I did know they were dangerous. Only because my older brothers told me so.

Most of the time, I tried not to think about it. I couldn't do anything, and I didn't know what would even happen should they find us. It was all one big irritating mystery.

I glanced at my phone again. Any more talking and I was going to be late.

"I'm going and I don't want you to follow me. Can you keep your mouth shut for at least an hour?"

"Your secrets are safe with me." Presley gave me a wicked smile.

"Whatever. I'll see you later." I turned to leave, and guilt stirred in my stomach. I was about to do something insanely reckless.

"It was nice knowing ya!" Presley yelled behind me. "I call dibs on your PlayStation."

I ignored him, picking up my pace and glancing behind me one more time to make sure he was out of sight. The library was huge and, thankfully, surrounded by a plethora of trees. Right before entering the library, I turned left and made a beeline for the fountain.

There were two fountains on campus. I assumed she was talking about the biggest one located in the garden. My guess was correct, and it didn't take me long to spot her pacing on the cobblestone. The sunlight danced on the strands of her hair, and the florals blew in the breeze around her in an assortment of colors. "You're late." She stared at me, unimpressed, arms crossed, foot tapping.

I glanced at my phone to confirm. One minute late. "Sorry about that. If you knew how hard it was to ditch my brothers . . ."

She may be the most intimidating woman I'd ever met. Her blazing hair matched the sense of fire she emitted. It engulfed me, stealing the breath from my lungs. Thankfully, I didn't need to breathe.

She spoke with strength, and her eyes narrowed. "Did you tell anyone you were coming?"

"Not a word." I ran my fingers over my lips, zipping them shut.

Her cool-blue eyes looked right through me, practically tearing into my soul. That's when I noticed police officers talking and laughing, with coffee in hand, not far from where we stood.

She came prepared. Of course she did. She was a fighter. Nestled between her white knuckles was a can of pepper spray.

My brain took it all in simultaneously. The Thing inside me assessed all possible threats without a second passing. Good thing I had the power to shut it up.

"Are you going to spray me with that? I promise that won't be necessary." Everything came out awkwardly, like the way people sing "Happy Birthday."

A strange pause lingered as she looked me up and down. I sensed her fear. It was weird. Definitely not a power superheroes had, as if I needed another reminder.

She didn't look scared, though. From the look on her face, she could kick my ass and eat me for breakfast. I liked that in a woman. But I shut that thought down quickly.

She finally spoke. "You talk. I listen. You'll answer my questions when I ask you, and I will decide if you are telling the truth."

I had no idea how that was possible, but I agreed. I couldn't hold back my urge to know one question. "Wait, can you at least tell me your name?"

"No."

Damn.

"What do you want to know? I'm an open book."

We stood like statues on the cobblestone path. Her arms were crossed, and she shifted her weight from one foot to the next. I guessed we probably looked like a bickering couple, since people mostly steered clear of us and the nearby solid granite fountain.

"You're a . . . vampire?" she said.

"Getting right into the hard questions first . . . Um. Yes. Technically. But I don't like that word."

"And you drink human blood to survive?"

"Yeah."

Her eyes hardened. "So, you kill people."

"What? No. No, I swear the drinking-blood thing is something we have to do, and I'm just not very good at it yet. I lost control for a minute. It doesn't usually involve anyone dying."

She eyed a couple as they walked past us holding hands, then whispered, "What do you mean by that? Be more specific."

"Well, I'm new to this. I haven't been what I am for more than two months. It's hard to control."

She wanted clear-cut answers for all of this to make perfect sense. Only problem was, I was completely in the dark about the whole vampire thing. On a scale of one to dumb, I was the dumbest when it came to knowing what was going on because my brothers had only told me what I "needed to know."

"I'm sorry. You have no reason to believe me when I say this to you, but the last thing I wanted to do was to hurt anybody. I didn't choose to be like this. I can't just drink the blood of squirrels or birds. I can't choose not to do it. I have to.

"We usually drink once a month, tops, and, usually, no one is seriously hurt. Most are drunks coming home from the bar, and they won't even remember. You were just a special circumstance because of me. I went up to the nature reserve because I wanted to try to do things alone, and it turned out to be a horrible idea. It's all because of me."

The word vomit poured from me like a gushing fountain. Something about this mystery girl made me want to reveal all my secrets.

39

Her expression softened. "Aaron, right?"

"That's me."

I prepared for a tongue lashing. For her to scream and throw the book at me. She'd never believe me. To her, I was just a monster who had attacked her, and I deserved that. I'd have to deal with whatever she chose to do.

"I'm not turning into a vampire. Am I?" She looked at me like cogs were turning in her head.

"What? Why would you think that?"

"Because of the scar on my shoulder. It's not getting better, and it hurts. I just assumed something was wrong."

I fought a smile. "I'm pretty sure you'd have to drink—"

A blonde chick dropped her book bag on the cobblestone with a thud and sat on the fountain two feet from us. Though I understood the reason for the public place, it wasn't ideal.

The fountain was large and well-kept. Celtic crosses were carved into the sides, with three cherubs holding jars that poured the water into the basin.

"Drink a milkshake. Drink a milkshake for that to happen. It's kind of a joint thing." I finished my sentence before turning my attention to the blonde. "Do you mind? She's kinda in the middle of breaking up with me. It's some sad stuff. Give me a few more minutes, and I might be crying all over the place."

I nodded toward the mystery girl, who looked like a deer caught in headlights.

She muttered, "Uh . . . yeah. Very hard . . . and sad." I stifled a laugh. Mystery girl was a bad liar.

The blonde stared at me for a minute before picking up her bag. "You probably deserve it."

"You have no idea," I said under my breath. I squinted, watching her leave in the midday sun.

The mystery girl sat in the blonde chick's spot. Her legs dangled as she took a deep breath and relaxed her shoulders. Every second, I could sense her fear settling.

I took a seat next to her on the deafening fountain. The gurgling water, the rippling waves, and the sputtering water pump all had distinct sounds. Tuning out all the stimuli was still practice for me. Lucky for me, the mystery girl spoke again.

"An infection. That's what the ER doctor said. If I had an infection, I needed to go see my primary." She sighed. "Did they know?"

"I'm not sure. Maybe. Maybe they knew it wouldn't heal and that you'd need to come back in. You don't need to worry, though. You're not gonna turn."

"Do your brothers know about me? That you saved me? Did you tell them anything?"

"No. It's not something they need to know."

She seemed to accept that answer, but I doubted she believed me.

"I can't believe this is happening. It doesn't feel real. How do I know this isn't some kind of fluke and you're not just some guy that calls himself a vampire and goes around biting people? I've seen the forums. I know it exists."

"Good point." I couldn't hold back my laughter this time. "I can show you one thing. I might be able to get away with it in broad daylight." I took a quick look around, making sure no one was intently paying attention to us. "What's your favorite flower?"

She eyed me suspiciously. "Peonies. Why?"

I was thankful she'd chosen one of the few flower names I knew. I took in a breath, and on the exhale, I let my instinct take over. I turned toward the stone archway at the garden entrance a few feet away and watched for my opening. The garden was a decent size, with tall hedges and stone statues that made it difficult to look clear across. I noted where everyone's line of vision was facing. Luckily, our campus wasn't completely open. Trees casting shade widened my window of opportunity. Once I had found my opening, I went for it. After running, I hid between tree trunks and dashed to the furthest end of the garden to pick her flower.

Within seconds, I was back, holding the delicate pink flower between my fingers for her to take.

Her eyes widened in fear, and the breath hitched in her chest, but her shoulders slackened from her ears, and she took the flower.

Her mouth stayed open as she analyzed every inch of the flower. "I know. It's weird, huh?"

Nothing I said would help. Nothing had helped me when I found out, certainly nothing my brothers said.

Her eyes were full of curiosity. "What else do you know?"

"Only what my older brothers have told me. Which isn't much." She was eerily quiet. Her face was hard to read.

"Where did you come from? I've never seen any of you here before."

"Um . . . we are new to the area. We moved from Brooklyn two months ago."

"How were you able to start in the middle of the semester?" Her voice sounded distant, but her eyes stayed trained on me.

"Kinda an unusual situation," I said, hoping she wouldn't push the subject.

"What do you mean by that?"

I didn't know what I was going to tell her, but I didn't want to lie. Not when I owed her the truth. The truth being: why her. Why I had moved was directly connected to why I showed up in Blackheart and attacked her in the nature reserve. Neither should have happened. But it did. Because of my brothers.

"There's a reason we left."

She raised her brows, waiting for me to say more.

"You see, the thing about that is . . . I can't tell you because I'm a little in the dark about it myself. My brothers didn't tell me anything, really. They just turned me and our little brother, and we left. They pulled some strings and got us set up here. I don't even know how they pulled that off either."

The familiar punch of anger hit my gut. It was a definite sore spot still aching two months later. My older brothers and I had countless fights that went unfinished for that reason. Why did they change us? Why were we running? Why wouldn't they just tell me more? It ended the same way every time. They'd never budge, and I'd always get angry.

"Do you expect me to believe that?"

Her tone didn't match her words. Her words were pointed, but her voice was patient.

I wanted her to have the answers, unlike me who was left worrying and wondering about what goes bump in the night. Maybe she could have the freedom I'd never have. She could have her answers—at least the best I could muster—and maybe she could move on and have a good life. Just like I'd imagined she'd have. "I didn't expect you to trust me, even after we talked. All I know is, it's dangerous, and I think I've already subjected you to enough of that."

She didn't miss a beat.

"Let's assume for a minute that I believe you. What kind of danger? Be as vague as possible without lying."

"Okay, people are looking for us."

"Can you explain people?" Her fingers gripped the edge of the fountain's stone wall.

The courtyard had emptied as the next classes started. The noon day sun was still high and bright.

I chose my words very carefully. "Um, a group of . . . nonpeople."

"So, there are more vampires out there."

"Yeah, apparently. And apparently, that's why we had to leave everything I loved and knew behind, and apparently, my older brothers think telling us nothing means protecting us. I think it's bullshit. Pardon my French."

"You don't seem like you know that much." A smile rested on her lips, and she sighed.

"Finally, you see it. I'm just here, trying to live my life and not kill people. And now, I've pulled you into our mess."

"I guess you do get the whole life-ruining thing." I did.

My hands would be sweaty—if I could sweat. "About that, there's a reason I wanted to talk to you alone . . . away from my brothers."

She eyed me suspiciously, her heartbeat picking up. "Go on." "You can forget this ever happened. Right here. Right now." I stood, hands to my side, looking toward the police officers enjoying their afternoon coffee. "I can walk right over there and turn myself in. I'll tell them I attacked you."

A wrinkle appeared between her brow again. "Why would you do something like that? You don't even know me."

"Because it's the right thing to do. I can't fix what happened. This is the only thing I can think of that makes any sense. Who knows . . . maybe I look great in prison orange?"

The words didn't flow like I wanted them to. I didn't want her to feel like I was guilting her into some situation. I wanted to want what she wanted. That was easier said than done.

The mystery girl was still watching me, though her eyes were glazed over in contemplation. She bit the inside of her lip and tapped her foot on the cobblestone.

I let her take her time and watched a group of students laugh in the distance. I couldn't help but think about how my life had completely catapulted into the sun. One day changed everything.

One minute I was studying and going to a community college close to my house. Presley had just turned eighteen, and he talked my ear off all year about how he wanted to go on a trip this summer. And then my brothers stormed in and ruined everything.

It wasn't all bad, though. I didn't miss the city. Surrounding our campus were redwood trees, and I never got tired of looking at them. I tried to soak in my last moments of freedom. The sounds of the birds and the breeze running through the trees.

"It doesn't make sense." She concluded. "You don't really mean that. You wouldn't do that. No one would do that."

I couldn't help but laugh. "You underestimate me?" I turned back toward the police officers and straightened my shirt. "I guess I'll just have to show you."

I started walking but stopped. "It was nice meeting you, by the way.

Sorry again for everything."

Her eyes were wide as I turned back to the policemen. I didn't want to think too much about what I was doing. I had to right my wrong, and I hurt this girl. Her life would never be the same because of me and my mistakes. She was innocent. I had to protect her. That was the most important thing.

"Officers, I need to report a crime I committed." I cleared my throat, puffing out my chest and trying to look as threatening as possible.

They didn't flinch at my words or even stop sipping their coffee.

"All right, go on." One of the officers shared a playful smile with the other.

"I attacked someone."

Everything in my body was telling me to run. The Thing in my head was fighting for my attention. But I left my feet firmly planted in the grass. This was my choice, and I wasn't going to let anything sway me this time. This was my chance to right my wrong and make the decision I wasn't strong enough to make in the forest. It was her or me, and I should have chosen her over myself.

The officers stared at me for a minute, one of them lowering his sunglasses to his mustache. "You attacked someone? Like you got into a fight?"

"Not exactly. I technically bit someone." The officers exchange glances, looking amused.

The one with the deep voice scratched his beard, stifling a laugh. "Son, you want to make a report stating you bit someone? Do you have the name of the person you bit? Do they even want to press charges?"

"Well, actually, I don't know the name. I—"

"What are you doing?" Mystery girl's voice caught me by surprise as she walked in closer to the scene. "I didn't think you'd actually go through with it. I'm sorry, this is my . . . my friend. He's doing this as a dare for his YouTube channel." She held up her hand, showing her phone.

"You two are aware that filing a false police report is a serious offense?"

The officer's deep voice boomed, but his expression was relaxed. He took another sip of his coffee.

"Yeah, I know. That's why I wanted to stop him before he actually said it."

I probably looked as confused as I felt. She narrowed her eyes at me before turning her attention back to the officers.

"Well, no amount of views are worth going to jail for. Kids these days." He chuckled under his breath.

"You are so right. I'm sorry. It won't happen again," she said before whipping me with her hair and motioning for me to follow her. We walked into a clearing away from earshot.

"What are you doing?" I said quickly.

"Me? What are you doing?! What was that?" she said through clenched teeth.

"I told you I was going to do it! I wanted to make it right. I thought this is what you wanted?"

"How could you possibly know what I want if I don't even know what I want?" She groaned and turned to look at the courtyard. "Just give me a second to think."

I stuffed my hands in my pockets and let the silence sit between us. She kept her eyes on the cars passing in the distance as she mumbled. Counting. One after another, she counted the cars. Not every one. Only the bright-colored ones as they drove up to the crosswalks and stopped for pedestrians before zooming down the hill.

"I don't want this on my conscience."

When she turned to me again, her eyes were softer than before, but worry settled in them.

"If you are telling me the truth, and everything just happened to you like it did me, then . . . then I don't want it on my conscience. I'm not done with my vampire questions, and if you go to jail, I'm never going to know if you were telling the truth about my shoulder or anything you just said."

I didn't know what to say, but she was clearly waiting for me to speak.

I wanted to say thank you, then hurl myself over a bridge.

I didn't deserve the mercy she was giving me. "What do we do now?"

She crossed her arms. "We keep living our lives as strangers. You don't know me, and I don't know you. If I have more questions, then I'll come to you for help, but we're not friends. You don't approach me. You don't know me."

I rubbed the stress knot on the back of my neck. "Well, what if I want to be friends?"

She smiled. "You look like you have plenty of people to keep you company."

I laughed. She was joking. For the first time, she relaxed. "Fine. You're the boss. Can I at least get your name?"

"Kimberly . . . Kimberly Burns."

She looked down at her hand before stretching it out for me. A flash of excitement hit me, and I grabbed her hand a little too fast, but she didn't flinch.

"I'm Aaron . . . just Aaron. We're using a fake last name. Coleman. You know, because of the people following us. It even says it on my driver's license now. I should definitely not be telling you that, but I didn't want to lie. So, Aaron Coleman, I guess." A sheepish grin spread across my face.

I was breaking every single one of the rules my brothers had set in place. But I didn't care. For the first time since I was changed, I felt like myself again. The me before I turned into the guy who stalked girls in the forest.

The smile returned to her face. "So many questions, but for now, I have to get to my next class."

"I guess I'll see you around, then, Burns."

She straightened herself, fluffed her hair, and gave me a begrudging nod. Then slung her backpack over her good shoulder.

"Sure. Maybe . . . We'll see." She waved at me awkwardly before heading back toward the lecture halls.

I stood, watching her leave, before strolling up to the library. I couldn't shake the notion that she may be the coolest person I'd ever met.

Five

"Thank you so much. Have a wonderful day." I faked a smile at my barista as I reached for my favorite Pink Drink.

"Not a coffee person? Maybe I should have suggested somewhere else."

William's voice startled me, and I jolted forward, nearly spilling my drink over the counter.

He laughed. "Still jumpy, I see. Sorry."

William appeared beside me, wearing a black-and-blue sweater, fitted with a white collar, and khaki shorts that were snug around his knees.

"That's okay. I've had a long day, and I'm already plenty jumpy, so no coffee for me." I smiled sheepishly.

I had almost forgotten about agreeing to meet him.

He leaned against the counter, and we waited for his black coffee before choosing a table next to the window. The sun was setting, and ripples of peach and cream painted the sky.

Our café was small and filled with books, books on shelves, books stacked in every corner. It was my favorite spot on campus, and they stayed open late.

William let out a nervous laugh. "I'm afraid I've already made an ass of myself here."

"Oh, no." I placed the straw between my lips and sipped. "Thanks for meeting me today. I really needed company."

That was an understatement. After my run-in with Aaron, my thoughts felt so heavy I thought I might explode. I couldn't tell William anything, but just talking to another normal person helped.

He pursed his lips. "Do you come here often?"

"Oh, all the time. On Mondays, they have half-off croissants. They're to die for."

His expression melted, and the corners of his mouth twitched into another smile. "You don't say? Oh, before I forget"—he reached into his pockets and pulled out my notes—"I brought these for you. But don't worry, I don't plan on asking you to tutor me."

I smiled. "I'm happy to help you if you need it."

He leaned forward, putting his elbows on the table and taking a sip of coffee before saying, "No, I wouldn't dare waste our time with something so boring. Let's talk about you."

"Me?" I coughed. My throat was ice after a long sip.

He leaned away from the blinding sun on his right side. "Yeah, you don't think I invited you out for coffee to talk about myself, do you? What kind of gentlemen would I be? So, besides holing up in coffee shops and not drinking coffee, what do you like to do for fun?"

"I like hiking. I usually go up to the nature reserve, but sometimes, when I have a long weekend, I love going to the Redwood National Forest."

"You go with your family?" He took another long sip of his coffee.

"No, I usually go by myself. It's fun usually. This weekend— there was a bit of a hiccup."

He raised a pointed brow. "A hiccup? What happened?"

I hesitated, picking my words wisely. "I got . . . bit . . . by an animal."

He moved his coffee from his lips. "Like a squirrel or something?"

"No . . . more like a bear or a wolf. I don't know what it was. It doesn't matter." I took another long sip of my drink.

"Wow, are you okay? You're saying that so casually. How bad were you hurt?" William's eyes grew wide, and I started to regret telling my half truth.

"I think I'm still a little in shock from it all. I'm okay. It's just a bite. I lost a lot of blood and went to the hospital, but I'm fine." My answer didn't budge the worry in his dark eyes.

"Are you sure? You need to take a rest. Maybe some time off. I can't even imagine what you went through."

I'll admit, the offer of time off sounded tempting. Even a weekend trip out of town would have been nice, but with upcoming finals, it made more sense to soldier through my suffering.

My phone vibrated in my pocket, and I leaned down to look. It was Chris finally returning my phone call.

"Do you need to take that?" William eyed the phone in my hand.

"No," I said, placing my phone on the table.

I turned to face the window just as I set my phone on the table, and my body froze.

Aaron was walking across the campus, backpack in tow, wearing a large, slouchy football jersey and a backward cap. He was moving fast, like he was late for something. This time, there was no one around him.

"Do you know him?"

I must have been staring too long.

I snapped my attention back to William. "No. Definitely not."

"Except, clearly, you do." William chuckled. "What is he, an ex-boyfriend?"

"Oh, God no. No, he's just a guy I met recently."

Not even a day in, and I had already broken my own rule.

William swirled his coffee around in his cup, watching me as if I were the most interesting person on the planet. "Where did you meet?"

"We me in . . . the hallway. I, uh . . . dropped my books, and he picked them up for me. That's it."

The vibration on my phone sounded again.

"Are you sure you don't need to take that?" William smiled. "It's okay if you do."

His words reassured me, and I smiled. "I kinda do. I'm sorry."

"Don't be," he said.

I grabbed my drink and a few napkins, then made a beeline for the door.

"Kimberly, wait!"

My hand lingered on the door handle, and I stopped.

"Come with me to the Omega Beta Alpha party tonight. I can meet you there."

"Oh, I don't know . . ."

I felt cornered. On one hand, William was nice, but I didn't want to give him the wrong idea. My life was an actual tornado, and I didn't plan on dragging anyone else into it. Even if he was cute.

"Humor me. I'll make sure you have a great time. Don't you want to pick my brain?" William smirked.

The phone in my hand wouldn't stop vibrating, and it slipped from my grasp. William was quick to hand it to me, our hands touching. Suddenly, my head was in outer space.

"I'll meet you there," I said, betraying my previous resolve.

I wondered why I had just agreed to do the exact opposite of what I said I was going to do, but that could wait.

"See you then." He held the door open for me, and I bolted.

I walked out to the bus stop outside my dormitory. The clouds broke into pools of burnt orange above my head. The wind blew my hair in my face, sprinting the soft scent of my rose perfume forward. My heart was in my chest again. This was it. I was finally going to get to tell Chris everything.

The dirt whisked in a cyclone near the yellow bench I was sitting on. I swirled my heeled boots around in the dirt and kicked it on top of my laces. The sun was beating down, and my skinny jeans were sticking to my legs. The bus stopped to unload its passengers.

One by one, bodies trickled out of the bus. Why was I so nervous? I sighed and let my shoulders fall away from my ears as I leaned back.

I went to redial, and the shrill ring of my cellphone snapped me out of my trance. I shuffled around to bring it to my ear.

"Hello?"

"Hey!" Chris said, muffled. The roar of talking and laughter made it hard for me to hear him. "There you are. I was starting to worry."

I was surprised by the spark of annoyance that zapped right through me. I'd been calling him for almost a week.

I closed my eyes and brought my fingers up to squeeze the bridge of my nose. "I'm fine—"

"You don't sound fine. What's up? You said you wanted to talk to me." My fingers were sweating as I gripped the phone.

"I did. Something happened. Something big."

"Don't tell me. You got that scholarship for your sophomore year—"

"No. It was something bad."

"Hold on." A long pause followed by a click of the door came through. The roar in the background of his call vanished. "You're not pregnant, are you?"

Nervous laughter escaped my lips. I squeezed the phone, feeling the blood rush to my cheeks. Pregnancy would be so much easier to explain. "It's not that. I went on a camping trip, and . . . I was attacked by a man."

"Oh my God. How bad were you hurt? What happened?"

"I'm not finished. It was a man, but he's more than that. He bit me . . . and took a lot of blood. I had to go to the hospital."

"What the hell? Like some psychotic drifter?"

"Closer but not it. I'm going to tell you something, and you have to promise not to think I'm a crazy person."

"Okay . . ."

I took one big breath, filling my lungs and letting the words pour out on the exhale. "I think the person that bit me was a vampire."

A pause stagnated, and I wondered if the call dropped.

"Kim! This isn't funny. I thought something actually happened to you. You scared me." Chris laughed. "But it's a good joke. I didn't know you had it in you."

"I'm not joking! Something did happen to me. I have proof. I'll send the picture."

I quickly scrolled through my phone to send the picture I had snapped of my shoulder that morning. I was waiting to go back to the doctor to get my shoulder looked at until I showed Chris.

It was the only bit of indisputable evidence I had.

Another pause.

"Kimberly, when did you learn to do special-effects makeup? This is amazing."

"It's not makeup. I'm telling you. I. Got. Bit."

"That doesn't mean it was a vampire. I know you used to watch that Buffy show when we were younger, but come on. What did the doctor say?"

"That it was an animal attack." I sighed. "But—"

"Exactly. You can't even be sure of what you saw. You're probably just traumatized."

But I met him. The words lingered on my tongue, but I couldn't bring myself to say them. He was never going to believe me. Even if he was here, it wasn't in his nature to believe things he couldn't make sense of. It was our constant source of tension. When I said the sky was the limit, Chris had a way of weighing me down and keeping my feet firmly planted on the earth.

I got up from the bench and smoothed my wind-blown hair. "You're right. I'm fine. Don't worry about it."

He sighed. "I didn't mean to upset you. I just don't want you there alone, scaring yourself with weird theories."

"What does that mean?"

"It just means you're alone there, and you don't have anybody. I want to be there for you, but it's hard sometimes. I've got my own stuff going on here. I got a promotion . . ."

"I had no idea . . . that's amazing. You should be proud of that."

"I am . . . but sometimes, I wish you would have just moved up here with me."

"New York was your dream. The city . . . big business. That's so you. You were made for it. I'm not."

"I know. I can't be there for you like you need me to be. I'm—I'm only going to keep letting you down."

"Yeah, I know." With my shaky hand, I wiped a tear from my eye. "You don't have to worry about me. I don't need someone to take care of me."

"That's not what I meant—"

"I better go. It's getting dark here at the bus stop, and I don't want to get kidnapped, so I'll talk to you later."

"Kim."

"Congratulations on your promotion. I'm happy for you."

Tears flowed from my eyes, and I dug my fingernails into my palms. Every time I tried to hold on to our friendship, it seemed to slip further and further from my fingers. I kept holding on because I wasn't sure I was ready to let go. Letting go meant admitting our friendship might not last.

Chris always talked about moving to the city. I thought things would be different. I thought it would still be like the old days, where I could call him for anything, and he'd be there. But it was obvious to me things had changed. He was ready for that change, and I wasn't.

A lump settled in my throat as I made my way back toward my dorm. I hated the word "alone." I didn't want to identify with that word, not when I was so many other things. But it seemed to follow me and show up at the worst moment. The moon lingering in the pink sky followed me with each step.

I took a deep breath and tried to steady myself. All those years of therapy had actually paid off. I glanced at the clock on my phone. I had planned to go straight to urgent care after showing Chris my shoulder. But it was that or the party. I couldn't do both.

My shoulder could wait till morning. What was a few more hours? The party could be fun, and I could even wear my new dress. As long as I wore a long-sleeved turtleneck under it, of course. That would definitely cheer me up.

Six

M y stomach was in knots as I made my way up the stairs to the large wooden doors of the OBA frat house. The tall windows and white pillars loomed over me like an omen. Dark-red bricks blended into the trees surrounding it. The cool night air buzzed with the muffled music and laughter. It was dark, and I felt a lot less confident than I had just a few hours before.

My hand on the doorbell, I hesitated, adjusting the hem of my plaid dress. Was this a doorbell-type occasion? What if that was the most socially awkward thing I could do at this party?

Thankfully, a short blond-haired boy with curls, who greeted me with a smile, interrupted my back-and-forth. He was interestingly dressed with a pair of bright-pink swim shorts, a neon green-and-white-striped button-up and Croc slides adorned with emojis and icons. It was a chaotic look that reminded me of the '80s, but strangely, he pulled it off well.

"Hi." His voice was light and enthusiastic. "Nice to see ya. Come on in."

"Oh . . . uh. I'm sorry. I was supposed to meet someone here. His name is William. He's the one who invited me."

His wide smile turned down. "Uh, I don't know any William. Did he say he lived here?"

"Well, not exactly . . . I . . . uh." I was getting frazzled. It was a combination of the sound bursting my eardrums and the thought that I may have just made a fool out of myself. "I'm sorry. He invited me. I'll just go."

"Wait! I'm officially inviting you." He held out his hand. "I'm Presley."

I must have hesitated a second too long since he said, "I don't bite. Promise."

Stifling a nervous laugh, I shook his hand. "I'm Kimberly. It's nice to meet you."

I relaxed as he led me through the front door and into what appeared to be a foyer. I didn't know what I had expected a frat house to look like, but this blew all my expectations out of the water. High vaulted ceilings, white crown molding, and dark-lacquered hardwood floors adorned each room. It was hard to notice anything other than the sea of people shuffling into the various rooms like schools of fish, but it was hard to ignore how expensive a place like that could be.

Presley led me toward the kitchen, walking in fluid steps, and had no trouble parting the crowd. He did so with a friendly smile, tapping people on the shoulder or striking small talk with them as we passed.

The kitchen had a huge stainless-steel fridge—bigger than any I'd ever seen—white marble countertops, and a center island occupied by a group of people doing body shots.

We stopped in front of a plethora of coolers littering the floor.

"What do you drink? We have every alcohol known to man."

"I'm good. I don't drink, actually . . ."

"No problem. We also have bottled water, sparkling water, and soda. Whatever you want, I'll go get it. Even if I have to drive to the gas station. Don't worry, my brothers and I aren't drinking tonight, you know, to keep an eye on things. Well, all except for—"

"Your brothers?"

I let my curiosity win.

Presley seemed nice and more than willing to talk to me. I wasn't sure what I was going to do once he left. The longer I could carry on a conversation with him, the better.

"Yeah. Do you know them? There's Aaron over there. Zach and Luke are playing poker, I think." Presley motioned over to the entry to a dining room.

And there he was, Aaron chugging something in a red SOLO cup. The room erupted in cheers as he threw his empty cup onto the floor.

All the cards fell into place. I had managed to find the one place on campus that Aaron happened to be, and it wasn't just him. His brothers were there too. How was it that the one time I tried to do something normal, vampires had to be there?

"No," I blurted. "I mean . . . kinda. I know Aaron. Barely. We met, like, once. It wasn't a big deal."

Presley's mouth stayed poised in a smile, his head cocked to the side. "Oh, yeah? What about Zach and Luke? I could introduce you." He wiggled his eyebrows playfully.

"Wait, you all live in the house . . . you're part of the frat?"

"Yep! It's a blast."

"Kimberly!" Aaron yelled, crashing into the kitchen like a tornado. SOLO cups on the ground scattered in his drunken wake, and he stumbled into one of the coolers. "What are you doing here!?" His smile beamed, red warmth peeking through his beige skin.

"It's kinda a long story. Boring one, though." The words came out slowly as he moved a little too close.

"All right, you kids have fun. I'm gonna leave you here. Kimberly, nice to meet ya. Let me know if you need anything." Presley snickered as he disappeared into the foyer.

Aaron was still beaming. "I was secretly hoping you'd show up, and here you are!"

Aaron was really drunk. That answered question one thousand and one. Vampires could drink.

"You didn't tell me you were part of a frat," I shouted over the loud frat boys entering the kitchen for their next round of drinks.

"You didn't ask." Aaron bounced on each foot to a beat entirely of his own.

"Aaron!"

Behind him, a large group of girls called to him, motioning for him to come over.

His lips curled up as he giggled and steadied himself against a wall. "I'm—I might have had a little too much. I usually don't drink this much, but it's just—the ladies keep giving me drinks. Like, what am I gonna do? Say no?"

I bit my lip, trying to hold back laughter. I could see why he would be popular with the ladies. No doubt, Aaron had a natural, boyish charm about him. Against my better judgment, I had to admit he was attractive.

"I had no idea vampires could drink things other than blood." He placed his fingers to his lips with a playful grin. "Remember, that's our secret. Just you and me know, okay? Don't tell anyone." His eyes lit up. "I gotta give you a tour. Don't worry, I won't show you the whole thing. Just the highlights." He turned to lead without letting me answer.

My options were standing alone in the kitchen or following the drunk vampire. Surprisingly, I chose the latter. We stumbled through a wall of half-naked girls and boisterous frat boys. The bass from the stereo moved my entire body. My sweaty hands slid along the wall as I tried to steady myself. Too many bodies were packed together in the dim light, and I tripped on an empty beer can and fell backward. My shoulder slammed into the wall, inducing a sharp pain in my fingertips.

As I rubbed my arm, couples danced around me, and the occasional drunk threw a plastic ball into the liquid of sloshing red cups. Everyone was grouped together, as if they all knew each other.

We finally stopped in front of a large staircase in the hallway. It was pretty standard, same hardwood for the steps and thin white wooden guard rails.

"Now this . . . this is the staircase. Personally, my favorite part of the house." He pushed his hair out of his eyes and motioned to the ceiling with a smile.

A chuckle escaped my lips. "The stairs are your favorite part?" I ignored the prying eyes and tried not to block the flow of people moving around from room to room.

"Uh. Yeah. It's dark and has all these little swirls. It's so sick. It's oak—okay, that's a lie. I don't know what the different types of woods are. I'm just trying to be cool." He giggled to himself and stumbled backward.

I smiled. "Well, I appreciate your honesty."

Aaron's eyes locked with mine. "I'd never lie to you. No way. You'd never speak to me again. I'm going to tell you everything. Seriously, ask me anything."

"So, you're telling me that you haven't lied to me yet? Everything you've told me is the truth?"

"Yes! All of it." His eyes were droopy as he moved his hands over his face.

"So, you weren't lying when you said you hadn't told your brothers about me?"

Realistically, that was my biggest fear. Aaron seemed honest enough and kind. But I knew nothing about his brothers. They might not be so happy if they knew Aaron had willingly told me who and what he was.

His demeanor changed, and he hung his head but kept his eyes on mine. "Oh, no. They would kill me if they knew. I don't wanna talk about them. This is all Zach's and Luke's fault. It sucks, but I'm trying to be okay. I'm doing it. Look at me. Don't I look great? Don't I look happy?" Aaron paused before chugging the rest of his beer.

In the lighting, I could finally get a good look at his eyes. They were soft and warm. In his current state, he couldn't hide the hint of sadness pooling in his irises and the crinkle in his forehead as he spoke.

"You look drunk." I smiled. "Come on, I want to see the rest of the tour."

The night wasn't going like I'd hoped, but despite the strangeness of my circumstances, I was actually having fun.

"You do? Here, I'll show you the pool!" Aaron's pitch spiked like a kid's at Christmas.

I laughed at his silliness and followed him through the groups of people. As we got closer to the pool, the crowd was more dense and, surprisingly, more drunk. The sweaty bodies started closing in, making my heart beat faster. Aaron was unfazed as he pushed through people, politely telling them to move.

We stopped in front of a large pool that was glowing with different lights. The rock waterfall hid behind the crowd on the deck.

"Aaron, this place is huge. I've never seen a frat house look like this." I casually left out that I had never been to a frat house.

"Oh, yeah, there's a lot of money invested in this place." He got up closer, and we faced the pool's neon lights. "I heard the founder is the one who is sinking money into it."

"The founder . . . aren't all frats in this campus really old? This is an old town."

"Go, go, go!" Aaron cupped his hands over his mouth and yelled across the pool. A group of men held Presley up in the air, carried him to the edge of the pool, then threw him in.

"Aaron." I waved my hand in Aaron's face.

"What were we talking about again?"

"We were talking about the person who pays for all this."

"Oh, yes. That guy. I heard he's rich. Hey, do you think all vampires turn out to be rich like the movies? God, I hope so." A smile stretched across his face. "Wow, we need to come up with a new word for vampire. I really hate the word."

As my brain processed everything around me, Aaron made a beeline for the main house. "Come on, I want to introduce you to the girls."

"What? The girls . . ." I planned to plant my feet and not follow, but I didn't want to be left alone with all the people around. He led us through a glass door into a living room that was fit with a large lounge couch. It looked to be the common room where most people hung out.

On the leather couch sat a group of girls who were talking with a few guys standing and sitting close. A blanket of anxiousness fell over me as we neared it.

"Everyone, attention—attention. This is Kimberly. Kimberly, this is everyone else." Aaron fell back onto the couch.

"It's nice to meet you all." I took my seat across from them.

I was met with warm smiles.

"Hi, I'm Jennifer." A girl with brown hair and warm skin twirled her fingers at me in a wave. The other girls took turns introducing themselves.

"I'm Heather." Her neon-purple hair glowed in the dim lighting, the only one to stretch out her hand to me in a handshake.

"Chelsea," the only blonde said.

The most prominent thing about her was her smudged red lipstick and the subtle dirty look she was giving me.

Chelsea inched closer to Aaron. "Tell us about how you guys met. I've never heard your name come up."

Aaron and I exchanged a tentative glance. He opened his mouth, but I cut him off.

"We actually met in the hallway between classes one day. You know, the whole drop-the-book thing. He picked them up for me."

"Not surprising. Aaron's a gentleman." Chelsea traced her fingers along Aaron's arm.

"Yeah, I can tell he's pretty popular." Their eyes were trained on me. "Jennifer, I like your shoes. They're super cute."

If there's one thing I had learned about living with women in the group home, it was to compliment them to gain their trust. It worked on almost everyone.

Her eyes lit up instantly. "Thanks. I got them down at the boutique on Main Street."

"Your dress is so cute, Kimberly. Did you thrift it?" Chelsea said, wearing a black bodycon dress.

"Thank you! I did."

Chelsea eyed me up and down. "I could tell. You just have that vibe." I couldn't tell from her expression if she was genuine or not, so I assumed she was complimenting me.

"That reminds me. I almost forgot to tell you about this new thrifting app I found." Heather ushered them into a new conversation.

I leaned into the couch, my shoulders relaxing away from my ears. Chelsea averted her attention away from us and talked to Aaron and some guys beside him. Every few seconds were met with her giggling laughter. Slowly, I started to feel like I always do in social situations. Like I was fading into the background. Every minute ticked by, and I imagined them all watching my every move.

"So, Kimberly, what's your major?" Chelsea's voice broke my concentration. The whole group hushed to listen. Their silence was deafening despite the loud vibration of music.

"I'm a Psychology major. What about you?"

"Oh, interesting. I'm in Criminal Justice." Her face was soft, but her tone was off.

"That's cool. Do you want to be a lawyer?"

"Yeah. I'm pretty good at arguing, so why not? Aren't I, Aaron?" She leaned her hand to rub his chest, but he wasn't paying attention to our conversation. When he didn't answer, she nudged him in the side.

Aaron's head spun around. "Yes to whatever you are asking."

"What about you? What's your big dream?" Chelsea uncrossed her legs and leaned in closer.

"I don't really know. I've never had a definite idea for a job I think I could do for the rest of my life."

I hated that question. Though I knew I wanted to graduate and be successful, I never felt settled into my major. I had already changed it once before. It was hard to narrow down one thing I was passionate about, but I was afraid to be left with nothing and crippling student loan debt. So, I settled at the end of the year with Psychology.

"Oh, I'm sorry. That sucks. Maybe you should talk to a counselor or something. I know there are a lot of people who can help you with that. I could never do that. I like to know where my life is headed."

"Yeah, it's okay. I have time." I shifted awkwardly.

"Isn't that what everyone says? Then you spend all your money for a major you don't want?" Chelsea grabbed a red cup from the table and took a sip, her lipstick staining the edges.

"Probably. I try not to think about it."

"Well, my cousin didn't even go to college, and he makes so much money now. I wouldn't worry too much." Heather gave me a reassuring smile.

I turned to Heather. "What about you? What are your majors?"

"I'm in nursing. I've wanted to do it since I was little."

Envy bubbled in my stomach. I wanted to be one of the people who had a strong conviction of what they wanted to do. I had the drive, knowing I wanted to support myself, but I lacked the how. The passion behind something I could go to school for.

Jennifer smiled at Heather and grabbed her hand, pulling her in closer. "Me too. We actually met in one of our classes."

Jennifer got up in a flurry of excitement and pulled Heather from the couch. "Oh my God, Angie just showed up. I didn't think she was coming. Come on!"

They said their goodbyes and shuffled into the foyer.

"Bye." My voice sounded like a whisper.

Chelsea furrowed her brow as they left. "Aaron, come on. Let's go with them and get some drinks."

"Uh. Okay. Lead the way." He smiled as she got up and dragged him off the couch. "We'll be right back. You're staying, right?"

Chelsea didn't give me time to respond as she dragged him into the other room.

"Yeah, I'll be here." My body sank back into the couch before I sighed. "I guess."

I was close enough to the speaker that it was rattling my entire body.

I grabbed my shoulder and winced with every vibration. The longer I sat there, the more relaxed I became. Scanning the crowd for any signs of activity, I noticed a large crowd huddled around a poker table. Every few seconds, the crowd would cheer and gasp. I had to fight the urge to check my phone as another song went by without them returning. I peered anxiously at the kitchen but couldn't see anything.

"Mind if I sit over here?" William slumped into the seat next to me, holding a beer, surprisingly a tad overdressed in his black blazer.

I couldn't fight the pang of annoyance resting in my stomach. "Oh, didn't expect to see you here, considering you invited me to crash a party."

"Now, now, I never said I lived here. Just that you should come." He was smiling again, watching my expression carefully.

"You got me." My attention floated back toward the kitchen.

A large number of bodies traveled in and out of the hallway, yet no one familiar was in sight.

"Well, I'm glad you came." He breathed through words easily and effortlessly. "Sorry I couldn't meet you here sooner. I got held up. I see Aaron kept you company in my absence."

I laughed. "Yeah, well. I didn't expect him to be here. Do you know Aaron?"

He grinned, his mouth twisting into an unusual expression. "Just in passing. Him and his brothers have thrown a lot of parties since they got here. Wild bunch, all right."

As we talked more, I leaned farther into the couch.

"Really? What makes you think that?"

"Well, they throw parties like this, for instance." He motioned up into the air, sloshing his beer around.

"Yeah, I've never been to anything like this."

He smiled. "Well, I'm thankful someone as pretty as yourself decided to grace me with your presence."

I wasn't used to the way he was staring at me. His eyes panned over my features, making my face hot with embarrassment.

"It's time for you to fess up. So far, all I know is, you're in my writing class and your name is William."

William never let his eyes wander from my face. "Ah, yes. Well, I'm currently studying Criminal Justice. I want to be a judge someday."

I took another look at him, analyzing his pressed blazer, clean-cut hair, and sable-colored dress shoes. He looked old enough to be a lawyer already. "Is that something you've always wanted to do?"

"Yes. My younger sister died when I was fifteen, and ever since then, I've wanted to dedicate my life to justice." His smile widened, his eyes scanning the crowd before sipping his beer.

"I'm sorry."

"Don't be. It was a long time ago." His eyes followed my gaze back to the kitchen. "Are you sure I can't get you something? Doesn't have to be a drink. They have food here too." I almost blurted out another rejection but stopped myself.

"You know . . . sure. I'll take some chips if they have it."

He smiled. "As you wish."

Excitement fluttered in my chest as he retreated to the kitchen. A sense of pride from my newfound people skills called for a celebration. Something good was coming out of one of the craziest days of my entire life. I was exhausted, and it was my way past my usual bedtime, but I was having more fun than I'd had in a long time.

"Hey, beautiful."

The words brought me back to reality. A tall, slender guy with moppy brown hair sat beside me, forcing me to move over. He was wearing a shirt I'd seen before, another BFU swim team shirt.

He didn't look coherent as he spoke again. "Wow, you're— you're so pretty."

"Uh, thanks." I squirmed back, the stench of alcohol on his breath stinging my senses.

He leaned closer. "No, you're like the prettiest girl I've ever seen."

"You're too kind."

"Would—would you like to come back to my place?"

"No, get away from me."

I got up and moved to the other end of the couch, looking toward the kitchen, but no one familiar surfaced. Everyone was drunk and stumbling into each other to the beat of the music.

He scooted beside me again. "But you're so pretty. I mean it. An angel."

"I'm not interested. Leave me alone."

He caressed my outer thigh, igniting rage in my chest.

I grabbed his wrist and twisted it. "Get off me."

"Ow, what the fuck!" he cried, weaseling himself away. "You crazy bitch."

His yelling shifted the crowd's attention. I got up and kept my head down. A dark silhouette cast a shadow over us. Two guys with broad shoulders came into view. It took one glance up at them to realize who they were.

Aaron's older brothers.

I could tell by how many of their features matched Aaron's. It was different for each of them.

The big bulky one, who was wearing a colorful button-down that hugged his huge biceps, had Aaron's soft auburn eyes. He also shared his warmer skin tone. The other—the shorter, dark-haired one—had Aaron's jaw and facial structure, especially right around the eyebrows. He was wearing a long '90s band T-shirt that swallowed him.

The larger, muscular one with the dirty-blond mullet looked at the guy. "Hey, Danny, do we have a problem?"

The other was a smaller build but no less muscular. His dark hair was long and curled at the edges of his ears. "Looks like someone is being rude to our houseguest."

Danny backed up with his hands in the air. "No problem. We were just talking, man."

"Bullshit," the dark-haired one spat with pure venom in his voice.

"You need to leave. Now." The large one grabbed him by the collar and shoved him toward the door, leaving the other brother standing next to me.

"Hey, where'd you learn that?" He motioned to his wrist.

A smile curled at the edge of his lips. He leaned casually into the leather armchair just a few feet away from me.

"I've taken some martial arts classes," I said, my heartbeat thrumming in my ears.

Cheers erupted as everyone watched Danny get thrown out, cutting my attention.

"Uh, I think I'm going to go."

"Are you sure? Fuck that guy. He won't bother you again. Promise," he said, his dark brows knitted together.

Before I could answer, the other brother walked up. "Are you okay?"

I couldn't take my eyes off them for a second. My brain was slowly rebooting, trying to comprehend how they could look and act so normal—and be vampires.

I didn't know anything about them. They could be dangerous. One slip up, and I could find myself in another tricky situation. I had enough for the night. I needed to do the smart thing and go home.

"Uh. Yeah. I was leaving anyway. Thanks." I sheepishly waved and made a beeline for the front door. My heart was in my throat, and I pushed my feet faster. With the slam of the door behind me, I breathed a sigh of relief. I think I've had enough embarrassment for one day.

Keys in hand, I searched for my car. Clouds covered the moon, making it hard to spot it in the yard. After weaving through the muffled maze for a few minutes, I found my car wedged between two large flatbed trucks, with another small white car blocking me from behind. I had to go back in there.

Pushing my hands through my hair, I turned my attention toward the campus. The streetlights were dim in the dark night. My dorm wasn't that far. It was against my better judgment to walk home alone, but it was a Saturday. Surely, there would be people around.

Making my way out of the yard and into the street, my heartbeat was loud in my ears. The streetlights were spaced far apart, leaving me to walk in the shadows. An unnerving feeling slowly overtook my train of thought.

My ears focused on the distinctive sound of my platform shoes hitting the sidewalk. With my purse strapped to my shoulder, I kept it close to my body, my hand gripping my phone. Behind my footsteps, another noise emerged, nearby tapping to the sound of my own steps. My heart jumped into my throat, and I spun around. There was nothing. Drizzle misted in the illumination of the streetlights. I took a deep breath and headed toward the campus's glowing lights, reassuring myself of my own paranoia.

Keeping my head up at all times, I moved faster. No one revealed themselves. Counting my steps, the tapping started again. It was almost undetectable, partially concealed by my own footsteps.

It didn't matter. I was almost to campus. I finally reached the courtyard, and my anxiety deflated. I checked my phone and kept my hand firmly on the lock button. It crossed my mind to call for help, but I hadn't seen anything at all, only heard the sound.

As I turned to leave, the flick of a lighter caught my attention. It was close behind, not even fifteen feet away. My body froze, and my breath caught in my throat.

Slowly, I turned to the empty air behind me, digging in my purse for my Taser. The wind blew burning embers into the air. I forced my feet to move, jogging back toward my dorm. I could feel a nearby presence. Every second felt like I was taking a step back. Goose bumps erupted on the back of my neck.

My momentum came to a halt. With my hand on my Taser, I squeezed the button, ready to go. The lights were too far, and whatever was pursuing me was too close. With my eyes closed, I drew in a breath. My whole body shook with adrenaline. For the last time, I turned to face the darkness behind me.

I was knocked off my feet, and my body braced for the fall. I placed my hands in front of me, but they never reached the ground. A strong set of arms stopped my tumble, and pressure engulfed my neck. I couldn't see anything.

My attacker's hand pushed my face in the other direction and covered my mouth, too strong for me to struggle under their grasp. Their arms were stone, tightening every time I tried to move.

We tumbled to the ground. Something knocked him off me. This time, I landed onto the freshly mowed lawn. I opened my eyes in just enough time to see the shadow of my attacker. Whoever it was had a hat covering their hair and a thick black leather coat. "Are you okay?!"

It was Aaron. Aaron saved me from someone—or rather, some-thing—and I had a pretty good guess of what that something was. I couldn't feel my body. I sat up and focused on the scrape on my leg. It should have hurt, but it didn't. I didn't feel anything.

Aaron's hands were warm on my face. "Hey, talk to me. It's okay. You're safe." He frantically looked me up and down. "You're bleeding a little bit. It doesn't look bad, though. Do you want me to take you to the hospital?"

He was talking to me, but I couldn't take my eyes off the light pole right next to us. Raindrops fell, leaving fuzzy streaks in the glow of the light. Everything was a swirling blur. My mouth still wouldn't form words.

"Kimberly! Please say something."

Slowly, I held out my hand to touch the raindrops. The water dis-solved into my palm, and I felt myself coming back to my body. Aaron's warmth helped as he rubbed my back.

"All right, that's it. We're going to the hospital." Aaron lifted me to my feet and moved his arm around me to make sure I didn't collapse.

"No. I'm okay. No hospitals."

I didn't let go of his arm at first. I was convinced if he were to let go of me, I might turn into a puddle on the sidewalk.

"What happened? D-Did you see who that was?" I said.

"No. I couldn't tell. They were too fast. I pushed them off you, and they bolted."

I blinked a couple times, letting the cool raindrops run over my face.

Every moment, I was more aware of where I was and what had happened. "Someone bit me . . . They bit me. Oh my God. Check me."

Aaron pulled my hair over my shoulder, and I wrapped my arms around my waist to steady myself.

"It doesn't look deep. I think I got to you pretty quickly. I don't think they took much blood."

"You got to me right on time. What were you doing? Following me?"

I scanned the courtyard, expecting someone to jump out from behind a tree. Everything was eerily quiet for a Saturday night.

He let out a nervous chuckle. "You made that sound weird. Technically, I was, but I heard about what happened at the party, and when I saw you leave your car, I wanted to catch up with you and make sure you made it home safe. I was worried about you . . . for good reason, apparently."

"You seem sober." I finally released the iron grip I had on his arm and dusted off my plaid dress.

The rain had picked up, and I was getting soaked. My body was still shaking with adrenaline, and the cool breeze wasn't helping either.

"Well, to be honest, I'm still a little drunk. But it wears off pretty quickly for us. Plus, I sobered up a lot when I saw someone jump you. I didn't even think—I just went."

I gasped. My attention turned to the empty sidewalk ground. My purse was gone.

"They took my stuff. What the heck? What kind of vampire steals women's purses? What am I going to do? My keys and everything are in there. Without my keys, I can't get into my dorm or my car." I buried my head in my hands. "What is going on? I thought this was over. Why does this keep happening to me?"

"It will be okay. I promise. We'll figure this out." Aaron smiled, and I could see how he was a little drunk; he was a little too excited when he delivered his next line. "In the meantime, it sounds like you need a place to stay. You know, a safe, warm place. With plenty of vamps to protect you."

I opened my mouth to protest but quickly shut it. I needed help. I couldn't do it alone, and I didn't want to. I was exhausted. I needed a place to sleep, and no other place around was offering vampire body-guard service.

I sighed. "All right. Lead the way."

Seven

AARON

The windows of the OBA frat house loomed ahead just as the rain picked up. Kimberly was next to me, teeth chattering and arms wrapped around her body. I'd have offered her the shirt off my back if it wasn't also soaked. But I felt bad for her sloshing around in her platform shoes. I'd offered to vampire run us to the frat house, and she declined. I was only slightly disappointed.

I tried my best to keep Kimberly calm and distracted as I scanned for any signs of danger. The rain made it hard to hear anything and left me blind. But I was determined, drunk or not. Nothing was going to hurt her with me around.

I still hadn't fully processed what had just happened. I never imagined Kimberly and I would ever talk again, let alone that she'd come to one of our frat parties and get attacked on the way home.

We trudged up the steps until we stood in the porch light, the rain around us creating a roar under our covered patio.

"Welcome to my humble abode. Yes, you've already been on the tour.

But there is still lots to see." I put my hand on the door handle.

She grabbed my shirt and yanked me back a few steps. "What? No, I can't walk through there. I don't want you to march me up there like one of your—your conquests."

"Who do you think I am? I totally don't do that. Plus, I told my brothers you're just a friend. If I told them what happened, minus the vampire part—"

"Aaron, you don't understand . . ." She looked at me with beads of water dripping from her hair to the ground below. "I don't exactly want everyone to know. You trust them, but I don't know them."

"It's okay. I get that." A sly smile curved my lips. "I have a plan for an alternative, but I don't think you're gonna like it."

"What is it?" She sighed and crossed her arms, her weight shifting from one foot to the other.

"I'm going to carry you up there, like, through my window. Now just come here and wrap your arms around my neck." I inched closer to her and patted my back.

"Oh, no."

"You don't have any other options. It's either the door or the window."

She kicked the air sheepishly and walked in closer. Her arms wrapped around my neck from behind.

"Don't say I didn't try to do it the normal way." I chuckled, effortlessly lifting her legs. "Ah, okay. I got you."

Nervous laughter escaped her lips as we stepped into the rain. The tall three-story house loomed above our heads. Her heartbeat radiated through my skin, the sound of her pumping blood flooding my ears.

"What's wrong?" I said, walking us over to a wall, where water was running like a waterfall over the red bricks.

"Not trying to be that girl, but I'm kinda afraid of heights." She buried her head in my shirt, shielding her face from the rain. Her legs squeezed harder around my waist, and I forced myself to think only about the wall in front of me and not the cute girl hugging my back. I definitely didn't want to think of how warm she felt or the feeling of her breath on my neck. No. The brick was a really nice shade of red, and the rain made the color pop away from the mortar. "I can't believe this is happening to me." Kimberly sighed, strengthening my resolve to keep focused.

I glanced behind me to make sure no one was looking, scaled the building in two seconds, and plopped us onto the steel fire escape near my window. Being a vampire was fun sometimes.

"You can't believe what? The vampires or scaling a three-story building in the rain?" I said, attempting to lighten the mood.

"How did I end up in some angsty teenage novel?" She looked up at me through wet eyelashes. "This is not what I wanted to do today."

I couldn't help but smile at her expression, and I led us to my window around the corner of the house. "Well, don't fall in love with me, and there won't be a problem."

We reached the window, and she swayed anxiously, waiting for me to open it. My window was locked but pulling it up and breaking the plastic was no harder than picking up a pencil.

"Don't worry. I won't," she said, teeth still chattering.

I offered my arm to her and motioned toward the window. "Oh, it's so easy for you, then?"

She turned her head to the side to look at me before putting her feet through my window. "Yeah. Simple. I don't have time for that."

I couldn't hold back my laughter as I stepped in after her into my dark room. "I'm pretty sure it doesn't work like that."

A small lamp on my nightstand illuminated a small corner of my room. Kimberly stepped forward and tripped over something in the darkness.

I grabbed her arm and steadied her. "Shit, sorry, hold on."

I dashed across the room in a split second and hit the light switch. My dorm was nothing special. It was a reasonable size, not much smaller than my room back in Brooklyn. The corners were still bare. Nothing but old nails hung on the white walls. My bed was pushed up close to the window, fixed with a cheap white bedspread I had bought on Amazon.

On the other side of the room was my TV, accompanied by a tangled pile of wires and a large stack of video games. The TV stand was a different color than my desk, which was littered with textbooks and loose papers.

In Brooklyn, my room was filled with knickknacks. My mom had a love of collecting things and passed it on to me. I had shelves filled with my childhood action figures I wouldn't part with and energy drink cans I thought looked cool. The blanket on my bed was a hand-me-down from the twins' room. A large quilt of different-colored patches. It was a chaotic space filled to the brim with color, including the walls that my mom let me paint neon green when I was in middle school. It contrasted with the stop sign hanging above my bed that Presley and I stole in high school.

My new room didn't feel like home, but it would do.

"Wow," Kimberly said.

"I know my room is dirty. You don't have to rub it in." I went to work, picking up various dirty clothes off the floor, being extra quick to pick up my old underwear first.

"I have to admit, I'm a little surprised." She leaned down and removed her soaked shoes. "Your room isn't what I expected."

I chucked my dirty clothes into a huge pile in my closet. "What do you mean?"

She marveled at the walls. "It's so empty . . . and boring."

"Oh, that . . . yeah, uh, when we moved, I didn't get to bring anything, even my rock collection, which was like my prized possession. I just haven't felt like decorating—it hasn't been my top priority."

That was an understatement. I missed all my things from home. Everything I had collected as a kid, I would never see again. All my Pokémon cards and the coolest rocks I had spent every summer combing local ponds for were gone. It was stupid, and I should have been too old to care, but I did.

She opened her mouth to speak, but a yawn took its place. Her wet clothes swallowed her.

"Way ahead of ya." I turned around and rummaged through my small dresser, picking out what I thought would be most comfortable: sweat-pants and the freshman orientation T-shirt I was given when we arrived. I then headed back toward the window.

"What are you doing?"

"You didn't want anyone to know, remember? If I don't come back, it's going to be pretty obvious I'm with you. I'll get you some food too." I opened the window and moved my legs out first.

"You don't have to do all that." She shifted nervously, clothes still in hand.

"Well, considering you're a guest, and I don't want to listen to your stomach grumble all night, I'll take one for the team." I winked before shutting the window and dropping out of sight.

Within seconds, I was down the wall and through the front door. My mission was simple. Get Kimberly a sandwich from the leftover party platter without my brothers noticing. It seemed simple enough, but it wouldn't be. Because my brothers were nosy.

Presley peeked his head around the corner. "Hey, how'd it go? Is she okay?"

I forgot I had mentioned to Presley I was going to check on Kimberly before I left.

"Yeah, she's fine. I walked her home. She got locked out of her car."

I went for the kitchen but stopped my foot before it hit the ground. Luke and Zach were in the kitchen cleaning up. I stood still and moved behind the wall. As I turned, I found myself face-to-face with Presley. I mouthed for him to be quiet, and he grinned. He clasped both of his hands together and pretended to shout for them. With the quietest motion I could, I hit him in the arm.

He mouthed a string of words slowly so I could understand.

"What's the big secret?"

I need them out of the kitchen, I mouthed.

Presley's eyebrows raised, and a wide smile stretched across his face.

"I'm not telling you."

He shrugged, and I knew what he was waiting for.

I got closer. "If you do this, I will write your English assignment."

I constantly questioned Presley's decision to major in Journalism, considering he hated anything that involved writing. I didn't think he fully understood that becoming immortal had axed his dream of becoming a TV talk show host. It was a nightmare trying to keep him off social media.

His eyes lit up, and he gave me a big thumbs-up before heading to the stairs in the foyer. The party was winding down, with the occasional human straggler passing through to get to the living room. Presley grabbed an empty beer bottle on the way and stopped midway up. He winked at me before dropping himself off the side of the banister. The shattering bottle and the loud thump of his body weight hitting the hardwood floor was enough to make some girls rush into the foyer and scream for help.

Like clockwork, their cries brought Zach and Luke into the foyer, and I could already picture the annoyed look on their faces. I snagged the sandwich and watched them help Presley, who was faking a sprained ankle, to the couch.

"Hope you like turkey," I said after softly knocking on the door.

To my surprise, she smiled upon seeing me, and her wet hair was perfectly combed away from her face. "Thanks. I found your hairbrush . . . and a semiclean towel to dry off. Hope you don't mind."

"What's mine is yours." I casually walked over to my desk and plopped down in my spinny chair. It felt good to be dry. I'd snuck into Zach's room and borrowed one of his band T-shirts and his favorite flannel pajama pants.

"I take it you don't sleep?" She took a big bite of the sandwich, her eyelids still heavy.

"I wish. I don't even get tired, so I'm up all night. It's not as cool as it sounds. I mostly just play games all night to help me pass the time."

"What kind of games do you play?" She motioned to my console. "I used to play before college."

"I like anything I can get my hands on at the moment. It's shocking how fast you burn through games when you're up for twenty-four hours." I leaned back, propping my feet up on the desk. "Why don't you play anymore?"

"I can't afford a console. The one I used to play wasn't mine." She took one last bite before scooting back into bed and getting more comfortable, but she didn't relax. Her hands moved to her shoulder, and she winced.

"We should check that bite again."

"Oh, no. I'm sure it's fine." She pulled the sheets up to her shin.

"I think we're a little past being shy, aren't we? I mean, this is as vulnerable as it gets." I smirked. "You're in my room. That's a huge step for me. Clearly, I'm the one who is suffering the most." She smiled, and I was thankful she understood my humor.

I sat up a little straighter. "I want to help."

She contemplated for a minute before nodding and scooting toward the edge of the bed. She moved her hair out of the way and revealed an imprint, similar to the one on my shoulder. It was a clean imprint but not deep.

"That's weird. It's like they bit you but didn't take any blood. It doesn't hurt at all?"

"Nope. Just my shoulder. Thanks to you. I planned on going back to the doctor tomorrow, but I've been dreading it because it didn't go well last time. Another joy of vampires existing, mention them one time, and everyone wants to ship you to the looney bin."

I chuckled. "You seem to be taking it well. I was completely mute for the first couple of days."

"That must have been hell, not knowing what's going on and being changed." Her eyes beckoned me to say more.

I contemplated how much I should say. Every bit of information I gave her would push her further and further down the rabbit hole. She'd be lost in wonderland.

The bite on her neck was a visual reminder it was too late for that. Besides, it was not like I knew that much, anyway. She deserved to know after everything I had put her through.

"What you need to know about my older brothers is that they have their own little secret life they don't like to share with the class. Not sure if it's a twin thing or an older brother thing, but it's been that way since we were kids. I never thought much about it until it was too late."

"How did they change you without telling you?" Her eyes softened.

"Since it's late, I'll give you the cliff-notes version. They came home one day, looking frantic. Told us to get in the car and wouldn't say why. Just that someone was after us. There wasn't time to grab anything or even call my mom. We threw away our cellphones, got these weird fake IDs. We drove for hours and hours without stopping until, finally, they took us to some safe house they knew about and then . . . changed us. Just like that. It was kinda a trust thing."

Saying it out loud only reminded me how stupid I sounded. Blind trust was something expected in my family. Family over everything else. I used to think it was cool, and being so close to my brothers felt like we were part of some secret club. But since, I've been regretting ever trusting them.

Her eyes traced the lines on my bedspread. "What about your mom?"

"She's safe. They took care of her somehow, and she's somewhere they can't get her. I don't know where she is, though."

I missed my mom. Her traits reflected in each of my brothers, and I couldn't go a day without thinking about her. Presley got her humor, Luke her warmth, and Zach got her endless determination and fiery spirit. Despite everything my brothers had put me through, it was hard to want to be away from them. They were the only thing I had.

"I'm sorry." Kimberly's voice brought me back to the present. "That must have been hard."

There was no ounce of sarcasm in her voice. She was genuinely being kind.

"Not as hard as being bit by a vampire twice in one month." I chuckled, hoping the new heaviness of our conversation would disappear.

A crooked smile played on her lips. "You're right. Tonight is all about me. I'm the only one in this friendship that's allowed to have problems."

I sat up in my chair. "Did you just say the F-word?"

"I wouldn't say that."

"You definitely said it. Admit it, Burns, you want to be my friend."

"Help me with my shoulder problem, and maybe we'll talk," she said, an extra sharpness lacing her words.

I didn't need to be told twice. "Yes, ma'am. I've got just the thing."

I opened the small wooden drawer in my desk. Within seconds, I held up a long sewing needle. "This."

Kimberly's eyes grew wide. "Oh, no. Absolutely not. What would you do with that?"

"It's for your shoulder. The way it works is younger, inexperienced vampires—a.k.a. me—have trouble controlling their . . . venom. Uh, yeah, let's call it that. It's supposed to numb everything, but if you can't control it, then it gets trapped under the skin, and it hurts."

"So, you use that needle to get it out?" She grimaced. "Are you playing a joke on me right now?"

"What? No. See, look." I grabbed the collar of my shirt and pulled it down, revealing my shoulder. "It should look like this. I'm just going to make small pricks, and it will help release all that pressure."

"I don't know . . ."

"Hey, if you don't want to, I understand." I turned to face her, making sure I could get to her at eye level. "I just want you to know that I'm indebted to you. I dragged you into this. I can't change that, but I can try to make your life better, and hopefully . . . you'll trust me after that."

She watched me for a minute. "Aaron, if I didn't trust you, I wouldn't be here. Besides, I think if you were going to kill me, it would probably have been easier like a week ago. And now, you've added my DNA into your room, so you're screwed."

I joined her in laughter. "Damn, I didn't think this one through. Now my master plan is ruined."

She took a deep breath and blew it out slowly. "Okay, let's do this shoulder thing."

"You sure?"

"Yeah. I'm tired of it hurting. Plus, I'll save money, so win-win. I have to warn you, though, I have a low pain tolerance."

"This will be quick. Okay, I'm going to move your sleeve over, so just don't freak out."

"Wait." She pulled away.

"Yes?"

"I just don't want this to be weird. You know, with vampires in the movies, it's all like . . . sexual." She grimaced, forcing the last word out.

"Whoa! You're the one bringing the S-word in here. I'm just trying to relieve the pain in your shoulder." I held up my hands.

"I'm just double-checking."

"This is a move-free zone. I'm going to touch your shoulder in the least sexual way possible. I'm just going to poke around your scar and then I'm going to gently press on the skin to massage it out."

"You never said that. You're going to have to milk it out of me like a cow?" She groaned before placing her head in her hands.

"Now you're just being gross. Hold still. I'm about to touch your arm, but it's just a friendship touch. F-R-I-E-N-D."

"Oh, shut up and just do it." A nervous laugh escaped her before she pulled her hands to her lap and squeezed them together.

I rolled up her sleeve. She looked a thousand times better in my shirt than I did.

"Ow!"

"Kim, I haven't started yet."

"I'm sorry. I'm nervous."

"I know, it's okay. I'll be quick."

I had to concentrate fully on the amount of pressure I was putting on her skin. Tiny little pinpricks brought little beads of blood to the surface. I wiped it gently with a napkin.

Her blood smells good. Do you remember the taste?

My hand slipped, and she yelped. I quickly apologized and readjusted my focus. The voice could talk all It wanted to. I'd just have to drown It out.

Kimberly's soft counting distracted me. I peeked up to figure out what she might be looking at. My guess was she was counting the hangers in my closet.

"Why do you do that?" I asked before pricking her with the needle again.

She grunted. "Do what?"

"Count. I can hear you under your breath." I pressed my hand harder into her shoulder. "Almost done."

"I don't know. I've done it since I was a kid. It calms me down."

"Take a deep breath." I waited for her to fill her lungs with air before I applied more pressure to her shoulder on her exhale.

"Ow. Ow. Ow. Ow. Ow."

"Done!" I got up from the bed and went for the first aid kit.

Luke insisted we each have one. Just in case someone in the frat needed help.

"You were right. It feels way better."

I placed a large bandage over her shoulder. "Told ya. You should listen to me more often." I winked and retreated for the trash can.

She groaned, pulled herself under the blanket, and propped herself up on the headboard. "I'm not so tired anymore."

I plopped down on the floor next to my scattered video game controllers. "Well, good thing you have me to keep you company."

After everything she'd been through that night, I was happy she seemed so relaxed. For a moment, it felt like we were in our own little world. A weird world. But one where no one else was watching us.

"Yeah, I guess you're, like, thirty percent my friend now." She smiled.

Silence introduced muffled music coming through the door.

"Uh, you gotta give me more credit than that," I said.

She sighed. "Fine, forty percent."

"Fifty."

"Forty-five."

I smiled. "So, does that mean I get to ask you questions now?"

"Sure. What do you want to know?"

I thought hard for a second on a good starter question.

"Do you have any friends? I'd kinda assume you'd want to tell someone after you got attacked."

"I do. His name is Chris. I've known him since I was, like, eight or nine. But I didn't tell him. Well, I did, but he didn't believe me."

"Does he go to BFU too?"

"No, he moved up to New York. He was the forward-thinking one." She turned her attention to the fluffy pillow on my bed.

"Is that a bad thing?"

"No, I'm happy for him. It's just not the same. He's basically moved on with his life, and he's the closest thing to 'family' I have," she said, hooking air quotes.

I leaned in. "What happened to your family? If you don't want me asking that, feel free to tell me to go to hell."

"Well, my mother abandoned me on the side of the road when I was four. There were no other living relatives to take care of me, so I grew up in foster care. I aged out when I was eighteen."

"Oh shit, I'm sorry—I don't know what to say."

"It's okay. Most people don't, but that isn't something I go around announcing to people. I've made my peace with it." She smiled, the warmth coming back to her cheeks.

My made-up life for Kimberly, back when she was still a mystery girl, must have been wishful thinking. It only added to my guilt. I couldn't imagine what her life must have been like. There wasn't a time when I was ever alone. But she had to face everything by herself.

"Yeah, we were in a group home together on and off until we both aged out."

"And you wanted to stay here in the mountains."

It was easy to tell how much Kimberly loved the mountains and not just because of the camping trip I had ruined. Everything about her screamed local, especially the various trail patches and enamel pins I had seen on her backpack.

"Yeah, this is my home. It's the only constant I've ever had. I wasn't ready to leave."

I was lost in her blue eyes and the way she was looking at me. She was opening up to me, and we were clicking. Talking with her felt easy. Easier than it had been with any girl I'd ever met before. The more I thought about it, the more my heart kicked my rib cage.

"Well, I'm glad you're here. Not glad you got mugged by a vampire or that I clearly ruined your life but happy that I'm talking to you now."

"Yeah, me too." She smiled at me, and a brief silence followed. Her heartbeat accelerated just like mine before she spoke again. "You sure I didn't interrupt any fun plans?"

"Ha. If you call sitting in my room studying and playing video games fun. I mean, I guess it is, but this is way better."

She rested back onto the pillows. The sleep was back in her eyes.

"You can get some sleep. I'll probably just go hang out in the living room all night."

"Okay. If you still want to play video games in here, I don't mind. I'm a deep sleeper, so you won't wake me up."

I was already up and headed toward the door. "Really? Okay, but when you wake up in the middle of the night because of my violent button mashing, don't say I didn't offer a solution."

"Aaron . . ."

I stopped just short of turning the knob. "Yeah?"

"Thanks for this." Her heartbeat was still beating in a steady rhythm.

"Anytime."

It was three in the morning. Walking around in the middle of the night was something I'd often do to curb my midnight boredom. I searched for Zach and Luke in hopes I might be able to kill some time with them for a few hours. I also needed to keep tabs on them and make sure my cover wasn't blown. When I couldn't find them, I cocked my head toward the ceiling and listened as far and wide as I could. It took a minute to sort through unwanted sounds—talking, laughing, the grunting from upstairs . . .

My best guess was that they were somewhere outside. I found a wall in the back of the dining room and pressed my back against it. The hum of the electricity buzzed under my fingertips. I pushed my attention further, listening intently until I could make out one of their voices. It was challenging to keep my full attention on the vibration of their voices, but I had a lot of experience eavesdropping on them as a little kid. My new vamp powers were just a cool, new extension of what I used to call my super spy persona.

"So, what now? I think we are down to plan, like, X." Zach exhaled sharply.

"He just needs time . . . just like we did." Luke's voice was softer and, therefore, more muffled and harder to hear. Despite being fraternal twins, they couldn't be more opposite.

I knew they had to be talking about me. No one gave them more grief than I did.

"Look at how good that turned out for us," Zach said.

Luke replied, "Well, he doesn't exactly have the best role models."

I could hear liquid sloshing, hitting the glass in waves. Luke was drinking. It made sense, since the party had died down, and he didn't have to worry about driving anyone home. But something about it never sat right with me. Luke never used to drink. "Okay, then. Plan Y, it is—to let our brother become a drunk. Sounds good to me," Zach said.

A brief silence wedged itself in.

"Oh, come on, I'm kidding."

Luke didn't laugh. "I know. It's not that. I'm just having a bad night."

The sloshing of liquid continued, followed by another sip.

"Well, I'm all ears. Shoot."

"Can you promise not to hate me after?" Luke's voice came out more clearly this time.

Zach laughed. "You know that's impossible. You can tell me . . . however fucked up it is." Another pause.

"Do you ever . . . miss . . . her?" Luke whispered, and I almost missed it.

My mom was the first person to come to mind.

"Fuck no," Zach replied.

"Oh," Luke said, deflated.

"You want to know why? Because that's what she wants. She wants to pin you and me against each other, and she wants us to fight over her because she's a sick, twisted bitch with a twin fetish. So, no, I don't miss her. She doesn't care about us. Fuck her."

It was definitely not my mom they were talking about. But who else could it be? They shared a lot of things as twins, but women weren't one of them. Zach had been with a girl named Ashley for more than five years until she moved to San Francisco and they decided to separate. I'd never seen him look at another woman since.

Zach spoke again. "I know it's different for you but, Luke. It's not real. The way we feel about her isn't real because it's been a lie the whole time. She fucked with our heads from the start. They all did. The sooner we forget them, the sooner we can all move on."

They definitely weren't talking about Ashley. Luke didn't actually date in high school, but he did have a girl he was interested in: his best friend, Sarah. Luke and Sarah had been inseparable since kindergarten. They did everything together. When Luke joined the football team,

Sarah joined the cheerleading squad to cheer him on. They even ended up as prom king and queen their senior year. But it couldn't be Sarah . . . because Sarah went missing a year prior and was never found.

"I just wish this feeling would stop. Sometimes, I feel like it would just be easier if they found us."

They weren't talking about girls at all. Well, they were, but it had to be someone I didn't know. Someone in The Family. Their gang.

At least that's what my best friend in high school, Enrique, called it. But even he was vague about what he knew.

Back in Brooklyn, our family had to be strategic. It was easy to get pushed around, so my older brothers grew up hard. Learned to fight. Covered our ass and kept us from getting in trouble or bullied. That's all I thought it was at first. That was—until I ran right into Damian in the hallway right before a sophomore year pep rally. Damian was someone everyone knew not to mess with because his family was big in the crime world. I heard a lot of stories, none I was interested in figuring out if they were true. I ran into Damian by accident, one that was entirely my fault. I was carrying Presley's mascot head, "Axe the Alligator," and I didn't see Damian rounding the corner in the hallway. Presley was always forgetting it at home, and I'd have to run to get it for him.

"Oh shit, sorry about that, man." I stumbled backward. I wasn't afraid of him beating me up because I knew my brothers would never let that happen. But I was afraid of what might happen to them if they did.

"No. I'm sorry. I shouldn't have ran into you. Please don't say anything. Let's just forget about it," Damian said.

I stammered in agreement and he scurried off behind me. I'll never forget his wide-eyed stare, like he'd seen a ghost.

After running to give Presley his alligator head, with two minutes to spare, I found my place in the gym stands next to Enrique. I told him everything that had just happened, casually yelling over the sound of the drumline.

Enrique's eyes grew wide. "You don't know?"

"Know what?"

After a little back-and-forth, he finally spit it out. "Well, don't tell your brothers I was the one to tell you, but Luke was gunned down two weeks ago. He was shot in the shoulder. Had to be admitted to the hospital and everything."

I let out a laugh. "You're kidding." I looked across the gym to where the seniors sat, and there sat Zach and Luke, casually leaning against the bleachers. They had their usual smiles and were talking as the cheerleaders performed. It wasn't uncommon for them to be out at night or for me not to see them for a couple of days. I thought back on the last few weeks and noticed how they had been gone longer than usual. My mom worked long hours as a nurse, so it was easy for them to come and go unnoticed. Plus, they were so close to graduating, she gave them more freedom. I guessed it could be possible, but could something like that happen, and they wouldn't tell me? They didn't seem like everyone else I knew in gangs at my school. They never dressed differently, and they didn't run around with other groups of people. It was just the two of them all the time.

"Dude, I wouldn't lie to you about that. It happened, and the talk is . . . whoever your brothers are hanging with is no joke. Their retaliation was brutal. It's got Damian's family scared. It's got everyone here scared."

"What retaliation?"

Enrique put his hands up defensively. "Nope. I'm not saying it. I shouldn't have told you. Your brothers have obviously tried to keep it a secret. Don't bring me up. I don't want them knowing my name."

"They already know your name, dumbass." I waited for him to say more, but he turned to watch the pep rally. And that was the first time Enrique had ever kept a secret from me. It was also the first time I ever suspected my brothers were a part of something sinister.

"I am literally the worst person in the world for saying that." I heard Luke's heavy sigh, and I leaned into the wall, drawing my attention back to the present.

"If you're the worst person in the world, there is truly no hope for me." Zach kept his tone light.

"Shut up."

"It's true. Plus, you're thinking too much about it. You can't trust your feelings, remember?"

Luke stayed silent, and a sharp clink of glass hit the concrete. "Relax a little. I'm going to get you another beer."

I stumbled away from the wall, and thanks to there being no humans in the kitchen, I was able to run back up the stairs to my room. I couldn't risk my brothers catching me listening to them. My mind raced with the new information, but I didn't have anywhere for it to go. It didn't make any sense. But it did strengthen my resolve. My brothers had their secret life, and I had mine. I could pull it off, just like they did. Kimberly needed my help and, in a way, so did my brothers. Kimberly needed to stay as far away from my brothers and their problems as possible, and Zach and Luke needed me to figure out this vampire problem. Knowing would only add to their stress. If there was another vampire in town, I'd need to be the one to track them down and figure out their motive for everyone's safety. I was doing the right thing.

Eight

KIMBERLY

A fter waking up, my hands searched for my phone under my pillow. Nothing was there. I had forgotten all about the night before and was reminded when I sat up and surveyed the room. Aaron's TV was dimly lit with a video game save screen on pause. A cool breeze hit my face, and birds chirped close to the window.

The door clicked, and Aaron appeared, looking cheerful as ever, holding a purple drink. "Wow, you look like hell."

"Thank you." I scoffed before turning my attention to the drink in his hand.

"Is that for me?"

"Yeah, I got you a smoothie. Thought you might need nutrition, considering you need food to not die."

"Thank you for that thorough explanation," I grumbled, my whole body sore.

He strolled over to sit on the edge of the bed. "How's the shoulder?"

I brought my lips to the glass to drink a bit of the cool liquid. "A lot better. I slept all night. It usually wakes me up a couple times."

"Good. Are you happy?" He was watching my reaction closely. "Uh, yeah, I'm happy. Why do you ask?"

"I was hoping your happiness might soften the blow of the mistake I made just now." Aaron flashed a sad puppy dog expression.

My smile dropped. "Uh-oh."

"I might have let it slip that you were up here in my room." He held up his hands in defense. "But I told them what happened, and it's cool."

"What?! Aaron, I knew you couldn't keep a secret. Is that all you said? Do they know how we met?"

"No, of course not. I said I met you at school and that we are just friends."

He tilted his head toward the door, his expression hard to read. "Would they be . . . mad? I mean, if they knew who I was?"

My imagination went wild, wondering how they'd react. I still had no idea what kind of family I was dealing with. They all seemed nice, but I had a hard time believing a family on the run from other vampires could be normal.

Aaron must have heard my heartbeat pick up.

"It's nothing bad. I think they would be really lecture-y about it. They're just protective."

I put my smoothie down on the nightstand and scooted closer to Aaron. "You keep saying that. I don't get it. Are your brothers some kind of mobsters or something? Who are they running from?"

"I have theories. They fit the profile for gang members, I guess. They got matching tattoos before they turned eighteen. People started treating them differently—"

"Different how?"

"People in town were scared of them. But I know my brothers are good people. They just made shitty decisions growing up."

I couldn't fathom trusting someone as much as he trusted them. But something in his voice made me believe him every time he'd mention them. He cared about them in a way I'd never cared for anyone. If I trusted Aaron, I'd have to—at least for the moment—trust the people he cared the most about in the world.

"You said you had theories. What theories? What do you know?"

He hesitated, kicking one of his college textbooks on the floor.

"Aaron, do you trust me? I know I'm just some girl that you met and attacked, so you probably don't yet, but our paths are directly linked now. You're literally my only hope in figuring out what is going on and who this vampire that attacked me is. We have to work together if we're going to get to the bottom of this. I need to know everything you know."

"I do trust you." He sat next to me. "I know that we're running away from something called The Family. I think it's a vampire cult. Presley calls it the Mafia. That's how my older brothers were changed. I don't know anything about it, their purpose, or what they do. I just know there's a lot of them, and they could be anywhere and that they're dangerous. So dangerous that we had to leave behind our life and go into hiding."

"What do they want with you?"

Aaron raised his brows without a response.

"Got it. You don't know . . . Do you think it's possible my attack could have to do with them?"

"Anything is possible at this point."

A large thump on the door broke our concentration.

In the blink of an eye, Aaron was pounding his fist on the door. "Presley, get away from the door."

I sucked in a breath, still completely enthralled with his abilities. It was going to take a while before I was used to anything that was going on.

"Sorry, they are normal, I promise. Let's head down before they pitch a tent outside. Remember the story. We are just friends who met at school."

"Well, don't forget you're only a percentage," I teased. A permanent crease settled between Aaron's brows since I had mentioned his brothers, and for reasons I couldn't yet explain, I wanted to see it disappear.

"Oh, ouch. Okay, mathematician, do you even remember what percent that is?" Aaron laughed as he watched me frantically brush my hair to look halfway presentable.

"I think it was something like twenty percent or some low number like that," I said.

"All right. All right. Stop mocking me. Let's go."

Aaron opened the door, and we walked to the edge of the stairs. I caught a glimpse of them as they disappeared into the living room. It was at that moment every lofty idea I had about vampires being elegant disappeared right along with them. Aaron should have been my first clue.

"Yep, those are my brothers." Aaron chuckled as we descended the stairs. The smell of wood polish filled my nose. I placed my hand on the smooth guard rail. "Look, Aaron. This is your favorite part of the house."

He flashed his teeth right before we reached the hardwood floor, and he ushered me into the living room. I expected to see a war-torn room filled with beer bottles and trash. Instead, everything was clean and pristine. Suddenly, I was contemplating how long I'd been asleep.

"Well, well, the infamous Kimberly Burns."

One of the twins met us in the entryway. He was the more muscular one, wearing what looked to be a Hawaiian button-up and gray sweat shorts. His mullet was curly and his beard looked recently trimmed and tamed. When he smiled, I was taken aback. He smiled just like Aaron. A big out-of-this-world smile brought a sense of warm safety to my chest.

"I'm Luke. It's a pleasure to officially meet you."

I held out my hand promptly. "Nice to meet you. Thanks for saving me from that guy yesterday."

"Happy to do it. He causes a lot of trouble here. He tried to fight Zach last week. But, you know, I've never seen someone try to break his hand before. That was pretty sweet—Hey, come over here." He turned around and pulled his other half out from behind the wall.

"I'm Zach. And you are Kimberly," Zach said with an unamused tone.

His hair was much darker than Luke's and longer. He, too, was muscular but much slimmer than his twin. What stood out the most was the dark circles under his eyes, making his ivory skin look hollow.

"You look nice in my brother's shirt," Zach said.

Everything about him was darker than his twin, including his entirely black outfit that consisted of black joggers and a Nine Inch Nails T-shirt.

"Uh, thanks?" Like clockwork, heat rose to my cheeks.

"Really, you're going there? Even though we just talked about this two seconds ago." Aaron's eyes were like daggers.

Zach chuckled, holding his hands up. "Hey, I thought it was a compliment. I was being nice."

With sweaty palms, I rubbed my hands together, looking for the exit.

"He's kidding," Luke said with a boisterous confidence and toothless grin.

"And I'm the cool one. Obviously." Presley walked in and propped himself against the wall. His clothes were even louder than the day before.

"Oh, you're the guy that got thrown in the pool." I smiled and held out my hand to shake his, hoping he would get the joke.

He squinted with a mischievous smile before shaking my hand. "Oh, you saw that, huh?"

He pulled up a chair, closing an awkward circle around the couch, leaving me on the outer edge.

"We all saw it," Zach said.

"Well, Kimberly, we're happy to have you. Is there anything we can do to help? Aaron told us about what happened to you last night. We'll accompany you to the police station if you need help."

Zach leaned over the couch's arm. "Or better yet, we could track them down for you and beat them up?"

"Again, he's kidding," Aaron blurted nervously.

But something in Zach's eyes didn't convince me. His posture was rigid, his shoulders back. He looked on edge, but his apathetic look told me he was good at hiding it.

"No, he isn't." Presley laughed, and Zach kicked his chair.

The wood splintered, causing Presley to crash to the floor. Their group shared a collective look. Aaron and I stole a glance at each other, while a strange silence sat between us all.

"Wow, these chairs must be cheap." Zach scoffed.

Presley picked himself up, dusting off his shirt. "That, or Zach's legs are freakishly strong . . . you know, because of the martial arts thing?"

They definitely weren't great at blending in. I decided to hand them a way out.

"I think I'm okay. Thanks, though. I probably need to get going and figure out my life." I turned to Aaron, shrugging.

"Yeah, hold on. I'll go get your stuff!"

"Maybe you can come over again sometime?" Zach was still leaning over the couch's arm. "Luke and I want to see some more of those martial arts skills you have."

I chuckled. "Yeah, I don't have that much skill in it. I just take a self-defense course every month. It's free on the first Monday of every month at the W. I take it you guys are pretty involved?"

"Yeah, we used to compete." Luke smiled proudly and crossed his huge arms across his chest.

"We miss it sometimes," Zach said.

I silently wondered if their martial arts had anything to do with The Family. Martial arts could be a useful skill, but I was pretty sure gangs didn't learn hand-to-hand combat. But a vampire cult might.

"Did you guys ever win any trophies or awards?"

"Zach did. He was the best in class," Luke said.

I concealed my surprise. Due to the sheer size of Luke, I'd thought he'd be the better fighter.

I turned my attention to Presley, who was sitting casually on the couch. "What about you? Did you and Aaron ever . . . ?"

"Oh, no. Definitely not. We did a lot more dormant activities growing up. Usually including staying home and playing video games until three a.m." Presley leaned back to talk to Aaron, who was coming down the stairs. "Isn't that right?"

Aaron sighed, a plastic grocery bag in his hand. "What are you telling her about me? I bet it's embarrassing."

"Just solidifying your laziness and love of video games. You know, to let her know what she's signing up for." Presley smiled just before Aaron elbowed him in the ribs.

I grabbed the bag from Aaron, waving to the group. "It was good meeting you guys. See you later."

"Likewise," Zach and Luke said simultaneously.

"Looking forward to it." Presley winked.

Aaron guided me to the door, and I followed closely behind. The house was bustling with other frat guys. Button-up shirts and khaki shorts everywhere. I'd almost forgotten there was an event on campus that Saturday. A lot of the fraternities and sororities were having their last get-togethers before summer.

He walked me to the edge of the stairs. "Are you sure you don't want me to walk you home or drive you?"

"No, I'm fine. I can handle it. I'm going to go talk to my RA. Have her help me get some things figured out."

"Well, I put my flip-flops in there for you. That way you don't have to wear your wet shoes back." He smiled, but it quickly faded as his attention shifted to the street.

"Thank you . . . thanks for everything."

I didn't have words for how I felt. Not only had I stayed the night in his room, I felt safe doing so. I'm not sure who was more surprised. Even more than that, I enjoyed our time together. It was confusing, to say the least.

Aaron's brown eyes glowed in the afternoon sun.

"Yeah, anything you need. I'm here for you."

I grabbed the too-big flip-flops from the bag and slipped them on. "So, what are we going to do? If there's another vampire out there, we need to know who they are and what they want. Do you think your brothers would be open to looking for the guy that mugged me? Maybe they can find him quicker than we can. We wouldn't have to say anything."

"Oh, no. I don't want them anywhere near this. If they think for a second that there's another vampire here, they're going to bolt."

"Like leave Blackheart?"

"Yeah, they're on edge." The little crease returned to Aaron's forehead.

A wave of anxiety washed over me. That was the last thing I needed. To be there, alone, with a vampire problem and no way to defend myself.

"Don't worry. That's not going to happen," Aaron said, rendering it almost believable. "We'll just have to deal with it ourselves."

"If it was someone from The Family, why did they bite me and not drink my blood? Why would they want my stuff? I don't feel like it makes sense. It doesn't fit the profile of some dangerous vampire super mob."

Aaron sighed and ran his fingers through his hair. "You're right. That's weird. I mean, I guess there could be a vampire using their abilities to steal stuff from people."

"How are we supposed to know if someone is a vampire? Is there a way you can tell? With a heartbeat, maybe?"

He shook his head. "No. We have heartbeats too. Maybe I can pick one of the twins' brains about it and see if they'll tell me anything useful. I doubt it, but I'll try."

"That's a great place to start. I'm going to cancel my debit cards today, and I'll be able to see if my attacker actually used them or not. That might help us figure out a motive."

I sounded like a crime detective. One look at Aaron in his scruffy bed hair and pajamas told me there was no doubt we were amateurs. But we were amateurs with combined brain power and similar goals. So, that had to count for something, even if the only thing Aaron contributed so far was an overly optimistic disposition.

"I'm going to go get my stuff. And when I pick up my car, do you want to hang out . . . maybe?"

The sun was higher in the sky than I would have liked it to be. I had overslept. I had a lot to do, including getting the locks to my room changed and picking up the spare car key in my dorm room.

Aaron beamed with a raised eyebrow, his disheveled morning hair almost covering it. "You're asking me? You want to hang out with me?"

"Yeah, I do. Unknown vampire on the loose. Probably best to stick together. Plus, I kinda want to see what video games you have."

"So, this means you and I are officially friends, then, Burns?" "Yeah, it does . . . Coleman," I teased.

A wicked grin spread across Aaron's face, and he held out his hand. I took it, and he leaned in closer to me. "Calem. That's my real last name. Aaron Calem at your service. Let's add that to our secrets list."

Nine

AARON

"Earth to Aaron. Hello." Presley waved a hand in my face. "You keep doing that."

"Doing what?"

I sat up in my chair. I was in the frat house's dining room with my books and assignments scattered around me. It was the middle of the week, which meant many people weren't around.

"Zoning out like that. Where do you go, and why can't I come to your planet?" Presley said, pulling on a highlighter-yellow pullover.

I hated that sweatshirt. Mostly because it was blinding but also because he insisted on pairing it with the weirdest clothes possible. Presley hated matching, but once he was in second grade, we pretty much gave up on trying to get him to dress any differently. Zach resolved to beat up anyone who made fun of him for it, and Luke didn't stop him.

"Where are you going?" I said, removing the papers stuck to my arm.

"I met some girls who invited me over to their sorority party. You should come. They have a pool."

"We have a pool," I said.

"Yeah, but this pool has women in it." Presley ruffled up his curls, eyeing himself in the big over-the-top mirror hanging on the wall opposite of me. "Unless you know any hot guys with an ounce of personality, then I'll swing over there instead."

"Aren't there plenty here?"

"Yeah, but they're all aggressively straight and not nearly as cool as me," Presley said, putting on his shades. "You wanna come?"

"I'm not going. I have to study." I turned back to the books sitting in front of me.

I had numerous finals to keep me busy, and that's all it was. Just to keep me busy. I wasn't exactly champing at the bit to start a career I could never advance in. Back in Brooklyn, I wanted to become a veterinarian. But I was stuck looking like a twenty-year-old. I didn't have much hope for that future anymore.

Plus, the newfound information of an unknown vampire on campus had me on edge, not just the immediate threat to Kimberly but also the possibility that, should my brothers find out, they would flip. All the effort we'd put to settling in and making a home here would fly out the window.

Presley laughed. "Whatever. Do your thing. We can all play Warzone when we get back."

He had truly never worried about anything, but I wasn't sure if I admired that quality or if I hated it. Nothing ever fazed him. Not even the sudden realization he was a vampire. Not moving across the country. Not having to hide from people who wanted to hurt us. He was still right as rain.

"All right, I won't be gone long. Three hours tops. Tell Mom and Dad I have GPS on my phone, and I'll check in every thirty minutes," Presley said before he disappeared toward the foyer.

Glass clanking against stainless steel broke my concentration. The sun was going down, and it cast a shadow into the kitchen where a few of our housemates were cleaning up their dishes. I looked down at the mechanical pencil in my hands. Somehow, I hadn't even noticed.

I adjusted my sore butt in my chair. Piles of notes buried my textbooks. The grandfather clock chimed from the living room, and I looked at my phone. How long had I been studying? It didn't feel long, but hours had passed without my recollection.

I tried to focus back on my textbook when a soft cry rang in the air. The sweet scent of blood flooded the room. The smell slapped me in the face. It was easy to identify, not only because of how potent it was but also in the way it lingered in the air, sucking up the potential for any other odors. Once it hit the air, I'd be smelling it for a week.

I got up quickly to follow the scent to the kitchen. A housemate stood with a bloody towel in hand, drops of blood dripping onto his flip-flops.

"I cut myself," he said, a little too calm.

His face was familiar, but I wasn't recalling a name. To me, he was the guy who loved to wear tank tops.

He checked his hand again. "It's not that bad."

The water drained the crimson smudges. I was frozen. Not because I couldn't control my thirst but because I didn't have a lot of experience with emergencies.

Within seconds, Luke pushed past me, and grabbed another towel, coming to the tank top man's aid.

I almost didn't realize he was dripping water all over the kitchen and in swim trunks.

"You're definitely going to need stitches, man."

Luke's voice was calm. Reassuring. My frozen muscles thawed, and I walked over to help.

"W-What do I need to do?" I said.

"Just hold pressure here while I wrap this." Luke smiled at me and grabbed the clean towel before wrapping it around the guy's hand.

Tank top guy's teeth ground with each bit of pressure, his heart rate skyrocketing as he let out a slow breath.

Luke turned to the guy's friend, who was still looking at us dumbfounded. "Are you going to take him, or do I need to?"

"Well, the thing is, I'm a tiny bit drunk, so . . ." the friend responded. A crowd had gathered, gasps of horror and awe amalgamating in an awkward shuffle.

"I'll take him!" Another housemate swooped in and dragged him away from Luke.

Bodies shuffled toward the front door, leaving Luke and me alone. Specks of blood littered the floor, stains of swirling red glued to the stainless-steel sink. I was thankful being a vampire wasn't like the movies. No burning throat or uncontrollable thirst. If that were the case, I was almost one hundred percent sure Presley would have accidentally killed our diabetic housemate.

I grabbed a towel to clean up but stopped when I saw Luke's face. His calm, collected smile was gone. His eyes bore a hole into his hand, where blood still lingered on his fingers.

"Luke? A-Are you okay?" I said.

He couldn't have been having a reaction to the blood. Luke was overly meticulous about feeding. He even had a calendar reminder on his phone.

I stepped in front of him and waved my hand in front of his face. "Luke, come on."

His body stood stiff, his eyes vacant.

My stomach turned. Something wasn't right. I'd never seen Luke react that way to anything.

"Zach," I said, barely audible. I knew he would hear me from inside the house. "I think something is wrong with Luke."

Within seconds, Zach was right next to me. One mention of Luke being anything less than fine always sent Zach into panic mode.

"What happened?" His eyes scanned the blood on the floor, like the wheels were turning in his head.

"This guy cut his hand, and Luke helped him. Everything was fine. But he just shut down or something. He won't answer me."

"Hey, look at me," Zach said slowly, grabbing Luke's shoulders.

I thought we might have been causing a scene, but everyone's attention had shifted to the bleeding guy outside.

"Come on." He dragged Luke to the counter and washed Luke's bloody hands. "It's just a little blood. You're okay. See? It's all gone. Everything is okay. We're safe. You're safe."

Without looking to see if anyone else was watching him, Zach snatched a towel from the other side of the room and wrapped Luke's hands up.

Luke responded to Zach's touch by blinking as Zach toweled off his hands for him. It reminded me of the shocked, unresponsive state in which I had found Kimberly in the courtyard, with the same vacant stare.

Luke's voice was unusually quiet. "S-Sorry. I just—I'm fine."

"You don't have to explain," Zach said, his voice sharp. "I'll take you back up to your room, and we can chill, watch one of those dumb comedy movies you like."

Luke shrugged him off. "No way. You have to go tonight. I'm okay." He straightened himself, using the towel to wipe himself off.

He ignored me completely.

"No, I'm not going. I'll go tomorrow."

Zach was still giving Luke a head-to-toe protective scan, raising a brow. It had been just two weeks. Zach hunted more than the rest of us. When I asked why, he'd say, "Because I have to." And that was that. Zach hated repeating himself. It wasn't worth the argument to ask him about it any further.

"No. You're going." Luke slapped Zach on the shoulder reassuringly.

Luke had spoken. And when he spoke, we listened. Even Zach. Something about the way he talked made us fall in line. Luke had been our natural-born leader since he came into the world two minutes before Zach. It was a role only he could do because he was great at it, and the rest of us sucked at it.

Presley, Zach, and I proved to ourselves repeatedly that our decisions either got us in trouble, or they were just plain stupid. Luke, on the other hand, had great ideas, and he had a good way of speaking to each of us in a way we understood. We didn't follow his lead because he was the oldest. It was because he was a great leader.

"I'll keep him company," I said quietly.

Zach gave me a disapproving smirk. "Can you keep your attitude to a minimum, Your Highness?"

"Yes." I gritted my teeth before forcing a big fake grin. That was my least favorite nickname.

Zach's expression softened, and he let out a sigh. "All right. I'll be quick."

He took a look around before grabbing one of the towels and speed-cleaned the rest of the blood from the floor and the sink. "There. I'll see you guys later."

He turned to leave but stopped before he rounded the corner.

"Be good."

I groaned. "I got it. I got it. Jesus, just go." Luke was already making a beeline for the stairs.

"Where are you going?" I followed close.

"I'm going to lay down for a minute." He peered over his shoulder, forcing a smile. "Don't worry about me, though. Nothing I can't handle."

Luke's weight shifted with each step. His invisible burden rested on his shoulders. I guess it was the worst part of being the leader. He had to be the strongest person in the room.

We reached his room, and he slumped onto his pristine bed despite still being in his swim trunks. Everything in his room was in order. Not a pen out of place. Sheets pressed, pillows perfectly symmetrical.

Luke would have done great in the military. It's all he ever talked about when we were kids. He wanted to save people. Fight for his country. All for the greater good. I scanned the empty shelves over his desk and contemplated how different life would have been if he had enlisted.

"You don't have to stay." Luke sat up and pulled his hands through his hair.

The mullet was a new style for him. Growing up, he'd sported a short military cut. It wasn't until we left Brooklyn that he started to let it grow.

There was no way I was letting what had happened in the kitchen slide.

I plopped down next to him. "I know. But I figured I'd annoy you for at least forty-five minutes before I go back downstairs to stare at my textbook for three more hours and get absolutely nothing done. Then I may play some games till my brain rots out of my skull and the sun comes up."

Luke smiled. "Sounds like a wild night."

"I like to live on the edge."

My attention drifted to the hardwood floors. The silence between us grew, and footsteps passed by outside the closed door. Just normal people doing normal-people things.

I wished that could be us. I wanted to be like them, and it would just be me and my brothers going to college together.

"Just ask." Luke watched me with a raised brow.

"What's going on with you? I've never seen that happen before."

I didn't look at him. I kept my eyes on the small little lines of the wooden floor.

A pause expanded before he answered.

"Look, I know that probably looked weird, but it had nothing to do with me losing control. It's nothing like that. I promise."

"Is this about The Family?" I blurted. "Did they . . . do something to you?" Luke sighed.

"Why won't you just tell me? I don't get it. Why do you have to keep this a secret still? Halfway across the country, and you still won't talk about it."

"Did it occur to you that maybe I just want to protect you?"

Luke's sincere gaze made me sink into the bed like a stone in water.

"From what? From them? I don't even know who they are because you won't tell me a single thing about them. I'm starting to wonder if they're even dangerous."

"They are," Luke said, his words cutting me. "The less you know about all of it, the better."

"How does that protect me from anything?" I scoffed.

The familiar anger swelled, and I was already eyeing my escape route.

"Not just from them . . . but from me. I'm not the person you think I am. I'm a lot worse," Luke said.

"You're the best person I know. You've been my go-to hero for all my essays since kindergarten."

He shook his head. "Not anymore. I'm no one's hero."

"I'd say you're doing pretty good. We're all alive. Mom is safe, at least. All this other stuff is just growing pains."

It wasn't enough. I wished he trusted me more to tell me, but it was the most real talk Luke and I had had in months. It felt good.

He nudged me. "When did you get so mature? I can't believe you're trying to make me feel better." I couldn't believe it either.

Kimberly shot into my mind, with her reassuring smile and her grace. She was undoubtedly the most patient, understanding person I'd ever met. The least I could do was to pass on some of her magic sorcery to my brother.

"What are brothers for?" I said, lying back on the bed to stare at the ceiling.

He smiled half-heartedly, but he didn't say another word.

I knew it wasn't that simple. We were brothers. But he and Zach had been much more to me. My only stable male figures, mashed together, made up a pretty good dad. Because of that, I'd never be able to be there for him the way he was for me. There would always be things he'd want to keep from me.

"Can I ask you something that's kind of random? And you can't ask me why I'm asking."

I proceeded with caution. If I was going to get any information, it would be from Luke.

He nodded.

"How would one . . . identify other vampires around? Like, say someone in our frat was a vampire, could you tell?"

His eyes narrowed. "Well, you wouldn't. It's easy to hide. Unless you can catch them not breathing, but it's rare. Now, I don't think I'd need to tell you that if you suspect someone you should come out and say it. Vampires around isn't a good thing. It's not like the movies, where they are everywhere and anyone can change whoever they want. Vampires are few and far between. They come from . . . places of power. I'm not even sure you could turn someone if you wanted to."

"What? Why not?"

"I'm not one hundred percent sure, but to put it simply, the blood that changed me was powerful and then you took mine. My blood wasn't as powerful as the last, and yours won't be as powerful as mine."

I started thinking out loud, trying to understand. "You're saying this isn't like *Twilight*, where there are little covens all over the place?"

Finally, a wide smile returned to his face. "*Twilight*?"

"Presley made me watch it." I chuckled, remembering that time.

Presley made me watch a week-long marathon of vampire movies and TV shows when we were first turned. It felt like torture at the time, but admittedly, it was kinda helpful.

Our conversation didn't ease any of my worries. Kimberly was definitely bitten by a vampire, which meant whoever it was could be the big bad. There were so many questions I wanted to ask him, but I had to choose my words carefully.

"So, you haven't suspected anything, then . . . about vampires in the area?"

Luke hesitated, watching my expressions like a hawk. "I haven't. Have you heard anything . . . seen anything?"

"No—"

"Because The Family is dangerous. They'll hurt you. They've killed people. People I know. So, if you know something, you need to tell me."

"I know. There's nothing. I'm just curious."

I held my tongue. Any more talking and I was going to blow the secret. This conversation wouldn't go unnoticed by Luke. He'd definitely tell Zach about it when he got home.

They kept their secrets under lock and key. I would too. I reminded myself of that every time I felt guilty. They had a lot on their plate. All I was doing was easing their burden and following up on a lead. That was it. They didn't need to be involved.

After a few seconds of silence, I sat up and said, "Want to watch me play Final Fantasy?"

Luke hated video games, but when we were kids, he'd watch me play. I wondered if I had blown my cover.

Finally, his shoulders dropped, and he chuckled. "Hell yeah."

Ten

KIMBERLY

With labored breaths, I ran along the busy roadside. My feet followed like a magnet. I checked my watch, squinting in the glare of the morning sun. I had been slowing down and needed to pick up the pace.

I pushed harder, staring straight ahead. My lungs pushed against my rib cage, begging for air. Finally, I went downhill. I jogged on and felt a rush of relief. My headphones drowned out the noise of passersby, and I kept pushing, leaning into the pain. All I had to do was make it to the end of my song.

A gentle tap on my shoulder stopped me in my tracks. I turned and ripped my headphones out of my ears. Nothing. Just the steady stream of cars on one side of me and a white wooden fence on the other. Thoroughly confused and extremely out of breath, I assumed I had imagined it.

I replaced my headphones and picked up my feet. They tried to find their rhythm again, but my body was slow and heavy. I turned my head to make sure no one was following.

Dizziness came over me, and I had barely stopped in time before tripping over my feet. I placed my hands on my hips and leaned down to try to catch my breath. Even though I was still, my eyes couldn't focus on anything. I tried concentrating on the cracks in the sidewalk before finally closing my eyes for a second to get ahold of myself.

"Hey, are you okay?"

A hand touched the middle of my back, and I shrugged it away.

I opened my eyes, and William was combing me over with worry. He looked like he had raided the campus merch store, with his BFU dark-green shorts and baseball tee.

"Yeah. I just felt dizzy for a second." I blinked a couple of times. The feeling from before was completely gone.

"Shouldn't you be taking it easy?"

He was kidding, but I could hear a hint of conviction in his voice.

He reminded me of what the doctor had said. I should be taking it easy. My body was still under stress, and I hadn't given it much time to adjust. I must have gone a little too far.

"Maybe I should walk you back to your dorm," he said. His hair was wet, with beads of sweat, his face flushed.

"Oh, no, you don't need to do that. I can walk by myself. I feel better, really. Were you out running too?"

"Yeah, endurance helps with swimming. Here, you can have my water."

He held out a flask of water that had been buckled to his hip, and I wondered if it was hygienic to drink after a practical stranger. I took the sip of water anyway and closed my eyes for a second to ground myself.

I thanked him, trying not to feel bad about another chance at getting my three-mile time back on track.

"Let me walk you up to the shops up there. I'm heading that way." William motioned up ahead.

I nodded, and we started walking. Our campus was located a short distance from the main town square. I picked my running location for that exact reason. It was populated, usually bustling with bike riders and students walking between classes to get lunch at one of the outdoor patios or an ice cream sandwich from the parlor on the corner.

"I missed you at the party after I came back from the kitchen. They told me you left."

My heart sank. It had been more than two weeks, and I'd completely forgotten about leaving William in the kitchen at the frat house.

"Oh my God, I forgot. It wasn't on purpose. It was a whole thing with this creepy guy, and I left early. I'm so sorry. I should have said something."

It had been two weeks since the night of the party, and in those two weeks, I hadn't seen William in my writing class once. I was starting to wonder if it was because of me.

"Please don't apologize. I was just checking to make sure everything was okay."

His smile seemed sincere as he pulled his hands through his hair.

"I did look for you in class, but I didn't see you. Is everything okay with you?"

"Oh, yeah, I was sick last week, and this week, I had another class to cram for. I'm pleasantly surprised you noticed my absence, though." A smile tugged in the corner of his lips.

"Hey, Kimberly!"

Aaron's voice was coming from up ahead. He bounded toward us in his white socks, flat sneakers, chest held high. Aaron's outfits were casual. Simple tees, and if I were to guess, he had a few different-colored pairs of the same shorts he cycled through. He wore a long-sleeved baby-blue sweatshirt layered with a white shirt underneath.

"Sorry, I got here early. I had nothing to do today, and I was excited."

He looked at William and immediately stuck his hand out. "Hey, man. I'm Aaron. Nice to meet you. I didn't know you knew Kim."

William grabbed Aaron's hand firmly. "I'm William. Kimberly knows me from class. I was just helping her up the sidewalk. She nearly fainted back there."

Aaron frowned. "What? Are you okay?"

"I'm fine. It was nothing. I think I just got dehydrated or something," I said before turning to William. "Thank you. Sorry again about the party. Maybe we can have a raincheck?"

"I'll hold you to it. I'm sure Aaron here will have another party soon. Then we can pick up where we left off. Right, Coleman?" William's dark eyes glistened.

"Uh, right. Sure. I'm sure we will. At my place. The perfect place for you guys to . . . bond. Great idea!" Aaron said at a mile a minute. "Anyway, Kim, are you ready to go?"

"You two have fun today." William cast a lofty expression at Aaron before jogging back down the hill we had just come up.

I shook my head. *Boys.*

"Someone's got an admirer." Aaron nudged me.

"Hardly. He's just a friend."

The sun was high in the sky, and the light reflected in Aaron's dirty-blond hair. I couldn't help but stare at him for a second. Aaron was light, and the sun's rays enhanced every one of his features. It reminded me of that early-morning feel, when I'd wake up in the mountains, the sun catching my skin. It was warm, and it woke me up and invigorated every cell in my body.

"You think he's cute."

Aaron skipped backward in front of me, his hands stuffed into his pockets. Despite the amount of people on the sidewalk, he had no trouble dodging them.

"No."

The words rolled out quickly, but I didn't want to lie.

"Maybe. But that doesn't mean anything. It means I have eyes. Just like everyone else."

"Should I expect wedding bells in the future, then?" Aaron said.

"Wedding bells? I think as far as life events go, right now, I'm a lot closer to a funeral."

Aaron laughed. "Whoa, dark! It's way too early in the day to be talking like that."

We stopped in front of my favorite boutique. It was painted pastel pink and had little hearts on the windows. It displayed the cutest clothes I'd ever seen, and if I could save up long enough, I could afford the block-colored long blazer in the window.

"Do you think I'm cute?"

Aaron's tone was still light and airy.

I wasn't prepared for the sudden rush of heat in my face.

"Why would you ask me that?"

"You're blushing, Burns."

"Can we focus? Please?"

He shook his head. "Right! You're right. I'm focused, and I have news."

We took a seat on one of the concrete benches that had a view of the street and the horseshoe drive across from it. A grassy park was just behind it, with kids playing and a couple having a picnic.

In the two weeks since the night of the frat party, Aaron and I had found zero leads for the vampire in town. Nothing in the news about animal attacks or any other attacks on campus when we had checked the sheriff's log. I had suspected someone had been in my room when I went back for the first time, but I didn't have any evidence other than an out-of-place sticky note and a shirt on the floor I didn't remember wearing. But I wasn't one hundred percent sure I was thinking clearly, considering everything that was going on at the time. I was thankful for the change of locks, though.

"Well, I had an opportunity to ask Luke some stuff. I guess vampires are a pretty big deal if there is one stalking you. They aren't very common, I guess. Not like the movies. He said they come from places of power."

That sentence could have meant so many things. Places of power could refer to anything. Government, money, religion.

"So, the chances of me being attacked by a random vampire are pretty slim, then?"

"Slim but not impossible, I don't think. There are probably outliers and strays. Take me and my brothers, for example. I doubt we're the only exception."

"Yeah, you're right. Did he mention any kind of spidey sense for vampires?"

"I asked about that too. Apparently, nada. And honestly, maybe it's wishful thinking, but I don't think it's The Family. Luke said something yesterday he's never mentioned before. He said they've killed people he knows. It just got me thinking . . ."

"Yes?"

"I just have a hard time believing a member of The Family would go through the trouble of stalking you on campus and not take your blood. Wouldn't they just kill you? And if they're so powerful, wouldn't they just come right out and take us? I mean, we're right here, in broad daylight. It doesn't add up."

"Good point." I kicked at the concrete. "At least we have a good place to start."

If Aaron was right, then that could be a good thing. One vampire we might be able to handle without getting anyone else involved, at least in the beginning. A straggler vampire made the most sense, and that made me feel better. One was better than a mob, and I was sure I didn't want to get involved where The Family was concerned.

"You don't have to worry, though. I won't let anything happen to you. I know that's the most ironic statement of the year, coming from me, but you can count on me."

His smile was warm again, doing that thing where it made me feel like I was floating. It came with no strings attached. No pressure.

"Yeah. I know," I said.

I trusted Aaron in a way I knew he wouldn't hurt me, but I wasn't sure I actually trusted his protection. But that wasn't his fault. I wasn't sure if I'd ever trust anyone else for my own protection other than myself.

"All right, I have to ask you something that's been bothering me, and you have to answer honestly." Aaron hung his head, and I nodded for him to continue. "Do you think I abandoned you at the party? Because, looking back, I'm annoyed that I got too drunk, and I feel like if I had stayed with you, then none of this would have happened."

"No. I don't think that."

"You're sure?" Aaron creased his forehead. "I didn't make you feel bad or . . . lonely?"

There was that word again, haunting me, even in the daylight.

I swallowed. "You don't have to worry that much about hurting my feelings."

"Why not?"

"I'm a big girl. I don't need you to worry about stepping on my toes. I can handle it."

"That's not even a question. I know that. But if I'm being an asshole, I want you to call me out on it. Because I'm stupid, and I'm going to make mistakes. Promise me you will?"

I was speechless at first, surprised by the seriousness in Aaron's eyes and the conviction in his voice.

"I promise."

Aaron slapped his legs and popped up off the bench. "Good. Now, what are we doing? I know we said the library was the move, but now, I'm thinking that sounds extremely boring and my attention span is not there today." A smile danced on my lips.

"Well, that's okay. We don't have to. We can do anything. I was going to head to the grocery store after."

"Can I come!?"

Aaron's eyes were wide.

"You want to come to the grocery store with me?"

"Yes, I want to go. Do you know how long it's been since I've been to the grocery store? Months! It's funny—when you don't need food anymore, you kinda miss the mundane."

Pure excitement radiated through every muscle in his body as he bounced.

I exhaled right before he grabbed my arm and pulled me from the bench. "I can't believe you want to do something so boring."

"It won't be boring with me."

"I don't mind. Come if you want to."

"Yes!" Aaron skipped around me like a kid. "Sorry, I am feeling really good today."

"Hm, you don't say."

"You've never noticed this place?" I said, pulling my car into park.

"Kim, grocery stores are the least of my worries right now." Aaron wasted no time bolting out the door.

I took my time gathering my things and my door opened beside me.

"For you, madam."

Aaron's voice carried and echoed from the mountains around. The grocery store was tucked off the side of the road and looked like every other building in town. They were all made of the same materials. White slatted wood panels and brown shingled roofs. It was one of my favorite things about town. It made everything feel cozy.

"Well, thank you, sir."

Butterflies soared in my stomach momentarily. I'd never had someone open my car door for me. Ever. There was a first for everything.

I grabbed my backup purse and swung it over my shoulder. "Now, don't get too excited. I have to eat pretty healthy because I'm training for a marathon, and I live in a dorm, so I don't have a lot of room."

"You eat healthy? Kim, you're in college. Live a little." He grabbed a cart from one of the outside racks and hopped on the back. "Away we go!"

Aaron was like a kid in a candy store, zooming around, looking over every display. I casually walked around with my cart, waiting for Aaron to come up to me and display some item he loved. To my surprise, I didn't find it annoying. It was endearing and fun.

For thirty minutes, he didn't get tired of showing me new items. "Kim, you have to get these. Please."

I turned around, and Aaron was holding not one but two packages of blueberry waffles.

"I don't need waffles. You're just trying to live vicariously through me."

"Yes, yes, I am." He threw both into the cart. "Oh my God— and these! I lived on these."

He grabbed a package of Oreos. "Double Stuf!"

"Aaron, they're going to kick us out if you keep yelling." I laughed.

Aaron gasped. "I need to go get you some milk for these!"

In a flurry, he threw the Oreos into the cart and left. I sighed, looking at all the junk food in my cart. One junk grocery haul wouldn't kill me.

I kept walking through the aisle and combed through oatmeal flavors. The hair stood on the back of my neck as I looked up expectantly. No one was in the same aisle as me. Looking back, I noticed there weren't many people in the store, just the overhead lights' green, fluorescent glow, which was unusual for the middle of the day.

An eerie feeling poured into the atmosphere like a fog. In all of Aaron's excitement, I had let my guard down. Something I had never done before.

I searched around for the threat my body perceived, but it was nowhere to be found. A weight settled on my chest. Gripping the cart, I pulled myself through the aisle. I glanced behind my shoulder once more. An empty aisle mocked me. Someone was watching me, but who?

I picked up my pace. Every few aisles, I skipped and peeked around corners. The large, circle mirrors on the ceilings revealed nothing. I couldn't put my finger on what I felt or why.

A man walking toward me on his cellphone caught my eye. I ducked into another aisle, hoping to conceal myself. I gripped my cart but kept watch on the bottle of wine on the display next to me, imagining how I could use it to beat the crap out of my attacker. It seemed unlikely that a vampire could be following me in broad daylight, but like Aaron and I said, anything was possible.

The man dressed in a lounge sweater and button-up collar turned the corner, following me into the aisle. My heartbeat was strong in my chest as I hunkered myself closer to the food shelf. I squeezed my fingernails into my palm as I grazed the white wine bottle. I was ready for anything. To my surprise, he passed me quickly, not even looking in my direction.

I relaxed my shoulders and did another quick sweep. The man was one of the only people in the store. No one was following me. I was truly just being paranoid.

"Hey, are you okay?"

I jumped at Aaron's voice behind me, surprised by the sudden relief I felt at his proximity.

"Your heart is beating really fast."

His warm, chocolate eyes panned over me, looking for any sign of danger.

"Oh, yeah. It's nothing. I'm not used to shopping with someone else. It's taking a little adjusting."

Aaron smiled before observing our surroundings. "You don't need to worry. I won't let anything happen to you here, and new things are good."

His words hit me like a ton of bricks, but I kept my reaction neutral. I fought an inside voice that wanted to tell him I didn't need his help. It was true I didn't trust anyone else to protect me, but another part of me—that was growing larger and larger by the day—did. I wanted to trust in the way Aaron did.

"New is really good."

Aaron cradled a giant red gummy bear in his hand. "Here. I got you something." He waited expectantly for my reaction. "Look what I found. Isn't it great?"

"It's . . . a giant gummy bear."

"Awe, you're not as excited as I'd hoped. Come on, let's keep looking."

We continued walking together down various rows before landing in front of the beverages. I grabbed a liter of Diet Coke and handed it to Aaron to put in the cart.

"You know that stuff will kill you, right?" Aaron smirked.

"Is that more probable than me being killed by vampires?"

"You've got a point."

I pushed the cart but stuttered to a stop. "Speaking of which, I've been kind of curious about something."

"Oh no." He raised his brow. "It's a doozy, isn't it. What is it?"

I checked to make sure no one was around us. "I was just thinking about how it's been a few weeks since you . . . you know. Do you have a plan for drinking more blood?"

Aaron groaned. "I knew it. Do we have to talk about that? I was having fun." He tried to push the cart away, and I quickly walked in front, blocking the aisle.

"Come on. You don't think about this stuff? What about your brothers? How do they do it?"

He kicked a dusty wrapper that clung to the floor. "Of course I think about this stuff. All the time. I get it, though. I would be curious too."

Hanging on the cart, he averted his attention, cleaning the dirt from under his fingernails. "I don't have a plan right now, I guess. I'll just tag along when my brothers go out again. They like to go together but I don't know. It feels too casual. Too weird. I don't like it."

I tried to imagine myself in Aaron's position. What it would be like to have to attack the innocent for their blood. The fear. The guilt. It hurt to even imagine. Despite being one of Aaron's victims, I knew it was harder to imagine him having to do something like that. As I got to know him, I could see how completely devastating it must have been for him to have to make those choices.

I nudged him to try to get him to perk up. "Come on, let's go check out."

Upon reaching the checkout counter, the cart was full of junk.

"What is all this stuff? How did you even get it in the cart without me noticing?" I hoisted the groceries onto the conveyor belt.

"I have my ways." Aaron snickered. "Don't worry, I'm paying for it all."

"Uh, no, you're not. I can pay for it myself." I leaned into the cart and fumbled for my purse.

"Kim, I'm paying for it. I put like eighty percent of the stuff in here."

Ignoring him, I continued to search for my wallet in my cluttered purse.

He walked around me to stand in front of the cashier. "Don't listen to her. I'm paying."

I snatched my wallet from my purse. "Don't listen to him. I'm paying."

The young cashier stood frozen, dumbfounded with our banter.

"Ah ha!" I grabbed my card and held it in the air.

Aaron spun around me, blocking the card reader. "Nope, nope. Not happening."

"Aaron, no, you're not paying for my groceries." My frustration was building as I sighed and folded my arms. "What are you doing?"

He held up his hands in surrender, his voice soothing. "I promise I'm not trying to win by trying to assert some weirdo dominance over you. I'm your friend, and I want to pay because I picked all this stuff out. I. Feel. Bad."

"Okay, I get that, but I don't need you to do that. I can pay for them."

Aaron smiled again. "Then, I'm sorry."

I raised a brow. "Sorry?"

"For this." In one fluid motion, he swiped the card from my hand and chucked it as far as it would go.

I could hear the distinct snap of the plastic as it landed two aisles away. I dashed after it with a grunt. As quickly as my anger came, it was gone. It disappeared as I combed through the dusty tile floors. Upon reaching the corner aisle, a girl with long brown hair greeted me.

"Thank you so much. I'm so glad you found it."

Her eyes were glossy, vacant. None of the muscles in her face other than her mouth moved.

"Here you go."

I slowly reached out to grab the card, observing her blank expression. "Okay, thanks again."

"Here you go."

Something about her didn't sit right. Her unblinking expression never left mine as I turned to leave and headed for the front door.

Aaron was casually leaning against the cart, waiting for me.

"You're a jerk." I crossed my arms.

"Sorry, Miss Independent. It had to be done." He watched me, probably expecting me to smile, but I turned back toward the aisle I had come down.

"What's wrong?"

"Something weird just happened . . . and it's happened before."

I had to turn away from him to think back to why that interaction felt so familiar. The blank stare on the girl's face. The lifelessness in her features reminded me of the guy from the gym, the one I had bumped into on the way to the water fountain. He had the exact same look in his eye.

"Kim? You're freaking me out."

"Tell me every vampire power you know about." I moved out of the way to the entrance and just outside the sliding doors.

"Uh, okay. Super strength, killer hearing, good sense of smell, speedy—"

"What about any type of psychic power, anything to do with the mind?"

Like the flip of a lightbulb, Aaron's face lit up.

"You know . . . my brothers did tell me about this thing. I can't do it yet. Kind of like a memory lapse thing."

I frowned. "And you're just now telling me? Tell me how it works."

"I forgot! Presley and I are too young to do it, and my brothers can only do it for a few seconds. So, it's pointless. Basically, I was talking to them, then, two seconds later, I noticed my arm hurt. They told me it was because they punched me. But I didn't remember. I still don't."

"When you said you're too young . . . do you mean that, the older you are as a vampire, the more psychic ability you might have?"

"I think that's a good assumption. Why? Tell me what you're thinking."

"It may be a good way to find our vampire. Think about it. The vampire who attacked me was likely watching me at the frat party. I bet there's evidence somehow at the party. Maybe he compelled someone there."

"Compelled? Like wiped memories, you mean?"

"Yes, or what if it's more . . . what if they can make people do things?" I ran my fingers through my hair and tucked it behind my ears. I desperately wanted to keep my train of thought going.

Aaron bounced from one foot to the other. "I don't know if I'm following but keep going."

"All we need to do is think back to the party and figure out if anything strange happened, anything out of the ordinary."

Aaron frowned. "Shit. I'm not going to be any help. I was drunk off my ass the whole night."

"I know. But think . . . can you remember anything weird anyone said or did at the party?"

Aaron rubbed his forehead. "What about that guy? That guy that grabbed you at the party. Uh, Danny!"

"He was probably just a creep."

"Maybe, but he did cause you to leave the party."

"You're right. Maybe when he touched me, it did something or maybe he was setting everything up to make me leave. You're a genius!"

"Me? No, don't give me the credit for your great ideas." Aaron moved us out of the way before an old lady was about to ram us with her grocery cart. "What do we do now?"

I smiled. "We find him."

Eleven

AARON

"This is a bad idea." I paced back and forth, my sneakers squeaking on the gym court.

Kim sat with her legs dangling over some dirty wrestling mats. It was the first time I'd seen her hair up. It was pulled into a ponytail, with soft wisps caressing her face.

For days, we tried to track down Danny. I had talked to all the guys in my hall and tried to find any mutuals, but no one knew him. Zach and Luke didn't know anything other than he wasn't welcomed back to the house for any reason and to tell them if I saw him. I didn't even bother asking Presley, since he would want to know why.

I thought we might be at another stall until Kimberly called me in the middle of the night. She remembered that Danny was on the swim team.

"Maybe, but we don't have another choice. If we want to know if Danny is our guy, then we have to get closer to him. This is the best way."

Her blue eyes were fixed, set on her intention. She wouldn't be taking no for an answer.

"Plus, it's the perfect setting. There are tons of people here."

"Fine, but we need a code word, something we can work into the conversation if we're feeling uneasy and need to bail." I cast a quick glance at the glass doors in the lobby.

Danny would be there any minute, according to the swim schedule posted on the school bulletin. "Good idea! What about . . . pineapple?"

"Why pineapple?" I smiled.

"It's the first thing that came to mind. Plus, it's my favorite fruit."

Learning one of Kimberly's favorites felt like a privilege not a lot of people got. I swallowed, the butterflies in my stomach fluttering. Luckily, the footsteps outside distracted me.

Danny strolled in on time, duffle bag in hand, and he headed toward the locker room. The way he walked and breathed all seemed normal to me.

Kimberly and I decided not to talk, in fear it might give us away. If he was a vampire, he'd be able to hear us in the lobby.

She raised her eyebrows at me, waiting for my approval. Another look toward the locker room, and I gave a thumbs-up. We started walking. A singular force.

Danny spotted us immediately and turned on his heels. Kimberly and I exchanged looks before running in front of Danny and blocking his path.

"What's up, Danny? Got somewhere to be?" I stuffed my hands in my pockets. I tried to take every note on how to be threatening from what I'd seen Zach do. Step one: be casual.

"I'm not talking to you. I don't want to be seen with you. Leave me alone."

Danny moved to go around us, but Kimberly and I had our hands firmly on the glass doors that led to the pool.

"What? Why?" Kimberly said.

Danny met my eyeline. "Your brothers made it very clear that I need to stay away from you guys. Especially you." He stepped back, eyeing Kimberly. "Zach threatened to break my arms if I didn't. Plural. That dude's a psycho, so I don't want to see if he's bluffing."

He probably wasn't. It looked like Zach had done enough threatening for the both of us, but I wasn't going to let him off that easily.

"We just want to talk to you."

I kept my shoulders pulled back and chest out. Step two: stay calm and act like the coolest guy in the room.

"Listen, I'm sorry I grabbed you, okay? Won't happen again. I was really drunk. I don't even remember being in the living room." He went for the door again, but Kimberly stepped forward, and he flinched away from her proximity.

I wasn't getting any good reads on the guy other than the fact that he genuinely seemed scared of my brother.

"You don't remember?" Kimberly said.

"No. One minute, I was out by the pool, the next, I was sitting next to you. I was really drunk."

I understood what Kimberly was getting at.

"What about after my brothers threw you out? Where did you go?"

Danny reared his head. "I called an Uber to get home. Why?"

"Can we see your Uber receipt?" Kimberly said, her eyes daggers.

The gym bag dropped from Danny's shoulder onto the ground, and he sighed. "Will you stop talking to me if I do?" We nodded.

We waited for Danny to take his phone out and scroll to his previous Uber transactions. Other teammates of his strolled in for practice. All three of us were met with weird looks as they weaved past us behind the glass doors.

After a few minutes, Danny shoved his phone in our faces. His story checked out.

"Now what?" Kimberly said.

We walked toward the weight section. The smell of sweat was everywhere. In every direction I turned, it was all I could focus on. The high ceilings and the echoing amplified the ambience. I could hear everything. Every splash of the pool, the girls sparring in the boxing room, and the clinking of weights hitting the floor.

The front lobby doors opened, and William appeared.

My chest tightened, and my stomach felt like lead.

William spotted us instantly and waved at Kimberly. He didn't look in my direction.

Before I could say some kind of joke, Kimberly's eyes grew wide, and she grabbed my forearm before ushering me out and onto the school lawn.

"What? What's happening?"

"William! William was at the party with me. He got up to get food, and once he was gone, Danny came over He's the only other person it could be." Kimberly paced back and forth in the freshly mowed grass. "I didn't even want to go to that party. I was going to say no, but I dropped something, and he touched my hand. And suddenly, I wanted to go. I never suspected him because . . . because I thought he was my friend." She went silent, blinking a few times.

"How could I be so stupid?"

I hated hearing the hurt in her voice and seeing the disappointment on her face.

"Whoa, whoa, whoa. I never want to hear you say that again. You are the smartest person I know. Who wouldn't want to be your friend? Plus, we don't know if he is our guy yet. We'll have to test him first."

Even though my dislike of William was growing by the minute, I didn't want it to be true. For her sake, I'd have to hold on to the hope that he wasn't the guy, which was the opposite of what I needed to do, since we needed to find the rogue vampire.

I was surprised when a soft smile returned to Kimberly's lips. I tried not to focus on it, but something about her smile drew me in. Hanging out with Kimberly made me happier than I'd felt in a long time. She was genuine. Strong. Brave. Everything I wanted to be.

Kimberly spoke, crossing her arms. "Well, if he's the guy, then he's smarter than I thought. We have to be careful. He could have been planning this from the beginning . . . from the first time I met him. That means he's cunning, and it sounds like he has some kind of plan."

"Shit." I spied my brothers walking toward the gym.

Luke and Zach strutted with their sparring gear in tow, mostly for show, Presley with a basketball under his arm.

Kimberly followed my line of sight. "Oh, no. Are we still sure we shouldn't tell them anything? I don't want them to know who I am, but at the same time, I keep asking myself if we're in over our heads here."

"I'm sure. If I tell them anything, we'll be on the road in the next hour. I'm not risking them leaving you here."

She looked relieved, and I swear she leaned into my arm a smidge.

"Besides, if our theory is right, and he isn't part of The Family, then one vampire shouldn't be hard for us to handle. Maybe there's a reason he's doing what he's doing. Once we know more, we can tell them."

"Hey!" Luke shouted, his voice booming between the stone buildings. "You guys should come with us to the gym."

Luke was back to his usual self, and I hadn't seen him so much as frown since his incident in the kitchen. He wrapped his arm around me and shook me with delight. "Zach and I are practicing some Krav Maga drills today."

Kimberly's eyes lit up as she smiled. "Really? I've always wanted to learn Krav Maga."

"Hell yeah. We'd be happy to teach you." Zach stuffed his hands in his pockets.

I elbowed her softly. "We can't, remember? We . . . have . . . stuff."

"Oh, right. We have stuff."

Zach smirked. "Stuff, huh? Presley, what was it we were talking about earlier?"

"I know! The formal. You're coming to that, right, Kim? Aaron already asked you, I'm sure. It's like three of the frats on campus coming together to throw a huge party at The Conservatory."

Kimberly looked at me for direction, and I shrugged. I had completely forgotten about the formal in all the madness.

"Uh. Yes. I'm going. When is it again?"

"Saturday night. We'll pick you up." Luke smiled. "It will be fun!"

"So much fun," Zach said flatly.

My brothers smiled.

"We'll meet you guys there in a minute, okay?" I made eye contact with Luke and motioned toward the gym.

"All right, we're going," Luke said.

My other brothers, thankfully, followed suit without too much of a fuss.

I turned to Kimberly and slowly let out a breath. "I was going to ask you. I—"

"I just had a really bad idea." Kimberly looked up at me with big innocent eyes. "You're not going to like it."

"Uh-oh."

"What if . . . we got William to the formal somehow. It would be the safest place because we'd be close to your brothers if anything went wrong. We could get William to expose himself somehow and then we'll find out what he wants. Maybe I can ask him to go with me?"

I grimaced. It was a great idea but way too risky. Kimberly was in enough danger as it was. "Oh, absolutely not."

"How else do you expect us to get close to him? I can be his 'date,' and we'll just see what he does. If he's trying to get me alone, we'll be in the one place it's almost impossible to do so. I've been to The Conservatory before for a local concert. It's not that big, and you could stay close by. We'll be able to see if he tries to compel me, and maybe we'll be able to catch him in the act. If our lone vampire theory is correct, we can get his motive and then turn him over to your brothers. He'll be done and dusted and then we can finally be done with this."

"Kim, that idea makes so much sense, but there is no way I can possibly agree to let you do that." My stomach turned.

"I know it's risky, but this may be our only chance to do this. Especially if he doesn't know that I've caught on yet. It will look like we're directly playing into his hand."

She was right. Of course she was. It was clear from the look in her eyes she wasn't going to take no for an answer. But I didn't have to like it.

I sighed. "Does this mean, we need to go crash swim boy's practice so you can ask him to the formal?"

She nodded, and we walked toward the gym. Her breathing hitched in her chest when we reached the entrance. I left to walk out of sight, my heartbeat matching hers. Erratic.

Once again, I found myself eavesdropping. I sat where Kimberly had been sitting on the mats and put in my headphones, with no sound. The gym was loud. On top of all the TVs and workout equipment, I had to tune out the sounds of the basketballs hitting the court in front of me. Thankfully, Presley wasn't on the court. In the next room over was a spin class. And, once again, the horrible echo of the pool room. I listened for Kimberly's heartbeat. I found it quickly. The night in the forest must have etched its unique rhythm into my brain. I would definitely not be telling her about that creepy, newfound information.

"Are you okay?"

William's voice made her heart kick like a horse, the faintest sound of water dripping almost masking his words.

"I'm okay. I just wanted to ask you something that couldn't wait." An edge tinged her voice. "Would you want to go to the big fraternity formal on Saturday? Aaron said I could bring someone, and I thought of you first."

"I have to say I'm surprised. I heard of the formal, but I thought for sure Aaron would ask you first."

He was smirking. I could hear it in the way he said my name.

Vampire or not, I did not like the guy.

"He did, but he's just a friend," she said in one breath.

I swallowed. A burning sensation filled my stomach. The edge in Kimberly's voice remained, and I hoped William would pass it off as nervousness.

"And I'm?" William said.

"Someone I'd like to get to know better," Kimberly said, this time with confidence. "It's Saturday at eight."

"Okay, I can pick you up at your dorm—"

"Oh, no, that's okay. I can just meet you there," Kimberly said, the words tumbling out too fast.

I buried my head in my lap. He had to be on to us by then.

"Are you sure? I'd be happy to," William said.

"I'm sure. I will see you there." Her tone wavered as she turned to leave. "Did you have a number I could reach you at?"

"Actually, my cell is currently broken. But don't worry, I'll be there on time this time, and I'll find you. It shouldn't be a problem, seeing you already know how to find me." He laughed, as if it was perfectly normal to not be reachable by cell phone.

In this day and age, it was less and less likely.

Kimberly's heartbeat was back to doing kick flips.

They said their goodbyes, and as Kimberly and I joined, still not talking, we shared a look. This was about to be our best idea yet, or our worst—I couldn't tell. But if the sick feeling in my stomach was any indication, I was going to regret it.

Twelve

AARON

"Are you sure you're ready for this?" I whispered in Kimberly's ear, holding the car door open.

"I'm ready." She smiled at me, and I marveled at her in her red dress. It hugged her in all the right places. It was short but not too short. She looked comfortable and confident, and I really needed to think about something else. Anything other than how amazing she looked.

"Why are you looking at me like that?" She narrowed her eyes.

"Your hair is fluffy," I spit out quickly. It was beautiful and fluffy. She went to smooth it down and I laughed. "It looks good. Don't worry."

Party buses were pulling into the narrow driveway, tree branches scratching the windows. Fraternity guys and their dates piled out onto the gravel drive, most of whom were already drinking.

An industrial building tucked into the tall pine trees greeted us. A soft, warm glow radiated from the two-story compound, showing the red bricks and iron architecture. A long line stretched all the way to the back of the building. The more people, the better, as far as I was concerned.

"Let's get this party started!" Zach yelled, practically bursting my eardrums.

I followed my older brother's lead on what to wear for the night. Luke and I had on black blazers, matching slacks, and a simple white shirt underneath, but Luke's blazer barely fit over his shoulders, and he had to leave it unbuttoned. Zach, of course, opted for an all-black look.

Presley groaned. "I think your party started way too early. You guys gotta sober up. You promised to get my drinks at the open bar."

Presley found a black-and-white-checkered blazer and opted for a pink bowtie, and thanks to Luke, we were almost late because of his drunken tutorial on how to tie a bowtie.

"Don't worry, little brother. We are here for you! You can count on us." Luke flung an enthusiastic finger at Presley, jabbing him hard in the chest.

"Ow!" Presley rubbed his chest. "You guys should just go and do your loner-twin thing, and we'll catch up later."

"Got it!" Zach and Luke said simultaneously, leaving us in peace. They disappeared into the growing crowd together.

I heard through the grapevine multiple sorority girls had been dropping hints for them to accompany them to the formal, but since we'd been in Blackheart, I hadn't seen either of them do anything more than flirt with a few girls here and there.

"They seem excited," Kimberly said.

"They were in a weird mood today and started drinking early."

I stuffed my hands in my pockets. I'd stopped trying to figure out the reasons for their moods a long time ago. Whatever the reason, it would stay locked away along with all their other secrets.

"Now that's an understatement." Presley chuckled under his breath, pulling out a pack of cigarettes, then popping one in his mouth.

"If Zach sees you smoking, he's going to freak out." I sighed.

"Please, it's not like it matters now." His eyes switched to Kimberly. "Besides, he's way too drunk to notice." Presley exhaled a large puff of smoke with a pleased sigh.

Kimberly and I exchanged another glance as we started for the back of the line.

We'd spent the last few days preparing the best we could. Our hearts beat together in our collective spiral of anxiety. I had to keep a watch on my brothers and make sure they didn't get too close, while also keeping an eye on Kimberly and William.

"Are we going to stand in this line?" Presley whined. "I'm already bored."

Outside, the crowd surged at the doorway, with more people than I had thought. A wall of cologne and perfume hit me like a freight train. My throat was instantly dry from the inhale.

Heightened vampire senses weren't always a good thing.

"What do you suggest?" I said.

"Well, I did have one idea. The thing we used to do to sneak into the movie theater . . ." Presley shot me a wicked smile. "We even have a damsel now. It will be way more convincing."

I frowned. "I'm not subjecting Kim to our stupidity. I mean, not unless she wants to be subjected to it?"

Her eyes searched us. "I have no idea what you're talking about. But I guess I'm open to it."

"You heard the woman. Follow my lead." Presley put his cigarette out on the ground and threw it into his pocket. He pointed out into the trees. "Oh my God. What is that?"

Innocent Kimberly fell for his trap, like I had hundreds of times growing up. She turned to look for the signs of dangers in the trees, and in one fluid motion, I leaned down to pick her up bridal style.

"What are you doing!?" she yelled.

"Shhh. Be chill. Act like you're dead or something," Presley whispered to her before cupping his hands over his mouth. "Everybody, move! Out of the way. We have a fainter over here! She needs to get inside!"

To my surprise, she played along, leaning her head into my chest and relaxing. Her warm skin emitted electricity against my chest, and I hoped she couldn't feel my heart beating like a hammer.

I did my part in maneuvering us through the crowd. "Everybody, please move! We need to get her inside to get some air!"

A slurry of voices talked around us, most whispering their concerns and wondering if she was okay.

"Do we need to call an ambulance?" someone said close to my ear. "She'll be okay. We just need to get her inside." Presley sounded so reassuring.

She was a natural, with her eyes firmly shut, her body limp in my arms.

We stepped through the entrance, and the music hit me even harder than the perfume had. I thought navigating large crowds was bad, but loud music would take some getting used to. I slowly tilted her out of my arms, letting her stilettos hit the floor. The venue held high steel beams strung with lights in every corner. I had imagined a sort of club with dance floors shifting colors, but everything was warm-mahogany wood. The bar was tucked off into the corner, and the stage stood front and center. The DJ was already in place. Next to him was a winding staircase that led to the second floor.

The smooth groove of the music vibrated into my feet and up my spine. It felt powerful, igniting my senses.

I glanced at Presley to see if he was feeling as disoriented as I was. His wide-eyed smile told me he wasn't. It was going to be a long night.

"And here we are. A fast pass to the fun." Presley smiled, looking proud of himself.

"Do you guys do that kind of thing often?" Kimberly brushed off her dress and readjusted her hair.

"More than I care to admit." I chuckled.

The venue wasn't packed yet, and I didn't see any sign of William.

"I'm going to go try to steal a drink from someone. Do you guys want anything?" Presley said, mid-sprint for the bar.

"No, we're good." I waved him off.

I turned to Kimberly, speaking louder. "A little birdie told me that you don't drink."

She smiled but never stopped searching the crowd. "No, I don't."

"Do you mind if I ask why?" I shifted my stance closer to her, letting our shoulders touch as we watched the door.

"I-I just . . . I don't know what my tolerance is, and I've never had anyone I trusted enough to drink with. You know, in case I got so drunk I couldn't drive home or something. Is that stupid?" She bit the inside of her lip.

"Definitely not stupid. You know . . . you do have someone you can trust now, though. I'd take good care of the drunk you. I'll even hold your hair if you throw up." I nudged her.

"Maybe when we aren't on an important mission." She looked up to me, her blue eyes sparkling in the twinkle lights ahead.

I wanted to drown in them, but I had to focus. I reminded myself of not only the task at hand, but the fact that the girl in front of me had been attacked twice in the last month, once by me. That made thinking of her as anything other than a friend off-limits. She needed me to help keep her safe, not have feelings for her.

Her attention shifted back to the door, and her face dropped. "There he is. You're going to stay close, right?"

"Don't worry. I'll be right here." I winked at her before William intruded into our circle.

"Good evening." He smiled in his crisp black blazer. Everything about him was well-put together. He pulled a red rose from behind his back, handing it to Kimberly with a short bow. "You look breathtaking."

Her voice caught in her throat, and her heart sped up. "Uh, thank you."

I wasn't prepared for the heat that rose from my chest into my face. Loosening my balled-up fist, I swallowed the lump in my throat.

Wipe that smirk off his face.

The voice was back with a vengeance, and I had a feeling It was here to stay. It only came up sometimes, and usually, I could push It away, but despite my resolve, the heat traveled up my throat.

"She likes peonies, by the way." I tried my best to force a wide, toothy smile. "Don't worry. You'll get it next time."

William chuckled, the whites of his teeth taunting. "Noted. Thanks for keeping my date company. Much appreciated. Say . . . where's your date, Coleman?"

It took me a second to realize he was using my fake last name.

Kimberly looked up to me, chewing the inside of her cheek, and I gave her a reassuring wink.

"Didn't bring one. Thanks for the reminder."

The events of the night would have been much more fun if Kimberly was my date. I imagined twirling her around on the dance floor, dancing like maniacs, and maybe even . . . slow dancing. Maybe in another life that would have been possible, but in the one where vampires existed, I was doomed to go stag.

William placed his hand on the small of Kimberly's back. "You ready?"

The proximity of his skin next to her felt wrong. Not just because he was potentially a brainwashing vampire, but something else made me want to snatch her away from him.

She nodded, and they made their way into the crowd. The music was loud, making it hard to hear where they were. I'd have to keep her in sight while not making it obvious. They slowly moved toward the bar.

As people piled into the building, the volume in my ears kicked up a notch. The smothering conversations everywhere were a dull roar. Announcements were just about to start, and I was already feeling sensory overload.

"Whatcha doing?" Presley appeared next to me, holding a Jack and Coke. His favorite. I diverted my attention to my shoes, but Presley caught my line of sight. "W-What's she doing with that guy?"

"That's her date," I said.

"I thought you guys were going together. That sucks. You must be mad jealous, huh?" Presley laughed before sipping his drink.

"No, we're just friends."

They were still standing next to the bar, due to the crowd, and William had Kimberly pressed against a wooden pillar. His arm was placed casually over her. He'd lean in closer to her every time someone passed behind him. I coughed a little, diverting my attention, before the voice started up again.

Presley smiled. "Whatever you say. You look jealous, though."

"I'm not. And, no, I don't," I snapped.

It couldn't be jealousy. If I were jealous, that would mean I liked Kimberly more than a friend, and I couldn't do that to her. Not after everything she'd been through. We couldn't be together. So, it was settled. I didn't like her.

"You don't have to get all defensive. If one of us was going to fall in love with a human, it was definitely going to be you. Zach and I already placed a bet on it. A thousand dollars says you admit it by the end of the month. Zach thinks you'll cave earlier than that."

"Where'd you get a thousand dollars?"

There were so many things wrong with his statement, so I homed in on the less offensive one.

"Betting, duh." He took another sip of his drink.

"You're one to talk," I snipped. "You also invited someone who happens to be human."

Presley's date for the night was Ellis Finch, but he hadn't arrived yet. A guy from Presley's Art History class who was at least six foot two with warm-brown skin and a thick mustache. He was a mellow dude who seemed way too smart to be into my brother.

"Oh, that's different. You've been giving her 'I love you' eyes since I first saw you guys together. Me and Ellis are completely casual. You look like you might propose any minute."

"All right. I'm done talking about this."

Presley snickered with his lips pressed to his glass. "Truth hurts sometimes, I know."

The announcement commenced, and we listened to the speaker, who was the president of another frat. He was tall and lanky and cussed like a sailor, which Presley found hilarious. I periodically diverted my attention back to Kimberly and William, who were also at a standstill, watching. Kimberly looked to be perfectly fine. Every so often, I'd tried to find the rhythm of her heartbeat or tune into their conversation, which was mostly small talk. Mentions of the weather. Nothing important.

Kimberly fluffed her hair, and her eyes searched for me. I reached up, acting like I was yawning, and caught her gaze.

My mind started to wander. What if William wasn't the vampire but just a charming guy who was into Kimberly? What if she ended up liking him too? The rage bubbled in my chest. I tried to stifle it, but the thought of them together kept bringing it to the surface. I didn't like William. Vampire or not. He wasn't good enough for her. I wasn't either.

She's ours.

The voice was a mere echo as the music picked up. The announcements faded and the partygoers broke out into dance while the lighting dimmed. Warm twinkle lights turned cool, and pools of blue and green hues flooded the dancefloor. A light fog poured from the stage, covering our feet.

I sighed. That was going to make my spy adventure much easier.

Presley had emptied his drink and chewed the ice. "I don't get the big deal, anyway. If she was your girlfriend, couldn't you just tell her you were a vamp and then maybe she could donate her blood to you? That would solve a lot of problems."

"What!? No, no I wouldn't tell her," I said quickly.

"But you'd drink her blood?"

Presley was clearly buzzing, and he loved to stir the pot. He was the cause of almost all our fights at home when drinking was involved.

"No! Can you go away so I can enjoy my night, please?" I moved into the crowd, keeping my peripheral on Kimberly.

"Fine. Ellis is almost here, anyway. I gotta go get another drink. I think I see Chelsea over there. I'll be sure to tell her you're going stag." He patted me on the shoulder, and before I could turn around to protest, he was gone. I rolled my eyes. *Little brothers.*

I caught sight of my mark in the fog. William had his arm locked with Kimberly's, and he led her into the crowd. Still looking nervous, she played it off well and let him coax her into dancing with him. William looked up, catching me watching them. The smile returned to his face, and he kept dancing.

I shook my head. I had to regain my focus. Keep William in a safe proximity to the rest of my brothers and wait to see if he made any kind of move. We outnumbered him, four to one. No way was he going to leave with Kimberly.

A hand grazed my shoulder, and I knew who it was by the smell of her sickly-sweet perfume. Chelsea was a beautiful blonde from Sigma Sigma Xi, but she wasn't my type. For one, she couldn't take a hint.

"Aaron, oh my God. You clean up well," she said, looking me up and down. Her dress reminded me of a disco ball, adding to the sensory overload.

"Chelsea, this isn't a good time." I patted her on the shoulder. "Cool dress, though."

I didn't actually like her dress but thought it might make her happy enough to leave.

She followed my line of sight. "You look lonely and a little sad. Dance with me."

Chelsea grabbed my hands and pulled me closer toward William and Kimberly, walking us into their direct line of sight. I exchanged looks with both of them while Chelsea pulled me closer. She put her hands to my chest before sliding them down my body.

I stopped her. "What are you doing?"

"Just having fun. You should try it." She winked.

Having fun was out the window. I glanced back at Kimberly, who was watching me. When our eyes met, she raised her eyebrows, and I shrugged. Chelsea and I continued to dance, while William spun Kimberly around. My heart jumped every time his hand met hers.

Every so often, I would see Zach and Luke fist pumping, drunkenly dancing, and jamming to the music.

Each song passed slowly, and I was relieved when Kimberly pulled away from him and excused herself to the restroom.

I mirrored her movements, stopping Chelsea from dancing on me. "I gotta head to the restroom. I'll be right back."

"Do you just want me to wait for you here?" Chelsea said, moving her body to the beat of the song.

"Uh, sure. Sure. That works."

Kimberly and I reached the hallway to the bathroom at the same time. A large red velvet door led into a hallway. The muffled noise felt like a warm blanket over my ears.

I opened the door for her, and we could finally talk despite the music shaking the walls.

"Are you good?"

"I'm doing okay." She grabbed my arm, ushering me toward the quiet corner. "He hasn't said anything definitive yet, but he keeps talking about what we are doing after this. I think he's trying to get me alone."

"Well, that's not happening," I said. "Do you think this is our guy?"

"I'm still not sure. I feel like I'm getting closer, but he keeps noticing you watching me. Maybe you should back off a little and stay out of sight? That way, if he is the guy, he'll be more likely to slip up."

"Kim, that seems like a horrible idea on top of our already risky plan. I don't like this guy."

She looked down, calculating. "I know, but there's something weird about this. I can feel it. It has to end tonight, or we may not get another chance. We have to draw him out. Once he does, I'll give the signal, and I'll make an exit and then you can get your brothers. Do you think you could stay in earshot enough that you could hear the code word?"

"I don't know. It's so hard to hear in here, but I think one word I can listen for."

She looked so sure of herself. It infused me with confidence. He couldn't take her anywhere I wouldn't see and couldn't hurt her in public without exposing himself. She was right. Our time was up. Everything had to end that night.

I accompanied her back through the crowd, returning her to her date, and I returned to mine.

Chelsea placed her hand on my chest. "Now, where were we?"

Kimberly and William disappeared farther into the crowd and into the fog. It was going to take a lot of mental power to listen for her signal, while also entertaining Chelsea. Not to mention, the music had picked up, and people grew wilder. Sweaty bodies moved me in every direction, while the music drummed in my ears.

"Chelsea, I don't know. I'm not in a dancing mood," I blurted.

"That's okay. Maybe we should get a drink instead?" I hesitated, and she caught it. "I know your mind is elsewhere, okay? But I still don't think you should be alone tonight. We can have fun."

Her words cut deep. From the moment I met her, I felt for her.

Her ex-boyfriend had tried to push her down the steps in front of our frat house when I stopped him. I stayed up with her all night as she cried off all her mascara onto my white shirt.

She could be pushy at times, but she also gave me the impression that she'd been through some things. At the same time, I knew the more attention I gave her, the harder it would be for her to let go of her image of me. I wasn't the man she envisioned. I wasn't even a man, really. She wanted something I couldn't give.

She didn't wait for my reply and dragged me by hand toward the bar. That was my cue to listen hard for Kimberly's voice.

Kimberly's voice rang through the crowd. "Are you having fun?"

"I'm having a marginal amount of fun," William said. "Are you?"

"I am. I just don't feel like I'm getting to talk to you," Kimberly said.

"Well, this was your idea." William laughed. "What do you want to know?"

"What do you want to drink?" Chelsea's voice cut my concentration.

"I don't know. My stomach kinda hurts, so I'm not sure if I want to drink."

"Two AMFs please." Chelsea slapped down her ID. It hadn't occurred to me that she was older than me.

I hid my face, hoping the bartender wouldn't see me lurking nearby, not that I had planned on drinking, anyway. Leaning against one of the large wooden pillars, I tried to listen again.

"What are you doing all the way over here?" Kimberly asked.

He chuckled. "The sunny views in California were calling my name. There are so many interesting people."

A longer-than-usual pause gave way, and I wondered if I had somehow lost their voices in the crowd until William said, "I'd love to tell you all about it. Would you accompany me upstairs, where it's a little quieter?"

Heat rushed to my face again, and before I could contemplate what I was feeling, Kimberly spoke again. "Uh, sure. I'd like that, but I think I'll take you up on your offer. Do you think you could get me a pineapple margarita?"

Shit. I spun around and searched for her in the crowd. As the night went on, the music was louder, the lights darker, and more people swarmed the dance floor.

"You don't drink, sweetheart. Why don't you tell me why you really invited me here?" William's voice was sharp.

Ice ran through my veins. He knew. She was right. He was the vampire.

"Here you go. This should help your mood." Chelsea thrust a tall glass of blue liquid into my hands.

My mind was going a million miles a minute. I needed to ditch Chelsea, and any attempt to get her to go away was bound to lead into an argument I didn't have time for. Kimberly needed me.

William's voice was a small whisper in the crowd. "You don't know what you've gotten yourself into."

Chelsea's white sparkling dress caught my eye. It was the way the lights from the disco ball danced and shimmered on the sequins. I knew what I needed to do. I brought the drink to my mouth and pretended to chug it. A few streams of the alcohol trickled down my neck, and I pretended to fall into a coughing fit. The liquid sprayed all over her dress. The blue glowed neon against her white dress, and Chelsea cursed under her breath.

"What the hell? Are you okay?" She placed her drink on the bar, grabbing mini towelettes to clean herself.

"I'm so fucking sorry. I'll get you more paper towels!" I said, knowing full well I would not be doing that.

I found myself in the middle of the dance floor. Kimberly's voice wasn't coming up. I couldn't tell if she wasn't replying or if I just couldn't hear her.

I peeked over the wall of bodies, then the bass exploded into a never-ending pulsing that wouldn't stop rattling my eardrums. The crowd thrashed from side to side, nearly knocking me to the ground. I cupped my hands over my ears, my eyes darting for the faintest sign she was near. With every second, fear crept into my mind, and I tried to search faster. Every corner ended up empty. I couldn't find my brothers, and I couldn't find Kimberly. The light show continued, and my heart beat faster in my rib cage. I stumbled into the crowd. The rhythmic thumping boomed harder and harder. Every sense that had once made me feel invincible dragged me down with it. No matter how much I tried to focus on anything else, I couldn't. I was drowning.

"What's wrong?" Luke towered over me. He grabbed my forearm and pulled me away from the view of the dance floor. Relief washed over me.

"Please help me. I've got to find Kimberly. Something's wrong."

I pushed my way through the crowd with a newfound confidence, caring less and less how hard I was pushing. I searched continually for any sign of her red hair.

Luke was hot on my heels. "Tell me what's going on."

"I will. I just have to find her first."

I called out her name, knowing it was futile with the whole dance floor pulsating with movement.

"There she is!" Luke pushed me in her direction before I could even see her. His height gave him an advantage I didn't have.

When I spotted her, she was moving toward the edge of the dance floor close to the stairs.

"Wait, stay here! I'll be right back, and I'll explain everything. Okay?" I said.

Luke nodded and I left him in a haze of bodies in the middle of the floor.

When I reached Kimberly, she was stumbling around on her heels, her eyes hazy and confused.

"Kim! Are you okay?" I couldn't hide the desperation in my voice. I scanned her shoulders to check for the faintest mark or bruise. There was nothing. She was unharmed. The world slowed, and I pulled her close to me. "Don't scare me like that."

She blinked a few times before speaking. "Yeah, I'm okay. It was just . . . I don't know what I was doing. We were dancing, and . . ."

The groggy look in her eyes didn't leave immediately, and my throat tightened.

Her head snapped up. "William! He went to get me a drink and never came back, but I saw him go up the stairs. Then it was like I couldn't control my body. But I wanted to go up there."

She pointed to the tall winding staircase next to us. Black iron all the way to the ceiling.

"You don't remember what he said to you?" I said.

The blue lights accentuated the worry in her eyes. Kimberly frowned. "No, what did you hear?"

"Don't worry about it. I'm going to take you to Presley and don't leave his side, okay? I'm going to go up there."

She grabbed my wrist as I turned to lead her. "Aaron, wait!"

I glanced down at her hand and then back up to her face. "Kim, you're going to be okay. I'll be right back. I'm just going to see if he is still here."

She kept a firm grasp on my wrist. "No, it's not that. You have to be careful."

A smile tugged at the edges of my mouth. "Are you worried about me?"

"Well, I mean . . . do you even know how to fight vampires or fight anyone?"

"I guess you have a point, but I have to go see if he is still here."

"Aaron, something doesn't feel right. I don't know."

Her blue eyes swallowed me whole, longing woven into her voice . . . for me. I wanted to bathe in the feeling.

"I'll have Luke come with me. We'll finish this."

Her eyes grew wide, and she squeezed my arm. "Don't tell him anything. Don't tell him about me. Promise me you won't. Please."

She was backing out of our plan. I opened my mouth to protest. Her desperation flooded my senses. I was pathetic, absolute putty in her hands.

"I won't. I'll be very vague. You will have to let go of the death grip you have on my arm, though." I motioned to my wrist, where she had been white knuckling it.

She let out a breath. "Okay. Yeah, that's a good plan."

I snuck her through the crowd, leaving her with Presley, who, to my surprise, wasn't too drunk . . . yet. He wrapped his arm around her, promising to keep her safe.

As I made my way back to the dance floor, Luke walked in step with me. "Are you going to tell me what's going on with you?"

"Kimberly has a stalker. He's been around all night, and I need to go and check and make sure he's gone. Will you come with me?"

It was a bold move, saying a lie directly to Luke's face. He wouldn't buy it, but he would come with me. That's all I needed.

Luke stared at me for a minute, looking completely sober.

"Why can't you just tell me the truth?"

"I don't have time. We have to go now."

I walked toward the iron steps looming in the distance.

Luke followed behind me, and my confidence rose. I didn't want to admit to Kimberly how nervous I was. If her theory was true, William was dangerous. Questions had to be answered.

As we neared the top of the steps, Luke slapped me on the back. A pat of reassurance. Guilt ruined any ounce of comfort it brought me. I hated lying to him despite every lie he'd ever told me to my face. This was different. He had those secrets to keep me safe. I was putting us all in danger.

As we reached the top of the stairs, I slackened. There didn't appear to be anyone up there. The lighting was dim, and the stage lights cast a light show over the ceiling above us, the cool blues and greens long gone. The ceiling was red, and the lights above danced a warm orange. We stepped out onto the wooden floor that made a distinct sound with every step.

"Is that him?"

Luke, the more observant one, spotted him leaning into the corner almost completely disguised by darkness. "To what do I owe the occasion?" William's voice was cold.

"I've seen you around before." Luke took a step forward, and I followed close behind.

"You have. I've attended some of your fancy parties," William said.

"What do you want with Kimberly?" Luke took another step forward, keeping a protective stance over me. "Whatever it is, I think we can come to an agreement here. You need to leave her alone."

I matched his stance. "He's right. This ends now."

"Oh, so he does speak? Hiding behind big brother, are we? Typical Aaron," William said.

"I'm not the one hiding," I said.

"You're right. How rude of me." William stepped into the red light, only half his face showing. Something dark lurked in his eyes.

Luke must have sensed the shift. He leaned in closer to me. His shoulder pushed me back a half step.

"Now, I thought this was a party? Why so serious all of a sudden?" William smirked, his eyes never leaving Luke.

"You're one of us."

Luke's voice was the one that was icy cold this time. I wasn't used to it.

William scoffed. "I'm nothing like you."

Luke talked through gritted teeth and looked at me. "This was your secret. You knew what he was, and you didn't say anything."

"Well, technically, I had an idea, but I wanted to be sure." William took another step toward us.

Luke's voice was shrouded in worry. "We need Zach."

"Too bad he's all the way across the building. I don't know much about you, Luke, but I do know that you'd never leave your poor little brother up here to fight alone." William's eyes bore into mine.

"Who are you? What do you want?" Luke said.

"Isn't that obvious? I want the girl," William said.

I shook my head. "If that was true, why didn't you take her before? You had plenty of opportunities."

William's pointed teeth peeked behind a confident smile. "Are you sure you're not just jealous you weren't the only one to taste her?"

I wasn't prepared for the wave of anger crashing into me.

Within seconds, I was shaking from head to toe.

Kill him. Kill him. Kill him. Kill him.

The voice seeped into my skull, making it harder and harder to think clearly.

"What's he talking about?" Luke gripped my forearm, but I couldn't feel it with the heat pulsing through my body. "Kimberly? The girl you've been hanging out with?"

William tilted his head, laughing at me. "Maybe I just like messing with you."

Killhim.Killhim.Killhim.Killhim.Killhim.Killhim.

The voice was getting louder and louder.

"You shouldn't have brought big brother, Aaron." William sighed. "Now I have to complicate this a little."

I wanted to comprehend what he was saying, but I couldn't get a grip. Every time I tried to hold on, it felt like a rope pulling me out to sea. My body was rigid, writhing with anger.

"Aaron, what's wrong with you?" Luke's voice sounded faint.

William's eyes locked with mine. "She tasted good too."

I lunged forward, letting rage take me. William moved toward us. A millisecond later, I found myself on the floor. Luke had pushed me behind him, and William was standing in the middle of the floor, bathed in crimson light. Luke stumbled backward slowly.

As quickly as it came, the rage and the voice were gone. I rushed to Luke's side, with my heart in my throat. His eyes were hazy and confused, just like Kimberly's, only they were cloudy and black. He looked right through me, as if I weren't there.

William's eyes stayed locked on Luke. "Now that was interesting. Just when I thought there was nothing you boys could do to surprise me."

"What did you do to him?" I said.

"He'll be okay. Just needed to jog his memory a bit. Oh, and I did you a favor. He won't remember any of this. Neither will you." William grabbed my wrists. His face just inches from mine. "You're not ready yet. But you will be soon, and when the time is right . . . you won't be able to save her."

He let go, and the world fell away. The floor opened up and blackness took over.

KIMBERLY

Waiting for Aaron was impossibly long. Every minute that passed felt like an hour. Presley was getting more drunk by the second, and I felt less and less secure. I had no view of the stairs, and all I was left with was a worried pit in my stomach.

My brain didn't feel right. I replayed the formal over and over again in my head to try to find the hole, and there was something I missed. I just couldn't put my finger on it.

Had I found out William's true identity? Was he actually dangerous? Signs still pointed to him being the vampire, but I had no clue why. I was missing something crucial.

The stairs were still empty, and my manicure was trashed. I had chipped off almost every single speck of paint in the span of five minutes.

"So, Kimberly, seen any good vampire movies lately?"

I turned my attention back to Presley, who was casually swaying with a drink in his hand. His date, Ellis, was at the bar, getting them more drinks.

"W-What? That's really random." I scratched my neck.

A smile spread across Presley's face. "Is it? Come on, tell me your favorite."

"Uh, I'm not sure. I don't like vampire movies."

"Hmmm. That's interesting because you're into my brother, and he's one, so I figure you must have a thing for vamps."

A lump caught in my throat. "He's . . . what? I-I don't know what you're talking about."

Presley's curls bounced when he laughed. "Come on. Cut the shit. I know."

Terror filled my body in a way I never felt before. My mind went over anything I might have done to reveal the secret.

I stole a look back at the crowd. "How did you find out?" I spoke in a whisper, knowing he could hear me. My hand was shaking at my side.

"What?! You know?" Presley yelled. "Aaron told you, didn't he? I knew it!"

Despite the loud music, he had gained a few sideways glances.

Shushing him, I said, "Presley, please be quiet. You can't tell anyone."

"I can't believe I was actually right! I knew Aaron couldn't keep a secret." He bounced.

"He didn't tell me. I found out . . . another way."

"You found out another way . . ." His head popped up. "What, did he bite you or something?"

The nightmare continued. I couldn't believe it. How could he guess? How could he figure it out?

His eyes were wide, and he bounced again. "I'm right, aren't I? He bit you! Holy shit."

"How did you figure it out?"

He held up his hand matter-of-factly, counting down. "Well, you're a bad liar, for one. Two, you didn't even flinch when Zach broke that chair in the living room. Let alone question it. Three, you guys have been sneaking around and giving each other the eyes. It was not that hard to decipher."

My face was hot, and my stomach was doing somersaults. It was too much. I wasn't ready for Aaron's older brothers to know about me yet. Something deep inside me was directly opposed to that idea, but I didn't know why.

"Presley, please don't say anything to your brothers."

He wouldn't let it go that easily. Like a five-year-old who just discovered the best secret in the world, it was written all over his face.

"Come on. This is the secret of the century. It explains so many things!"

"Please. I'm literally begging you not to tell them."

I spotted a familiar face making his way through the crowd. Luke beelined for the bathroom, only he was alone. Aaron wasn't following him. I turned my attention back toward Presley. "I have to go. Just don't say anything yet. Please."

His smile softened. "Don't worry, your secret is safe with me."

I had no idea if I could trust him enough to believe a word from his mouth, but it would have to do. I had done enough begging for one night. I pushed through bodies, much slower than I'd hoped. Sweaty people were packed together like sardines closer toward the stage. I made an exit for the hallway that led to both bathroom doors.

"Luke?" I peeked my head in, trying not to startle him. "Is everything okay?"

He stopped at the sound of my voice but didn't turn to face me. I moved in, trying to get a good look. Luke's once-warm complexion was cold. His expression had turned into a blank slate. His hands were shaking. The blue neon sign above us cast a dark shadow on his face.

He was silent as he stared off into space. His forehead creased, the reflection of pain registering into his frown lines.

"Hey, what's wrong? Are you okay?"

Luke closed his eyes for a second and took a step back. When his back hit the wall, his eyes were forced open. "I don't know. I'm sorry. Just give me a second."

Immediately, his reaction registered. He was having a panic attack. I'd seen it many times growing up in foster care, though I'd never had one myself.

My heart sank, and panic grew on his face. He crumpled to the ground, pulling his back up against the wall.

"Hey, it's okay. You're okay," I said softly.

He gripped his chest and cried in pain. "I'm okay. I'm okay. I'm sorry." He exhaled sharply, as if he were struggling to force air out of his chest. "I-I'm sorry just—just give me a second."

The creaking door let in a flood of music, and Luke laid his head on his knees, covering his ears.

I blocked Luke from any prying eyes. "Hey, can you give us a minute?"

The group of sharply dressed, sweaty men met me with blank faces.

"Seriously, give us five minutes, please?"

They finally retreated, and I leaned down next to Luke. "It's going to be okay. You're safe."

He pulled his hands to his head and covered his eyes. His body rocked with each stifled sob. "I'm sorry. I can't do this . . ."

I was careful not to touch him.

"Do you want me to get Presley? I think I saw him—"

"No! I just need a second. I need a second." He buried his head into his knees, exhaling. "I just need it to stop."

"You're okay. Everything is okay," I said. I tried to keep my voice low, but the music echoed in the hallway.

"I need my brother. I need—"

The door swung open, the thumping of the music shaking the walls.

Zach appeared, his eyes full of panic. "Hey, I'm here. I'm here."

I backed up and let him sit next to his brother. He sat on the floor, and Luke held out his hand for Zach to grab.

"I saw her. I saw her." I could barely make out Luke's voice among the sobs. "She was here. She's in my head again."

"She isn't here." Zach dug his hand into his pocket and pulled out a piece of gum. "Come on, chew on this. Focus on the taste."

Luke pushed his hand away, but Zach persisted. "Come on. It's going to help. This will pass."

Luke took the piece of gum and buried his face into his knees. "She was here. I felt it. Maybe they're here somewhere. We need to check."

Zach gripped his hand and whispered, "They aren't here. We're okay. She can't find us."

I'd never seen Zach so soft or Luke so vulnerable. It reminded me of the feeling I got when I'd taken the picture of the family in the hospital. Their love for each other felt tangible, so strong I could reach out and touch it.

Zach looked up, as if he had forgotten my existence. "Thanks for keeping him company. I think I've got it from here."

The dark circles under Zach's eyes revealed a man worn beyond all recognition. They told thousands of stories all at once. I didn't know what the twins had been through, but I knew it was something that must have never touched Aaron or Presley. I was starting to truly realize why Zach and Luke had kept secrets from their little brothers.

Zach gave me a shy smile before the door swung open again. A few guys and their girlfriends stopped to stare at us.

"Hey, give us, like, ten minutes, okay? Then we'll be out of your hair," Zach said.

One random guy huffed. "We've been waiting. You can't—"

"Dude, does it look like I give a shit? Get the fuck out!" He grabbed an empty beer bottle and chucked it at the door. Its shattering spilled all over the floor, leaving remnants twinkling in the hallway's dim lights.

He sighed, turning his attention back to me. "Sorry."

"Let me know if you need any help." I smiled and walked back toward the door.

As I opened it, the same group tried to walk past me.

"I swear to fucking God, if you try to walk in here again before that ten minutes is up, I will kick your fucking ass. Stay the fuck out!"

I eased past them, and they reluctantly closed the door.

"Ugh. I hate that guy," they complained, planting their feet firmly by the door.

And I thought my life was complicated enough with a vampire trying to kill me. I couldn't even contemplate the things Luke said. The questions kept bubbling up in my mind. Who was the girl Luke was talking about? What happened to him to make him so scared? All of that was overcome by the growing fear that I needed to find Aaron as soon as possible.

"Hey! Sorry about that. I cleared everything up."

Aaron's voice startled me. Relief washed over my senses, seeing him perfectly fine next to me. I did a quick once-over to make sure he was still in one piece. His hair was a little wild, but he looked fine.

"What do you mean? What happened to Luke?" I said.

"Luke?" Aaron looked behind me and responded like he was citing a well-rehearsed speech. "Luke's fine. He got upset before we talked to William and left."

"I saw him come down the stairs," I said.

Aaron shrugged. "If he did, then it must have been after I left."

"That doesn't make any sense! None of this is making any sense," I said.

Something in Aaron's expression didn't look right, and every time I tried to dig into my memory to try to investigate, I couldn't pull anything up.

"There's nothing to worry about at all. He is not the vampire. I'm one hundred percent sure." Aaron smiled, but it didn't match his eyes.

His words didn't comfort me like I'd hoped. I looked back toward the stairs, and as I did, William descended the stairs. Without a word to Aaron, I pushed through the crowd. I had no idea what I'd say, but I knew he had the answers I needed. In the blink of an eye, I lost William in a sea of dark-haired boys.

Aaron was hot on my heels. "Where are you going?"

"To find him. There's something we're missing. I know it."

As I made my way through the crowd, yelling outside the building stopped me in my tracks.

"Come on." Without any explanation, Aaron grabbed my hand, leading me through the crowd and toward the back door. I knew I should have been more focused on the surrounding chaos, but I couldn't focus on anything other than Aaron's hand on mine. It was warm. Comforting. Heat flushed my cheeks.

Despite the music, the sound of commotion grew louder and louder as we neared the door. One by one, people funneled outside to look at something.

Once outside, we arrived at an open circle in the mob. Guys were mauling Presley, at least ten of them. In the midst of his shuffle, Presley lay on the ground, protecting his body with his legs and arms.

It was a relief knowing he wouldn't be seriously hurt, but that didn't stop my stomach from churning. Aaron left me at the edge of the circle and went in to pull the group off his brother. A gasp of horror escaped my lips as they relentlessly punched and kicked Aaron as he tried to pull Presley off the ground.

A fire ignited under my feet, and I went to step in. For a moment, I lost all sense of reasoning. He didn't need my help, yet my body leaped into action.

Chelsea grabbed my arm. "You don't want to get in the middle of that."

I wanted to push her off, but I knew she was right. The two were becoming overwhelmed. Probably too afraid to fight back in fear of exposing themselves.

"What happened?! Why are they fighting?" I said.

Chelsea grimaced. "I don't know. Some guy just punched Presley out of the blue and then everyone started jumping on him."

Ellis tried to jump in and help but was also punched and thrown to the ground a few feet away. I ran to his aid.

I pulled him from the gravel driveway. "Are you okay?"

He dusted himself. "I don't know what happened. We were walking to the car, and this guy just sucker-punched him. They won't let me through."

Ellis wiped the blood from his chin with labored breaths. This looked bad. I wished I could tell him he didn't need to worry about Presley. He looked like he was about ready to jump back in.

"Wait here. I'm going to get help," I said.

The music was still blasting from inside, and I went for the door to go get more help, when Zach appeared.

"What the hell is this?" Zach barreled through the crowd, wasting no time flinging people off Presley and Aaron.

His body was fully alert, with his shoulders back. With two hands, he flung the guys into the dirt with sheer force. They flew back, knocking bystanders down in the process. When one would go to punch him in the head, he'd easily counter and shove them to the ground. He was a natural. This time, the guys didn't come back for more. Once they'd picked themselves off the ground, they disappeared into the crowd.

Zach picked a guy up from his white collar and pulled him close to his face. "Want to tell me what the fuck happened here?"

"I don't know! He just made me so angry, so I punched him." The guy struggled beneath Zach's grasp, but there was no escaping the iron grip he had on his shirt.

Zach turned to Presley. "What the fuck did you do?"

"Nothing! Ellis and I were just talking outside."

Zach's eyes caught fire as he turned back toward the guy, who was still trying with all his might to get Zach to let go of his shirt. "Please, don't tell me you just punched my brother because you're a homophobic asshole, or I swear to God—"

"No, no, no, no! That's not it. I don't know why I did it. I just got angry."

A guy in the back got up, bloodied from Zach's assault. It took me a minute to recognize him as the guy from the party. Danny.

Zach dropped the other guy to the ground and met Danny face-to-face. "I should have known this was you. You better get to talking. Fast."

Danny's face twisted in horror. "Okay, I know what this looks like, but

I didn't mean to do this."

A light bulb went off in my head but illuminated an empty room. Something about this was strange. Danny was terrified of Zach when Aaron and I questioned him earlier that week. There was no way he would have done this on purpose.

Zach's expression turned sinister. A complete deadpan with a lifeless look in his eyes. "I'm in a really bad mood. So, I'm going to say this once. You hurt my brother. I will fucking kill you. I don't care about your reason or why you did it."

"Zach." Luke appeared next to him, putting his hand on his shoulder. "Let me talk to him." Danny's whole body was shaking.

"What was this about?" Luke said.

Luke looked worn, but that didn't make him look weak. He towered over Danny.

"I-I just was angry. That's it. I'm sorry."

"Sorry isn't fucking good enough," Zach spat.

"Stop." Luke stilled Zach with his hand before turning back to Danny. "I don't want to see you around us anymore. If I see you, we'll have a problem. This is the final warning. Understand?"

Danny nodded and tore off into the crowd. Aaron appeared, looking freshly untouched, with only messy hair and a dirty blazer to show for his fight.

He looked worried. "Are you okay?"

"Me?! What about you?" I reached for his forearm, but I caught myself just before my fingers touched his skin.

He leaned in, whispering in my ear. "Vampire, remember?" He pulled back and winked.

Aaron's brothers were huddled in a group, all looking mentally thrashed. The fact that there wasn't a scratch on any of them didn't bode well for their cover.

"I think we should go." I tugged on Aaron's blazer, and he nodded.

I peeked at the dance floor inside. As the night wound down, the crowd dispersed, and it was easier to see. William was nowhere to be found. My stomach felt empty but not from the lack of food. Our big experiment had come up inconclusive. If anything, there were more unanswered questions. Aaron's answers about William didn't add up. Nothing made sense.

Presley took a few minutes to check on Ellis, and Chelsea pulled Aaron aside to make sure he was okay. "Hey, Kimberly, can we talk for a sec?" Luke's voice startled me.

I nodded and followed him to a light pole that illuminated a portion of the pine trees. The music was still going inside, but some people were stumbling back into their buses and getting ready to leave for their after-parties.

"I, uh. I'm sorry about earlier. Truth be told, I don't even like showing my brothers that side of me, so I feel weird that you had to see that."

"Oh. Please don't feel that way. It's nothing to be ashamed of. I understand."

He laughed nervously and rubbed his neck. "I'm glad you feel that way. Maybe someday I will too. Thanks for being so cool."

"Well, thanks for . . . raising your brothers to be the way they are. You've done a pretty good job. I'm sure you've dealt with a lot. It's not easy being the example, I'm sure."

His eyes lit up, and a huge grin spread from ear to ear. "That's probably the best compliment I've gotten in a long time. Thank you. Glad to have you around. I gotta go check on everyone, but you're riding with us, right?"

I nodded, and Luke disappeared toward the car as I waited for Aaron.

The night's events repeated in my head. I couldn't shake the feeling I had forgotten something important, but I couldn't put my finger on it. I thought of the look on Danny's face and how strange his behavior had been, then went back to Presley. Presley knew my secret. I had to warn Aaron as soon as possible.

After a few minutes, Aaron was done talking to Chelsea, and we walked toward the car. He was oddly quiet.

"Presley knows," I said. "He knows I know you're a vampire."

Aaron went to open his mouth, and I continued. "It slipped out. He tricked me, and it doesn't matter. He knows, but he promised not to tell."

Aaron sighed, and the car was fast approaching.

"Well, that's not good because Presley is notoriously bad at keeping secrets."

"There she is!" Presley jumped with a beer bottle in his hand. "Guys, I found her!"

The alcohol must have finally caught up to him. Luke put his hand over Presley's mouth to keep him from talking further.

"Yeah, Pres, we see her." Zach groaned. He sat on the hood of the car and ran his hands through his hair before taking a pack of cigarettes from his pocket.

"Can you get off the car so we can go?" Aaron snapped. His shoulders were rigid as he struggled to pull the keys from his pocket.

"Here we go." Zach took a drag of a cigarette. "What is it now?"

"Did you have to cause a huge scene like that?" Aaron said.

"I didn't cause a huge scene. The people trying to beat Presley to a bloody pulp did."

"Bloody." Presley snickered in his own little world.

"Yeah, I know, but do you always have to come in and do the thing where you walk around like some psychotic asshole?" Aaron said.

Zach groaned. "Please. Spare me. I don't want to hear your holier-than-thou monologue today."

Aaron shook his head. "Typical."

"You're both being rude." Luke's voice cut the tension. "We still have a guest. Your bickering can wait till we get home." Luke smiled at me and put his large arm around me. "Sorry, about that, Kimberly. I thought I taught them better."

Luke's half hug was oddly what I needed at that moment. My previous reservations about him had disappeared. He radiated a sense of safety and warmth, yet the thought of telling them who I was flooded me with pure terror. I didn't know why, other than the obvious reasons. Something felt different.

We piled into their car, and I laid my head against the cool glass window and breathed in the scent of the vanilla air freshener hanging from the rearview mirror.

My brain was still playing wrapped up in what I was missing. No matter how close it felt, it was out of reach.

Should I have just believed Aaron and what he said about William? We came to the dance to put everything to rest, but somehow, I found myself back in the car with no answers.

"Aaron, crank it up!" Presley was the only loud one. Zach and Luke sandwiched him in the back seat.

Aaron was driving and hadn't said anything since his conversation with Zach.

"Shhhh. Kim is trying to sleep," Luke said in a hushed voice. "No, she isn't. Come on, I just want a little music."

"No." Aaron groaned.

"Fine, I'll just sing, then."

"No!" they all said simultaneously.

My eyes fluttered open. I loved being in the car at night. Something about it was so calming, seeing lights in a blurry haze. But they didn't give the same comfort this time around. A deep, unsettling sensation had crept its way into my body, and I had a feeling it wasn't leaving anytime soon.

"Presley, if you're quiet, I'll get you a present tomorrow," I said, without moving my head from the window.

"Really?! Okay. I'll be good, I'll just hum." His voice trickled with excitement between slight slurs of speech. "Hmmm. Hm, hm, hm, hm."

"Oh, she's good at this." Zach chuckled.

The car's roaring blended with Presley's loud humming. I took a deep breath, compressing all that had happened. My eyes opened just enough to watch the lights pass by in the window again. Sparks of light in the infinite dark sky.

Thirteen

Aaron

T he carnival lights' buzzing only strengthened the nervous energy
pulsing from head to toe. I walked in step behind my brothers as
we strolled the boardwalk. The ocean breeze was comforting, along with
the nostalgic scent of fried Twinkies and turkey legs. I wished we were
there for the carnival.

It was late, and the full moon hung overhead, lighting our path between abandoned stands at the edge of the carnival. We were following
a group of four guys, who were drunk and belligerent. We'd spent the
better part of two hours scouting the perfect group, pretending to be
normal people. Zach smoked a cigarette and shared a casual conversation
with Luke, while Presley tried his best to beat every carnival game we
walked past. He carried around an empty fountain drink container,
which he would loudly sip on occasionally. I, on the other hand, had not
uttered a word since we got there.

The events of the dance loomed over us like an omen. Zach and Luke
were particularly stressed about the brawl's unneeded attention. Their

strict rules were even more rigid. I was constantly trying to find time away from them and meet with Kimberly, who seemed just as fearful as Zach and Luke. I couldn't get myself to feel much of anything. A strange sense of numbness chilled me when I remembered the dance.

The Ferris wheel stood in the distance, and my mind wandered back to Kimberly and her fear of heights. I imagined how different the night would be if I had come with her. Her red hair blowing with the cool night breeze as we swung from high up. She might have grabbed my arm and told me how scared she was by the swaying, and I could have said something cunning, like, "Do you think there is any universe in which I'd let something happen to you?" Yeah. Something cool like that. The dance was a steady blur but had one shining moment I couldn't stop replaying. Her hand on my wrist. The way she looked up at me. The heat from her body as she begged me not to go.

You just want to kill her. You don't really care about her.

The voice had been nagging me all day. Every time I tried to think of Kimberly, the Thing would turn it around.

We need her.

I tried to focus on her face and the way she laughed. How much I enjoyed her company.

Her blood. Think only of her blood.

The Thing wouldn't go. I looked across the lot at a group of people chatting. I focused on their pumping blood. Their hearts were beating in unison, but the voice didn't respond, almost as if It wasn't interested in them at all, just Kimberly.

I tried to put the thought out of my mind and focus on the task at hand. The drunken group continued to walk on by themselves, and as fate would have it, the large crowds in the carnival stayed away from the outer edges. It was good for us, bad for them.

"How are you doing, Aaron?" Luke nudged me.

He hadn't been the same since the dance. Kimberly told me about his panic attack. I'd already asked him. He wasn't sure what triggered it. Only that he thought he saw someone, but he wouldn't say who.

I should have been worried about it and figured out the thing Kimberly insisted we were missing from the formal. But I couldn't focus on anything other than what was in the present. The night I'd been dreading all month had finally come. It was time to hunt.

"Peachy. I'm having a great time," I said.

"It will be better this time. We're right here with you." Luke placed a firm slap on my back.

"Yeah, we'll knock this out in just enough time to ride the Tilt-O-Whirl!"

Presley's enthusiasm was annoying, but I couldn't help but be a little envious. I wanted to puke, and he was already thinking about what he was going to do after.

"All right, there they go. Let's do this." Zach watched them disappear down an alleyway made up of large steel storage containers. He flicked his cigarette on the ground.

"You're really going to litter, huh?" Presley said.

Zach scoffed. "I think as far as moral dilemmas go, I've got bigger problems. But go ahead and add litterbug to the list."

Anxiety buzzed in my body. We picked up the pace and went completely silent. I hated that hunting people was so easy. It was easy to hide the sound of my footsteps. Easy to move out of the way when they looked behind them. It was too easy.

Kill. Kill. Kill.

That voice stopped me in my tracks. Luke stopped up ahead and motioned for me to come. I walked in closer, trailing the back.

Blood. We need blood.

With every step, the voice got louder and louder.

It happened like we had planned. Zach went first, taking out the lead and blocking the way, in case any others tried to run. They were too drunk to run. Luke grabbed two and pushed one in Presley's direction and the other to me.

Kill him.

It was impossible to drown out. I grabbed the guy by the collar and shoved him up against the wall. He was blackout drunk. There was no struggle, and he was easy to overpower. I just needed to drink a little blood. That was it. I brought my lips to his neck, the blood pulsing along the jugular vein so close I could almost taste it.

We need to drink him dry. You need more than that. Kill him. Kill him, now.

I pushed him away, knocking the guy into a pile of trash. He groaned, flailing on the ground. I couldn't do it. I was going to kill him by drinking his blood.

"Aaron, what's wrong?"

Luke was next to me, his face already clean, the scent of blood smeared across his forearm. My eyes focused on the red, and my body shook. I was about to lose it. My control was slipping.

"I'm fine. I'm done. Can we just go?" I sprinted out of the alleyway and toward the nearest streetlight.

"What the hell happened?"

Zach was hot on my tail and was the first to reach me. If it wasn't for his speed, I would have kept running.

All three of them waited for me to speak, watching me with worried eyes. I thought the feeling would stop, but a boiling rage was coming to the surface. Whether it was the Thing inside me screaming for attention or my own emotion, I couldn't tell anymore.

"I'm going home. I'm done."

I stepped toward the carnival, but Zach grabbed my jacket from behind. I thrust him off me, tearing my sleeve in the process.

"We can't go yet. We still have to hunt more."

Presley was right. Because we hadn't killed our victims, one wasn't enough blood to sustain us for a month. I knew the consequences of that too well. I was living it.

"No, fuck this. Fuck all of you and your ability to be okay with this."

The words spilled out, and I couldn't stop them. This time, I wanted to hurt them. Every one of them.

"Not this again." Zach sighed.

"Fuck you. You want to talk about me staying in line and being a good brother when you're the one who betrayed me?! You did this to me, and you didn't tell me. You didn't prepare me. I'm fucked because of you and your selfishness!"

Zach grabbed me by the collar and forced me back against the light pole. "You are such a prick. What would you know about sacrifice!? What do you know about being selfless?! Absolutely fucking nothing because all you do is sit around and bitch and moan."

"Zach," Luke cautioned.

"No, he needs to hear this." He turned back to me, our faces deathly close. "I've sacrificed everything I've ever wanted *for you*! So you could fucking live and have a decent life. I'm not perfect, but I'll be damned if I'm going to sit here and let you call me selfish."

I pushed him off me, my mind spinning. I wanted to stop talking, but the rage poured out of me. "Well, it was all for nothing. This is your fault. You ruined our lives."

"Eh, don't bring me into this." Presley had his arms crossed and looked to be inching farther and farther from our group.

"Of course. How could I forget? You don't care about anything! This is all easy for you. So, fuck you too."

"Aaron, come on. I thought we were past this." Presley looked defeated. "Let's just finish and—"

"Past it!? I'm just getting started." I snarled. "You have no idea how I feel. How could any of you? You only care about us. But what does that make us? It makes us monsters! We're bad people, and I used to be a good person, but I can't be anymore because of you and shitty decisions!"

I couldn't convey the betrayal I felt since the day I was changed. They were the reason I was forced to hunt people in the first place and risk killing them. I was tired of the burden. Tired of the fear.

Luke's solemn face washed over me, pulling me out of the flames and straight onto ice.

The pain in their eyes felt like an ice bath after a dip in the hot tub. It looked different in each of their eyes. Zach was pissed at me. Presley desperately wanted peace, and Luke just looked disappointed. I hated the bond we had sometimes. I wanted to be mad at them. To hate them for all the times they let me down, but I couldn't. No peace came from loving or hating them.

"Are you done?" Luke waited in silence, the carnival sounds playing an amalgamation of melodies in the background.

I didn't say anything, and turned back toward the carnival lights. They didn't try to follow me. I fought the knot in my stomach and the urge to turn back. For the first time in my life, I wanted to be alone.

Fourteen

KIMBERLY

I tapped my foot as the clock on the wall ticked by in an achingly slow crawl. The professor proceeded to overexplain the requirements for our finals. His monotone voice only made my eyes heavy with boredom. I rubbed my sweaty palms together and counted each tick of the clock. A change had taken place in me. It was as if a hidden part of me was coming alive. Things grew more important than school. I wasn't spending all my time thinking of the next thing. I was completely present in my own life.

"All right, class. You're dismissed." He furrowed his eyebrows.

I got up and fought my way to the door. Once in the hall, I barreled toward the exit. The courtyard was booming with a flurry of activity. It was the week before finals, and students who were previously less invested started to show up again.

"Boo!"

Aaron's voice startled me.

"Jesus! Be careful. Don't you know there are dangerous vampires afoot?" I joked.

"How could I forget?"

Aaron was dressed in his hiking boots and flannel shirt. He had a tattered canvas bag strapped across his shoulder that looked almost exactly like the one I had thrifted years ago. I'd since decorated it with various patches from all the places around the mountains I visited and hiked.

"I can't believe I can't go camping alone now because of vampires." I sighed as we walked toward my dorm.

I had just a few more things to pack for our trip up the mountain. We were planning on staying all weekend, and Aaron had convinced Luke to let him go despite the seclusion.

"You should probably get used to that, seeing as you're a vampire magnet and all." Aaron smiled.

My phone vibrated in my backpack pocket, and I checked it.

It was Chris. Again.

I turned it off and put it back.

Aaron raised an eyebrow. "Are you ever going to answer him or keep him in suspense?"

"I don't know. I'm not his biggest fan right now."

It was easier to ignore him and focus on more important things like dangerous mystery vampires.

"Well, you did try to convince him vampires exist. Maybe the guy needs some time. You can't ignore him forever," Aaron said as we passed through the school garden. The smell of fresh flowers and pollen drifted in the air.

"Why are you being so levelheaded right now?"

"You're right. That's your job, and I'm truly the last one who should be giving you advice right now." Aaron stopped to pluck a huge white peony. He brought it up to his nose to smell it before handing it to me. "You're doomed to receive flowers from me now until the end of time since I know which is your favorite."

Butterflies swarmed my stomach, and I sniffed the delicate flower. The petals were ivory, velvet between my fingers. "I think I can live with that."

There was goodness growing among the darkness and confusion. My relationship with Aaron had brought me more joy than I wanted to admit. Something about his internal optimism

quelled the fear of opening up. He relentlessly pursued me and my happiness. That was more than I could say for anyone else in my life, including Chris.

It made the world easier to take. Even the most confusing parts.

"Have you seen William anywhere?" I asked, peeking over my shoulder.

Worry had settled permanently in the pit of my stomach since the dance. I was afraid to go anywhere by myself anymore. I felt delusional again. Nothing indicated William was our vampire, but I couldn't shake the fact we had missed it at the formal. I was having trouble remembering our original plan and why we even thought it was William in the first place.

"Kim, how many times do I have to say it? He's not the guy."

Aaron didn't know, but I noticed his change in demeanor when he came back to find me in the crowd that night. Since the dance, he looked more troubled than usual. I noticed the weird shift in his voice every time he recited the same monologue back to me of what happened when he left.

It was the same each time. They went to find William, then something triggered Luke, then he left. Aaron swore he had talked to William and concluded there was nothing to worry about, but when trying to get direct pieces of dialogue from him, he'd repeat the same thing back to me.

Yet, I still trusted Aaron's cloudy judgment. At least I trusted that he felt he was telling the truth.

"I just think there's something we are missing about the dance. He never came back, remember? And we haven't seen him since. That's weird," I said.

Aaron and I had done a few "covert ops missions," as Aaron liked to call them. We'd checked the swim team schedule posted on the bulletin in the gym and waited for William to show up for practice, but he never did.

I kept replaying the same scene in my head. When I started to feel nervous because William wanted to get me alone, I used the code word. Everything after that wasn't clear. I remember walking toward the steps, and Aaron looked panicked.

"You're right. It's weird. We shouldn't rule anyone out." Aaron nodded matter-of-factly.

I loved Aaron's refusal to gaslight me despite the doubt in his eyes.

"What are we going to do about Presley?" I said.

Aaron shrugged. "He swears he can keep the secret this time."

"And your brothers—how have they been since the fight?"

"They're fine," he said quickly. "Kim, come on! It's a beautiful day. Can we just go enjoy it? I'm kind of looking forward to our little getaway, just to have a break from everything." Our getaway. The butterflies were back.

"You're right. Why worry about dangerous, life-altering events when you can ignore all your problems and sleep in the mountains?"

The grin returned to Aaron's face. "Exactly."

"Hey, wanna see me climb that tree over there?" Aaron bounced in step with me, pointing to the tallest tree on our horizon. The giant redwoods surrounded us and kept us company on our journey up the trail. It was magical.

"Uh, no, actually." I laughed.

The wind sang through the trees in the distance and stirred the pollen and petals. I took a deep breath and admired the aroma. There was still a good bit of daylight left.

"Do you need to stop to rest? Tell me if we're going too far." Aaron walked beside me, casting a long shadow over my face.

"You're too worried about me. I'm not made out of glass."

"I'd say humans are pretty fragile. Hey, I can carry you on my shoulders if you want." He wiggled his eyebrows, tempting me.

"No thanks, I can walk by myself." I snickered.

"Suit yourself, then." He looked up, admiring the sun peeking through the trees.

"I didn't know you liked to hike. I can't imagine there are many places to hike in Brooklyn."

"In Brooklyn, no, but my brothers would take us hiking upstate for special occasions when they could."

"Your brothers were very charming at the dance." I slid slowly back into a conversation Aaron refused to have with me.

He apologized for how he acted after the dance. I told him he got a pass after spending five minutes being kicked and punched in the head. But I wanted to bring it back up to get a read on Aaron's true feelings on his brothers.

"Oh, yes, they were *so* charming, weren't they?" Aaron's voice oozed sarcasm. "Was it Zach threatening to kill someone or maybe Presley figuring out our secret and blackmailing me to do his homework *again* that screamed gentlemen?"

"That's not what I meant. I just saw a different side to them that I wasn't expecting."

We picked up the pace and headed for higher ground. Thanks to my long-distance running, I wasn't out of breath yet.

I spoke again. "When Luke was having his panic attack, Zach came in a few minutes later to comfort him. It was sad . . . but sweet. If I hadn't seen that, I might have a different opinion of what happened."

He eyed me curiously. "And what was your opinion?"

I shrugged. "I get it. If I had a family I loved that much, I'd probably act the same way."

Aaron's laughter carried through the canyon walls. "I find that hard to believe."

"You've got a lot to learn about young Kimberly. You'd be surprised. I once hit someone over the head with a lunch tray for taking my diary."

His mouth fell open, and I continued. "These girls liked to steal my stuff, and I had to show them I meant business. So, I attacked this girl, and Chris had to pull me off her. I wouldn't let go of her hair."

"Holy shit! You're hardcore, Burns. I had no idea." Aaron was smiling from ear to ear.

I savored that look, knowing everything that was going on. His natural state was this carefree, fun person—only, lately, he never had the opportunity. Neither of us did. But there, in the shadow of the trees, it felt like we were completely alone for once. The world was falling away and our worries along with it.

"Tell me a good memory you have of your brothers."

We pushed farther into the ravine. The rocks greeted us with an assortment of colors. Steel grays and blues mixed and contrasted with the dark-chocolate dirt beneath our feet.

"Well, they never missed a single one of my baseball games. Don't be too impressed; I was the worst one on the team." Aaron laughed. "They also never missed any time Presley appeared as a mascot, and I truly mean not one. Even when they moved out after they turned eighteen, they picked us up from school every day because my mom was always working."

Aaron kept his gaze ahead, a sense of sadness lingering in his words. "I could count on them for everything. If I got too drunk at a party, they'd drop everything and come get me. My dad left when Presley and I were young. He was never there for them, so they wanted to be there for us."

"They sound pretty great, and I can't believe you played baseball."

I smiled, thinking about what his childhood must have been like. Very different from mine. Filled with family Christmases and fun high school memories. When I was younger, I might have felt jealous. But I just felt bad for him. It was one thing to never have it and another to have it get ripped from you.

"I give them a hard time now, but I know they didn't mean for any of this to happen. I've been kinda an asshole to them lately, and I feel bad about it. I'd still do anything for them . . ." Aaron turned to me. "Sorry,

I'm getting cheesy again."

"No, it's okay. Cheesy is good." I kept my eyes trained on the rocky path spread out before us. "Wow, this is some rough terrain."

I was partly joking, though I had never hiked in that part of the mountain before. I normally picked grassier areas closer to the woods. I analyzed the assortment of rocks all around our feet and spotted a grayish-blue one, entirely unique from the rest. I picked it up. It was smooth and had small golden flakes.

"Too rough for the greatest hiker that ever lived?" Aaron's wide smile was back.

"Ha! I wish. If I could just stay up in the mountains all day, I would."

Aaron chuckled. "Why don't you? It's not too late to change your major."

The dirt clumped beneath our feet. The sound of my soles hitting the ground brought a comforting melody to my ears.

"I just don't see myself making a lot of money in that. You have to make a lot of money here to support yourself, and I don't want to struggle. Doesn't it seem smart to choose the option that makes more money?"

Aaron shrugged. "Not if you'll hate it. Don't get me wrong, you'd be a great psychologist, but you won't find this in an office."

He gestured to the expansive wilderness around us. Tall pines and redwoods stood like giants and complemented the canyon walls. The rushing waterfall roared in the distance. Its echo beckoned me forward into the wonderland. He was right. Fresh air was hard to beat.

"You've got a point." I paused. "Here. For your rock collection. Maybe we can start a new one." I placed the rock in Aaron's hands.

He looked at it, turning it over a few times. "You've got a good eye, Burns. Thank you. I like that idea."

We peacefully walked in cadence until a huge stream separated us from the other side of the trail. The water rushed in and out, covering almost all the rocks. There was no definite way across.

"Uh-oh, maybe we should go around." I peered down the bank. "I bet if we head down, it won't be as rough."

"Nonsense." Aaron rushed toward me, and I found myself suspended in the air. He grabbed my legs and pulled me to his back. I had no choice but to hold on to his neck. "Is this necessary?"

He was steady as he waded into the rushing water. The cool water splashed up and hit my exposed legs, sending a shiver down my spine.

"Probably not." He chuckled.

The atmosphere was still and tranquil in the wake of the setting sun, the sound of the water peaceful and smooth.

He was right. It was easier. My body relaxed into his, and every muscle melted in his warmth. The soft breeze brought a whiff of his mint shampoo to my nostrils. It wasn't an uncomfortable place to be.

Soon, we made it to the campsite. Aaron helped me unpack everything and set up the tent. He cooked me some hot dogs and cracked jokes. I wrapped a blanket around me as we settled by the fire. The fire lit up his face in a warm glow that complemented his eyes.

"Ah, nice, warm fire. One might say it's a little romantic." Aaron rested his back against a tree stump.

"Yeah, I'm sure that's what you say to every girl by the fireside." I raised my eyebrows, taunting.

"Oh, please, you're exaggerating my skill with the ladies. Plus, I'm not putting 'the moves' on you. I'm just stating a fact."

My face felt hot, and I blamed it on the fire. "Ouch. I'm not good enough to put moves on?"

Aaron sat up. "Whoa, whoa, whoa. That's not what I meant. I just don't want you to see me as some creep."

"Well, I don't think you're creepy. I'm happy you're here."

His eyes twinkled in the shadow of the fire. "Wow, someone's feeling open today. I'm happy too. You're fun to hang out with. Kind of a stubborn pain in the ass sometimes—but fun."

I was convinced every word Aaron spoke was true. Even his jokes had a level of truth, which was rare in a person.

I leaned back and listened to the sounds of bugs chirping in the night.

Our silence wasn't hollow. A warm feeling surged in my chest. It was calm yet exhilarating. A sense of familiarity came with the smell of the pine. Warm. Comfortable. Happy.

"What are you thinking about?" Aaron's gaze was heavy with curiosity.

"I think . . . this is as close to home as I've ever felt."

My heart skipped a beat at the thought. The moment was perfect, but I couldn't put my finger on why. I had been out there so many times before. What made this time so special?

"Does this include me?" He narrowed his eyebrows expectedly. "Yeah, I think it does."

The smoke twirled up and disappeared into the night sky above us. I inhaled the smell of burning wood and savored it.

Aaron spoke again. "Have you ever had anyone hike with you? Did any of your foster families take you?"

"Chris used to come with me sometimes, but no one has ever enjoyed hiking as much as I do. Some of my foster families brought me with them, but you'd be surprised how many take in kids but exclude them from the rest of the family."

"They excluded you? I find that hard to believe. You're like the most perfect rule follower I know."

"I wasn't always that way. I was put in a lot of homes when I was younger, but they weren't good. One of them even accused me of stealing. Which I didn't."

"Jesus, that's harsh. Do you have any good memories of it?"

"There are a few. Once, when I was around maybe ten years old, I got put into a home with another little girl my age. Her name was Dusty, and she was like a sister to me. Probably the closest I ever got to feeling like I had a sibling. I stayed with them for a little more than a year. We still write to each other sometimes."

"Wow, maybe she can come and visit, or you could go visit her. Hey! We could go on a trip. It would be fun."

"She lives in London now."

"London? All the more reason to plan a trip. Do you not ever think of traveling?" Aaron scooted closer as the wind blew the smoke nearer to his face.

"I guess I didn't. Not alone anyway."

Aaron's smile widened, and I knew what he was going to say. "Well, you're not alone now, are you? You have me . . . and my brothers. Not sure if you want them, but they are there."

I contemplated the truth in his words. I wanted to believe them. But Aaron's brothers didn't know about me, and I doubted Zach and Luke would be happy about me knowing their secret. But the small hopeful part of me dared to imagine a life where they did.

If we were to have told them, then they'd find our rogue vampire a lot easier. Best-case scenario: once we solved our mystery, we'd get to move on. We could continue to go to Black Forest University together and go to football games in the fall. Maybe the people following Aaron and his brothers would give up eventually, and we could all be safe . . . together.

I shuddered at the thought. That was the first time I had allowed myself to contemplate a future with anyone else for more than a few seconds. I sat for a minute and allowed myself to think on it and hope.

Aaron's laughter turned cold as he stared into the fire. "Kim, I need to tell you something."

I hugged the wool blanket wrapped around me a little tighter. "Okay . . ."

"No matter what happens . . . if we have to leave, I promise that I'll come back for you. I would never leave you here alone, and I won't just leave without telling you. So, if I disappear because something happens to me, I just need you to know how important you are and that I wouldn't abandon you."

"You're leaving?"

"No! Just. I don't know how this is all going to play out, and I wanted you to know that just in case."

My heart was beating harder in my chest, and I couldn't look away from Aaron's gaze. No words would form on my lips.

"I'm sorry I dragged you into all this." He smiled softly, little bits of his blond hair resting on his brow.

"Come on, no more apologizing. I think we are past that, aren't we?"

"I guess you're right." He was close to me, our knees touching. "W-Would you be okay with telling my brothers? I'm kinda wondering if that needs to be our next step here. We're out of leads, and I don't want you to get hurt. It's harder and harder to get my brothers to keep you safe without telling them anything."

"I've had the worst feeling about telling them ever since the formal. I don't know why. But I think it logically makes sense to tell them. Do you think they'll get really mad?"

Aaron grabbed a twig and drew a smiley face in the dirt. "Mad at me, definitely. But you, no."

"Okay, let's do it, then," I said, my heart beating faster at the thought.

"Cool. We'll tell them tomorrow, then." Aaron studied me. "I still don't get why you're not totally freaking out and running away from me after everything I've put you through. You're so calm."

"I'm just happy with my choices. I don't want to run away from this . . . from you."

Aaron's eyes pierced right through me. Crickets echoed in our silence.

"You don't want to run away from . . . me?"

"Yes, believe it or not, Aaron, I enjoy your company." I pushed out a laugh, feeling a little breathless.

"I enjoy yours too, Burns." He smirked, closely watching my face.

I admired him for a moment, and the way his eyelashes touched the wisps of his hair. His golden-brown eyes sparkled in the glowing flames. My heart thumped louder in my chest. Aaron had an incredible magnetism to his soul. I often struggled to get out of his gravity, but my attempts were futile. Aaron's warmth was inescapable, unavoidable . . . inevitable. I wanted it close. To warm up the coldest parts of my soul.

A smirk danced on his lips. "You know, the dance was a disappointment for a lot of reasons, but it disappointed me for another reason entirely."

I waited in the silence, still not fully understanding.

"Will you dance with me?" He stood and brushed the dirt from his pants. He beckoned to me graciously, holding out his hand.

"You're kidding." I grimaced. "With no music?"

"Humor me."

With his signature wink, I took his hand. He waltzed me away from the ground and into the glow of the fire. He wrapped one hand around mine and the other on my waist. We swayed, and as we took our first stride, Aaron stepped on my foot.

"Ow." I giggled.

"I'm sorry." Aaron exhaled nervously. "I never said I was good at it, just that I wanted to."

"That's okay. I'll show you." I rested my hand on his shoulder and gave his other hand a reassuring squeeze. I imagined what it would be like to dance with a boy growing up. I hoped it would be at prom, but I never went to mine. This was better than that.

"Now you just feel the rhythm and sway."

Chirping crickets played our symphony. The soft silence between us didn't matter.

For a few minutes, we were just present. Enjoying every step of our dance. Our eyes met at the same time. It was almost like we were the same person sometimes. Like puzzle pieces, we just clicked.

"So, Aaron . . . crayons or colored pencils?"

He narrowed his eyes. "Uh, what?"

"If you could pick only one to use for the rest of your life, which would you pick? I'm just curious."

"Is this a test?" A wicked grin spread across his face.

"No. I'm just trying to get to know you better. There are a lot of things to learn about a person. Technically, I could start anywhere."

"Hmmm. Okay. Colored pencils, definitely."

His hand was firm on mine as we continued to move to the music of the forest. Everything around us fell away. Aaron's feet would bump into mine every so often with his off-rhythm swaying. "Oh, bad choice.

Crayons are way better."

"Yeah, whatever. You lose all color choice with crayons. There are a million shades of colored pencils."

"I guess you're right, but crayons are dark and more opaque."

"Okay, I'll give you that one for using the word 'opaque.'"

I knew it was ridiculous to talk about something so trivial, but somehow, it was fun. All our conversations were so heavy. This one was light.

"What about food?" I said.

"Oh my God, I miss food so much!" he exclaimed. His voice mixed with frustration and excitement

I laughed. "Hamburgers or hotdogs?"

"Um, I'm a true American, so hamburger."

"I think you could make an argument for both there but agreed. Hamburger."

"Hamburgers were so good . . ." Aaron's eyes glistened as he talked. "What about icing. What's your favorite?"

He opened up to me like a book, pouring out long-forgotten quirks and lost loves. I loved every bit of it. Not just hearing his, but also getting to share my favorites with someone who was interested in hearing them felt nice.

"Cream cheese. I love red velvet cake," I said.

"Me too! I'll have to make you one for your birthday. I used to love cooking and food. Luke taught me most of everything I know."

"I didn't know you cooked? Did you want to be a chef or something?" I tilted my head up to look at him.

"Nah, I just loved to cook for my mom back home. She loved it."

"Your mom. What is she like?"

We had never talked about it. I bit my lip, hoping I wasn't prying too much.

"She's the most amazing, supportive, strong person I know. I miss her a lot . . ."

I caressed his shoulder. "We don't have to talk about it if you don't want to."

"No, it's okay. I like talking about her."

He gave me a half smile as we swayed to the rhythm. Calm washed over me. With each step, everything felt right with the world. It was late, but I didn't feel tired. I didn't want to break away from him.

"I wish I could see her again." Aaron's tone grew more serious, and his grip tightened around my hand. "Do you think she could ever forgive us for this? We can't call or visit—we just left. She's probably worried. Sometimes, I wonder if I will ever get to talk to her again, and if I do . . . I wonder how mad she'll be." His shoulders tensed at the thought.

Mothers were not usually my favorite talking point. I often teared up in movies where the mom would tear down the world to get to her kids. I'd never felt such love, but Aaron had. Aaron had a mom who was probably doing everything in her power to get back to her boys. If Aaron had love like that, then I knew it would find him again. Nothing could stop it.

"Well, even though I've obviously never had any parental figures, I've always believed moms have sense when it comes to their kids. She knows you love her, and when you see her again, she'll take you back with open arms."

"R-Really?" His eyes searched mine. A sudden desperation appeared in his voice like I had never heard before. "You say the most perfect things."

"I don't think so."

I was taken aback, left breathless by the way he was looking at me.

"You do. It shouldn't be a surprise. You're perfect." Aaron's eyes locked on mine for a moment, and our dancing came to a pause.

We stood close to each other, completely still, waiting for the other to move away or to say something. But for some reason, I couldn't avert my eyes. We couldn't look away. The fire lit up his glistening brown eyes and the flecks of amber in his irises. My breath caught in my throat, and my attention shifted to Aaron's lips and his to mine.

"You should probably go to bed. We've got a big day tomorrow." Aaron released my hands and stepped away from the light.

I let out a breath, forfeiting any hope that had been building in my chest. "Yeah. Okay."

Hot disappointment prickled my face. What was I doing? What had I expected to happen? Aaron was potentially leaving—not to mention he was a vampire. We couldn't be together. What was I thinking by allowing myself to get close to a person who, in every scenario, would be destined to leave me in some way?

My neck stiffened. The once cuddly, warm air turned hard and frigid.

One crack broke the dam, and all the worries I kept out came back with a vengeance. My mind flashed to me, alone in my room. The old, familiar pain and envy radiated in my chest. I felt so different from that version of myself. I hated her. I didn't want her back. I swallowed the lump forming in my throat.

"What's wrong?" Aaron was next to me, giving me puppy-dog eyes.

I wanted to collapse into his arms. I wanted his comfort. But I didn't know how. Every minute I spent getting attached would lead me down the same path as before. One where I'd end up alone.

"Nothing." I spat, retreating into myself.

It didn't matter. None of it mattered if he was just going to leave, anyway. I didn't know why I envisioned a future where things could turn out or where his brothers might accept me. Even if they did, things wouldn't end the way I wanted them to. It was always going to end in a goodbye of some kind.

Aaron frowned. "Don't lie."

Genuine hurt welled in his eyes, compounding my guilt. I squeezed my mouth shut to lessen the damage.

He stood in front of me, lightly grabbing my shoulders. "Talk to me. Please."

"I just misunderstood. I thought . . . I don't know what I thought. It doesn't matter! Because you're going to leave and everything that has happened will just be some wild memory. I shouldn't be here with you. I should have just gone alone like I wanted to do. I shouldn't have done all this stuff with you. I don't know what I was thinking."

"What did you misunderstand? I never said I was leaving. I just wanted to warn you of the possibility, so you wouldn't think I abandoned you or something." Aaron pressed in, but I pushed him away and gathered my stuff. "What are you doing?"

"I'm going to bed. I don't want to talk about this." My old wounds had split open, leaving me sore all over.

"Come on. Fight with me. I'm an idiot. Just tell me what I did, and I'll fix it." Aaron stayed by the flickering flames.

His compliance and yearning only made my head spin harder. I just wanted to do what would hurt less, and being alone hurt less.

"No. There's nothing to fix. It's fine. I can handle it."

"You promised you'd fight with me." Aaron walked closer to me, and I stepped back.

"I don't want to fight with you. I don't want to talk about it. This was all a mistake. We'll tell your brothers tomorrow, and once the vampire is found, we'll go our separate ways again. I just want to be alone."

Aaron's eyes widened, his brows furrowed, and his mouth was agape.

"What? I don't und—"

"Tsk. Tsk. Tsk. Are the love birds fighting?" William's voice crashed into our conversation.

My breath caught in my throat, and before I could blink, Aaron grabbed me by the waist and pulled me behind him. I couldn't see William in the dark, but I knew Aaron could hear him. His gaze was fixed on the tree line.

"What are you doing here?"

Aaron's voice shifted into an aggressive tone I'd never heard before.

"Aaron, just the man I was expecting to see."

Though he was far away, I instantly recognized a change in William's voice. My memory sparked. He had an accent. Irish. I faintly remember talking about where he was from at the dance, but any specifics of the conversation were blurry.

"You didn't answer my question," Aaron said.

"Do I need a reason to come see you?"

William was standing next to the tree line. Leaning against a large pine tree, he was hiding just out of sight from the light of the fire. He wasn't the same guy. He no longer sported his pretty white shoes and striped preppy sweaters. Instead, he wore thick-soled boots that he had tucked his high-waisted trousers into. He was layered in a mixture of different hues and patterned shirts and a long black jacket that went to his knees. Nothing like what I'd seen him wear before. His eyes were dark as he pulled out a cigarette. With the familiar flick of the light, I stood, frozen. The flame flared across the bridge of his nose.

We were right.

William was the vampire.

"Will you cut the bullshit? What do you want with her?" William's attention turned to me. "Ah, the leadin' lady." He spoke with venom in his voice that made my skin crawl.

"Kimberly, you're looking lovely, as always." He kept his eyes solely on Aaron as he took a puff of his cigarette.

"What do you want with her?" Aaron repeated, still standing in front of me.

"How'd last night go? Rumor has it, you left early on your hunting trip." William smirked and pushed himself off the tree before stepping into the light.

Aaron's body stiffened. "How would you know that?"

"Your brothers are a lot of things, but subtle isn't one of them," William said. "They're easy to keep tabs on."

Hunting? Aaron never mentioned hunting. The last time we'd talked about it was at the grocery store. William straightened himself back up, regaining his posture and blowing out another puff of smoke.

His black eyes finally settled on me. "How ya feeling? Last few times I've seen ya, you haven't looked so good."

That's when I remembered the thing I had forgotten. Only I hadn't forgotten. William made me forget. He made Aaron forget. The reason Aaron and I suspected Danny. The very person who made us suspicious of William. William compelled us.

With a new fire under my feet, I said, "Because of you! Aaron, we were right. He is the vampire."

"I've gathered that one, Kim."

"No! We figured it out! At the dance. But he made us forget. He wiped our memory. You still don't remember?"

William clapped a long, slow clap. "Wow, I'm impressed. I knew it wouldn't last long on you. You're too strong-willed and smart. Aaron, on the other hand . . ."

"I still don't remember." Aaron looked back at me.

"You will, eventually. I can't place permanent blocks on your long-term memory. I'm guessing you won't remember our little conversation at the top of the stairs for a while either."

"Why are you here?" Aaron's voice was cold.

William moved forward, advancing with a calculated shuffling of his feet. "I'm just having a bit of fun . . . enjoying nature."

With a flick of his fingers, his lit cigarette flew to the ground, and he stomped it out. Aaron grabbed my hand, pulling me back behind him. My heart was beating out of my chest. I could sense something shift in Aaron. His whole body was shaking.

"You know, I'm curious about you, Aaron. You didn't tell your brothers about this secret you've been keepin'. That's an interesting choice for someone like you."

A brief silence followed, and I squeezed Aaron's shoulder.

"Come on, you don't want to talk? It's not fun that way." William chuckled, his jaw set and serious. Hatred flashed in his eyes with the flames of the fire.

Aaron scoffed. "I'll answer you if you answer me."

"Why am I here? Isn't that obvious . . . vampire. She's got blood." He pointed to me. "Come on. Ask me a hard one."

"You're not going to touch her." Aaron snarled.

William took another step forward. "Do you think you could protect her from me? Don't you think if I wanted to take her right now that I could?"

Crunching the leaves with another step, I flinched, and my heart leaped in my chest.

"Wanna bet?" Aaron moved away from me, taking a step toward William, until they were inches from each other. He was acting like another person, his hands shaking uncontrollably.

William smiled with his black eyes shimmering in the light of the fire. "Can you feel it? Your blood is boiling and rising to the occasion."

Aaron glanced down, looking at his hands, watching them silently.

"Aaron, you have so much to learn," William said.

I couldn't see Aaron's face, just his clenched, shaking hands. His eyes locked with William's. I stepped back toward the tent.

An aura wafted off Aaron. It wasn't fear. It was dark, sinister, pure evil.

The feeling made me quiver. William emitted the evil too. The menacing aura radiating off them tainted the air, and everything around me grew colder, darker.

"It's because you know you can't fight me. You cannot win. So, you let that thing take over." William's lips pressed together. "You don't look so good, Coleman."

"Stop." Aaron's voice sounded far away.

"What are you doing to him?" I clenched my fist.

For the first time, I couldn't think, fear seizing my thought process. I was frozen like a frightened, cornered deer.

"I'm not doin' anything. This is all him." William had a grin plastered on his face, and he turned back to Aaron. "You can't control it, can you?"

Aaron moved his hands over his face and groaned. I kept careful watch on William's proximity. It wasn't looking good. I couldn't protect Aaron, and I couldn't run. I fought the negative voice in my head and my stiff muscles. I'd fight with whatever I could.

"Shut up!" Aaron groaned and placed his hands on either side of his head.

"How long has it been since you've tasted blood? I'm guessing it's been quite awhile," William said.

Aaron's hands shook harder at the mention of blood. His body stiffened as he glared at William.

"I just love the young ones. You are so easy to mess with." William was speaking to Aaron in almost a whisper until his gaze landed on me. I clenched my fist to stop them from shaking.

"So reckless."

White-knuckling, Aaron pulled his hands through his hair. "You need to leave."

William's lips curled with insidious laughter. "You're making this too easy. Maybe I should just go ahead and—"

As William turned to push Aaron, I stumbled back. In the blink of an eye, Aaron placed his hand on William's chest, stopping him completely. His once-slumped shoulders pulled down and back. Aaron's head no longer swung low, as he was fully alert. He didn't look like the same man I knew as he stared William down.

"Stay away from her, or I will fucking kill you."

A shiver went down my spine. The words came from Aaron's lips but sounded nothing like him. He stood like a statue. His once-violent shaking had stilled.

The forest went silent.

William stepped back, keeping his eyes on Aaron. His face was more serious. "Now, now, no one has to die today."

He placed a hand softly on Aaron's shoulder and leaned in close to his ear. With black eyes, he stared at me, whispering something unintelligible to Aaron. Aaron stepped backward, his rigid body relaxed. He deflated before my eyes until he seemed small in comparison to William.

William licked his lips with a chuckle. "This has been fun, but I think it's time I leave you two to enjoy the rest of your night. Just wanted to pop in for a quick hello." He walked toward the trees and paused right by the tree line. "I will see you guys around." He turned to me with a crooked smile before disappearing into the brush.

Relief washed over me, and I let out a breath.

Aaron stood by the fire, staring at the ground with hunched shoulders. I rushed over to him.

"Aaron! Are you okay?"

The warmth returned to his skin. His face was a mixture of confusion and worry.

"Talk to me. Come on," I said.

He grabbed my arm to steady himself.

"I'm sorry. I don't know what that was." He stared past me into the trees. "That was . . . weird."

"Aaron." I waved my hand in front of his face and looked behind me, fearful William would come back any second.

His head snapped up, and I could tell he was really looking at me again. "I'm sorry. I'm so sorry. Are you okay?"

"That's the question I'm asking you!"

His fingers were soft as he held my arm. "No, I'm okay. Are you hurt?"

He frantically searched me, squeezing my shoulders.

"Do you not remember?" I said.

"I do. It's just . . . my head feels foggy."

The color returned to Aaron's eyes, and my wobbly legs stilled. He looked like himself again.

"Was what he said true? You haven't been hunting?"

"Kim. I've got it under control." He pulled away from me.

"That didn't look like control," I said.

"We need to go. Now. I can't protect you up here." His words still sounded harsh. Too cold for his own lips.

"What? What's happening? Tell me what he said to you."

"No. It's better if you don't know." He went to the tent, pulled out my stuff, and stuffed it in my bag. "We're going back to my house. You can stay with me. I thought I could protect you here but I can't. I have to get you somewhere I can figure out what to do."

"You're really not going to tell me?"

The breeze made me shiver as I took my bag. I searched the trees behind him, nervously expecting something to pop out. My stomach was still in knots. A fog was settling into the forest and weaved in out of the darkness.

"Kim, can you promise me you won't say anything to anyone about this? I'm going to figure this out. I'll make sure you get to go back to the life you wanted, and you won't have to talk to me again. This will be over for you."

Sadness stung my eyes. I instantly regretted my flare up of emotion and our argument. I didn't want to stop talking to Aaron. That was the problem. I wanted to be near him.

After our run-in with William, I was more sure than ever that I was scared of losing Aaron. I opened my mouth, the words lingering on my tongue. But I didn't say them. "Yes. I promise."

Fifteen

KIMBERLY

"Are you okay?" I eyed Aaron as he held a frying pan to the stove's flames.

The smell of hot oil and butter loomed in the air. We were back in the frat house kitchen, using an old cooking pan that had seen better days. The kitchen was nice and fully stocked, but it was clear no one had been taking care of the cookware.

"I've told you. I'm fine," he grumbled as he flipped a perfectly made grilled cheese sandwich. "Please stop asking."

He wasn't his normal self. He hadn't spoken much since the campsite. Since we'd met, a day hadn't gone by where he wasn't laughing—at the very least cracking a joke or two. I never thought I'd say it, but I wished Aaron was talking more. Our argument was long gone, and my sudden urge to bolt was a bad memory. I wanted to take back all the things I had said, but it never felt like the right time.

I leaned onto the counter. "Are we still telling your brothers?"

"No. Just give me some time to figure this out." His voice cut through me.

Aaron was still refusing to tell me what William said. He said it was because he didn't want to involve me anymore than he already had. It was so unlike him. Even when I insisted, because it involved my life, he stayed silent.

I sighed and moved to sit at the table. The room bustled with people. Tons of boys I didn't know passed by me, dismissing me as if I was another piece of the modern art deco furniture that littered the house.

"You just couldn't stay away from us, could ya?" Presley tapped my shoulder from behind and startled me. He grabbed the chair beside me and twisted it around to sit.

"I thought I smelled Aaron cooking in here." Luke was suddenly on the other side of me. I hadn't seen him come into the room.

The smell of food was thick in the air. The sizzling oil on the griddle filled our small silence. Their energy breathed much needed life into the room. They even seemed happy to see me, which was oddly comforting.

"So, Kimberly, you and my brother seem to be hanging out a lot. What are your intentions with our boy?" Zach laughed at his own personal joke, leaning against the doorframe.

He watched me with cautiousness. Though it sounded like a joke, the conviction was apparent in his voice.

"Is it the muscles or the hair?" Presley nudged me.

"Don't listen to them. They are just trying to be funny, as always." Luke greeted me with a big toothy grin and sat across from me.

"Hey, assholes, Kimberly is our guest. Let's not bombard her with questions." Aaron dropped a bowl of tomato soup in front of me, then placed a grilled cheese in my hand. "And we should probably let her eat first."

Luke leaned back in his chair and folded his arms with a wide grin. "I think Zach had something he wanted to say."

Zach bit his bottom lip before pulling up a seat next to me. "I'm . . . sorry about the other night. I had a little too much to drink and then the fight—"

"A little?" Aaron rolled his eyes.

Zach pointed at Aaron. "Don't interrupt me." He looked at me again. "As I was saying, Kimberly. I'm sorry if I made things uncomfortable."

"You didn't hurt my feelings at all. It was nice hanging out together," I reassured him.

"Is it good?" Aaron watched me as I sipped my soup.

Everyone's eyes were on me. I wanted to say so much and even more needed to be said. But I couldn't say any of it, so I picked the first thing off the top of my head to talk about.

"Yeah, thanks. Did you tell them that we went camping in the ravine?"

"Whoa, whoa, wait. You guys went camping together?"

Presley's face twisted into a wicked grin.

"That sounds . . . secluded." Zach exchanged glances with his brothers.

"Oh, shut up." Aaron groaned.

"So, like, what did you guys do up there . . . you know, with all the free time?" Presley asked, steering the conversation in a completely different direction than I intended it to go.

"Okay, that's enough, Luke?" Aaron motioned for his help.

"He's right. We don't want to make Kimberly feel uncomfortable. Right?" Luke stared down Zach and Presley.

"Right," they said in unison.

"Are you still feeling grumpy today?" Zach nudged Aaron, who was standing right next to him.

Aaron turned back toward the kitchen. "I would love it if everyone stopped asking me that."

Clanging pots and pans startled me as Aaron threw them into the sink to wash them. I took a bite of my sandwich, enjoying the toast's crunch. With every minute that passed, I doubted Aaron's judgment. His brothers needed to know something. What if William showed up again at their house? What if he was already trying to trick them into being friends with him or something?

"Well, I do have something interesting to report to you guys," I said midchew.

"Oh, yes, do tell." Presley was excited again.

"I think I have a stalker."

Aaron turned to glare at me. I tried ignoring it and turning my chair toward the others. "Yeah, do you guys remember William? He's come to a few of your parties."

No recollection crossed Luke's eyes. He must not have remembered anything either. I secretly hoped it would jog his memory, but if it's like William had said, it would be a while.

"Dude, yes!" Presley smacked the table. "I think he's on the same swim team as that Danny guy."

Zach added, "That fucker gave me a bad vibe."

"Why do you think he's stalking you?" Luke said, rubbing the stubble on his beard.

"He keeps popping up in weird places. He was even camping in the same ravine we went to."

Aaron's gaze was heavy on my face. I hated lying, but a lot of truth meshed with the lie. If William was dangerous, they needed to know.

"We can say something to him if you want." Zach motioned to Luke.

"Oh, no. Definitely not. It was just weird, and I wanted to tell you, just in case you saw him around. Be careful." I stuffed the rest of my grilled cheese in my face to avoid any further questions.

Zach scoffed. "Careful? I think it's him who would need to be careful."

"Now you've done it." Aaron sighed as he finished up the dishes and returned to the table.

"You knew she had a stalker, and you just didn't say anything?" Luke said.

"Hmm. Wonder why that is? Maybe because I knew terminators one and two would overreact," Aaron said.

The group turned to face him.

"He's been like that all day," I said softly.

Guilt crept into my chest. I couldn't tell them anything without betraying Aaron's trust. But something was seriously wrong with him. He was acting like another person entirely. My stomach turned with worry.

"Oh, no." Aaron groaned and buried his head in his arms on the table. "I don't want to hear it."

"Uh-oh. Aaron's in trouble." Presley snickered.

"I'm fine! How many times do I have to say it?" Aaron lifted his head, his eyes foggy. But his voice was full of aggression.

Luke got up from his chair, walked over to Aaron, and put his hand on his shoulder. "Why don't we go talk about it in the other room?"

"Let go of me," Aaron warned.

"Nope, family talk. Come on." Luke grabbed Aaron by the shirt, forcing him up.

Aaron eyed me as he made his way to the other room. I gave him a half smile and watched him walk away.

"Don't worry. She is safe and sound," Presley called into the other room. "Now onto the good stuff. Tell us about you. What do you like to do? Aaron tells us you're a bit of a loner."

I was actually relieved with his question. I expected Presley to blow the secret any second. But he leaned back in his chair and put his hands behind his head.

"You're not supposed to tell her that," Zach said.

"Who cares if Kimberly is a loner? Lots of people are like . . . uh, that lady who writes poetry . . . or wrote poetry," Presley said.

It occurred to me they have probably never had to deal with loneliness. From Aaron's stories, it was safe to say they always had each other. From morning until night, they were stuck together.

"Shut up. Don't try to act like you know things." Zach placed an elbow on the table and rested his chin.

"Aw, don't be jealous. Some of us actually paid attention in high school," Presley mocked.

Zach opened his mouth like he was going to argue more, but I cut him off. "It's okay. It's the truth. I kinda stick to myself." They directed their attention back on me.

"All right, all right. I'm asking the questions here. So, what is your favorite thing about Aaron?" Presley's eyes narrowed.

That's when I knew things were getting serious. I expected it sooner or later, seeing how close they all were. They were definitely grilling me.

"What kind of question is that?" Zach groaned.

"Hey, I wanna know! We have to weed out the gold diggers and self-centered broads." Presley smiled. He leaned in closer, waiting for my answer.

"How could she be a gold digger if we aren't rich?" Zach rolled his eyes.

"My favorite thing? Aaron's a good person. He's got a kind heart. I can tell. I'm sure you all had something to do with that," I said, still nervous.

My voice hung in the air. The house was oddly quiet for a Saturday.

Zach smiled at my answer but laughed under his breath.

"Actually, despite us, I'd say. But yeah, he really is."

"Is there anything we should know about you?" Presley said, wiggling his eyebrows.

"Um, I'm a pretty reasonable, forgiving person. I like reading . . . hiking—"

"Oh, Aaron told us you were an orphan too," Zach said.

"Zach!" Presley shouted.

I was beginning to understand their dynamic.

Zach pressed his lips together, annoyed. "What? I'm just trying to make conversation."

"Ignore him. We all do." Presley ruffled up his hair, leaning back.

Zach stood abruptly and moved toward Presley, his shoulders squared.

It was obvious they'd all spent copious amounts of time together. They were closer than any family I'd ever encountered, not that I'd had many good examples.

Presley almost fell backward out of his chair. "Ah! No, sorry, sorry!"

"It's okay. Yes, I'm technically an orphan. But that doesn't mean much to me anymore. The only thing you need to know is I'm good at reading people. So, don't lie to me."

"A threat. I like it." Zach took his seat again, relaxing his shoulders.

"Looks like she'll fit right in," Presley said, a sly smile spreading across his face.

The doorbell's loud chime broke our conversation, and we all turned our attention to the entrance.

"Who could that be?" Presley jumped up and ran toward the door.

Aaron rushed out of the room. "No, don't open that!"

"Too late." Presley swung the door open. "Hey, Chelsea!"

"Oh, there he is! Aaron, your girlfriend is here." Presley motioned for her to come inside.

Spit caught in my throat, and I wondered if, somehow, I had missed something. She walked into the room slowly and stopped once she saw me sitting at the table.

Her once calm demeanor turned sour. "Oh, hey. Kimberly, right? What are you doing here?"

I finished chewing the last bite of my grilled cheese, then answered. "I'm just hanging out." I smiled and waved.

"Oh."

She stood there and stared at me for a moment, and our awkward silence grew. I glanced over to Aaron, who was still glaring at Presley. Presley's muffled laughter echoed in the foyer.

Chelsea turned to Aaron. "Are you still going with me to buy my new car today or not? I know we planned it a while ago, but you said you would. I've been trying to get a hold of you."

Aaron and I shared a look before he answered. "Uh . . . yeah. Just let me get my stuff. Can you wait out in your car?"

She squinted. "Yeah, sure."

"Oh, wait, Chelsea, we are all still going to that thing tomorrow, right?" Presley called to her before her thick-soled heels clomped with another step.

"It's going to be great. We invited Kimberly too." Zach nudged my elbow.

"It's out in the woods. There is camping involved," Presley said.

"We heard a lot of college students go the weekend before finals. And our tests don't come until after Tuesday, so . . ."

"Um." I stood out of place, not knowing what to say.

On one hand, it seemed completely reckless for me to agree, with William on the loose doing God knows what. But technically, finals weren't going to stop because of my vampire problem, and being with Aaron's brothers was the safest place we could be. I just had to get Aaron alone and convince him that telling his brothers was the smartest thing to do.

The fear I felt about telling them dimmed, and I was wondering if William had planted the idea in my head, that telling them was a bad idea to buy himself more time. But why would he need to do that?

"Great! It's going to be so much fun." Presley wrapped his arm around my shoulder and stared at Aaron. "Chelsea, you're coming too, right?"

"Of course I'm coming." Her eyes met mine as she spoke. "I'll be in the car."

We waited in an awkward silence for her to leave. As soon as the door shut, Presley went running.

Aaron chased after him. "What was that!?"

They ran through the kitchen and all over the living room, knocking things over.

"I couldn't help myself!" Presley's voice echoed by the stairs.

"Hey, this looks fun!" Luke appeared at the side of the room, leaning against the wall, holding a beer.

"Are you kidding?" Zach laughed and headed to the fridge.

"What? What did I miss?" Luke asked.

"The opportunity was staring me right in the face! It was worth it—Ow!" Presley groaned.

Aaron had grappled Presley into a headlock. Presley grunted with the tight grip. Aaron maneuvered him around to punch him a couple of times in the arm. When he let him go, Presley skipped away with a smile.

"All of you are to blame for the drama that is about to unfold," Aaron said through clenched teeth.

"I didn't know she was your girlfriend . . ." I smiled, keeping my tone light.

I didn't want to think about Presley's comment, not when there were so many other things going on, but I couldn't help it.

"She's not. She's just been telling people that," Aaron said.

Presley laughed. "She knows it's not true either. I just thought I'd humor her."

"Well, I don't think she likes me very much." I gave Aaron a sheepish grin.

"Oh, don't worry, she doesn't like anyone." Zach placed his beer bottle up against the counter and hit the top of it. The bottle cap flew to the other side of the room.

"Yeah, even us sometimes." Presley rubbed his arm.

Aaron sighed, searching for his keys. "Kimberly, I will come pick you up in an hour, okay? Two hours, max."

Our eyes met, and I wondered if he could see the fear in my eyes. Being split up felt wrong.

He gave me a reassuring look before turning back toward his brothers. "Will one of you walk Kimberly home?"

"You don't have to do that." I got up from my chair.

"Oh, of course." Presley smiled. "Allow me. I'm a perfect gentleman."

"Do you think we'd let you do that after you just got mugged? What kind of men would we be?" Luke strode toward the front door, beer still in hand.

There was no use in arguing with them. All three of them walked me to my dorm, and I spent the next two hours in the common room where there were plenty of witnesses.

Luke put the car in park and placed his hand on the passenger seat's headrest to look at me and Presley. "All right, we're here!"

In a hurry, we piled out and pulled our stuff from the back of their car. It was an older Honda that had seen better days. Once we were in the parking lot, I knew exactly which park they were talking about. I had seen it in passing.

Large billboards lined the roads, coaxing us to come visit. Though I had lived in the town all my life, I'd never been. It was a one-of-a-kind adventure park geared toward adults. There was normal camping, rafting, swimming available but also common areas where you could eat and drink. I could see why it was a favorite spot for finals-fatigued students.

It was in a different part of the mountain from what I was used to. We traveled on long winding roads farther away from town. It was more secluded than I had expected, and also less kitschy. I expected an amusement-parklike structure, with huge gaudy signs and maybe a few animated animals. Instead, it was the mountain itself that greeted me. The park appeared to blend into the scenery, as if they were made together.

"Hey, guys."

Aaron's voice came from behind me. He had his arm wrapped around Chelsea's shoulder. She stumbled over her long, flowy cover-up. Her long blonde hair was perfectly curled underneath her sun hat. They rode separately, and I was having a hard time gauging how I felt about the whole thing. Aaron was acting more and more strange by the hour. Despite staying the night in his room again for protection, he left me alone all night and only said a few words when he came in to check on me. It was safe to say I didn't get any sleep.

Aaron met my eyeline. It was brief, and he averted his gaze to Luke. The look in his eyes was unsettling, and it left me with a cold chill.

"Trying to turn a few heads, I see." Presley chuckled, looking Chelsea up and down.

She smiled and moved herself to take Aaron's hand. "Always. I'll probably need to borrow one of Aaron's hoodies later. Are we ready to go inside?"

I caught myself in a troubling thought. Was I . . . jealous? It was the same feeling I had at the dance, watching them dance together. But there was no reason for me to be jealous. Aaron wasn't mine, after all. He was free to do whatever he wanted and date whoever he wanted. But it was still strange seeing him interact with her, even stranger that it came out of nowhere. If I didn't know any better, I would have guessed he was doing it on purpose.

Still, I found myself averting my eyes from his hand on hers.

"Kimberly needs to change!" Presley grabbed my shoulders from behind.

I examined our group, realizing I was the only one not ready. I packed so fast I forgot to change into my bathing suit. The boys were already wearing their board shorts and shirts in different colors and patterns. Presley's were the brightest.

"Uh, no, that's okay. I can wait until we get inside." I shifted my feet uneasily.

"Yeah, but the faster you get changed, the faster we can get to the fun," Luke said.

"Fine." I caved and grabbed my bag from my shoulder. It wasn't hard to find the changing area. A little building in the corner of the parking lot hosted a swarm of girls hanging around the entrance.

I caught a few glimpses of the river flowing through the trees in the distance. Loud, thumping music coming from the cars in the parking lot drowned out the rushing water.

"I'll come with. I need to check on my hair." Chelsea was hot on my heels and wrapped her arm around mine as we made it through the door.

I knew it had to be a trap. My heart was in my throat when she led me next to one of the dress stalls.

"Okay, let's cut the shit. Do you like Aaron?"

Warmth pooled in my cheeks. "I—why are you asking me that?"

Chelsea sighed and ran her black acrylics through her hair. "Because I'm not an idiot. I can see it going on right before my eyes. I just want to clear the air because I'm not trying to step on anyone's toes. If you like him, I'll back off."

"I-I . . ." I desperately wanted an out. I wasn't ready to answer that question.

Not when my world quite literally felt like it was falling apart, and the last real conversation between Aaron and me had ended in an argument.

Aaron meant more to me than I wanted to admit. He was definitely my friend, but did I want more? I thought back to the forest, to us swaying in the moonlight, crickets chiming their symphony. For a moment, I wanted more. In a fleeting moment, I wanted his lips on mine.

But he pulled away. He pulled away, and I pushed him away. That's how I needed to leave things. It would be a lot less messy for the both of us. I'd just had to forget about that fleeting moment. Forget I ever allowed myself to get sucked into that fantasy.

"We're just friends." I saw myself in the reflection as I said it. My eyes were hollow, and my cheeks tugged into a tight-lipped smile.

"Good." Chelsea turned to the mirror and pulled her hair into a high ponytail with her sparkly scrunchie. "Because I thought he liked you. That's the vibe I got from him at the formal, anyway."

My heart steadily beat against my ribs. I had no idea what she was talking about. I hadn't noticed anything. Aaron actually went out of his way multiple times to make it clear everything was platonic. I was the only one who slipped up for a second and thought I was feeling something more, or at least that's what I thought.

"Well, now that that's out of the way"—Chelsea dragged lip balm across her lips—"I'll let you get dressed, and I'll wait outside with the boys."

She sashayed out of the changing rooms with a new pep in her step, and I stood silent for a moment.

I had to stay focused. None of this was going to matter if we were all dead. I wasn't sure what William was capable of, but I knew he was an older vampire, and I knew he was strategic. I wasn't one hundred percent sure of his motive either. He stated I was his only goal, but he'd had so many opportunities to take me before. Like in the coffee shop. But maybe he was playing a game in which Aaron and I posed as his little pawns. Maybe he liked to see us squirm and suffer. I had to convince Aaron to tell his brothers, and to do that, I needed to know what William whispered to him.

I quickly changed my clothes and headed out. It definitely wasn't a place I wanted to be for a long time. Something about the crowded changing room made me nervous.

To my surprise, as I walked out, my friends were waiting by the front. The boys' faces all twisted into smiles.

"Are those board shorts?" Presley smiled bigger than I had ever seen.

"What?" I opted for board shorts and a long-sleeved shirt. It seemed more practical to me. Plus, I had a scar to cover. "There are rocks and stuff . . . you know?"

"Totally. Makes perfect sense." Luke held up his thumb.

"You look great!" Presley and Zach said simultaneously.

But I was starting to pick up on their cues and their mischievous tendencies. "Are we going to go in, or what?" Aaron avoided eye contact and turned toward the entrance.

Chelsea giggled and squeezed herself closer to Aaron. She smiled in my direction, more relaxed. I was thankful there wouldn't be any more animosity between us.

"We aren't trying to make fun of you." Zach walked around to my other side. "Promise."

I stumbled around awkwardly and let them lead us through the parking lot and up to the ticket booth. Aaron and Chelsea walked ahead, and I tried not to stare.

I scoffed. "Oh, I know exactly what you were doing."

"Do tell," Zach said.

"You wanted me to come out in a skimpy bikini to make Chelsea jealous." I smiled a little at the thought, then shoved it deep down inside. It wasn't a competition.

"Holy shit. She's a psychic." Zach chuckled, sounding almost proud.

"Or she's already getting scary good at reading us," Luke said.

"You guys just want a front-row seat to a real-life soap opera," I said.

"Yes. Definitely, that's it," Presley said.

Aaron and Chelsea walked hand in hand ahead in front of me. "Is that why you invited me?"

"Oh, no. We invited you because we like you." Luke sandwiched me between him and Zach.

"I don't know. It seems like you guys just worship chaos," I said.

Zach smiled. "I can see why you'd think that. But sometimes, chaos must ensue for the greater good."

"She gets it! Damn, Kimberly, you're already fitting in perfectly." Presley nudged me.

Happiness bubbled up in my stomach, but I tried not to let it show too much on the surface. It was comforting to be included in their group. But also guilt-inducing. I wanted them to know the whole truth and rid myself of the heavy weight in my chest.

The air was warm as the breeze hit my skin. The trees swayed, their branches bending softly with each gust. I was stopped abruptly by Aaron's back.

I stumbled backward apologetically. "Sorry, I wasn't paying attention." Aaron ignored me and stared straight ahead. His shoulders were rigid, his fists clenched.

"Is that the guy?" Presley leaned around Aaron.

"What guy?" Chelsea's voice chimed.

I peered around Aaron, where William was casually buying a ticket at the counter. He had a big bag and a tent strapped to his shoulders, and he was back to wearing his school attire.

"Yeah, that's him." Aaron's voice was cold.

"What do we do?" I muttered. My heart started beating faster as I remembered the night before.

William turned around and spotted us. He smiled nonchalantly and waved at our group.

"Oh. He is definitely following you, huh?" Presley's voice was concerned. "Isn't that the guy you were dancing with at the formal?"

"Who is following you?" Chelsea's face lit up with excitement. "Uh .

. . yeah, he turned into a stalker."

The words came out awkwardly, the simplest definition I could muster.

"Stay behind me," Aaron said.

"Uh-oh, someone's getting protective." Presley snickered.

Luke and Zach huddled in closer, shielding me from my surroundings.

Aaron propelled forward, and Chelsea stayed closer to the back of the group.

I struggled to keep pace as we pushed forward indefinitely. Just when I thought my life couldn't have been more complicated, William had to show up.

Sixteen

KIMBERLY

"**W**hat the hell are you doing here?" Aaron's voice echoed in the canyon walls. He stopped in front of William with a straight spine. William and Aaron were virtually the same height, but Aaron had a slightly smaller build. That didn't stop him from getting in William's face.

"Oh, hello, I just noticed you guys over there." William peeked behind Aaron to speak to me. "Traveling with the pack today, I see."

He was flipping a coin between his fingers. His lingering accent was long gone. He was back to hiding and playing the role of a regular college student.

"Yeah, you could say that." I forced a smile.

I was thankful Chelsea was there. Things might have gotten a little messy if she hadn't been.

"Are you following Kimberly?" Luke said.

"Why would I do that? You must be Aaron's brother, Luke. I've heard so much about you." The smug smile never faded from William's face.

I watched Luke's face closely. I wanted him to remember what happened on the stairs, but after a few seconds, I gave up on that hope.

"From who?" Zach studied him.

"Come on, you're holding up the line!" a random guy from behind yelled.

I hadn't noticed, but we were standing right in front of the entrance booth.

"Oh, don't worry. I already paid for them." William held up the passes and flailed them in the air. "Here, keep the change." He took the coin and flicked it toward Aaron with his thumb.

In the blink of an eye, Zach grabbed the coin before it reached Aaron's face. He held it tightly in his fist before letting it drop. His shoulders grew stiff, and his frame moved to protect Aaron.

I couldn't see his face, but the tension grew.

Luke placed his hand on Aaron's shoulder. "Come on, Aaron—Zach, let's go inside."

William's smile grew, and his eyes darted between the three. Aaron grunted but let his brother push him forward and away from the booth. Zach loosened his stance but kept his eyes firmly on William.

We entered the park, and I nearly stopped in awe. I had seen the mountain but not like that. A lush enclosure towered above, casting shade over us in front of the walking area. The canyon walls surrounded us on both sides. Somehow, the park was wedged right between the entrance of the canyon. As the walls expanded, so did the park. There was tall iron fencing stretching along the border that disappeared into the trees.

We followed the walking trail and stopped in front of a large tree. Vines wrapped around its trunk and covered it in little pink and white flowers. A division forked the trail, and we huddled at its crossing. I could finally get a good look at William. His hair was smoothed back, and he had on dark long sleeves and black board shorts that displayed the university swim logo in big white letters.

William's dark eyes ran through me. "I think camping is this way."

Aaron stepped in front of me again. "Why are you here right now?"

William matched his distance. "Same as you. Just a little fun."

"It's okay, let's just keep going," Luke said, watching Aaron.

"You don't know him like I do," Aaron spat back.

"Yeah, I don't know about this, Luke." Zach kept his eyes trained on William.

I shifted my feet. I was safe among the group, but I wasn't confident in their ability to stay calm. We were on the edge of causing a scene when the park guide spotted us.

"Hello, are you new to the Mountain Top Park?" A burly man with a blood-red park T-shirt interrupted us. "Sorry to startle ya. I just noticed you guys are packing some luggage. Are you here to camp?"

"Totally!" Presley cleared his throat and placed his hands in his pockets.

"All right, everyone who is camping, come over this way! Be sure to have your ticket stubs ready." He guided us through the trees and closer to the riverbank's soft trickling water.

Other guides were ushering in the strangers, and their voices carried in the echo of the canyon walls. The scene at the riverbank was pure chaos. Guides waded knee-deep in the water, pushed off its banks, then filed into the blue rafts.

Our guide gathered his hands in a single clap. "Okay, bros, this is how this is going to work. I'm going to need to do some bag checks. Don't worry, I'm not here to judge. Just gotta make sure you're not here with any illegal substances."

His voice was mellow as he continued explaining the list of illegal things. Our group was still staring daggers at each other. We weren't paying attention. "All right, enough talking. Place your bags on this cart here. We will get them checked out, and they will be left for you to pick up at the campsite location. You can locate your assigned campsite by the number on your ticket."

Afterward, we followed instructions and handed over our bags before he ushered us toward another table of life vests and helmets.

All the nervous energy was getting to me. My stomach dropped as I stared at the blue being tossed about in the rushing water. "Are you guys needing any help with your gear?" The guide stopped in front of us.

"No, we got it. We've been rafting tons of times," Presley said as he grabbed his helmet from the table.

Luke grabbed another one and handed it to Aaron. He leaned in to whisper something in his ear.

"Uh-oh," I mumbled. I held up one of the neon-yellow vests and tried to watch the others around me put theirs on.

"Have you never been before?" Zach was in front of me, putting on his vest. "I figured you had since you've lived here so long."

I had moved my vest to my shoulders, fussing with its buckles. "Uh. No, I think I got it, though."

"I can help you." Zach watched me with amusement. "Or watching you struggle is pretty funny too. I could continue doing that."

He grinned despite the deep indentation between his dark brows.

I threw my hands up in defeat. "Fine. Yes, I need your help."

"Ah, you broke so easily. Here." He helped me put it over my shoulders. "Then these straps will go under you. That's the only real difference. I'll get you a helmet. Hold on."

"Hey. Zach?"

He stopped and turned around to look at me. "Yeah?"

"Can you just watch Aaron? I'm worried something is off." I motioned to William, who was also getting his gear on.

I wanted to tell him everything. The danger. The fear. The uncertainty.

Zach smiled sincerely. "I'm way ahead of you. And don't worry about that guy. He won't get near you. That, I can guarantee."

With those words, he turned around and headed for another table. I waited and tightened my vest, looking around. Presley was playing around, with his vest already on.

Chelsea had her stuff on and was standing by Aaron and Luke.

The boys were talking too low for me to hear.

William stayed on the other side of them. He stayed casual but caught a glimpse of me and winked.

I sighed aloud and turned away. There was no relief from the stress I was feeling. I was about to start my counting when Zach appeared.

"Here it is." Zach appeared next to me and put on my helmet. I moved the strap under my chin and clamped it loosely.

"All right, you guys all check out. Are you ready to board?" The burly guy came back up beside us. I could barely see his lips hiding behind his unruly beard.

"Yeah, we are!" Some of the boys let out excitedly, mostly Presley and Luke.

We moved closer to the rafts, and I fell behind. Luke and Zach were leading the way toward the roaring river, and Chelsea was busy asking the guide about summer jobs. A hand grazed the middle of my back. Aaron was ushering me forward. He didn't say a word and kept his eyes on William. I longed for us to find a place alone. To slow down and figure everything out . . . together. We all stopped in front of a rubber raft that was beached on the thousands of small rocks covering the water's edge. The water was clear and smooth underneath the calico rocks.

"Hey. Wait." Aaron moved his hands to my helmet and pulled the strap tighter. His finger grazed my chin, and my heart jumped in my chest. Somehow, he felt like him again. Our eyes met, and despite the cloudy skies, his eyes burned like liquid honey. "There. That's better. Safety first."

My cheek was on fire where his finger lingered. "Thanks . . ."

"All right, your group is next." Our guide was knee-deep in the water, holding our raft steady for us to enter.

"Looks like we will all be able to fit. Perfect." William smirked as he turned to Aaron.

"We're not going anywhere with you," Aaron spat.

His brothers were instantly at his side. Zach and Luke took to his shoulders, and even Presley flanked him.

It was shocking to me how quickly their body language changed. "Come on. What's he going to do with all of us here? It's just a raft ride. We're here to have fun, remember?" Luke grabbed Aaron's arm, but Aaron didn't lose determination.

"Why's he acting like such an asshole, then?" Zach scoffed.

"Guys, I don't think this is the place to be doing this. We have some lovely ladies with us, who I'm sure didn't come to see us fight." Presley's voice was soft.

"Really, come on." Chelsea huffed. "He seems like a normal guy, and he paid for our tickets."

"There, listen to their reasoning. You wouldn't want to cause a scene." William smiled and stepped onto the raft.

"That's right, come aboard. Watch your step. I need strong rowers to come right over here." Our guide was still extremely energetic despite sounding like he was reciting from a well-rehearsed script.

Aaron's brothers filed in the boat after William, and I followed Chelsea.

Aaron stayed on the shore, watching us with disgust.

"Come on, bro! We don't have all day. These waters are moving with or without you." Our guide flashed him a toothy smile, moving the raft into position. Aaron moved reluctantly to the raft without saying another word.

"All right, guys, my name is Jared, and I'm going to be your guide today. Someone told me that you guys have done this before, so I'm sure you're familiar with our movements. I'm going to be in the back, steering and telling you guys what to do. So, follow my lead."

The boys chattered excitedly as we started to move. I grabbed my paddle, pulled my elbows in, and braced for our journey.

As the sun beat down, it became blatantly clear my day's struggles were not over. I sat casually next to Chelsea, who was much more interested in talking to me, and told me about her studies and expressed her readiness for finals. I was pleasantly surprised that we had some things in common, but I couldn't enjoy the small talk.

Aaron and William sat on opposite sides of the boat, right in the very front. They were in competition with each other from start to finish.

Our guide constantly had to stop and talk to them about working as a team. Though, it didn't help us from spinning our raft around and hitting things. Zach and Luke were busy watching William like a hawk, while Presley was constantly poking me in the back, telling me jokes. It was amusing, though, and after a while, I was ready to get off the hot piece of plastic.

It took us twenty minutes longer than the rafts around us to reach the shore.

"All right. Your stuff should be available to check out with your ticket stub. Thank you, guys." Jared sounded much less excited.

Our first step on shore introduced us to an open area, where food carts created a small food court with wooden tables and benches and an area leading to a couple of swimming holes.

"I guess this is where we part. Thank you, guys, for having me. Enjoy your time." William collected himself, and my "bodyguards" shuffled me toward the back. Despite being smothered by them, William continued to make eye contact with me. "See you around."

We watched in silence as he disappeared toward the swimming holes. A lump settled in my throat.

"Nothing we can't handle." Luke spoke slowly as he ushered our group in the opposite direction.

"I don't like him." Zach wiped the tip of his nose and rocked back on his heels.

"The guy did buy our tickets. That's a couple hundred dollars." Presley moved around excitedly.

"He had money. Does that make him a good person?" Aaron's emotionless expression never faltered.

"He's gone. Kimberly's safe. So, for now, I don't think we should focus on him anymore." Luke walked over to Aaron.

"Besides, I think he is just trying to get under your skin."

"Oh, it's working." Presley chuckled with a mischievous smile.

"Food. Did anyone bring food? I'm starving," Chelsea said from behind.

We shook our heads.

I still felt a little sick from rafting, not to mention the constant emotional whiplash of dealing with William.

"Aaron can take you to the food court. We can take Kimberly to the water." Presley's voice raised in excitement.

I tapped my foot and looked around. I didn't want to split up. Splitting up meant one or both of us were in danger.

Chelsea smiled. "Come on, Aaron, let's go." She dug her other arm into her bag and pulled out her wallet.

Aaron stared at his brothers as if they were talking telepathically. "All right. I'm coming."

After one final look behind me, we walked toward the springs, and the boys erupted into casual conversation.

"Hey, do you think something is wrong with Aaron?" I turned to Luke. "He has been ignoring me all day, which I assume is because of Chelsea, but he is just acting strange."

Luke's gaze floated to Zach and then back to me. "Yeah, we noticed that. It's not just you. He's been—"

"An asshole," Zach reassured.

"Well, I just don't know what to do." I kicked the dirt as we walked toward the springs. "It's so unlike him."

"I grilled him in the kitchen, but he wouldn't tell me anything," Luke said.

"Did something happen at the campsite?" Zach walked next to me with his hands in his pockets.

I paused a little longer than I should have. "No, everything was . . . fine."

"I just ask because when you guys came back, he seemed off."

"But he's been off in general, so . . ." Presley said.

"What do you mean?" I said.

Echoing laughter, splashing, and yelling rang through the mountain's walls as we continued on.

Something shifted in Luke's voice. "He just hasn't been our biggest fan lately."

"Well, all families have issues." I tried to sound as nonchalant as possible.

"Yeah, that's us. Normal family with normal family problems." Presley walked a few steps ahead of us, but he turned around to share a twitch of his eyebrows.

"I was hoping this trip would cheer him up, but I think it's having the opposite effect." Luke smiled at me half-heartedly, his gaze straight ahead. "Speaking of, are you okay being here with that guy walking around?"

"Um . . ."

I wanted to scream. I wasn't okay. I had a vampire stalker who was probably there to kill me and possibly anyone else that planned on getting in his way.

"It's not ideal . . ."

"Are you sure you don't want us to say something to him? We could probably manage to get him to leave you alone," Zach said.

"No," I said a little too quickly. "That's okay. It's probably nothing to worry about."

I didn't want them digging. Digging could be dangerous. My mind flashed back to William's black eyes as he whispered in Aaron's ear. *I just need to get Aaron alone for a second.*

My thoughts were interrupted as we reached the beach area. Natural pools of water blended into tall weather-painted cliffs. The water was an array of blues blending into a deep green. In the distance, I spied various waterfalls and water slides. More than a hundred people were scattered around, but there was room for more.

"I don't know about you guys. But I'm ready to actually have fun today." Presley's smile beamed. "Let's go!"

Presley ushered me toward the springs. I stumbled forward, almost losing balance. The others followed in a roar as they charged toward the water.

The water was cool on my skin. I let my hair down, immersing myself completely.

A cold silence rejuvenated my body. I enjoyed my one moment of peace. Upon returning to the surface, chaos ensued.

"Oh yeah, that's the stuff." Presley let his body float on the water's surface.

"Finally."

Luke waded in, and the rush of water hit me in the face, causing me to lose my footing.

"Kim, you can hold on to me if you want to." Zach was a few feet away. He swam effortlessly in a backstroke. His obnoxious splashing stirred the water.

"Wow." I laughed, letting my legs do the work of keeping me afloat. "You can talk to me like a normal girl, you know? I'm not some delicate little flower."

"Yeah, I know, but we can't let Aaron's special friend drown." Zach submerged half of his face under water, only revealing his eyes.

"Nah, I think Kimberly can hold her own. Right, Kimberly?" Luke chuckled.

I nodded in agreement. "See? Someone believes in me."

"Fine, but how else are we supposed to annoy Aaron? He's so protective of you." Presley spun in circles, letting his arms trail around him like an octopus.

"Trust us. Aaron hasn't brought any woman around that he gets jealous with," Luke said.

"I don't think I've ever seen Aaron get like this." Zach cast a look in Luke's direction.

"I mean, Aaron's had girlfriends . . ." Luke started.

"Quite a few, actually," Presley yelled enthusiastically.

"He's also had girls that are friends. But never has he brought someone around like you," Luke said.

I swam around to hold on to a rock. My shirt bubbled up as I moved half of my body out of the water, and I shook it out of my ears. "What are you talking about. What's so different about me?"

Luke smirked. "I don't know. What is so different?"

"I don't know." I leaned back, letting the water wet my hair again. Anything to avoid full eye contact with either.

Zach appeared on my other side. "Hm. You seem to be telling the truth. But . . ."

"We don't buy it." Zach and Luke talked in unison.

"We know there is something you guys aren't telling us. We can feel it." Zach moved in closer, closing the circle around me.

I dared to glance over at Presley, who was silently enjoying my struggles. He bit his lip, and his face was red from holding back laughter.

"Point is we need details. What are you guys hiding?" Luke leaned up against the rock I had propped myself on, his wrist visible.

Three parallel black lines that extended three inches onto the forearm. They were slender and wobbly and a little uneven. I peeked over at Zach's wrist that held the same ink. I'd never noticed them before.

"Nothing."

I kept my tone calm, but internally, I was screaming. There was no way I could convince them I was telling the truth.

Zach relaxed. "Don't worry, we will figure it out."

"They're really nosey, huh? You get used to it." Presley propped his elbows up on the rock and let his body hang. He turned and looked behind him. "Quick, get on my shoulders."

"What? Why?" I said.

"It's that game, you know . . . Marco Polo."

"What?" Zach said.

"Not even close. It's called Chicken." Luke laughed.

Presley shook his head. "No, that's not it."

"How would you know? We never had a pool." Zach splashed Presley, causing an outpouring of chaos.

I leaned farther into the rock as they splashed and pushed each other under the water, once again failing at their job of looking human.

Their special bond engulfed me. Being with them made time pass quickly. They made me feel comfortable and accepted, even if they'd

215

spent half the time grilling me. I knew it came from a place of love and protection.

Aaron walked up to the water bank with a perky Chelsea at his side. "What are you doing?"

His heavy gaze penetrated our carefree circle.

"Nothin'," the boys said simultaneously.

A strange silence settled among us. Happy, young adults passed with their yelling and splashing. I wished that could be all of us. Carefree. If only Aaron and I had met in another life, maybe things would have turned out differently for his brothers too. Maybe they wouldn't have ever gotten mixed up in bad things, and they would have never had to suffer as much as they had. Maybe I wouldn't have spent so much time alone. We could have been at the Mountain Top Park just like normal college kids.

"All right. Let's go cliff diving." Presley practically sprinted out of the water.

"Cliff diving?" I fidgeted.

"Yeah, it's right over there." Zach pointed to a tall cliff nearby, a rocky ledge. Some guy in hot-pink swim shorts hurled himself off the edge and past the rocks below.

"Are you afraid of heights?" Luke said.

"Um, a little," I admitted.

I waddled to the shore. My clothes stuck to my skin, the hot sun beating down on my back.

Luke took off his wet shirt and wrung it out. "Don't worry. It's perfectly safe." Easy for them to say.

That was my first chance to get Aaron alone. I went up behind him to try to tap on his shoulder, but he was already leading the charge up the cliffs. I sighed. I'd just have to wait till we got up there. I looked around, making sure my vampire stalker wasn't following.

Water sloshed around in my shoes, and they squeaked with each step. The sun was high above the trees and peeked through the branches and dried the beads of water on my skin. I followed behind the shirtless group of men—and Chelsea, who still looked as perfect as the moment she stepped foot in the park.

My attention drifted to Aaron and Chelsea again. It might have been good for Aaron to stay focused on someone completely normal. A normal girl. Completely removed from our world. I didn't feel like a normal girl anymore. I couldn't be. Once I was bitten, my life had changed forever.

Chelsea stumbled forward every few seconds and cursed her shoe choices. Aaron patiently helped guide her up the path. I didn't like the feeling settling in my stomach as I watched his hand graze her back.

Presley trailed behind me, and I slowed down to meet his pace. "How did Aaron meet Chelsea?" I tried to keep my voice low.

I couldn't help my curiosity. Chelsea was the polar opposite of Aaron. My brain couldn't handle them being so close.

Presley watched them with amusement. "They met when we first moved here. We have a lot of sorority girls over for parties. I guess some guy tried to push her down the stairs after the party was over, and he stood up for her. She's been obsessed with him ever since."

My heart fluttered uncomfortably. "Wow, I could definitely see Aaron doing that."

"Welp, the story is—or at least I've heard—Aaron was the first guy to ever be nice to her." Presley shrugged.

Chelsea stumbled again, and her shoe flew off beside her.

"Hey, hold on!" I called, and the boys came to a halt.

"What the . . ." Chelsea stood unevenly with one foot bare. Her flip-flop was broken and wedged between some rocks. "That's just great."

"What's the holdup?!" Zach's voice carried through the trees.

"We've had a blowout!" Presley said.

I pulled my bag from my shoulders and rummaged for my water shoes, figuring we would be the same size.

"What kind of blow out!?" Luke chimed.

Presley chuckled. "Like flip-flops!"

"Oh, okay . . . Hey, Presley, tell those ladies to hurry it up!" Zach's voice echoed in the canyon.

"Ugh, we can hear you! Just shut up." Chelsea's voice was so shrill, even Presley covered his ears.

I skipped up the trail. "Here. You can have these."

It was my pair of old, tattered water shoes I used for my camping excursion when I needed to get close to the water. It wasn't much but better than nothing.

She held the shoes with her mouth agape for a moment before the corners of her mouth curled up into a smile. "Thanks."

"It's okay. Better than walking through the dirt and rocks," I said, thankful she'd taken my olive branch.

"All right. The princess has been tended to. We may resume the procession!" Presley yelled.

It didn't take us long to reach the cliff. The trees gradually became sparse, and people gathered all in one place. One by one, boys and girls danced their way to the edge and took a big leap. My stomach dropped as their bodies disappeared out of sight. I made my way to the edge, my feet inches away from the drop. The water rippled in a perfect circle as one person plunged their body straight into the water. I let out a slow breath as they swam over to the embankment.

"Kim, over here," Presley called before disappearing into an opening in the trees.

I reluctantly followed him through the small opening. Pine branches pricked and scratched my skin.

We walked out into a more secluded spot, where no one was jumping. The grass was lush, and there was plenty of room to get a running start.

"We're the only ones here." Chelsea folded her arms.

"Yeah, that's the point. One of our friends told us about this spot. Don't worry, it's perfectly safe, just a little more rocky." Presley's smile beamed, and he flung his flip-flops off to the side.

"Will we get in trouble?" I said, knowing the boys probably had no problem doing something that might get us all kicked out.

"I think we'll be fine. Live a little, Kimberly." Presley nudged me before walking closer to the cliff. It was the most ironic statement, coming from someone who was practically invincible.

"Don't you trust us?" Zach shot me a wicked smile as he moved his arms around his body and limbered up for show.

"Absolutely not," I said, smoothing a smile over my lips. "Someone go first, then I'll follow."

I stayed close to the trees and kept my attention on Aaron, who appeared to be in a different world. He stared off into the trees, his body not moving an inch.

"Suit yourself." Zach ran for the water without hesitation and did a front flip.

"See, the trick is to run, squat with your knees, and throw yourself into the air." Presley demonstrated the flip extremely close to the edge.

"Are you sure you want to jump?" Luke was watching my face. "You don't have to. I can walk back down with you if you need me to."

"No, that's okay. I'm just scoping it out. Don't worry about me," I said.

"Luke!" Presley jumped up excitedly. "Do the back flip."

He pointed out into the vastness of the water below. Up on the cliffs, we had a view of the top of one of the water walls. A series of alternating rock ledges were smooth and flat enough for some people to slide down.

Luke gave me a soft pat on the back. "See you down there." He went over to the edge and flung himself backward, easily missing the rocks below. A feat that might not work for someone who didn't have superhuman strength.

A large splash sounded below, followed by an uproar of cheering. Music blared and echoed up the mountain walls along with the constant smell of a burning campfire.

"Come on, Aaron, let's jump together," Chelsea said, with more pep than I had anticipated. She grabbed his forearm. "We can head back to the campsite early."

He was turned away, his body completely still, looking into the woods.

Chelsea nudged him to get his attention, but he didn't reply.

I strolled over to Presley seconds before he was about to bound off the cliff. "Presley, can I ask you for a favor and you not ask me why?"

His brows pressed together curiously. "Sure, but it will cost ya. For friends, it's free. For family, it costs."

"What? Presley, you just met me."

"I know, but I only trust the people in my family. I trust you. So, therefore, you're family. Therefore, it costs."

I sighed. "Fine, can you distract Chelsea for a few minutes so I can talk to Aaron . . . alone?"

He chuckled. "You got it, boss. Just remember, I'm going to collect one of these days."

I didn't have time to think about what that meant, but knowing Presley, it probably meant I'd be doing his schoolwork, or he'd be asking me to do something embarrassing.

Presley playfully waved to her. "Hey, Chelsea, let me show you something over here."

She spun around. "Do you think I'm stupid? You're going to push me off."

"Me? No, never," Presley said. "Come on. I'm having a girl problem, and you're the only girl I trust to give me an honest answer. No offense, Kim."

Chelsea reluctantly followed him closer to the ledge, the fringe of her white cover-up soiled.

I made a beeline for Aaron and wasted no time grabbing his arm and pulling him between an opening in the trees, just out of sight from the others. He didn't resist. It was a tight fit, with only a couple of feet between us. Our backs pressed up against the trees, and we faced each other.

"Aaron." My voice was firm. "Tell me what's going on."

A small wrinkle separated his brows, and he spoke slowly, his eyes distant. "I feel kinda weird . . . foggy."

"We have to do something. I'm serious. We're getting you help."

I tried to hide the fear from my voice, but I knew I couldn't hide it from my face. I never contemplated the burden Aaron had to bear. He had a side he didn't want me to see. A side he couldn't keep from bubbling to the surface. It was eating him alive, and that made me unbelievably angry.

There was something different about being angered for the protection of others. At fifteen, the embers of anger were red-hot in the pit of my stomach. Longing for malice and revenge. This kind was different. It was a fire that lit up my entire body, which made me want to run to get help. It sprang my feet into action.

I'd keep pushing for whatever it took to get him better.

"I just want it to stop," he said.

I gripped his shoulders to steady him. Our bodies pressed together. "Come on. Let's just go down there and tell your brothers everything."

"No." His voice grew cold again. "We're not doing that."

"Why not?"

"We just aren't." He tried to divert his gaze, but I held him in place.

"What did William say to you?"

He stared at me, lips pressed together. After a few seconds, he shook his head. "Kim, I can't . . ."

His voice softened. Then he was the man I knew again. Soft, enticing smile and rich, warm-brown eyes. Less than a day without it, and it felt like a lifetime. His cute, fluffy hair and blushing cheeks were a sight to see.

I wrapped my arms around his neck and hugged him. "It's going to be okay. I promise we'll figure this out. You don't have to do this alone."

He hesitated, his arms pinned to his sides. His entire body felt like a rock, but after a few seconds, he wrapped his arms around my waist and buried his head on my shoulder.

He melted into me, and I nuzzled into his neck. My chest pressed firmly against his, and the world went silent. His heartbeat stayed in a steady rhythm with mine.

In the shadow of the trees, it was just the two of us. Aaron was just like me. Alone in the darkness, trying to find his place in our new world. From the very beginning, that's who we were. We were the same in so many ways I'd never seen before.

No matter the consequences, I was going to stick it through till the end. Even if his skin on my skin felt like the most comforting, perfect thing in the world, and it would soon be a distant memory. It would be worth it.

Soon, another splash sounded below, and Chelsea's voice was close. "Come on, Aaron, Presley was just—"

I pushed away from Aaron, but it was too late. Chelsea was already staring at us with her big blue eyes.

"This isn't what it looks like," I blurted.

"I knew it. I knew something was going on." She snarled. "Just friends my ass."

She bolted for the cliffside, and we followed.

"Chelsea, wait!" I said, my voice echoing in the trees.

She turned on Aaron. "Here, you had me fooled. You like to play like the cute, innocent type. But you're just like the rest of them. Some loser who has nothing better to do than to get drunk and fuck with women and their feelings."

His eyes darkened, and his voice cut through the warm spring air with a cold shill. "Maybe you were the delusional one. Why would I like someone like you? There is nothing special about you. You're controlling, and you can't even take a hint. I never wanted you around. I just felt sorry for you."

Chelsea's face fell, her mouth agape. She was completely unguarded, astonished at the verbal assault. Her pain washed over me like fresh gasoline, igniting the guilt in the pit of my stomach.

She was an innocent bystander left in the wake of our mess.

"Aaron, stop," I said.

He ignored me, his gaze searing into hers. He cast a shadow over her petite frame. "It's sad. All the things you do for my attention. Pathetic." His lips curled into a smile. He was enjoying her pain.

If I hadn't seen him say the words, I never would have believed they were capable of coming out of his mouth.

With lips trembling, she held her head high. "Fuck you."

Her hair whipped around as she made a dash for the trees, and I followed. "Chelsea, wait. He didn't mean that. He—"

She turned with a slap to my face. "Never speak to me again." Her eyes glistened with tears. I knew the pain in my cheek was nothing compared to the pain Aaron had inflicted on her. Chelsea leaned down to remove my shoes and threw them at my feet. I rubbed the warmth in my cheek as she disappeared. The sting imprinted the truth on my face for the world to see. What we were doing was reckless. Dangerous. It was time to tell the truth.

I turned around, expecting to see Aaron. He was nowhere in sight. The only sounds came from below. The splashing carried into the trees behind me, and carefree laughter fluttered like a songbird.

"Kimberly!" Presley's voice was easily identifiable. I followed the sound to the cliff's edge where our group was waiting near the beach area.

I waved back to Presley. My stomach was still in my throat. Would Aaron's brothers accept the truth? Would they still allow me to hang out with them? Maybe they would leave without a word. Without a trace. Leaving me here. Alone. I pushed the thought out of my head. None of it mattered. I couldn't think about myself anymore.

As I turned to look for Aaron, his frame towered over me, stopping me. His eyes still looked hazy and lost. "Are you okay?" His hand touched my cheek, and I flinched. The warm amber still wiped from his irises.

"I'm fine," I said.

"You look . . . scared." His voice still sounded far away despite our proximity. I could smell his cologne and feel his body heat.

"Aaron, there's something very wrong with you." I watched Aaron's footsteps as he moved closer, forcing me back a step. The cliff's edge loomed in my mind. He closed the distance between us. My feet stuttered backward, and he grabbed my waist, pulling me closer to him.

"W-What are you—?"

He brushed my hair from my shoulder, bringing his lips close to my neck. I stood, frozen. Swallowing a breath. "You smell so good."

His words dripped with longing, the sound foreign to my ears, his breath hot on my skin. He twirled his fingers in my hair. Judging by my sweaty back and damp hair, he wasn't talking about me or the sunscreen I had put on that morning.

Placing both hands on his chest, I tried to force him back. His muscles were stone. Tense and rigid.

"What's the matter? I thought you'd like me like this?"

His breath was still hot on my neck as I shoved his chest again, this time much harder.

"No. I don't. You're being an asshole."

I fell back. Only, this time, there was no ground left to catch me. I fell into the open air. My only thought was on the rocks below.

Something firm hit me and wrapped me up before I made impact with the water. I flailed around, feeling trapped as I submerged deeper into the spring water. My hand stung, and I pulled it close to my body. With no effort of my own, I found myself pulled to the surface of the water. Water filled my throat, and I coughed, struggling to swim. Somehow, someone had pulled me up, as if I had a life preserver.

Upon opening my eyes, Aaron was pulling me toward the shallow end of the water. When I got my bearings, I pushed him off to swim by myself. Cheers and applause erupted around us. My stomach dropped as their eyes weighed me down.

Aaron didn't stop walking toward the shore as countless people applauded and patted him on the back. I swam, then walked till the water hit my knees, pulling my hair out of my face and wringing it out. A stabbing pain radiated from my hand. A large cut lined my palm. I closed my hand and wrapped it around my waist. That was the last thing we needed right then.

As I struggled to get my bearings and tried to comprehend what had happened, Aaron's brothers circled me.

They talked in a flurry around me, their voices running into each other.

"Are you hurt?" Luke's jaw was set and serious.

"What happened?" Zach said.

"Dude, you scared me." Presley grabbed my shoulders.

I couldn't help but chuckle at the sound of worry in their voice.

"Funny to hear you guys being so serious."

They relaxed with sighs of relief and nervous laughter.

"Well, if you wouldn't be so dramatic and throw yourself off a cliff, we wouldn't be in this mess," Presley said.

"He's right. What were you thinking? Who does that?" Luke placed his hand on my back, guiding me to the shore.

"Wait, where's Chelsea?" Zach said.

"It's kinda a long story," I said as Aaron barreled past us and out of the water.

Luke and Zach shared a look before following after him, not speaking a word.

Presley and I stood dumbfounded for a second. The breeze filled the silence, and we watched as college students ran around in hoards. Their laughter and screams carried through the air.

"Uh-oh, you're bleeding." Presley motioned to my hand that was still wrapped around my waist.

I released my grip, revealing the long gash oozing across my palm. It looked worse than it felt.

"I better go clean this up."

"I'll come with you!" Presley gave me a sheepish grin. "And you can explain to me this long story of what happened with Chelsea."

I reluctantly agreed and told him the bare minimum of truth, skipping the part where Aaron's eyes had turned black, and he looked at me like he wanted to eat me. I was so close to telling him. The words were right on the edge of my tongue, yet I held back.

We had to tell Zach and Luke what was going on. Everything had gone too far. But Aaron was serious about them not knowing, and I didn't know why. Would he stop me if I tried? I just needed to get Aaron alone and talk some sense into him. I was so close to getting him to open up.

Presley and I reached the restroom, and I went inside to clean my hand up. My shoes squeaked in the water that wove its way between the tiny tiles. The sick smell of dirty toilet water motivated me to quicken my pace. I grabbed a few paper towels and walked to the sink to examine my hand. The cut wasn't as deep as it looked. I put my hand under the cool water, searching for something to cover it with. My only option was my shirt. I pulled it over my head and held it in front of the hand dryer.

After ten minutes of awkward stares, I wrapped it around my hand and over my wrist. I left the bathroom with a sigh and kept my attention on the wet floor to keep from slipping.

"Guess you decided to take that shirt off after all." Presley nudged my shoulder with a carefree smile.

Thankfully, my wet hair provided a good scar cover-up.

I couldn't fight the look on my face. I was drowning.

"What's wrong? You know, other than the obvious bleeding hand you have there and getting slapped in the face."

His frown didn't suit him. If Aaron was the sun, Presley was the wind. Always moving. Free. The drooping corners of his lips tied him down in an unnatural way.

"There's something wrong with Aaron," I said.

"Yeah, I know he's been on one lately."

I stopped him. "No, you don't get it. There's something seriously wrong. I don't know what to do, and I'm freaked out. Your brothers are going to freak out, and . . . and . . ."

Presley squinted, waiting. "And?"

"I don't know what to do. Help me!"

"Okay, okay. Chill." Presley steadied me. "I think you're overexagger-ating Zach's and Luke's reactions. Sure, you lied, but it's not like they haven't. I don't get why you're so scared for them to know. The sooner you rip off the Band-Aid, the better. For the record, I'm happy you know about us, and you don't hate us. That's pretty badass."

I smiled at his sentiment but quickly overwhelmed myself again with thought. "I just need to talk to Aaron first."

Presley leaned in and whispered, "The truth is, they're actually big softies. Zach, especially. Underneath that hard outer shell is a man who used to write poetry to his high school sweetheart. The long sappy kind."

"Wait, Zach had a high school sweetheart? What happened?"

It didn't shock me he had a girlfriend. He was attractive and seemingly athletic, so, of course he did. But I was curious about the details.

"They ended up breaking up when she went off to college. I think she wanted to stay, but Zach basically told her he couldn't be with her because of . . . you know." He shook his head. "Anyway, Aaron will cool off eventually. He always does."

"He's been like this before?" I said.

"Yeah, kinda. Standoffish—and not to mention the big fight he got in with Zach just a couple days ago."

"He didn't say anything about a fight."

Just like he hadn't mentioned anything about going hunting.

"That's not surprising. It was intense. He yelled. Zach almost broke a light pole. Then he just stormed off. He hasn't been right since."

"Was this on your hunting trip?" I said, lowering my voice a bit.

"Oh, so you know about that kinda stuff, then, too? Sweet. Yeah, it was."

"Did Aaron drink blood on your trip?"

The words felt weird coming from my mouth, but there was no way around the question. I had to follow the thread.

Presley eyed me suspiciously. "Yeah, we all did. We don't kill people, though. You know that, right? He told you?"

"Yeah, yeah. He told me." My mind spun in circles.

Was it possible William lied about Aaron? At that point, anything was possible, and it explained a lot. Aaron did seem off on our camping trip. Maybe this was just a trickle-down effect and not as serious as I had thought, or more likely an idea William had compelled in some way.

If that was the case, Aaron might never agree to tell his brothers, and

I'd need to be the one to do it. I hated the idea of doing something like that without Aaron's agreement or help, but I couldn't wait anymore. Whatever was wrong with him, his brothers had to know.

"You don't need to worry about Aaron. He'll come to his senses. As for Zach and Luke, I don't think it will be a big deal. I mean, it's not like you guys did anything dangerous. You're obviously not going to tell on us."

A lump caught in my throat. If only we had just one secret. They were all dangerous.

I spotted the twins in the distance, who were walking over from the food court. My hair was drying and falling away from my shoulders. One swift breeze, and the scars on my neck would stand out. Dropping the bomb on them in the middle of the park with tons of bystanders was probably not the best idea.

"I have another favor to ask you."

I couldn't hide my fidgeting, and Presley spun to see where I was looking.

He smirked. "You're running up quite the tab. Remember, you owe me."

The twins were closing in.

"Okay, fine. I owe you. Give me your shirt." I tugged on his blue shirt that had a little embroidered logo on the sleeve.

He laughed. "Weird request but okay."

I wrestled the thin cotton number over my bathing suit. After a few moments, Luke and Zach appeared, looking less solemn.

"There you are. Wait, why are you wearing his shirt?" Luke searched for the missing link between us.

I held up my wrapped hand. "I had to sacrifice mine for the greater good."

"Yeah, and Kim's embarrassed of her bathing suit." Presley's voice had no hesitation.

"Why didn't you just say that earlier?" Zach said.

"Aaron's calmed down a lot. He told us about what happened with

Chelsea. We tried to catch up with her, but it looks like she took her stuff from the campsite and left. I know we haven't made this all that fun for you, but we promise no more slapping." Luke's grin radiated eternal optimism.

"Except, if you want to slap us to let go of all that pent up anger, go ahead." Presley leaned his face close to mine.

A soft laughter escaped my lips. "Yeah, I'm up for anything at this point."

Their attempt to lighten the mood worked, and for the first time that day, I could see things working out. I just needed to get them alone. I resolved to tell them at the campsite. With or without Aaron, I was going to come clean. They'd be upset, but maybe they would understand. We could figure out the William problem. We could do it all together.

Dark pools of purple and red filled the perfect portrait above. I never grew tired of seeing the sunset over the mountain treetops. I loved watching the sun disappear out of view, entrenched in silence. It made me feel small but secure at the same time.

The calm sound of the sleeping forest came out to play shortly after. I sat alone by the campfire and Presley and Zach argued about how to set up the tent a few yards away. I sighed and let the warmth of the fire wash over me. The cloth felt heavy on my hand. I removed the shirt and stretched my hand open and closed.

We had two campsites reserved about fifty feet apart. The other campsites were full, and it was oddly quiet and calm. After a long day of swimming and rafting, everyone must have been too tired to keep the party going. My whole body ached from the jump, and all I wanted to do was crawl into my sleeping bag.

A branch crunched behind me, followed by Luke's voice. "Can I get you anything? I was going to make dinner."

"Uh, sure, I could eat. I'm not picky."

"Great, um . . . I just wanted to tell you that I'm happy you came today. I know it wasn't the best day, but it was good to see Aaron smile again. I know I have you to thank for a large part of that." Luke smiled, watching my expression.

"I wouldn't say . . . large."

"Oh, I would. It's been hard for us lately, and since you came along, Aaron—he just seems happier. So, thank you."

His words warmed me with the fire. "Thanks, Luke. That means a lot."

"Don't mention it." He patted me on the shoulder and walked back toward the others.

I allowed my legs to bring me to my feet. It was right then or never. I hoped I could get through the whole conversation without puking.

I spied Aaron walking across the yard toward me, and I stopped. He had left to get us some more firewood and to scope the place for any signs of William.

"Hey, can I talk to you?" Desperation leaked in his voice, his mouth twisting into a deep frown.

"Okay, sure," I said slowly.

He didn't speak another word, and I followed after him. I expected him to stop at the tree line, but he didn't. He kept walking farther and farther into the forest. I stumbled over a few branches and unearthed roots, wading through the twilight.

"Where are we going?" I asked, trailing behind.

"Just to where they can't hear us."

After a few more minutes, Aaron stopped abruptly and turned to face me. His features surprised me. His eyes were soft and filled with worry. Pieces of his dirty-blond hair fell into his face. "Kim, I'm so sorry about today. I-I don't know what happened."

I walked a few steps closer. "It's okay. Are you feeling better?"

"No, there's something wrong with me. I don't know what to do."

His voice caught in his throat.

Seeing him in pain, hurt. It blindsided me. All I wanted was to make it better.

"Come on, we're going to fix this. We're going to tell your brothers."

"No!" Aaron called out desperately. "You don't understand."

"Then, tell me. What is it? What did William say to you?" My voice echoed through the trees in sync with the birds, who were singing their last song of the day.

His eyes searched mine. "I can't—I'm scared. I don't know what will happen. I don't know what to do. This is all my fault. First, dragging you into my shit, and now, my brothers . . ."

"William mentioned them, didn't he?" I closed the distance between us and took his hand. His skin was cold, and I placed my other hand on top of his to warm it.

"He said if I told my brothers, he would kill you. And if I told you, he would kill one of them. I just needed some time to figure out what to do, but I can't think straight. I don't know what's happening to me."

"I know. That's why we need your brothers' help."

"Kim, I can't protect you. I thought I could. I want to, but—"

"You don't have to protect me. I'm not scared."

I surprised myself with how true that statement was. All the fear I'd been working through since figuring out I was being stalked by a vampire, paled in comparison to the thought of losing who Aaron was.

The world needed people like Aaron, someone who could find the good in any situation, someone who risked everything to save me twice. I couldn't let his light go out.

His eyes never left mine. The hints of warmer-lighter brown had come back into his irises. It was comforting, just like his presence always was. He shook his head. "You're never afraid."

"That's not true. I get afraid all the time." I cupped his shaking hands in mine. "I need you. You have to get better."

"Okay." Aaron's voice was stronger. "We'll tell them. We can still fix this."

Relief washed over me as the color returned to his face. Everything that had once fallen into the darkness had come back to the light. We could fix this. We still had time to save Aaron and keep his brothers safe. After all, there were four of them and one of William. This nightmare could soon be over, and I could experience the relief of coming forth.

"Come on, let's go back to the campsite." I pulled away, but Aaron had a firm grip on my forearm. I tried again to break his rock-hard grasp. "What is it? What's wrong?"

He stayed silent for a moment, his gaze settling on my hand. "You're bleeding . . ."

I looked down at my hand, only then realizing I had taken off my makeshift bandage. My wound had reopened, and the tiniest bit of blood smeared onto his hand.

"Aaron . . ."

My heart leaped into my throat as the color drained from his face. In the blink of an eye, his skin was lifeless. Hollow. The whites of his eyes black. Gray rings glowed around his irises. Void of any color. His canines sharpened into fangs.

He tilted his head, licking the tinge of blood from his fingers. It was quick, so quick he thrust me into the tree with a hand over my mouth before I could scream. The bark tore through my clothing, and I groaned in pain. Every part of my body vibrated. Aaron was shaking uncontrollably.

I shook my head, my muffled screams of protest hidden with me in the shadow of the trees. Aaron bit down on my wrist, and a white-hot searing pain tore through my forearm. Every attempt to wiggle made it hurt worse, but I managed to free my mouth.

"I know you're still in there. You have to stop." I winced as the pressure increased on my wrist. "Aaron, let me go!"

Without warning, the pressure and pain were gone. I fell against the tree and pulled my bleeding wrist to my body, holding it with pressure. The surrounding area was still, save for my staggered breath. In a matter of seconds, it was over. Aaron had disappeared into the night.

I crumbled to the forest floor. Every movement made my wound sting, and the throbbing wasn't letting up. Inhaling through my nose, I took in a long breath and let it out slowly. I knew what I had to do. Getting back to the campsite as quickly as possible was imperative. For me and for Aaron.

My adrenaline helped me get back to my feet, but the dizziness had taken over. Taking another deep breath, I attempted again, only this time, I flew forward into a tree, knocking the air from my lungs.

It was completely dark out, and I found myself walking in circles. My head was spinning, and the more I walked, the more turned around I felt. I stopped, my eyes darting in every direction, everything unfamiliar.

"Can anyone hear me?" My voice wasn't as strong as I wanted it to be. Nothing but silence followed. I made my way to the ground and cried out at the pain in my wrist. Blood trickled down my arm, and I hugged it close to my chest. My rapid breathing was the only sound in the quiet trees.

Rustling leaves and cracking of twigs broke the silence.

"Aaron?" I said.

A silhouette emerged through the trees. It took a few seconds for me to make out the face in the dark. My heart dropped.

William was standing in the clearing, looking at me with black eyes.

"I'm afraid not, love."

$\mathcal{S}$eventeen

AARON

A strange ringing filled my head. It wasn't just loud. It was everywhere. I grabbed my head and pulled my hands down over my ears. Incessant ringing filled every corner of my mind. The pressure that came with it was intense. Internally, I screamed for it to stop.

Just like that, the ringing was gone. I blinked a few times and tried to get my bearings. The area didn't feel familiar to me. I was walking through a clearing in the trees. It was dark, the glow of the fire casting silhouettes on their trunks. It was a campsite. No. It was our campsite.

The fog in my head lingered. I blinked, trying to focus. Somehow, I still felt like I wasn't in reality.

"Hey, Aaron." Presley jogged toward me. He met me with a smile, but it quickly turned to a frown. "Where's Kimberly?"

My body moved in slow motion. "Kimberly?"

"Yeah, short . . . red hair . . . our friend?"

His tone didn't match his words. Worry had dispersed in his eyes, and he panned to the woods.

I still had no idea who he was talking about. My mind was still playing catch-up. I strained my brain, trying to push back the fog and think harder.

"Guys. Get over here. Now," Presley called out.

"What? What's wrong?" Zach appeared, and I stumbled back onto my heels.

"Something's w-wrong with Aaron . . ."

Presley had only stuttered a handful of times in my life.

"Luke. Get over here," Zach muttered.

"What?" I said slowly.

Their seriousness was unsettling.

"Aaron, where is Kimberly?" Luke pulled me close to his face.

"Kimberly . . ." I closed my eyes, trying to remember. Kimberly. Of course. Kimberly Burns. How could I have forgotten her?

Luke shook me. "Can you hear me? Where is she?" His grip was firm on my shoulders.

"Why do you keep asking me that? I don't know! What's happening?" I pulled away from them. I didn't like the wide-eyed stares they were giving me.

"Aaron." Luke's voice was strong, and he stood in front of me. Time was passing quickly, and I didn't even see him appear. "I need you to focus. What happened?"

"Wha—what happened, when? Why are you looking at me like that?"

He shook his head and got closer to my face. "You left with Kimberly. What happened to her?"

Like the snap of a rubber band, my thoughts fell into place. Everything came back at once. My dull senses kicked back into overdrive, and I could smell the sweet scent coming from my shirt. I'd know that smell anywhere. Blood.

I looked down, afraid of what I would find. Red stains shining brightly in the dark night smeared my hands, almost as if it were glowing. Shock hit, and I threw my hands in disgust.

"No! No, no, no. This isn't happening. What the fuck!?" I fell backward, but Zach stopped me.

"Tell us what you remember," Luke said, his voice sharp.

They crowded me, and I closed my eyes. "I-I walked with her, and we were talking . . . I think it was getting dark and . . . I don't remember."

Her blood was so sweet it was almost repulsive. I couldn't take my eyes off my hands.

Luke and Zach were staring at each other. "You smell that, right?"

"Blood," Luke said as he peered back toward the forest again. They weren't talking about the blood on my hands.

"We have to go get her." My voice shook with fear that was consuming me. I had hurt her. I was sure of it. Nausea erupted in my stomach.

"Okay, show us." Luke moved us out of the circle, and we headed for the forest.

As I ran farther into the trees, memories resurfaced. I followed the familiar feelings until we reached an opening. The stench of blood was all over the ground.

"Kim . . ." I meant to say it loud, but it didn't come out as more than a whisper.

"Kimberly!" Presley yelled, his voice echoing in the trees.

Zach and Luke searched around in the trees, but my feet were frozen. Blood spatter littered the ground. It confirmed what I had already known.

I attacked Kimberly. This was her blood, and it was everywhere.

The weight of those words hit me, and my knees buckled. Fear paralyzed me. My head was pounding, and my body ached all over again. It was too much.

"Hey, we didn't find her. The trail of blood cuts off not far from here." Zach's voice was barely registering.

The ringing came back, and I buried my head in my hands.

Their voices were blurring into a cacophony, and I couldn't tell who was saying what anymore. I didn't care to know.

"What does that mean?" a frantic voice called out.

"I don't know. But we didn't find her . . . you know, so that's good."

"How is that even remotely good?"

"It means she's alive."

"We don't know that."

"Or something . . . or someone carried her off."

"Or maybe she just got away on her own!"

I opened my eyes, and Presley was leaning in front of me.

His voice was far away. "A-Are you okay?"

The ringing was getting louder every second. I couldn't hear the breeze flowing through the trees or the crickets chirping. My vision was darkening, as if the moon was dimming.

A strange presence crept forward. Evil radiated from the dark figure that kneeled beside me in my peripheral view. White hair was falling down, almost touching my hands. It was an apparition of a woman. I refused to look in its direction. It put its face right next to mine, and smelled of rotten flesh. Her eyes were pure white.

"Are you ready to give up?" a dark, morphed voice spoke from the apparition next to me.

I opened my mouth to speak but couldn't. My fingers had no feeling as I laid my hands in my lap. The vision in my right eye blurred. Everything around me was cast in red, slowly fading to black.

My brothers' voices were barely audible in the darkness.

"H-Hey, what are you doing?!"

"Stop! Stop!"

"Come on, get him off!"

"I can't. He won't let go!"

Deep rage bubbled within my stomach. I was about to explode.

It was spreading to every cell in my body. "Are you . . . trying to . . . kill me?"

The voice of my little brother soothed the flames of rage.

Everything snapped back into reality once again. I found myself leaning over him, my hands squeezing his throat. If he were human, he would have definitely been dead.

"Pres?" I said in barely a whisper.

He smiled as he coughed. "Hey, welcome back."

"I'm sorry. I don't know what that was." I jumped off him and grabbed my chest.

My heart was hammering against my ribs, and I was seconds away from a full-on mental breakdown.

"Okay, what the fuck was that?" Zach's voice was close behind me.

Luke forced me to sit up, and he leaned on his knees in front of me. "I need you to tell me the truth. Have you drank blood in the last month?"

This time, I didn't hesitate. "No, I lied at the carnival. I couldn't do it. I couldn't control it, and I was afraid. I should have just said something."

I ended up hurting the one person I most wanted to keep safe. The irony wasn't lost on me. Nausea shot up to my throat.

"I've never seen anyone not drink." Zach directed his conversation toward Luke.

"But he just had blood when he bit Kimberly." Presley was back to his feet, combing his hands through his hair. "Why is he still all . . . scary?"

"That probably only helped him regain a little control." Luke frowned. "He needs more. A lot more."

"I'm done. I can't do it anymore." I shook my head, wanting to wake up from the nightmare I was living.

"Aaron—"

"No. I'm done. This is too much. If she's dead. I'm dead. If I killed her, it's over for me. I can't keep killing people . . . especially the ones I care about." I touched my hot face. "You're just going to have to go on without me because I'm done. I can't live with myself anymore. I want this to be over."

"Look at me." Luke pulled my hands away. "You didn't kill her. You want to know how I know? Because you are you. You are still Aaron. You care about her. I know you do. So, that's why I also know she is out there somewhere, and we're going to find her." I searched for doubt in his eyes. There was none.

"But . . . how . . . how do you know? How are you so sure?" I choked back tears.

I felt five years old again. Begging my brother to help show me a way to get back on my feet. But out of all my rock bottoms, this was the lowest. I didn't think there was a way to keep going.

"Because I'm your older brother. It's my job to be sure. We need you." He gently held out his hand, palm facing up.

But I knew it wasn't meant to help me up. I placed my hand on top of his, and he sandwiched it with his other hand. I completed it with my left hand. It never failed. When Luke held out his hand to me, it felt like he was giving me some of his strength.

"No one is dead. We're going to find her. I promise." Luke smiled.

I wiped the wetness from my eyes. Luke always kept his promises.

"What if she ran away and went to the police?" Zach said.

Presley was next to him, still rubbing his neck.

"Then, we will figure it out." Luke pulled me up from the pile of dry leaves and prickly branches.

"I-I don't think she would do that." Presley shifted nervously.

"She just discovered vampires exist. It's probably her first instinct," Zach said.

Presley talked through gritted teeth. "I was going to keep this secret for longer, but considering the circumstances have changed, I feel like I have to say it . . . Kimberly knew we're vampires." My older brothers both turned to me.

"You told her?!" Zach snarled.

"No, I didn't! Well, I did but not like you think." I interjected.

"Aaron bit her." Presley gave me a sorry expression. "I'm just trying to help."

"What? So, she's known this entire time?" Zach said.

"I called 911 that day in the forest when you guys found me. I never thought I'd see her again and then I found out a few days later that she went to BFU. It was like fate. I don't know! I apologized, and after talking, she didn't want to press charges or anything. Then she got mugged, and it just progressed from there."

"Aaron, what the hell were you thinking?" Luke sounded more disappointed than angry.

Zach was on the verge of blowing a gasket.

"If you're taken to jail, they will find us and our location immediately. You could have gotten us all killed."

Presley stayed silent but went to stand beside me for moral support.

"I know! Okay, I know. I was just so happy that I didn't kill her, and I wanted her to know she was safe. I messed up. A lot, apparently." I sighed, pulling my head into my hands again. The ringing was ever present. "And . . . you're about to get a lot more mad at me."

Zach was giving his death stare. "There's more?"

"Kimberly's mugger was a vampire . . . and that vampire is named William. He almost attacked me and Kim on our hiking trip, and I couldn't say anything because he told me if I said anything about it that he'd kill her."

"I fucking knew it." Zach snarled and threw his hands up.

"Okay, Aaron's giving me a run for my money for the most reckless brother award, and I don't like it," Presley said.

"That could be where she is. Maybe he took her." Luke perked up.

"Wait, he's here?" I tried to think back on the day, but I couldn't reach it. I could make out small moments with Kimberly, mostly, but they were all a blur.

Luke nodded. "Yes, he followed her here. You really don't remember?"

I shook my head.

"What else do you know about him?"

"He's smart, and I think he's got some kind of plan. He's had a lot of opportunities to take Kimberly and me, and hasn't. We figured it out at the formal, and before we could say anything, he did some kind of mind trick and made us forget. When Kimberly was attacked, I was afraid you guys would just want to leave, and I didn't know if he was after her, and I didn't want to leave her without any help. I'm sorry . . . I'm such a burden."

"Do you really think that little of me? We wouldn't have left her to deal with a vampire on her own. I'm sorry you felt you had to do this all by yourself. I know we haven't exactly inspired trust." Luke grabbed my shoulder. "But now. Please. No more secrets. Okay? Zach, want to add?"

"You're an asshole, and you almost got us all killed," Zach spat.

Luke eyed him, waiting for him to say more. "Five-words-or-less apology."

Zach groaned, holding up five fingers on one hand and counting. "I. Don't. Think. You're. A"—he held up his middle finger on the other hand, counting six—"burden." Surprisingly, it was one of his best apologies.

Luke cracked his knuckles. "All right, let's assume that William took Kimberly. Zach and I will go back through the camp and check for any sign of her. I'll be calling hospitals and feeling out the police stations to see if she has appeared anywhere in town. Pres, you stay with Aaron, and you guys circle around to the front of the park and search for clues. Watch for William and, if you see him, do not approach. Call us."

"So, you don't think he's a part of . . . The Family?" Presley was pacing back and forth between tree trunks.

Zach shook his head. "No, we'd know. This guy sounds like a loner. Which is unusual. He's been playing the long game. Definitely not The Family's MO."

I turned swiftly at the sound of laughter ringing through the trees. I blinked, trying to peer farther into the dark, but a fog set in. It couldn't be real.

"Did you guys hear that? Sounds like someone laughing." My brothers all stopped talking to look at me.

"Buddy, there isn't anyone laughing out here." Presley sheepishly smiled.

"He's hallucinating," Zach said.

"Presley, keep him sane?" Luke said.

"Roger that!" Presley pulled my head back around to focus on the group. "Please don't start talking about some little creepy girl following you or something."

My entire body was weak. I decided to focus on moving one foot in front of the other. I lost my balance a few times and almost landed on my face. Everything was exhausting. I had almost forgotten what exhaustion felt like. Zach and Luke grabbed my shirt to keep me upright.

In the tree line, I saw a flash of white hair again. The same haunting apparition of the woman in a long-slip dress appeared. She turned around to wink at me. A giggle escaped her lips, and her eyes taunted me.

"Oh, no, this is much worse," I said.

"Right. Okay. Call if you find anything. And, Aaron?" Luke stopped just short of the tree line. "I promise We'll get her back." He gave me one final smile before disappearing with Zach into the fog.

"I don't feel good," I said as we started walking. I forced every muscle to bend to my will. My feet were cement blocks as they pushed through branches and debris. I sniffed the air, constantly searching for the scent of Kimberly's blood.

I was emotionally numb, and I could only focus on the possibility of finding her.

"I can tell. Considering you are shaking." I turned to look at Presley, and he smiled. "What sort of things are you seeing right now?" He locked arms with me and dragged me through the trees. "Well, it's a lot scarier than your fear of little ghost girls." *You're weak. That's why you will die.*

"Doubt it. Don't knock it because you haven't even seen half the scary movies I've seen."

"I don't think I need to watch any more for the rest of forever, considering I'm basically living in one." *This is all your fault.*

As we walked on, the voice was harder and harder to tune out.

"Thank God you never workout, Aaron." Presley held onto the other side of me. "It's way easier to carry your scrawny body."

"You're one to talk." I closed my eyes, feeling sleepy.

The trees morphed together in a big blob. I blamed it on the blurry vision slowly drawing my attention. Footsteps scurried between the trees, and I sensed someone was watching us, but I had enough sense to know it was just another hallucination.

Kim came to mind. Light bathed her. Her skin glowed, and her hair was always in her face. Guilt was quick to snatch my warm feelings. I couldn't believe I had let her down.

We quietly made our way through the forest. Despite me slowing us down, Presley was helping us make great time.

After a few minutes, he spoke again. "I'm sorry I've been such a shitty brother. I should have listened to you . . . I should have listened to her. She tried to tell me something was up with you."

I shook my head. "It's not your fault. This is all me."

"You don't get to play the martyr here. I think we can all take a share of the blame in this one." Presley kept his gaze firmly ahead.

I sighed. I didn't want them to take the blame. I wanted to drown in the guilt. I wanted to take the pain of it all. I deserved it.

"Well, I don't think she is out here. We should check the front and the parking lot. They have staff we can ask," he said.

I nodded, and I was thankful Presley's navigation skills had always been better than mine.

I felt the strangest urge to look up at the sky. I obeyed the quiet voice and tilted my head. I couldn't see anything on the ground, anyway. But it was also because this voice sounded different from what I was used to. It felt good and hopeful. The beauty of the night sky was overwhelming. Little sparks of light lighting up a blue sky. Kim would have loved it.

Chirping crickets came back, as well as the wind whistling through the trees. The breeze tickled my cheeks, bringing a smile to my face.

"Look, there's the fence," I said.

An iron fence was interwoven in the trees, massive as it towered over us.

"You think it would have electricity or guards or something." Presley scoffed.

"Well, I doubt they accounted for the undead scaling the twenty-foot fence." I walked up and placed my hand on the bars.

Barbed wire lined the top.

"Let's go. I've wasted enough time."

I imagined a clock slowly ticking. Kim was out there somewhere. I knew the longer it took me to find her, the worse things would be. As I pulled myself over the barbed wire, pain stung. I knew there would be no blood or cuts. With each moment, I was stronger. I turned to look at the park behind me. In the darkness, the gloom faded, or at least I hoped it would. I pushed my feet away from the fence and thrust myself to the ground. I didn't land gracefully, and neither did Presley.

"Oh, hell." Presley cried in pain, and he grabbed his ankle before falling over me.

I grabbed him and stumbled to pull us to our feet. My body still ached, but I wanted to hurry.

"Come on, I think the parking lot is to the right."

We jogged through the trees with a new determination. It wasn't long before the gleam of streetlights revealed the hoods of cars littering the parking lot, but it was sparse on the edges. I searched the empty lot for any sign of movement. A couple leaned against an old red Trailblazer. They turned with annoyance, and their red eyes seared into ours. Their skin was sunken in, and their thin arms grabbed at each other.

"Uh. Have you guys seen a red-headed girl come by here?" I smoothed my hair down in my best attempt to look like a normal college kid.

"If we did, I wouldn't tell you, kid." The male snarled, showing the gaps in his teeth.

I turned to Presley with an unamused expression. "So, I'm going to take that as a no."

"How much money do you got?" The slender woman stretched out her hand.

"Yeah, that's a no." Presley sighed.

"Okay." I pushed past them, looking out into the empty parking lot.

The moon was high in the sky. I had no idea what time it was, but judging by the lack of people, it was late.

I sighed. "There isn't anyone out here."

"What if we went by the front gate? There has to be a security guard or something. Come on." Presley hit my shoulder, and we jogged toward the ticket booth.

As we got closer, none of it felt familiar. I didn't remember the signs, the colors, the smells. Nothing. How much did I miss?

What else had I done that I didn't remember?

"There's someone over here."

I followed the sound of Presley's voice to an alleyway located in the back of the entrance.

A security guard with a thick gray mustache and olive skin was tucked into a small room. He didn't appear to be paying the slightest bit of attention. His eyes were glazed over, watching the surveillance monitors. Deep dark circles added to his hollow, sickly appearance.

I caught up to Presley, and we ran up to his window. "Hey!"

The man turned his head to face us.

"Have you seen a red-headed girl come through here? Or maybe she's on one of the cameras? She's my friend, and I . . . I lost her in the forest."

"We have reason to believe something bad has happened to her," Presley said.

"What is your name?" The security guard's voice was cold. His words came out slowly.

"I'm Aaron."

Our eyes locked onto each other, and my heart sank.

His face was void of expression.

He moved his hand across the desk to hand me a business card. "Here you go."

His voice was monotone, his eyes unblinking.

"What? No. I don't need that! Have you seen her or not?"

"Here you go." He moved the card toward me again.

"What is this?"

"Here you go."

"Is he possessed or something?" Presley leaned in, watching the man's face.

"What? That doesn't make any—oh."

"Here you go."

I took the business card. Underneath the guard's name read a scribbled address.

113 Chesapeake Rd. Come alone.

"Oh." I turned back toward the parking lot.

My stomach knotted at the thought of her alone with him . . . bleeding. There was no telling what he might do with her.

I had to find her.

"What does that card say?" Presley followed me into the car lot. I stumbled back and shoved it in my pocket.

"It's nothing."

He sighed. "Let me guess, it says to not bring anyone with you."

I ignored him and moved my hands to my thighs, searching for my keys.

"I don't have to tell you that this is a trap," Presley said.

"Nope." I grabbed my keys and headed for my car.

Presley stepped in front of me. "You don't think I'm going to let you go by yourself, do you?"

"I think we're going to talk about it for a minute and then you will inevitably realize I'm right and let me go."

Presley didn't smile back. "If you go there alone, if he could do that"—he motioned back to where security was—"that means—"

"It doesn't change anything. I'm going."

"It changes everything! If he can do that, then there's no telling what he could do to you . . . what he might do to her. We gotta talk about it. You need someone to go with you. Let's just think of a plan."

"You know as well as I do, the moment Luke and Zach catch a whiff of this—if they ever saw this address, no matter what—they would go busting in. There's no plan with them. I can't risk that, and we don't have any leverage."

"So, you just want to walk in there and do what? What if he is a psycho and just wants to kill you?"

"If something happens, if I don't come back. At least it's just me. It's not everyone we care about. I just have to get her out of there, and I have a much better chance if I go alone."

"Don't even talk like that," Presley said.

"You know this is the only option. You are the only one who would let me go." I walked in closer, suddenly feeling heavy.

"If Zach and Luke found out I knowingly let you go, they would kill me. Literally."

"No, they wouldn't."

I moved forward to pat his shoulder. "Just take care of them, okay?"

He smiled and reached in to hug me briefly. "See you later?"

I patted him on the back, fighting the lump in my throat. "Hey, it will be so quick you'll hardly know I'm gone."

We moved away, and I nodded before turning to my car. It was too much to think about. I didn't let myself ponder for more than a second.

Twenty minutes from the park, a small dirt road led to an opening in the trees. A complete dead end. There were no lights and no cars around.

From my years of watching crime movies, I knew I was walking into a trap. "Come alone" always means there's someone waiting to kill or torture you. I just didn't have any other options. To my surprise, there was no convenient stroke of genius that happened seconds before I arrived. I had no plan. No stroke of luck. No fancy way to talk my way out of this.

I arrived at the address with my heart in my throat. My heartbeat felt fifty pounds heavier. I flung the car door open and stepped out into the grassy green area. My headlights illuminated the night in a limited space. I searched for any sign of movement.

"I'm here. Just like you wanted!" I didn't let the fear show in my voice as I took another step. "Come and get me!" Only silence answered.

"Kim, are you out there?" I walked closer to the trees, trying to peek around the branches.

It was strange walking alone. With each step, it occurred to me I had never had to feel true isolation. What I wouldn't give to have one of Zach's classic "Hey, asshole, get behind me" lines.

As minutes passed, my nervousness faded and I wondered if I was in the wrong place. There was no way I could have typed it in the GPS wrong.

I sighed and turned back toward the car. When it swung open, I stopped.

"Sorry, I'm late." William watched me with a wicked smile, seated and leaning over my steering wheel. "You're alone, smart boy."

I didn't have time to think before he touched my hand.

Eighteen

Aaron

My eyelids were heavy as I fought past my disorientation. I blinked a few times until my vision focused on an ugly piece of art on the wall. It was colorless, just like the wall it was hung on. I was in a small room that reminded me of a funeral home with an old, faded carpet. The strange scent of dead flowers and wax cleared my brain fog. I had no idea where I was or whose ugly painting I was staring at. The smell of rain was faint in the air, and my clothes were just barely damp.

Finally, my senses came back, and my eyes landed on a patch of red lying on a cream couch a few feet in front of me.

"Kimberly." I sprang from my chair and ran to where she was draped across the couch.

Her heartbeat was identifiable, thundering. It was beautiful music to my ears. The best sound in the entire world.

I sighed and collapsed at her side. A joyful relief washed over me as I stroked her hand. "I'm so sorry. I'm going to get you out of this. I'm going to fix this. I promise."

She was breathing peacefully. A bandage wrapped around her hand and forearm with a tinge of blood coming through the cloth.

My stomach dropped, and another lump settled in my throat.

What I feared most had happened. I lost control. I hurt her. "Oh, you're up! It took ya quite awhile."

William's voice was laced with arsenic as he entered the room looking like a combination of a school professor and zombie killer. His thick-soled boots crunched the dirt on the hardwood floors and matched his plaid waist coat. "Don't worry. She's fine. I can assure you the only marks she has are from your dirty work."

"What is this?" I got up and stepped in front of her.

His eyes scanned me. "I've finally got you in a place where we can talk."

"I'm here, just like you wanted. Now, can you please let her go?"

"Please? It's a little early to start begging. You're not so tough now without your big brothers." The menacing air compounded around him, and I could tell he was sizing me up.

I was in no way prepared for a fight. I had to stay calm. Talk my way out of it.

I opened my mouth to say something witty.

"Shut up."

In the blink of an eye, he was sitting next to her, stroking her hair. I sucked in a breath. He could kill her in an instant if he wanted to. Whatever I did, I had to make sure she made it out of that room alive.

"You can't protect her in the state you're in. When you don't drink, you get weak." He got up and circled me like an animal circles its prey.

I hated that he was right. My body was slow. I could normally take in the scene in eighty different ways in a matter of seconds. But even my mind felt slower. I couldn't think of anything other than the fear I had for Kimberly.

"What is this about? What do you want with her?" I couldn't take my eyes off her. Her heartbeat was the only bit of comfort I could find.

"Don't you get it yet? This isn't about her. It's about you. She's here because of you." He was suddenly behind me, almost breathing down my neck.

"Me? What about me?" I turned around with nothing but a gray wall staring back at me. "I don't understand what you want."

He pushed me from behind, and I moved deeper into the room.

"Come on. I want to see that anger you had earlier. Show me that anger, Aaron." He pushed me again as he appeared in front of me, and I stumbled back into a small wooden table.

Come on. Fight him. Kill him.

"I don't have it anymore. It's gone," I said slowly, choosing my words.

Kill him.

"Don't lie. I know it's there." He started pacing back and forth, coming closer to me each time.

He's mocking you.

"Shut up," I tried to say under my breath, but I knew William heard me.

His smile stretched wide. "You're not talking to me, are you?"

"If you don't want her, what do you want with me?"

He stepped forward, and I shuffled back. "Tell me, what do you know about The Family?"

Shit. I wasn't surprised. I had a feeling that, one day, everything would come back full circle. All my secrets had come out. It was only natural my brothers' would too.

"Uh, I-I don't know anything."

He tilted his head curiously. "You expect me to believe that? Your brothers are part of the biggest criminal cult in America, and you're . . . innocent?"

"I don't know anything about it." I backed away. "They've never told me anything."

"That's what you're claiming? Oh, Aaron." William's brows pressed together, and malice wafted off him in waves. "Don't. Lie."

"What? We haven't done anything."

William pressed his lips together. "I can feel the guilt radiating off of you. You're practically sweatin' it."

Come on. Do something.

"I-I . . ."

My head was spinning. Every muscle in my body felt stiff.

William moved in closer to me. "You can't even say it, can you?"

A flash of white caught my attention, and the haunted apparition appeared again. Her long hair dangled around her face, and she floated from one end of the room to the next. I swallowed the lump in my throat.

"Your brothers have to pay for their crimes. For centuries, The Family has done nothing but spill blood and brought the plague of evil. That includes you."

My attention snapped back to him at those words. "What crimes?"

"They've been linked to a number of deaths in the Brooklyn area. Not to mention various crimes of stealing, their involvement in money laundering . . . I could go on," he said with a stupid smirk still on his face.

"I don't believe you. My brothers don't kill people. The other stuff . . . maybe. But they wouldn't kill anyone."

His eyes bore a hole into mine. "You don't sound so sure about that."

The apparition appeared next to his shoulder, and I fell back a few steps. It traced its fingers across his shirt. The white hair was blinding.

"What are you lookin' at?" His face was only inches from mine. A smug smile danced on his lips. "Seeing things, are we?"

"No."

I flinched as it stalked farther into the room to sit next to Kimberly, who was still lying peacefully on the couch. Its skin was hollow and translucent.

"It's that thing in your head. You're losing it. That's what happens when you don't feed. You get weak. It found your weakness. Now it's here to collect."

"To collect what?" I said, still watching my own hallucination.

The white-haired apparition sat over Kim and moved its hands over her hair. Panic hit me instantly. I knew in my head it wasn't real, but everything about it looked that way. It felt like reality.

"Your body. Your soul. It doesn't matter. You won't be alive much longer to feel it. Who knows, maybe I'll leave you alive long enough to let you suffer."

Numbness traveled up my hand. The apparition was gripping my arm. I pulled my hand away. She was closer than I had ever seen her. Her white eyes pierced, and I jerked away in panic, but William grabbed the sides of my face and forced me to look straight ahead. Searing hatred and a wildfire of rage behind his irises.

He pushed me into a floral lounge chair that was situated in the corner. A layer of dust flew up into the damp as he spoke. "Stay with me. Don't pay attention to it."

He pressed his palms into the sides of my face. I struggled to turn my face away, but his grip was strong.

"Don't struggle. It will be over soon."

A disorienting feeling washed over me. A thick film filled my vision. And then everything was black. My world faded in an instant.

The room was gone. Like being hooked into an amusement ride, my mind flew off. Flickering light induced pain in my head. I knew I had no control as flashes came up in my mind.

At first, my head was throbbing, but in seconds, it turned into searing pain. Whatever the flashing was, it flickered too fast. Heat flushed my body. A range of emotions hit me all at once, over and over in a reel, making me nauseous.

My limbs tingled. Electrical pulses surged through my veins. It felt as if my body was being torn apart from the inside out. William was in my head. It wasn't a subtle occupation. He was stomping around and turning up the mattresses. I couldn't feel my body anymore. I was completely in my head. His searching made me frantic. My brain couldn't take the intruder.

William's voice was close. "The more you struggle. The more pain you will feel."

The floor dropped out, and my chest ached with that familiar pain. I could feel my fingers again. I tried to pull my arms away from the chair with all my might. My eyelids were heavy and refused to open, and I was locked in my own body.

A wobbly image pulled into my vision. Everything was tilted back and forth. Everything was too vivid. Too sensitive.

Something caught my attention. Flowing locks of white hair, bending and blowing in the light. It was a woman. She felt oddly familiar.

"No need to be upset. You can relax."

Her voice sucked me back into the image. It wasn't the words she said but the way they affected me. Her voice was magnetic.

I was in my old living room. It was all there. Our mismatched couches, the pencil we broke off into the ceiling, and the smell of cheap vanilla candles my mom loved.

The comfort of that nostalgia didn't last for long. My hands were restrained behind me. The muffled sounds of Presley's groaning came from somewhere. The muscles in my arms burned as I struggled to get free.

It looked like a memory, but it wasn't anything I recognized happening before.

"Don't worry, he won't be harmed. I just need to see your face. I need to look into your eyes."

Her cool hands traced my chin and up to my brow. My entire body was shaking in fear.

The full image still wasn't coming into view. But I could hear my ragged breath. "W-What do you want with us?"

Her face was beautiful porcelain, her lips flushed with red. But it was her eyes that froze me into place, white and glossy. Void of any hope or light.

It was the woman who I'd been seeing in all my hallucinations. Was she a real person?

"Aaron, you have so many good qualities. So innocent. I can see you'll be a valuable member of The Family one day."

"What? Who are you?" My hands were still being held down by something as she moved over to Presley. "No, stop! Leave him alone."

She ignored me and ran her fingers through his curls. Her white dress, almost see-through, dragged along our shag carpet. It was flowy, elegant, and clung to her hips. Around her were men with cloths covering their faces, adorned in all black. Slacks and blazers with pointed loafers. They watched the woman like a hawk. Her every movement. Every word.

"Such handsome boys. No doubt your older brothers will be much happier with you by their side."

Her face almost reflected sadness, her eyes fell to the floor, admiring her soft, sheer gown.

Who was this woman? I didn't remember meeting her, yet she knew my brothers. And then it hit me. This was the girl they were talking about outside the frat house, the one Luke missed, the one he wanted to go back to.

Her eyes fell back on mine, and fear swallowed me. Her presence felt otherworldly. Bloodlust fell from her lips. *What* was this woman was a better question.

In the blink of an eye, she was in front of me again. Her lips grazed my ear. Despite her beauty, a feeling radiated off her I couldn't explain. Impending doom swallowed me as she caressed my skin. The room started to slow. My body was wobbly, and I couldn't move my head up. A smile appeared on her red-stained lips. She brought a pale finger to her lips and bit down. A stream of black tar-like blood flowed down in droplets. In one graceful sweep, she brought that finger to my lips. The bitter taste of iron landed on my tongue.

"Copula quae numquam solvi potest."

My world spun once more, and my old living room dissolved. I awoke to William biting into my neck. My hands were glued to the armrests of the floral chair. Kimberly was, thankfully, still resting peacefully. Weakness carried itself through my upper body until my arms were numb. It was a struggle to keep myself upright. I couldn't catch myself from falling forward. I squeezed my fingers on the armrests to try to catch myself, but my body weight was too heavy. Everything hurt.

William reached my chest just in time to stop me from sliding out of the chair. "There. Now let me look at you."

He grabbed my face and brought my chin up to look at him. "That's as close to death as I'd like you to be."

He was such a fucking prick. I wanted to say something, but I couldn't stop replaying the scene I had just seen over and over again. That was the first glimpse into my brothers' secret life I'd ever seen. I had imagined so many different possibilities, but I never imagined . . . her.

"W-Was that a memory? I don't get what's happening."

"The body has a hard time adjusting to the mental recall. Reliving old memories is like experiencing them for the first time. When you experience moments, they pass without a second thought. It's only when you are forced to relive them that you see and feel everything as it should be."

None of the words he said made any sense.

"Oh, yeah, I forgot you enjoy being a cryptic asshole." My eyes drifted back to Kimberly, who was still unconscious on the couch. I squeezed the armrests, trying harder to pull myself up. My body shook as I forced my muscles to bend to my will.

"Still making jokes, I see." William's smirk softened as he placed a hand on my chest and held me down. "Don't struggle. Your pain will be over soon."

"Don't say that like you care," I spat.

"I don't relish makin' a kid suffer the agony of a torturous, slow death, no. But there's no other way to kill vampires. It can't be helped."

Said the guy who just bit a hole in my neck.

"I take it you do this often." I fought hard to keep my eyelids open. But every so often, my head would fall. I still didn't know who William truly was or if that was even his real name. And I was growing too weak to care.

"I specialize in killing vampires, yes." William looked far away as he analyzed a fresh set of flowers on the table next to me.

"But you're a vampire . . ."

His fingers grazed the petals on a white rose. "But I'm nothing like you. The easiest way to kill one is to be one. A fitting sacrifice to make for the greater good."

"Hmm." I closed my eyes for a second and reopened them.

William was watching my face closely, but his face was devoid of anger, expressing sympathy.

"You made it easy for me, though. Without you, none of this would be possible. I'm sure your brothers will come after you."

"Exactly like you planned." I groaned.

His words hit deep in my chest, only adding to my physical pain. My heart leaped into my throat. A strange but familiar sensation bubbled into my stomach. Of all my fuckups, this was my worst. There was a lot I should have done differently, and I couldn't change it.

He motioned to Kimberly. "You are a lucky kid, though. I've seen thirsty vampires rip off limbs and break bones of humans when they lose control. They kill their own husbands, wives . . . children."

My body lurched forward, and my chest wouldn't stop heaving. Another wave of pain hit me, and I leaned forward, resting my body in my lap. The nausea was back with a vengeance.

"Is this normal for ya?" William was beside me with a hand on my back.

I shuddered between the muscle spasms. "When I was a kid . . . I used to—to throw up when I was stressed." I groaned, bringing my arms close to my body. "Vampire me"—I lurched forward again, feeling the burning muscles in my chest—"hasn't gotten the . . . memo."

I used my hand to cover my mouth and braced for the next round of nausea.

"Just relax. Here, lay back." William gently helped me move my head to the back of the chair.

I didn't have any choice but to receive his help. My body was spent, and my eyelids kept drooping. A soft brace supported me as he placed a plump white pillow underneath my head. "W-Why?" I closed my eyes, unable to keep them open for a second longer.

"Well, I can't have you dying before your brothers get here." He laughed, grabbed my arms, and placed another pillow on my lap. "Now, just rest for a minute. Stop talking and just rest."

Every second, the spasms in my chest lessened and the nausea faded.

"I'm tired," I whispered.

The soft sounds of rain hitting the rooftop were the loudest thing in my ears. I tuned into the soft symphony. I didn't have any other choice.

"Then, sleep." William's voice was far away as I drifted off, and for the first time in a long time, I slept.

Nineteen

M y eyes opened, and the fog cleared. It took me a few minutes to get my bearings and assess where I was. My wrist was wrapped in gauze and tape, and to my surprise, I no longer felt any pain.

None of it mattered when I saw Aaron draped over a wooden chair with black blood staining his shirt like dark pools of ink. Droplets littered the floor around him and stained the ornate fabric he was sitting on.

I leaped to my feet. "Aaron! Please wake up. Please."

His eyes were shut, his body motionless. My heart kicked my ribs, and I put my head to his chest, checking for a heartbeat. I couldn't hear anything other than the blood throbbing in my own skull.

"Wake up. I need you to get up." I wrapped my hands around his arms, shaking him.

We were in an empty, windowless room with dusty wooden floors and stone walls painted in thick gobs of white paint. The room was large enough to be a decent size bedroom, with nothing to signal what type of building we were in. Thunder cracked overhead, and the faintest taste of salt lingered on my lips. We were by the coast, if I had to guess.

Aaron's eyes fluttered open, and he blinked before focusing on my face. For the first time, I felt like I could take a full breath. I kneeled at face-level, taking his blood-soaked hand.

"Oh, thank God. You're awake. I was so worried."

"Yeah, yeah. I'm fine." His tone wasn't convincing, and he struggled to keep his eyes open. He looked to be glued to his chair. Every movement of muscle didn't move him an inch. "Ah!"

Aaron's cries brought a lump to my throat. I fought back the threatening tears. Things weren't looking good for him. Even if I had any idea what was going on or how to get help, no help was coming.

"You're bleeding." I touched his shirt close to his neck, where a bite mark was still wet with fresh blood. I didn't have to guess who did it.

"Oh, that? Just a scratch." He tried to straighten himself but any attempt to move was futile.

"We have to get out of here." I struggled to get back on my feet. My own blood loss was still apparent.

"Don't worry about me. I don't think I'm going anywhere anytime soon."

"What? No. I'm not leaving you here. Now, get up." I grabbed his arm, trying to pull him up and onto my shoulder. He winced with each pull.

"Kim, you gotta get out of here before he comes back." Aaron groaned.

His defeated eyes only ignited the fire under my feet.

"Don't get all noble on me now. There's no way I'm leaving you here." Pure determination fueled my muscles to try to pull Aaron up again. He was deadweight. I groaned in frustration. "Why are you so heavy?"

"Kim—"

"No." I dropped to my knees beside him. "I won't leave you."

I sucked in a breath and put Aaron's hand in mine. I wanted to warm the cold slowly overtaking his skin. His light, usually glaringly bright, felt dim.

Aaron's voice was soft. "Why?"

It made sense to me why he would ask me that. For the majority of our relationship, it had been about me. He had done everything he possibly could to right his wrongs and put my wants ahead of his. But something had changed. I had changed.

"Because, if this is the end . . . at least we won't be alone. I won't leave you here alone to die. No way."

Tears streamed down my cheeks, and I squeezed his hand.

He squeezed mine back. "I'm sorry for everything. I really screwed your life up."

I smiled, wiping a few tears. "No. You didn't. I'd do it all again. All the good. The bad. To meet you."

He chuckled. "You're delusional. You lost too much blood."

Every minute that passed, I knew it might be our last. But I was at peace. I looked at Aaron, soaking in his features.

I could say one thing that could describe the way it felt to be in Aaron's wake. The warmth. The laughter. The undeniable happiness. It felt like love. Love that showed in the way he cared for his brothers and they cared for him. And I was there, in the wake. Engulfed and enamored with it. I didn't want it to ever leave me, and I wanted to hold his hand forever.

The door clicked, shifting our focus.

Aaron's eyes glued to its frame. "Get behind me."

I looked at Aaron's utterly defenseless posture. "Oh, hush."

"Oh, you're up? That's a surprise."

William wasn't the only one to file into the room. Two others followed. One was female, the other male, all wearing fitted black cloaks that touched the floor.

I didn't recognize their faces.

"Leave her alone." Aaron tried moving again with no luck. "Fuck!"

William didn't say anything else, and they encircled us.

"Aaron, it's okay." I kept my voice steady. My hands shook slightly, but I clenched my fists.

"Don't touch her." Aaron strained again as he desperately tried to stand.

261

A cloaked figure came up behind him and wrapped fingers over his mouth. In the blink of an eye, I was met with the same fate.

A set of stone hands clamped my mouth. Another set of hands grabbed my waist to keep me from moving.

"Settle down, kids. I've got good news and bad. Good news is, your terrified waiting is over. Bad news is, Aaron has to come with me." William nodded once, and chaos ensued.

The man dragged Aaron from his chair. A trail of black blood smudged the floor with each kick of Aaron's sneakers.

If he was still fighting, I would too.

I shoved my foot down onto my captor's foot with no luck. No amount of pressure was being taken off my ribs. I used every ounce of strength in my muscle to try to wiggle free from the iron grip. I exhausted all the air from my lungs.

Aaron disappeared through a wooden door across the room, our eyes meeting one last time. A scream curdled in my throat. I threw my head back in anger, and pain radiated through my skull. Dizziness hit me, and for the first time, I relaxed, letting the hands keep me up.

"You're goin' to give yourself a concussion if you don't stop. Give her to me," William said.

As they passed me off, I bolted for the wooden door I'd seen Aaron disappear into. I slammed into it with my body weight and fell to my knees.

The smell of dirt and old cedar wood greeted me from the darkness. Candlelight flickered throughout the room.

With a groan, I pulled my aching body from the creaking floor. It was running on empty. A large wooden cross loomed in front of me. We were in a church. It was small, with only about ten wooden pews lining an aisle adorned with white candles. The walls were made of stones, and they went all the way to the ceiling, only stopped by a small worn mural.

Lightning struck outside and rattled the floor beneath me. The large stained-glass window in the front of the church illuminated the room.

"Aaron!"

My voice echoed into the high ceilings. His black blood smeared across the floor, marking his location next to a pew, where someone was shoving a gag in his mouth. My forearms stung from the impact as I went to run for him. Someone grabbed me from behind, and I flinched forward in a last-ditch effort to reach Aaron on the floor. Aaron and I collided, our heads smacking onto the dusty hardwood.

I groaned and held my head on my way back up. My world was a vivid blur. Aaron was still unable to move, so I removed his gag.

"What are you doing?" Aaron's eyes searched mine in desperation.

"I don't know!" I blurted as something blocked the dim light. We looked up to see a cloaked man staring at us inquisitively. He was bearded, with salt-and-pepper hair, some of his natural dark brown peeking through. It was short and cropped. His robe was white and ornate, adorned with gold embellishments and crosses.

My heart stuttered, and I leaned into Aaron. I found his hand and squeezed a little too hard.

"I'm not going to hurt you."

The cloaked man's voice was pure steel. Sharp and cold.

William was at the door, bowing before entering. "I'm sorry. That was my fault. I can take her."

"No, leave her. For now."

"Kim, I think we're officially fucked." Aaron squeezed my hand back.

I swallowed. The air was unnaturally dry, considering the rain pelted the stained-glass window.

The robed man crouched in front of us. "My name is Kilian. You must be Kimberly and Aaron."

Up close, I could see the crow's feet by his gray eyes. His hands rested on his knees casually. He had large gaudy rings and long scars on the backs of his hands.

Naturally, I took the lead. "What do you want with Aaron?"

"You were right. She's definitely strong-willed." Kilian smiled.

But it wasn't warm in the way Aaron and his brothers smiled— it was solemn. A smile that came from someone who bore great responsibility and had seen some things. I didn't want to know what those things were.

"Kim, don't let him touch you! Be careful." Aaron struggled to get onto his elbows. His arms shook with the weight of his own body.

Kilian turned his attention to William, who was standing at attention with his hands behind his back. "How much blood did you take from him?"

William smirked. "Only what was necessary."

"Prop him up," Kilian said.

William and another girl in a black robe grabbed Aaron on both sides, pulling him up from the floor. They scooted him back and leaned him at the foot of one of the wooden pews.

"I'm sorry you're so uncomfortable. It's not how I like to do things." Kilian stood. His long thick robe dragged on the hardwood, nearly missing a few candles.

"Can you please tell us what's going on?" I said.

"In order for me to do that, I must know what you know. How much do you two know about The Family?"

William stepped up and opened his mouth to speak, but Kilian held up his hand. "Please. I want to hear it from them."

I looked at Aaron, who seemed to be putting all his energy into staying conscious. I wasn't surprised to hear the name come up. The Family felt like an omen hanging over the Calem brothers. Therefore, it was hanging over me as well. It was only a matter of time before it caught up. I just didn't expect it would be so soon.

"Kimberly doesn't know anything. Just what I've told her, and it's not much. So, you can leave her out of this," Aaron said.

"I repeat. I'm not going to hurt you." Kilian stood in front of the cross. Despite his calm disposition, he wasn't very convincing.

Aaron scoffed. "You know, I might have believed you if I wasn't bleeding all over the floor of this nice church."

"If there was ever a time when this church was nice, it was long ago," Kilian said.

"What choice do you have?" William walked next to Kilian, his arms still poised behind his back.

He reminded me of a soldier. His shoulders were pulled back and waiting at attention.

"Fine. I know that The Family is dangerous. I know that . . . my brothers are somehow involved in all this, but I don't know how. They never told me anything. Probably to prevent situations like this."

"William informed me that he pulled a memory for you. Tell me about it."

"Memory?" I squeezed Aaron's cold hand. "What's he talking about?"

"Yeah, it was back in Brooklyn. At my house, some lady was there, with these weird eyes. They had me and Presley tied up, and she gave us her blood, and they said—"

"Copula quae numquam solvi potest. It's Latin. It means a bond that can never be broken." Kilian kneeled in front of us again with what appeared to be a handkerchief he had wetted from a bowl on the altar. With the linen cloth, he moved toward Aaron. "May I?"

Aaron hesitated. "I guess."

Without another word, he sponged the blood that was stained across Aaron's neck.

I never let go of Aaron's hand.

Kilian spoke again. "You don't remember because you were touched by a queen. She's the purest, strongest form of what we are. The history of The Family is a long insidious one, so I will tell you only what pertains to you.

"The Family began in the Renaissance Age, when politically influential elites would practice necromancy and try to summon demons. They wanted to use their power to obtain riches and knowledge not known to humans. After many attempts, they were successful in the transferring of a powerful demon into the body of a woman. They used women, usually orphaned or poor, as their test subjects and tried duplicating the transfer in men but were unsuccessful. The men did not predict the hold that the demon would have over them. They found themselves enthralled with Her.

"Their devotion turned into an obsession, and thus the first Queen was born. From there, the Queen made Her Guard, and the Guard made up their lower members. The original is long gone, and only six other Queens remain in existence, and it looks like you've met one." Aaron and Kilian locked eyes.

I cleared my throat. "Wait, so if you're not The Family, who are you?"

The double doors at the end of the aisle burst open. Zach and Luke stood with fire in their eyes. Soon, Aaron and I were being dragged backward. William grabbed both of our shirt collars and hurled us at Kilian's feet next to the altar. My bones ached as I crashed into the wooden block. Two robed figures placed a gag in our mouths and quickly tied our hands behind our backs.

"Stop right there. Unless you want the rest of your dear little brother's blood to be spilled." William tugged at Aaron's shirt.

Five robed figures, including William, surrounded Zach and Luke. The last two filtered in from behind, limping.

"I'm surprised you were able to get through our watchers. You are skilled," Kilian said, holding his hands in front of himself patiently. His face was unreadable.

The two guards rushed them, and I braced myself for their impact, but combined, they worked like a well-oiled machine. They stood back-to-back and fought them off one by one. When one twin dodged, the other one countered with a punch.

Kilian raised his hand, and the fighting ceased. The robed guards stood a few feet away with their hands behind their backs.

Zach wiped his chin. "Who the hell are you?"

"We are Legion. A movement founded a little more than a century after The Family. Our true purpose is to bring balance back to the world by exterminating members of The Family and exposing them for crimes they have caused."

William's voice cut the air. "Someone had to hold them accountable."

The twins shared a tentative look.

"How did you find us?" Luke asked, making eye contact with me and

Aaron, his jaw set and serious.

"How do you think? Little brother right here. He attacked a girl and sent her to the hospital. We search constantly for places with abnormal activity and places where idiots like you may be stupid enough to feed." William smiled. "But it was our leading lady who did most of the work for me. She led me right to him, and from there, you can imagine how easy they made it for me."

Luke puffed out his chest with an eerie sense of calm. "Well, then, you know that Aaron doesn't know anything and therefore Kimberly either. So, why don't you just let them go?"

"They're not going anywhere."

William's voice was cold. His grip tightened on my shirt collar.

"Cut the shit. This is about us. If this is truly some overly righteous cult hell-bent on rallying for justice, then why do you even need hostages?" Zach spat.

William tilted his head. "Justice? There will not be justice until you're wiped from Earth."

"Oh, really?" Zach squared his shoulders. "Why don't you come over here and do it, then? I'll let you get the first punch."

"My apologies for William's behavior. He has more reason to hate members of The Family than most," Kilian said. "The Family's actions are often overlooked by many government agencies, so justice often never comes for their victims or their families."

William's eyes bore a hole into Zach's skin. "We have no interest in bartering with you. We have you outnumbered. We can take you right now."

To my surprise, Luke smiled. He reached into his pocket and pulled out a switchblade. "I thought you might say that."

He threw the knife into his left hand before plunging the knife into his forearm and pulling it down toward his wrist. Black blood sprayed the floor.

My body felt cold, and a scream curled in my throat, muffled underneath the thick cloth in my mouth.

Aaron's muffled groans sounded next to me.

Luke chuckled to himself as he passed the knife to Zach, and Zach repeated the same on his arm. A long ribbon of blood dripped to the floor and spread to a puddle soaking into the dry wood. The determined smile never left Luke's face, though his scrunched nose told me he was in pain. "See, I think you're bluffing. You need us."

"You didn't think we'd come prepared to die, did you?" Zach moved his hair, revealing a bite mark.

I connected the dots. Vampires needed to be drained of blood before their skin could be pierced. That's why the blade would penetrate their skin. Losing blood meant they'd grow weak, just like Aaron.

Luke's body convulsed. "You want us. Let them go. It's a fair trade. We die, and everything we know dies with us."

"Better make your decision quick. We're bleeding out over here." Zach squeezed his hand, and more blood fell.

"You'd leave little brother and Kimberly here alone?" William tightened his grip on my collar once more, and I groaned.

Luke turned to Kilian. "You won't kill them. If you're who you said you were, then you wouldn't kill innocent people."

The scene was surreal. Just hours before, we looked like normal college kids, enjoying our time and swimming in a natural spring. Afterward, we'd stepped into a horror film.

The robed figures stood around the room like statues, most of whom were hidden by the dim light.

"I'll barter with you." Kilian looked intrigued. "But you can only choose one. Kimberly or Aaron. The other must stay here."

Aaron and I shared a look. Aaron squirmed under his restraints and tried to scoot forward.

Luke shot him a smile, blood still oozing from his arm. "Don't worry. I got this."

Another crack of thunder vibrated the walls.

Zach and Luke shared a look. Silently reading each other's minds. My heartbeat was in my ears again as I contemplated what it meant. The thought of one of us being left behind took the breath from my lungs. Let alone the thought of only one of us was making it out of the church.

Luke watched Kilian. "How can we know you're going to keep your word?"

"You're still alive, aren't you?" William said.

I couldn't see his face, but I could tell he was smirking.

"Let Kimberly go." Luke's eyes met mine.

William grabbed me by my shirt, lifting my feet from the ground. I struggled against his grip, but I wasn't allowed to look back at the altar.

"As you wish."

William dragged me toward the double doors. The two other guards grabbed Zach and Luke and pulled them toward the altar in my place.

"Can I talk to her first? Please." Luke shrugged them off with his big shoulders. "Just for a second."

"I'll allow it," Kilian said, a barely there smile appearing on his lips.

William didn't remove my gag and just flung me in front of Luke without a word while Zach was gagged and dragged toward the altar to join Aaron.

"Kim, Presley will come and find you. If you want to, you can go with him and get away from this place. I won't be there to protect you guys, but you're smart, and I know you'd be able to make sure he doesn't do anything stupid. But it's up to you. Whatever you want to do. Thank you for keeping our secret and caring about my brother. If I don't see you again, I'm happy to have met you."

Luke smiled in a way that made my stomach turn. Despite his world crumbling, he was still trying to give me some of his strength. To instill me with hope, that I would carry on.

All I could focus on was their blood falling to the floor, the same way Aaron's was, and the sinking feeling this may be the last time I would ever see them. Tears formed in the corners of my eyes, and I made eye contact with Aaron one last time. In the dim light, I could see the glistening reflection in his eyes. Relief. "All right. Goodbyes are said. Dominique. Come with me."

William brought us through the doors and to a hallway. A dusty, abandoned space with nothing but old, tattered paintings hung on the walls.

The tears kept falling, and William removed my gag once we rounded the corner.

"Let go of me!" I screamed, and it echoed in the empty hallway. He chuckled. "Gladly. Once you're out the door."

A wooden door was just up ahead, with an oil lantern illuminating the brass fittings.

I struggled to free myself again, only causing more pain and bruising to my already sore arm. The one named Dominique was right on my heels.

"What are you going to do with them?"

I didn't want to know the answer. I couldn't save them. Tears ran from my eyes, and I fought with everything I had to refrain from sobbing in front of them. I didn't want to give him the satisfaction.

We reached the door, and he stopped. "Kimberly, I understand this has been hard on you. I do. So, I'm going to give you an option. The deal was, you get to go and find Presley, but I could make you forget this ordeal for a while. You won't remember what happened here for at least a couple weeks, even with your strong will, and by the time you remember, they'll all be long gone. You'll mourn them, but it will be easier. You can move on with your life. Let all this go. With no more connections to the Calem brothers, The Family won't have any reason to come find you. You'll be free."

I was dumbfounded by what he had offered. Something so unbelievable and out of this world, even for a world where vampires existed. Forgetting would be bliss. The blood on the floor, the fear in Aaron's eyes. The pain ripping through my chest.

The thought of Aaron and me swaying in the forest came to mind. The soft scent of pine, and Aaron constantly stepping on my foot. His smile and his laughter changed me. It made me believe in a life I had given up on. Aaron's brothers were part of that too. I didn't want it to be easy. I wanted it to be hard and messy. Because that's how love and family were.

"No. I want to go with Presley."

His jaw tightened, and his dark eyes pinned me against the wall. "If you go with him, we will hunt you both down. Not to mention, if The Family doesn't find him first. You will be on the run. Come on, you and I both know Presley won't get very far without his brothers. You're condemning yourself to a life you don't belong in. Don't let them drag you further into their mess."

"Presley won't have his brothers, but he'll have me." I smiled through gritted teeth. "Their mess is mine now."

William sighed and grabbed the sides of my face. My breath caught in my throat. His eyes were cold. In them, anger burned, bubbling under the surface, waiting to explode. "Fine. As you wish."

Twenty

AARON

Every minute passed strangely, consciousness slipping and returning. Some moments I felt alert and scared. Then my eyes would close for a few seconds and something else entirely was happening.

My older brothers chatted, and every once in a while, they'd attempt to wake me up again.

My head lay on the floor that smelled of old cedar. The candles around me were starting to drip puddles of wax onto the dry wood. The assortments of colored wax swirled together into streams. Zach and Luke were chained just a few feet away. Rusty chains hooked into steel rods underneath the floorboards. This place was a prison.

It took me a minute to remind myself where I was, which was, apparently, on the floor of an old church, about to bleed out. My brothers looked like they were going to suffer the same fate.

But Kimberly was safe, and so was Presley. Somehow, my mangled body didn't hurt as much with that truth. The two people I needed to protect were safe. No matter what happened to us, at least I could die knowing that fact.

"How did you find me?" It took more effort than I anticipated to speak. The cloth from earlier was gone.

"You left your phone location on, dumbass." Zach smiled, but his eyes were still scanning me and the trail of blood I left beside me.

"How bad is it?" Luke's voice was more secure and, somehow, made me feel a little less worried about our situation.

"Pretty bad." I groaned.

Kilian and the other robed figures were setting up what looked to be some type of ceremony, with a large silver bowl full of some kind of liquid, set by the large cross. That's when I realized how tall Kilian was. He had to duck every time he walked past the corners of the cross.

One of the girls in a black robe motioned to me, white hair peeking beneath her hood. "Does he need to be chained?"

"No. He's lost a lot of blood. He isn't going anywhere." William's eyes bore into mine.

In the dim light, I could see his expressionless face. His eyes were glued to Kilian, awaiting his instruction.

"Can we get this over with?" Zach groaned. "If you're so holy, why drag it out? Don't you want to be merciful?"

Kilian turned to Zach after lighting another candle at the altar. "You see, this isn't an execution. While it's true, we are dedicated to finding and hunting down members of The Family. William has discovered something very interesting in your case that I think may be useful. Therefore, this is your trial, a place for your sins to be laid out before our council. Then we will decide what to do with you."

"That's fucking fantastic." Zach sighed. He turned his attention to me. I could feel his worry.

Luke's voice was softer. "Why does Aaron need to be on trial here? He hasn't done anything."

"I know. But he has been marked . . . meaning he's of great value to The Family." Kilian's robe dragged behind him as he paced the floor. The wooden boards squeaking and the occasional flicker of the flame were the only things heard in the otherwise silent room.

I sighed. My head was pounding, and all I could think of was getting on with our impending doom. "What does that even mean?"

Zach's eyes were wide. "That's impossible."

"Our brothers never met anyone we knew in The Family. How could they be marked?" Luke said.

"Aaron's memories revealed something he did not remember. A memory of . . . Her."

The twins sat up straighter, their eyes trained on Kilian, who was still slowly pacing the floor. "In this memory, She offered your brothers Her blood. We believe She planned to turn them herself and induct them in The Family, but it sounds like She was waiting . . . for what, we don't know."

"Does She have a name?" I asked.

"Since the Renaissance Age, they have been called many names. None are accurate. Her worshippers don't sully her with a name."

He stopped pacing and stood directly in front of Zach and Luke. I wondered what She had to do with my brothers. In my memory, She was haunting. Terrifying. Not exactly someone I imagined you could actually have any type of relationship with. Were they obsessed with Her too?

Luke spoke. "No. She was going to kill them. That's why we did this. That's why we ran away."

"Is that why you changed us . . ." I met Luke's gaze. "You thought The Family was going to kill us?"

"We didn't think, we knew! We've fucking saw it happen! It was all bullshit. Everything they ever taught us and showed us when we were kids was a lie and manipulation." Zach's face was red with rage. "That's what they do. If anyone has a family, they kill them. Because they want your loyalty. But we didn't know that, and when we found out, we left."

"And you played into their plan all along and sentenced your brothers to death." William was no longer smug. I couldn't see his face, but I could hear it in his voice. He was dead serious. "How does that feel?"

If looks could kill, William would be a dead man.

"Come closer, and I'll show you," Zach said deadpan.

"I don't believe The Family's plan is to kill you. Though, historically, you're correct. That is why I believe, even now, though, you have defected and therefore have committed treason against them. They're still looking for you. Not to kill you. But to take you back . . . the reason for that we will hopefully find out." Kilian stopped passing and stood in front of the cross, shoulders back and head high. "We will begin the trial. The results of this trial will determine the fate of your entire family."

I knew I should have been scared, but I couldn't bring myself to feel anything at that moment. My attention drifted to the puddle of my blood on the floor again. Black liquid soaked into wood grain. Tingling and numbness bled into my fingertips. I spat black blood onto the floor while trying to keep my balance sitting up.

The sleepy feeling was settling into my muscles again. I shook my head. "Let's just get on with it. Let me guess, you'll push your way into my head too?" I reached out my arm for him to take.

"Go ahead."

"Aaron, don't," Luke said, stirring in his chains.

"I like to give everyone a chance to plead their own case. The Family specializes in the mind manipulation of their members. They often mess with their memories and experiences, making it very hard to decipher the true intentions of the individual. That makes solely looking at memories quite difficult. I'm also opposed to pressing into the minds of others without consent, especially those like yourself, who have undoubtedly suffered a great deal," Kilian said.

"If we tell you what we know and you think we're innocent . . . We'll go free?" Luke said.

A crack of lightning illuminated the room and Kilian's face when he spoke.

"Precisely."

William pulled us to our feet. I swayed, and William caught my arm. Kilian walked to the front of the altar and grabbed the silver bowl. Placing his hands in the dripping water, he then marked a cross on Luke's forehead.

Luke flinched away as Kilian grabbed his face and hands and recited a prayer. "In this judgment, may you find peace, and your soul be set free."

"Amen." The robed members, who stood at the edges of the room, all spoke at once.

"Jesus, out of one cult and into another," Zach said, as Kilian placed the holy water on his head and repeated the same phrase.

Kilian walked up to me last, placing the cool water into two lines on my forehead. His gray eyes bore into mine as he repeated the prayer. "In this judgment, may you find peace and your soul be set free."

"Amen." The echoes of their voices rang in the dark room, solidifying their ceremony.

"Aaron, I will be addressing your brothers for most of the trial. It's important that you do not speak out of turn. I will address you directly if I need to." William placed me back on the floor, where I sat on my knees near my standing brothers. Probably to prevent having to hold me upright for the entirety of the trial. I was thankful, nonetheless.

"Luke and Zach Calem, you've been brought here under our council in your involvement in the death of the Hogert family and the disappearance of Sarah Garanger."

"What the fuck?" The words flew out of my mouth before I could catch them.

William clasped his hand over my mouth and leaned close to my ear. "Do not speak."

He kept his hand securely over my mouth, and I had no energy left to struggle. My stomach turned with anger and fear. Fear that my brothers were truly exactly like William claimed they were. My heart refused to believe those accusations. Luke would have never hurt Sarah. They were inseparable. She was like my Kimberly. He'd never lay a finger on her. I knew that. The room full of total strangers knew more about my brothers than I did in my nineteen years with them, and for a moment, I doubted my own conviction.

I was alert again.

"Zach, tell me what you know about the Hogert family."

Kilian stood tall. His shoulders pressed away from his ears, his body fully alert.

The Hogert family. Despite the brain fog from the blood loss, I was still certain I didn't know who that could be. The name wasn't ringing any bells in my memory.

"Raymond Hogert is the one who shot Luke our senior year of high school . . ." Zach's eyes panned to me, then back to Kilian. "Luke was in the wrong place at the wrong time, and he almost fucking killed him."

I sucked in a breath. It was true. Everything my best friend told me had actually happened.

"I see. I can imagine that made you angry."

"I didn't kill him. But believe me, I wanted to . . ." Zach's voice shook. "I wanted to kill him for what he did, and I probably would have if Ezra hadn't told me not to."

"And who is this Ezra to you?"

"He was a member of Her Guard, but to us, he was like a mentor. He's the one who helped us escape. That's how we were able to get all of our fake documents and shit and hide in Blackheart."

"A member of the Queen's Guard helped you escape?" William scoffed.

Luke spoke. "It's true. Ezra was the closest thing to a father figure we had. He helped us a lot."

"When Luke was shot, he promised they would handle it. They didn't want Luke and me involved in certain things. The Family worked like a real family. Someone hurt us, we hurt them. What did they do to them?"

"You don't know?" William scoffed, still sitting on the pew beside me, holding my mouth shut.

"Honestly, I don't. We never saw Raymond again. We never heard anything. After I cooled off and Luke got better, I let it go." Zach's voice was more solemn. "That's the truth. We didn't kill anyone."

Kilian cleared his throat. "The Hogert family were massacred in their own home. In that event, Raymond was killed along with his three siblings and his mother. The only survivor was his ten-year-old sister. The Family often leave survivors to send a message to another family member and give them an option for retaliation. Most don't."

A lump caught in my throat. How could my brothers be involved with people so sinister? I racked my brain, combing through old memories. All I could see were the smiles of my big brothers. Every time they picked me up from a party because I was too drunk or every Father's Day we spent celebrating just having each other. They couldn't be killers. They couldn't be the same as these people.

Zach gritted his teeth. "We didn't know."

"Of course you did," William spat. "Don't lie here." The robed figures stirred, whispering together.

"Check my memories, asshole. We didn't get a choice. They never let us see all the awful shit they did. All they had to do was make us forget. And they did. Over and over. Until we finally figured it out one day. That's why we left."

Kilian put his hand up, and the room stopped stirring. "I want to hear from Luke now."

He walked over to Luke, who was staring a hole into the floorboards. "What happened to Sarah Garanger?"

I never knew Raymond. I didn't even know what he looked like. But Sarah I'd known for almost my whole life. She was funny, inquisitive, and she treated me and Presley like her little brothers. She had long shiny brown hair and a dimpled smile. She made the best chocolate chip cookies. When she went missing, the whole town was littered with her face. My mom cried. We all cried.

It never occurred to me that my brothers might have something to do with her disappearance. But they refused to talk about it. I just assumed it was too painful for Luke, and I didn't want to make him bring it up.

Luke's eyes fluttered at her name. "I didn't hurt Sarah."

"Do you know where she is?"

I waited anxiously for Luke to speak.

He looked over at me with solemn eyes, then back to Kilian. "She's dead."

It was like the wind was knocked out of me. I thought knowing the mystery would make me feel better, but it just made me feel like I was going to vomit. Sarah, who made Presley and me cupcakes for every birthday, who loved her big family more than anything else in the world, was gone. Why would anyone want to kill her?

Anger ignited under my feet, and I stirred, but William kept a firm grasp over my mouth. His other hand was resting firmly on my shoulder. How could my brothers let anything happen to her?

She was practically family.

"She died because of me," Luke said.

"Stop saying that." Zach was quick to correct him. "We didn't kill her. She did."

I swallowed. A cold chill ran down my spine. I was starting to truly understand how deep my brothers were in over their heads.

It only made the anger in my chest burn hotter.

William's hand tightened over my mouth. "They're lying."

"You weren't fucking there!" Zach yelled.

"Would you rather show me than tell me?" Kilian reached, and Luke flinched away. There was no anger or judgment in his voice.

Just pure patience.

"No. No, I can't," Luke said. "I can't go back there. I can't."

Kilian spoke again. "Then, tell me what transpired."

Luke's face grew red, as if mentally recalling it was physically painful. "Sarah meant everything to me. I wanted to save her. I tried to keep her away from me so she'd be safe, but it didn't matter. She killed her right in front of me . . . to punish me because I cared about someone more than Her. She wanted to teach us a lesson."

The anger I felt was short lived. I was right. Luke would do everything in his power to keep her safe. That's probably why they never actually got together. Luke had tried to protect her, but it wasn't enough.

I couldn't imagine the pain Luke must have been in, unable to tell me or just unwilling to. Kimberly came to mind. If I lost her, especially like that, I don't know if I'd be able to recover. Let alone keep on with my regular responsibilities. I wasn't much different from my brother. After all, I'd done the exact same thing with Kimberly. I tried to keep her safe but ended up dragging her down with me. Something that had almost killed her multiple times.

William scoffed. "We need to confirm his story. We can't just take his word for it. How do we know he didn't lead her there as a trap?"

"What benefit would we have from killing her?" Zach was growing more and more angry. "Come over here and confirm the story, then. I volunteer. I can show you what happened to Sarah. I was there too. And you can look back in my head as far as you want to make sure we're telling the truth."

Luke's head snapped up. "Zach, no."

Kilian's features softened. "You don't need to be afraid. I won't mess with your minds the way they did. Only with your permission will I look upon your memories."

Zach hands jangled in his chains, and he held up his bloody arm. "Do your worst."

A smile appeared on Kilian's face. He moved in closer, closing the gap between them. "I can feel your fear. You don't need to be afraid. Just relax."

Zach opened his palm, and the man cupped his hand. Immediately, Zach's chest heaved inward, and he closed his eyes. I never took my attention off his face. He was calm at first, but he stifled sobs. One by one, tears fell from his eyes.

William tightened his grip on my shoulder. He probably expected me to react in some way. The joke was on him. My legs were completely numb, and I was about eighty percent sure I was about to lose consciousness.

Kilian let go of Zach's hand after a few minutes. "So much pain. A terrible thing to witness."

I didn't need to know the exact story. The look on Zach's face was enough. It all made sense. The reason Luke was having panic attacks, the reason they kept everyone a secret. I thought I was the one who was in way over my head, but my brother's had me beat by a long shot.

Luke looked at me across the room, the candlelight flickering light on his face. "I didn't want the same thing to happen to you and Presley, and I didn't want you to ever know about this. I'm so sorry. Zach and I just wanted to help Mom with the money. That's why we joined when we were young. We thought it was harmless. Just stealing and pickpocketing in the city."

Zach sounded more melancholy. "We met Ezra when we were ten years old. He caught us stealing groceries. He promised us a life that didn't exist, one where we would never worry about money if we just did what he said. We didn't know what he was or who he was. They lied . . . a lot."

William released his hand, and I could finally speak. "He didn't tell you he was going to change you?"

"No," they said.

"We didn't know that was part of initiation. They drug you beforehand. We just woke up . . . different. That's when we learned that She shared Her blood with us," Luke said.

And there it was. My brothers were manipulated into joining a vampire cult. The answer I'd be waiting months to hear, and it wasn't all that surprising for some reason. I think a part of me knew it because they cared and wanted to take care of us. They'd do anything for us, but I was seeing how far they'd go and the toll of what their decision meant. Zach and Luke had protected us, mostly, but it cost them everything. All their hopes and dreams. The girls they loved. They gave up everything they wanted for me.

"She is the one who turned you?" Kilian walked to the center of the altar. "You're sure?"

They nodded. A strange silence settled into the room. Everyone was more alert. More interested.

"Why? What does that mean?"

My days of keeping my mouth shut were done. Sadist swim boy be damned.

"The Family has a hierarchy of power. Lower recruits are not fed Her blood for the change. It's too sacred. Too important." Kilian was pacing again. His robe was gathering a layer of dust. "You must not be lower recruits to them . . . you must be much more precious to them."

"Precious . . ." Luke repeated under his breath, his eyes on the floor.

"How would you describe your relationship with the queen?" Kilian said.

He leaned forward with a string of prayer beads rolling between his fingers anxiously.

"Didn't I just show you that?" Zach snipped.

"This question in particular is for Luke," Kilian said as he watched Luke's face.

The room turned dead silent, other than the rain rushing along the stone walls.

I was reminded of what Luke said when I was eavesdropping. He said he missed Her. His voice dripped with longing. But how? After killing Sarah, how could he not hate Her like I hated Her?

Luke shook his head like he didn't want to answer, but after a few minutes in the silence, he did. "She's important to me. I'd be lying if I said I didn't feel connected to Her. But it's not real. It's just because we shared blood. But I never let the way I felt about Her come between what I knew was right. It's like Zach said. It's all just . . . manipulation."

His connection to Her was all blood, which meant that's all mine was too. The reason she showed up in my hallucination was all because of that tiny speck of blood.

I knew there was more to their story. There was no way all their stories could possibly be told in the course of one trial. I didn't know the extent of how deep their ties to The Family were or who She was to them, but I knew who my brothers were to me. I knew the extent they'd go to keep us safe, and in the end, they chose us. That was enough. It was finally enough for me.

"Gentlemen, I believe we've reached the end of the trial. You will now be able to say your final pleas."

My heart pounded. I leaned forward involuntarily, and William grabbed me to sit me up. The light of the flames blurred, causing haze to fill the entire room. A metallic taste lingered on my lips. I was scared. Yes. But also, I was barely holding on. If this was the end, at least we'd all die together.

Kimberly danced back into mind, with her fiery hair and laughter. I was going to miss her. There was so much more I wanted to do with her. Things I wanted to say. But her safety would have to be enough. She was with Presley, and they were safe. My job was done.

"I've collected sufficient information to make my final verdict and deliberate with the council. Please tell me your final plea." Kilian stood in line with the robed members who lined the walls, his hands outstretched as if he were worshipping.

Luke turned to me. "I'm sorry we can't get you out of this one. I wanted to tell you everything, but now you see why I didn't. I didn't want you to see how bad we messed up. Just because we didn't kill Sarah or Raymond doesn't mean we aren't guilty. We are. If I could go back, I would."

Zach sighed, watching Luke. "We're not guilty."

Kilian finally turned to me. "And you . . . What do you plead?"

I cleared my throat. The small movement hurt my chest. "I can't speak for my brothers . . . You'll probably say I'm biased, but they are good people. But in two months' time, I lied, put my brothers in danger, and then attacked an innocent girl twice because of my own stupidity. So, I'm guilty."

Zach put his head in his hands. "How did I know you would say some cheesy shit like that? You two and your morality really pisses me off sometimes."

I smiled. "What can I say? It's kinda been my job since birth." To my surprise, Zach laughed. In a strange way, I felt at peace. I'd finally fixed my mess. I righted my wrongs. That alone was enough to keep me calm. Kilian held up his hands, and the robed figures followed him to the altar. With their backs turned, they deliberated. I tried to remember every detail of my brothers' faces, hoping that, if death wasn't swift, I could have that as my last comfort. I thought we'd have eternity together, but forever turned out to be pretty short.

My voice was barely a whisper. "I'm sorry I was such an asshole. I think I get it now, why you kept all those secrets."

"We know. You don't have to apologize," Zach said.

"No, I mean . . . you literally joined a cult when you were ten, so we wouldn't go hungry and then, somehow, you were able to escape that cult despite some weird connection to a vampire queen and try to save us. Granted, it didn't exactly work out but . . . Zach, you were right. I don't know anything about being selfless, nothing that you haven't taught me. Thank you both for everything. Maybe in another life we'll stay clear of the cult thing."

Luke's eyes glistened, and he held up a fist to Zach, who bumped it, then held up his fist to me. Our unspoken bond could never be broken. Not even in death. I was convinced wherever I went after death, they'd find a way to get to me. It was our unspoken promise to never go alone.

As the meeting adjourned, two more robed people each came to stand by us. William stayed next to Kilian. The candles were little wax stumps on the floor, the large candelabra dripping wax in little red pools next to the cross.

"Our deliberations have been made. Through the majority vote of council, you have all been found guilty for your involvement with The Family," Kilian said swiftly.

My heart sank as the room stirred around me.

"However, it is by my decision your final verdict is made. I was quite moved by your displays of affection earlier. I did not expect you to choose someone other than your family to live. To condemn your innocent brother to death is your ultimate fear, and yet you looked it in the face and accepted it because it was the right thing to do. I've met many members of The Family. I've been battling them for centuries. Many of them are cold and unfeeling. Their obsessions are forced into them at a young age, and they are loyal only to their queen. I see that is not the case here. Having seen the memories . . . I was quite moved by your resilience to evil and your love for your family."

He turned to Luke. "I do not know Her plans for you, but I do see what She saw in you. Someone valiant, innocent, and virtuous. The Family loves corruption. They need people like you, Luke. They chose you because you are good."

"And, Zach, you as well. Your loyalty to your brothers is what they ultimately want from you for them, but you would not give it freely. So, they take."

"Despite your failings, I've concluded that your connection to The Family is by blood only. This manipulation, along with the tragedy it would be to convict the rest of your family of your past crimes, has made it very clear for me. Your final verdict is not guilty."

My brothers and I shared a joyful smile. Relief washed over me.

"Does this mean you'll let us go?" Zach said, stirring in his chains.

"You are wanted by one of the only six queens left in existence. We will require your help to bring Her down. You and your family will be allowed to continue on with your normal lives on campus with . . . supervision. I must stress the importance of your involvement with The Family. In all of my years hunting them, I have never seen their queen show such interest in Her disciples. They want you for something. We can use this to draw them out of hiding."

"You want to use us as bait?" I chuckled, my body wobbly.

"You will be protected. You will not be allowed to go anywhere that members of The Legion cannot. The Family will hunt you whether we are involved or not. We can use this opportunity to bring down the last queen in the western hemisphere. It will not be easy, but I believe you all have great potential to be productive and valuable members of society once more."

We had babysitters. It was better than waiting around for The Family to find us and do God knows what with us. This was a major upgrade. The tightness in my chest loosened when Kilian spoke again.

"With that conclusion, we must start with the removal of your tattoo. We cannot risk you being identified in public."

At the sound of his words, the two members closest to Zach and Luke unchained their hands. Without another word, they pulled small silver blades from their robes and took it to my brothers' skin. Carving out the little black lines tattooed on their wrists. My brothers didn't fight it, but their cries of pain echoed up into the walls of the stone church.

The shock of what was happening hit me like a train. My brothers' screams of pain echoed in my ears. Dizziness hit me, and it took me a moment to realize what was happening. The ringing was back in my ears, and the room faded. I brought my hands up to my head, trying to get it to stop.

"Stop. Please. Stop," I said.

My own words felt far away. The room spun, and I no longer felt any evidence of reality. Pain was my only reality and an unreal feeling of terror took over my entire body. I couldn't find my way back. That Thing in my head was clawing its way out of my head and taking over.

"Aaron, you need to drink blood."

William's voice was my only companion in that dark place.

He pulled me back into the world, and he placed something in my hand. "Drink this."

"I-I can't. I don't need it."

"Oh, you don't? The look on your face is telling me otherwise." He raised a blood bag in front of me. The red liquid made my mouth water. "You're spiraling. You need to drink if you want to live."

His face was blurry and hard to see. I could feel other eyes on me, but I couldn't focus on anything but William.

"Drink. It."

I moved the plastic around in my hand and watched as the wave of blood crashed inside. A deep longing surfaced within. My eyes trained on the red color, and it took over my vision. I brought the bag to my lips and bit down. The first drop on my tongue sent my mind racing. I squeezed the bag harder and tried to get more. Blood was the only thing I could think about. It was everywhere all at once. It was everything. Time passed quickly, and I snatched the other bag from his hand without a second thought. Blood. Blood. Blood.

A carnal thirst ripped open my chest, and every drop filled an infinite void. I opened my eyes, but all I could see was deep red. My hands shook as I squeezed harder until the bag went limp in my hands. It dropped, and I stared at the smearing of red covering my hands. More. More. *More.* I needed more.

The fog lifted, and I could finally see where I was. I had been brought back to the empty room Kimberly and I had been in. William and another robed man watched me with worried expressions.

The longing I had for blood wasn't fading. My muscles moved on their own, and I flew out of the chair. The men grabbed my arms and held me down.

"I need more." The words escaped my lips, and I shut my eyes and glued my back to the chair. I wouldn't dare let my body move another inch.

"No, you don't. You don't need more. Listen to my voice."

William's voice was calm, and I tried to focus on that despite the strange numbness traveling up my body.

"Don't think about the blood. You have to focus on something else."

That was easier said than done. Panic was setting in, and I couldn't think of anything other than the fear in my head. I was losing control.

"Here." William grabbed my hands and dug his fingers into my skin.

The pain sent a shock wave through my body. The sudden jolt was enough to stop the numbness from traveling farther and for my mind to prioritize.

"There. It should be stopping. You're okay. This is your body. You're in control of it."

"This is my body. I'm in control." I repeated the phrases until I believed it.

"You feel that? That release? It's letting go of ya."

The numbness disappeared completely. The empty room came back into view. Somehow, everything seemed brighter. I looked at the chair next to me. Kimberly's absence felt like a gaping hole. But soon, I'd see her again. I couldn't wait to get out of that godforsaken church.

I wiped my mouth and tried to still my trembling body. "Thank you."

"You need to get yourself under control. Honestly, waiting this long to feed . . ."

Kneeling beside me, he sighed. "But I suppose I have to give you a pass, considering your idiot brothers turned you themselves."

"Yeah, they meant well. I know they did," I said, every muscle in my body aching and fatigued

"Must you always defend them?"

I shrugged. "I think they did all right with what they had."

William scoffed. "Well, remember this. When you drink, you can't think about the blood. The blood isn't for you. It's for that Thing you share a body with. It's dark and evil. So, you drink, but only to shove it back into the hole it came from. You got that?"

"Yeah." I cleared my throat, my body feeling like a truck had run me over.

"This is just the beginning. We have blood bags to help you, but you're going to need to feed more now for the rest of your life because you let it get this bad. Surely, you've learned your lesson, finally."

I nodded. My mind couldn't comprehend what he was saying. There would be consequences. That much I gathered.

"You will be weak for a few days. It's normal to be sleepy. Just rest. You'll need more blood, but we can help with that," William said.

He turned his attention to the robed girl with white hair in the hallway.

"They're causing a fuss again." She motioned back toward the hallway.

"Tell them he's fine." William growled. "Thanks to me."

William pressed his fingers into the bridge of his nose. "You guys are going to be a handful. I can already tell."

"I guess I'll be seeing you around a lot more."

He smiled as he placed his hands on his knees and hoisted himself up.

"Yeah, guess so. It's a shame, though. I really wanted to kill you."

I mustered up the strength for a laugh. "Sorry to disappoint you, psychopath."

"Good night, Aaron." William smirked, reaching to touch my forehead, and everything deteriorated again. But no pain followed.

Only rest.

Twenty-One

Excitement bubbled up in my chest as I walked up the sidewalk toward the frat house. The sun peeked through the trees in the most beautiful way. Rays of sunshine painted the bricks. Warmth hugged my entire body, and I danced up the steps with a decadent bouquet of wildflowers in my good hand. My left hand was still wrapped up and would stay immobile for a while. I'd already gotten used to doing a lot of my daily tasks one-handed. As the doorbell rang, I pressed my head against the thick wooden door, listening to the stirring inside. The muffled sounds of yelling and laughter.

Aaron answered the door, wearing his khaki shorts and soft cotton button-down, his socks impressively rolled and complementing his white Converse.

He greeted me with a warm smile and grabbed the bouquet from my hand. "Hey! Are you ready to go? Let's go."

"Wait. I wanted to say hi to the guys before we leave."

Little lines appeared on his forehead. "Eh, right now isn't a great time."

My curiosity instantly piqued. "Why? What's happening?"

I pushed the door open, and Aaron led me inside. Zach's loud yelling was identifiable and coming from the living room. Aaron's brothers were all gathered there with a scattering of other guys I couldn't identify. William was leaning over the couch, watching Zach with a bored expression. All The Legion members had the same clothing aesthetic. Plaid, beige, and trouser pants.

"Fuck you." Zach's words echoed in the empty frat house. His shoulders were hunched as he glared at William.

"Kimberly's here!" Aaron jumped in front of me.

"Hey, Kimberly!" Everyone greeted me with excitement and smiles. Even those in The Legion were starting to get used to seeing me around. It was going to take time to learn all their names and faces, but the summer break would be the perfect opportunity.

Presley wrapped me in a hug and spun me. We had quite a lot of bonding time in the car after I was let go and we needed to get out of town. We talked about strategy, future plans, and cried together. We were overjoyed when we got the call and we didn't actually have to become runaways.

"Oh, Kim, I was just explaining to William how excited I am that they will be living here with us." Zach forced a smile in my direction. A small gust of wind blew his hair, and he ran his hands through it to tame it.

A long faint scar replaced the spot where the tattoo used to be. Luke had the same one. A reminder for all of us of the lengths they would go to keep us safe.

All the windows in the living room were open, and the summer air was wafting throughout the room, and the smell of freshly mowed grass was everywhere.

Finals were over. Aaron and I had to ask for an extension due to medical reasons and ended up taking our tests a week late. I passed all my classes with flying colors. Thankfully, my classes for the last semester had been pretty easy. Aaron struggled a bit but passed with mostly Bs and Cs. Luke was proud.

Luke was beside him. Laughter escaped his lips. "Yeah, we are super excited, if you can't tell. How's your hand?"

"You know you don't have to ask me that every time you see me?" I joked.

"He can't help it. It's his dad instincts." Presley shot Luke a wicked grin as he balanced himself on the back of the armchair.

Luke grabbed Presley by his hood and pushed him off the chair. "Shut up."

"Where'd you get the flowers? Are you guys going on a date?" Zach nudged Aaron playfully.

"No, they're actually for someone else." I smiled. "Another girl, actually."

"Damn, Aaron, what's wrong with you?" Presley crawled on his stomach toward us. "Don't worry, Kim, I'll get you some flowers."

"Thanks, Pres. You're the best." A playful smile danced on my lips as I turned to Aaron.

"Do you guys ever shut up?" William rolled his eyes, turning his attention back to Zach.

"Don't worry, you'll get used to it." I smiled.

William winked at me as he leaned against the wall. I didn't completely trust him. But neither did Zach, and I knew I could trust Zach to keep an eye on him.

Zach and Luke filled me in as Aaron recovered, leaving out no details. Even ones they didn't need to tell me. I wouldn't be forgetting anytime soon how The Legion actually felt about the Calem brothers and how they had been found guilty. I was thankful for Kilian, though, and his ability to see a fraction of what I saw in them. It made me a little more willing to trust them, but I wasn't fully convinced.

"Where is everyone? I know it's summer break, but it's really quiet," I said, eyeing the empty staircase and kitchen.

"That's the problem." Zach scoffed.

"They relocated all other frat members and are moving in all of their people." I could tell Luke was choosing his words carefully.

By the look on Zach's face, I guessed it was to avoid another fight.

"Whoa, you can do that?" I said.

"We can do a lot of things. It will be a new chapter. One no one has ever heard of before." William smirked.

Aaron reached the door and quickly turned the handle. "We should probably get going."

"Wait! Kim, you're still coming over later, right? Luke was going to cook you one of his old favorite dishes," Zach said.

"Wow, thanks, Dad." Presley joked.

"Oh, I'm definitely coming." I dashed over to Aaron's side.

"See you guys later."

Their voices ran into each other in a loud roar as they said their goodbyes. Aaron quickly shut the door behind me.

"Oh, thank God. Sweet freedom!" Aaron jumped from the stairs and spun in the yard.

"You were eager to get out of there." I chuckled at the exasperated look on his face.

"They've been driving me crazy. They cannot agree on a single thing, and Zach and Luke are constantly arguing back and forth with them. I cannot go *anywhere* without them needing to know an exact location and for how long. I don't know how I'm going to last the summer, not to mention the next school year."

I imagined all the parties Aaron and his brothers loved that year. From the looks of the members of The Legion, I didn't peg them as the partying type.

"Oh, it will definitely be interesting."

Aaron sighed. "I'm sorry. I just had to get that all out."

"I thought we agreed you weren't allowed to say that word to me anymore." A small smile tugged at the corner of my lips.

"Shit. You're right. I'm so happy to be here with you and don't want to ruin it by talking about my brothers."

It felt good seeing Aaron back to his fun, happy self. I hadn't been allowed to see him for the first five days since he was so blood deprived.

The sorority house was coming into view. Giggling laughter escaped my lips as our feet peddled along the sidewalk. I turned to the bright bouquet of wildflowers Aaron had bunched in his hand. The smell was intoxicating.

Aaron's sunbathed face turned white in an instant. "Kim, I'm scared."

"Oh, hush, you'll be fine." I tried to stifle another laugh.

"You don't think it's a little early? She's probably still pissed. She only slapped you, like, a week ago . . . Wait or was it two weeks? Shit, I need a calendar for this stuff."

We stopped in front of the Sigma Sigma Xi sorority house. It was a beautiful tan color with white shutters that blended nicely with the greenery behind it. The entryway had long, thick pillars, and we hid out of view.

I leaned in. "No, this is perfect. She's had time to cool off but not so much that she can completely resent you yet."

"You are the smartest, most cunning woman I know. How do you do it? Tell me in extreme detail," Aaron said.

"Stop stalling."

"I know. I know. But does this apology even count if I don't remember saying what I said?" Aaron looked up at the house, the crease returning to his forehead.

"It will matter to her. Trust me." A smile danced on my lips, my eyes gazing at the muscles on his forearms. "I don't think I've ever seen you look so . . . dashing."

He squinted and tried to hide a slight blush in his cheeks. "This is a trap. I know it."

He took a deep breath before bouncing up the marble steps. I followed close behind and moved over to the edge of the porch. He rapped his knuckle on the large door, and my heart jumped in my ribs. Aaron flashed me a worried expression before the door opened.

"Hey, is, uh, Chelsea here?"

I couldn't see anything on the inside as I hid my body next to the wall.

"Yeah, hold on. I'll get her for you," some girl said.

I tried to keep a brave face for Aaron, but even I was a little worried. Butterflies fluttered around in my stomach, making it harder to wait. The sound of heels clicking against hardwood echoed in a rhythm.

"What are you doing here? Come to yell at me again?"

Aaron cleared his throat. "Uh, actually I wanted to bring you these and apologize."

He flung the flowers a little too swiftly, causing some petals to fall to the ground.

"I don't need an apology. I'm a big girl. I can handle it."

"Of course you can, and if you never want to talk to me again, I understand. Just know, who I was on that day . . . It's not reflective of who I am. I never wanted to hurt you. I'm sorry for all of it. I really am."

A long pause followed by the swing of the door. "Goodbye, Aaron."

He turned toward me, letting out a long breath. "Well, that could have gone better."

I smiled softly and patted him on the shoulder.

"No, you tried. You apologized. That's all that matters. Now, it's my turn." I reluctantly grabbed the bouquet from his hand and walked toward the door. It was a lot more fun being the one who was hiding.

I knocked on the door, only this time, seconds passed before a very distraught Chelsea opened the door. Her hair was wild and out of place, but her makeup was well-kept.

"Great. Have you come to plead for Aaron. Because it's not going to work."

"Actually, I just wanted to see how you were doing. I, uh . . . hated how things went, and I just wanted to check on you."

She leaned against the door, watching me. "Why? I'm the one that slapped you in the face."

"Well . . . just . . ."

My chest tightened. I glanced over at Aaron who motioned for me to continue. "I'm not good at this. So, I'm just going to say what I'm thinking."

"This should be good."

"I know we haven't gotten along very well, and we had a misunderstanding, which was my fault. But I'd love to hang out with you sometime because I feel like we have a lot in common."

Her face was unmoving, and her dark circles had overtaken her prettier features.

"I know I'm awkward. I don't have a lot of experience in this type of thing." I held out the bouquet to her. "Whatever you choose. We are good in my book."

She sighed as she eyed the flowers in front of her. "Yeah, this is kinda weird." Her expression softened, and she grabbed the bouquet from my hands. "But that's okay. Thank you."

For the first time, she smiled at me. Really smiled at me with her sparkling white teeth. It looked good on her despite it being a rarity.

"You're welcome." I flashed her a smile before turning back to Aaron, who was hiding behind the pillar.

"Kimberly. You live in Rogers, right?"

"Yeah, I'll be here through the summer."

"Okay. I'll come by, and we can go shopping or whatever. I've noticed you have pretty good taste."

"Uh, yeah, that would be awesome."

She turned to leave but stopped. "And no, you can't come, Aaron."

"I know. I know." Aaron winked at me.

"Bye, Chelsea." I waved, and Aaron and I returned to the pavement.

Relief washed over me as I let out a breath into the wind. The weight of guilt was lifted.

"Looks like someone made a new friend." Aaron nudged me, causing me to stumble off the sidewalk.

"Yeah, it's kind of cool. I've never outright asked someone that before."

"If only I had similar good news. I get it, though. I wouldn't forgive me either." He kicked a tiny pebble, and it skidded between fault lines.

"She'll forgive you. She just needs time."

The smell of freshly cut grass rode the breeze. Every gust gave way to that sweet scent again.

"So, what do you want to do with the rest of our day? Frolic through the mountains, read a book, talk about how utterly doomed this life is?"

"Actually, I kind of want to stay in. Do you have any good movies?"

"Ha! Please, do I have any good movies? I'm the smartest of my brothers and have much better taste when it comes to the cinema." His words curled together in a melody.

"Yeah, I believe that."

My phone buzzed in my pocket, and I let it go to voicemail. It was Chris again, but this time, I had guessed he was just calling to check in. I had called him and cleared the air, leaving out all vampire-related details. He wasn't a perfect friend, but he had been there for me growing up. Letting all that go would be a mistake. After nearly dying, I realized how life was too short to hold a grudge. Our friendship changed. That didn't mean it had to end. The distance between us was a blessing. I didn't want to risk bringing anyone else into the Calem brothers' wake.

It was too late for me, but I wasn't complaining. Aaron's smile warmed me again. It was even brighter than the sun. The weight of darkness was gone . . . mostly.

"You seem better. How are you feeling?" I said.

My words stopped his fluent walking.

"Yeah, I'm dealing. Slowly. But I've been talking to my brothers about it. I think I'm going to get a few more blood bags from William, then they are going to help teach me how to control it so I can feed on my own. You know they have the mind-control thing that should help."

"That's a relief. We can't have you turn Mr. Hyde again. That was . . ."

"Scary. I think I'm always going to struggle with it a bit, but I've got all the time in the world to figure out my inner torment." His grin returned to his face.

"Yeah, you're already a little too much." I smiled. "But seriously, I'm proud of you for putting in the work. I honestly can't imagine how hard that would be."

"You're giving me too much credit." Aaron chuckled and wrapped his arm around me as we carried on. "Come on, I want to show you something. I hope there are no vampire hunters following me!"

I put my hand on Aaron's mouth. "What are you doing?"

"I just don't want any of those guys following us." His teeth gleamed in the sunlight.

"Where are you taking me?" I said as he steered us off the sidewalk.

"To show you all the mysterious wonders of BFU."

We walked through the grass in the parking lot behind building C, the same one with the clock tower and the high arched windows.

"Isn't this where they keep all the garbage bins?" I joked.

Aaron's walking turned into a skip. "That's what everyone wants you to think but really . . . "

We rounded the corner to some trees that cleared a way onto a path, a little sign hung loosely that read, "Twisted Oak Point."

"What is this?"

"Well, I thought to myself, what's a unique location I can bring the girl who has lived here her whole life, and after rigorous searching . . . and, by that, I mean asking a few random people on the street, they told me about this old trail."

"Wow." I stood in shock for a moment. "Yeah, let's go."

My sundress and strappy sandals didn't stop me. I ran up to him, and we locked arms.

He chuckled. "Don't worry. It's short."

We'd only grown closer since our near-death experience, and I found myself relishing every minute together. Time was precious. "I may have scoped it out beforehand. I had to see if it was lame," Aaron said.

"Why did you go through all this trouble?" I looked up at him, squinting into the bright sun.

He patted my hand as I wrapped it around his forearm. "Because. Because it makes you smile. You get this look on your face . . . I love it."

I couldn't take my attention off the feeling of his hand on mine. His touch was warm and sincere, but most of all, it felt natural. We reached the clearing into a wide-open space. A little pond was set ablaze by the setting sun. An old bench was perched right on the water's edge. The golden sunshine hit the water at just the right angle, and the peach sky reflected in the soft ripples.

"Well, what do you think?" Aaron was watching my face.

"It's so beautiful—come on." I pulled him to the bench. Its bright, tattered blue finish caught my eye instantly.

It was the perfect picture. The perfect gift. I wanted to drink it all in. Aaron's expression melted into one of peace, and we sat close together. My mind wandered back to our meeting place in the campus cafeteria. If anything hadn't lined up perfectly, I wouldn't have been sitting there. I would probably be in my dorm alone.

My chest tightened at the thought. I turned my attention to Aaron, and the light tinged every feature on his face an ambient pink. Even the pale-blond streaks in his hair were tinted like a glow from a fire. He turned to me without any words. His winning smile took over his lips.

"Aaron, what are you doing?" I chuckled. "You keep looking at me like that."

He let out a quick breath and averted his eyes. "What are you talking about? I'm not doing anything."

"That look . . ." I said, with a wide smile.

"Well, you're nice to look at, Burns. What can I say?" He wiggled his brows.

Nervous laughter escaped my lips, and I kept my gaze out on the water. I pulled my hair behind my ear as heat rose to my cheeks.

"You're blushing again." He grinned.

"Well, so are you."

He tilted his head back and laughed. "So what if I am? I think it's you that's giving me the eyes. It's like you're secretly in love with me or something."

If I wasn't blushing before, I was right then. My breath hitched in my chest, and my heart beat faster.

"So what if I was . . . hypothetically. Would that be bad?"

There were a handful of reasons why it would be bad. The most glaring one was the fact that Aaron was immortal and I was not. But in the crux of the prettiest sunset I'd ever seen, I didn't care. There was no way to deny the way I felt when he was near me.

Aaron looked shocked by my seriousness and was instantly nervous. "Uh, no. I'd be really happy if that were true. Even though, hypothetically speaking, it might be a bad idea. Probably not the smartest thing we could do. But I might say that . . . I felt the same way."

I smiled. "All hypothetically, of course."

He smirked. "Totally."

His attention was on my lips. The air buzzed between us with electricity. Fireflies were starting their night. Slowly floating around us. He leaned forward, and my heart responded. After a long pause, he reached over, grabbed my bandaged wrist, and softly traced his fingers over mine.

He wouldn't forgive himself easily, if he ever would.

"We have time," I said, leaning my head back and letting what was left of the sun warm me.

But we did have time. I didn't need to rush it. I could let it burn. Grow. Enjoy the moment and not think too far ahead. Every minute that passed, my heart grew softer and more used to the idea of him being around for good.

"Oh, I've got all the time in the world." Aaron was all smiles again. Our expressions were a perfect reflection. The longer I stared into his eyes, the more it hurt to turn away.

Aaron stretched his arms and let out a big yawn. "Gosh, I'm just so tired. Must be leftover trauma."

He placed his arm around my shoulder, and my heart leaped in my chest.

"Yeah, yeah." I scooted closer and rested my head on his cotton shirt.

Every muscle in my body relaxed. Our hands touched in the amber light, and the soft echo of Aaron's heartbeat reverberated in his chest. I knew there was one truth I would always hold on to.

Everything was better when we were together.

Epilogue

THE
FAMILY-
THE
GUARD

"California? What the fuck are they doin' there?" Akira said, sitting on a table from the French Revolution.

His thick-soled boots scuffed the finish.

The queen's Guards were sitting in the library, every wall filled with towering book shelves that went clear to the ceilings. The shelves were lined with century-old reads with tattered spines and old parchment. A large lavish rug brought warmth to the velvet couches. The soft glow of the fireplace lit up their brief reunion.

"They're being protected by The Legion." Sirius walked the length of the room, his hands shoved into his high-waisted trousers, his warm skin contrasting the white sweater that covered his neck. Dark-brown locks covered his ears. The gears turned in his head like a well-oiled machine. As third in command, his smarts kept the Guard in line.

"Legion? Protect? Who the fuck are they going to protect? They're weak bastards." Akira pulled his hands through his jet-black hair, his arms covered in tattoos. His style always changed, but he'd found a love in tech wear. He loved the overlapping fabric jackets and the large over-the-top baggy shorts he could tuck into his boots.

"You're awfully quiet." Sirius looked over at Ezra, who still had his nose in a book.

"Just thinking," Ezra said, wearing a fitted black blazer and a white undershirt. He preferred to wear something less fussy.

Akira's eyes bore a hole into Ezra's neck. "I'm still trying to figure out how they got out in the first place? Eh, Ezra?"

Ezra set his jaw and didn't let an ounce of emotion show on his face. He knew Akira suspected him. If he ever had a minuscule piece of evidence, he'd turn him in for treason. Akira, though a bit of a wild card, was the second in command for a reason. He was fiercely loyal to the queen.

"She needs to know right away." Ezra placed his book down on the end table Akira had been sitting on.

"Then, let's go." Akira jumped up. They knew their assignment at once.

They followed Ezra down the hall. One on either shoulder. The hallway was lined in an ornate flower rug that moved when they walked on the dusty hardwood floors. The walls were laid in gray-and-red brick, framed by a warm wooden trim. The Family's young members stopped as they passed by, averting their eyes and bowing their heads. They clung to the edge of the walls to leave more than enough room for the Guard to walk. At the end of the hallway was a long winding staircase that disappeared into the ceiling above. They ascended, heads low and shoulders back. Every muscle held a level of discipline and reverence.

They stayed silent. Each of their minds in another place entirely. Until they reached Her room.

They opened the door to Her chamber, a place only they were allowed to go freely. It was crafted to Her liking and had all the furnishings She could want, including a white canopy bed and a handcrafted vanity She would use to comb Her hair. Velvet couches and soft rugs from all over the world. She stood staring out the window to central Manhattan. Long black curtains blocked the sun's rays from Her skin. Her long white hair stretched down to Her waist, and Her porcelain skin contrasted with the red bricks that stretched to the ceiling. A thin veil grazed Her translucent cheeks, shielding Her eyes.

She turned to greet them, Her satin white dress dragging across the rich hardwood floors. Her fingers danced on the top of the sleeping grand piano in the corner. There was always an occasion of great importance when all three guards were gathered in the same place.

They stood in front of Her and took a knee. One hand reached for the floor while the other hid behind their backs. The Guard always waited. Always willing.

Ezra, the leader of the Guard, spoke. "We've found them. The Calem brothers."

The other Guard members dared not speak a word. Ezra was the only one freely allowed to speak with Her. He was Her ultimate protector. Not just Her physical body but of Her will.

"I knew you would." She smiled beneath Her veil. "It's far, but I can go—"

Her voice pierced them. "You will not. Akira will."

"May I ask why?" Ezra swallowed, his mouth suddenly dry. "Zach and Luke were my responsibility. Having been the one to recruit them and train them, I believe I could bring them home."

"I need you with me. The time is coming where the old Guard will pass away, and the new shall take its place." She walked in closer and ran Her fingers through Ezra's brown hair, noting the bits of silver. "Our time together wanes, and I need to make sure you'll be here to lead them."

For the last hundred years, the Guard had known their time was ending. Her prophecy stated the change and that two Gemini twins would secure Her Guard, with the addition of two more.

"I understand. I'm happy to stand by your side." Ezra closed his eyes, savoring the feeling of Her skin on his.

She smiled, Her lips perfectly pink. "Akira, are you able to complete the task? I want them all brought back here. Alive."

"Yes. I'll see that it's done." Akira pulled his arm tightly to his chest and nodded.

Sirius lifted his head, signaling he needed to speak.

"Yes, dear Sirius?" She walked forward and kneeled before him before placing a delicate hand against his cheek. His body shivered in Her proximity.

"They are being protected by The Legion. I saw it with my own eyes." The smile left Her delicate lips. A silent rage burned. "I see. That will make your journey more treacherous, Akira. But I have full confidence in your abilities. Please bring members of your squadron with you."

"Of course." Akira kept the excitement bubbling in his chest at bay. He loved a challenge.

Sirius raised his head again, waiting for his permission to speak. "There is one more thing. The Calems appear to be with a girl. Possibly a girlfriend to the younger brother, Aaron."

A long silence stilled as She paced. Sirius tried to avert his eyes from Her face, but he couldn't. He admired every inch of Her skin. Every strand of hair that flowed from Her head was a sight to behold.

She stopped and removed the veil from Her eyes to face Her Guard. Jealousy laced in beat with her cold heart. Her Guard stood at attention, the ecstasy of seeing Her washed over them.

A sinister smile crept on her lips, and Her venomous voice filled the room. "Kill her."

The series continues...

THIS BLOOD THAT BURNS US

BUY NOW

Scan Me!

I didn't know how many other universes there were out there, but if there were more, I'd bet I tried to make her mine every time.

-Aaron Calem

READ ON FOR A SNEAK

PEEK AT THE NEXT BOOK

IN THE SERIES.

One

AARON

I'd never been a big believer in destiny. I hated movies where the hero was doomed by the fates above, but meeting Kimberly Burns felt a lot like fate. The good kind, where there was one person in the world you were meant to meet, and everything had to go right for your paths to cross at the perfect time. I wished I could change the circumstances of that encounter, but I was thankful, nonetheless.

The true significance of meeting her may have forever been out of my reach, but as I stood in the middle of our fraternity mixer, I wondered if I'd still be right here if I hadn't. Something in the pit of my stomach told me life would be shitty if I hadn't met her. I probably wouldn't be slightly tipsy at a college party enjoying my Saturday night like a normal college student. Maybe The Legion would have killed us in that church . . . or maybe The Family would have already found us. I'd never know. But as I caught sight of her across the backyard, all the fears I'd had about the future disappeared. She saw me and smiled with rosy cheeks, and my heart kicked my ribs. She was magic like that.

The mist on the mountain sent a chill into the air. The dusk was upon us, and the light warmed her features. The scattering of trees around, painted in hues of orange and yellow, gave way to the most beautiful fall I'd ever seen. Brooklyn couldn't hold a candle to the beauty here. I could see why she never wanted to leave. Trading these views and these smells for concrete slabs and high-rises seemed criminal.

"Come on, let's go over there!" Presley said while he dragged me in the opposite direction, past the steaming pool. I groaned my reply, cursing the fact that our hands were zip tied. The sun disappeared over the horizon, casting an orange glow on the pine trees that surrounded the backyard of the OBA frat house.

We passed our fellow fraternity members, mostly comprised of The Legion's plants that rushed at the start of the fall semester. They, too, were subjected to our current mixer with the Sigma Sigma Xi sorority. Which required each guy to be zip tied to a girl until they both drank a fifth of alcohol, but Presley thought it would be hilarious to have me linked with him all night. It was annoying, but I was a little thankful. The one girl I wanted to be linked with wasn't part of the sorority, but she was here. If only I could get to her.

We passed William scowling in our direction. He was linked to a blonde talking his ear off, and I guessed it would be a matter of minutes before he compelled her to think they'd met their requirements. Drinking parties were prohibited at William's request at the first of the semester. I suspected it had something to do with his disdain for drunk college students' untidiness and messing with his precious plants he'd filled the house with. But since we were required to participate in school events and mingle with sororities, he didn't always get what he wanted. Presley had put in extra effort to pull some strings with the sorority president to ensure the theme.

The Legion's quiet occupation of our frat house over the summer was part of a bigger plan. OBA was always a smaller fraternity and paled in comparison to some of the larger ones on campus. With more than half of our members graduating last year, it made The Legion's invasion easier. Especially with Kilian's connections in the big wide world of academia. He wasn't very forthcoming with details, but I'd heard he knew a guy who knew a guy that could ensure any dealings in the fraternity were met without trouble. It also helped that the elected president of the fraternity transferred schools, leaving his spot open for a revote. Luke was able to get on the executive board, considering on his fake transcript he was technically a junior, and he was elected president. He took his job very seriously.

I'd finally understood what William meant about a new chapter. OBA would never be the same after their occupation, at least not the chapter in Blackheart.

Presley brought us to a group of girls who had been unlinked, and I couldn't help but stare off into space while remembering the first of the summer.

It was the day right after the night in the church. Due to the blood loss, I'd spent most of my time in bed sleeping, but I never got any good rest since I was constantly waking up because of nightmares. I'd desperately wanted to see Kimberly, but it wasn't safe for her to be around me until I'd gotten my thirst under control. It was torture.

"You want us to stay in Blackheart?" Zach had said.

I'd rubbed my tired eyes and tried to keep myself upright while we'd had a meeting with Kilian in the study. The tension in the air could be cut with a knife. Luke's foot tapped relentlessly as Kilian sat at his desk across from us, and we were forced on the velvet couches. I felt like I was back in grade school being scolded by the principal.

"I mean. I don't wanna leave, but . . . if The Family knows where we are, shouldn't we get out of here?" Presley said.

My heart sank. I couldn't leave Blackheart. I couldn't leave her.

"They don't know where we are. We'll know when they do. Trust me," Luke said, leaning back and pushing his hands through his hair.

"You really trust that Ezra won't tell them where ya are by now?" William said as he paced behind Kilian. He was always with Kilian, clinging to him like a lap dog.

"He wouldn't." Luke shook his head. "He could have easily prevented us from leaving, and he didn't."

Kilian spoke with strength in his voice. "Running puts you more at risk. They have the numbers. If they want to find you, there's nowhere on this Earth you can run."

"So, we're fucked." Zach groaned. "You want to wait here for them to find us?"

"No. We can't outrun them. But we can outsmart them. They will come for you, and we need to be ready when they do. They will not march armies and drag you. The Family must adhere to human laws just like us."

"I don't get it. If they're ultra powerful, can't they just overthrow the government or something? Take control of stuff. Why would they need to worry about laws?" Presley squirmed next to me.

"The Family has no interest in that. Each coven is different, and the only thing they care about is their queen. Some live quite peacefully within their communities, only killing a few locals a couple times a year. They may outnumber us . . . but they've learned from experience that creating unlimited amounts of members only brings them grief. The more bodies vying for Her attention, the more they fight. It always ends in bloodshed and the annihilation of Her coven."

"What's your plan?" Luke squared his shoulders and furrowed his brows.

"There will be three phases. One, the set up. Two, integration. Three, defense. You will stay here, and we will integrate into the fraternity. Here, you are surrounded by witnesses, and you will be safe to continue your education. Next, you will learn our ways while we teach you what we know. We will put all our resources into defending you . . . I can make some calls and get some people to help."

"Why?" It was the only question I had. The most important one. Why would they go through the trouble? What angle was he playing? There had to be more he wasn't saying.

"Because, figuring out why you are so important to them is the most vital thing. For years, we've been waiting for a way to bring down the North American coven, and it looks like you might be the key."

I didn't much like being a key. Something about being referred to as an object didn't inspire confidence. What use was a key once the door was unlocked?

There were other issues. A major crux of his plan hinged on me and my brothers adhering to The Legion's rules and learning how to blend into the world. But over the summer, I'd found it mostly meant they wanted us to listen as they bossed us around. I was thankful for their help, but the events in the church were still fresh in my mind. Trusting them had been out of the question, but my older brothers were oddly on board with Kilian's half-baked plan, and I hadn't complained because there was one beautiful redhead I hadn't been ready to say goodbye to.

"Aaron." Presley waved his hand in my face. "Uh, dude. She asked you a question." Presley motioned to the girls in front of me.

"Uh . . ."

"She wanted to know what your major is." Presley took a sip of our drink as he watched me squirm.

"General Studies." When we arrived at OBU, I stared at the list of majors for over an hour and had to choose something. So, I picked the only one that meant I didn't have to actually make a decision. There was still time to change it, but my career choice was the last thing I was concerned with.

Presley finally got the hint after I tugged on his wrist for five minutes, and we retreated into the crowd.

"Are you okay? You sure you don't need to . . . you know . . . feed?"

He said it almost like a joke, but I knew he was being serious. I had to feed more often, and it wasn't something I wanted to discuss with him in the middle of the party.

"I'm fine."

"You're doing that head-in-the-clouds thing again. I wanted to make sure." He pulled up his hands which pulled up my left arm, and I sighed. "I know what you want."

He handed me our bottle. I took a drink, wanting to get out of my predicament with Presley as soon as possible.

He turned toward the house where two fraternity members were mingling by the sliding glass doors. There weren't many humans left in our frat, but there were a few, including tank-top guy, who I'd discovered was named Jackson. He'd been in our pledge class in the spring, and I was surprised he'd survived his time on academic probation.

"You see that? He's eyeing your girl." Presley wiggled his eyebrows at me, and I tried to hide the heat that built in my chest when he said it.

"She's not my girl," I said, watching him study *my* girl. And he was way too drunk to be looking at her like that. I could see why, though. She wore her BFU sweater paired with these cool plaid pants that hugged her hips and legs. She made everything look good.

I tried not to let it bother me. If she wanted someone, she should pursue them. I wasn't her best option. Why shouldn't she be with a normal guy?

There might still be a way for her to have some sense of normalcy, but not with Jackson. Anyone but him.

Kimberly sat with Chelsea, who had been unlinked, across the yard. Earlier, she bribed Zach to drink some of their bottle when her date wasn't looking because she couldn't stand him.

I couldn't hear what the girls were saying over the music, but it seemed like Kim was trying to force some water on her.

"Why not? All you gotta do is ask."

He said it as if that were simple. As if I hadn't hurt her more than once. As if I wasn't immortal. As if it were truly that easy.

I opened my mouth to speak, but Presley dragged me across the yard before I could say anything. I wanted to snap that little zip tie and be rid of him for the night, but he hauled me to the one place I wanted to go.

"Kim, Aaron isn't feeling good." Presley slung me toward her, and I steadied myself with my hand on her shoulder.

She stared up at me with her brows drawn together while clinging to my shirt. "What's wrong?"

"His stomach hurts," Presley said before chugging more of our fifth.

Her nose crinkled, and her eyes narrowed. "Oh, really? And when did this start?"

"Couple of minutes ago, actually."

"Well, Aaron's a big boy. Maybe he just needs some Tums." Chelsea snickered, and I flashed her a fake smile. Despite her friendship with Kim, she still hated my guts, and I didn't blame her.

"I don't know. He looks pretty sick to me. I think we better take him inside the house before he starts puking everywhere."

"I'll take him," Kimberly said, grabbing my hand and sending a shiver down my spine, which felt weird while being tethered to my little brother. She let Chelsea know she'd be right back, and I shot Chelsea a weak smile, and she replied with a middle finger. Okay, maybe she had warmed to me a little.

She guided us through the crowd of people on the lawn and through the open glass door where Jackson got an unobstructed view. I finally understood Presley's plan all along, and I couldn't help but smile at the pinched expression on Jackson's face. She led us to the kitchen where Zach and Luke were still cuffed to their dates, making them laugh so loud it echoed through the house.

"My party people!" Presley said, pulling our hands up in the air.

"Hey, losers." Zach smirked, and he waved his free hand while his other pinned his blushing date to the wall. He was tipsy enough to be having a good time.

Luke was playing cards with his date, and from the wide smile he gave her, I'd have guessed he was losing. He loved a challenge. When he saw us, he chuckled. "Who told you guys you could link together?"

"Come on, Aaron's my buddy. My pal. What would a night of drinking be without him?" Presley passed me our bottle, and I swallowed a few gulps.

"What about that *thing* tomorrow?" Luke said, furrowing his brow.

And I pressed my finger to my lips.

Kimberly grabbed my forearm and whispered into my ear, "You didn't tell them?"

"We . . . have not mentioned it. Tomorrow is all about you," I said, and she squeezed my arm. "Don't worry about it."

A worry line settled between her brows before disappearing with the most adorable nose scrunch. She stayed pressed to me, her fingers grazing my arm, and I inhaled her rose perfume. After our near-death experience in the church, her hand found mine more often when we were walking on the street. She'd rub my back when I got too stressed out and clung to my arm when we watched scary movies. It was easy. Simple. Like breathing. Back when I used to have to do that.

Though we hadn't mentioned anything more since that yellow bench in the park, something about our relationship had changed. I'd be lying if I said I wasn't happy about it.

"Assholes," William said as he burst into the kitchen. "Pool. Now."

"Can't, officer, I'm a little tied up." Zach lifted his hand still zip tied to his date.

"Yeah, my hands are tied." Luke chuckled.

"Fine. You three"—William pointed to Kim, Presley, and me—"pool. Now."

We followed him, and I led Kimberly with my free hand. As we opened the door to the backyard, foam filled the yard and pool.

"What the hell is that?" William said as he flicked the foam that had settled on his sleeve.

"Uh, looks like a foam machine, sir." Presley smiled.

"No shit. Which one of you stole the money for that?"

"We didn't!" Presley and I protested.

"The sorority girls rented it," Kimberly said. "They wanted to surprise the boys."

"Jeez, we get in trouble for stealing one time, and now you think we're criminals." Presley folded his arms in a pout.

At the beginning of the semester, Kimberly had been a little short on money for her textbooks. We talked about it briefly, not expecting my older brothers to show up the next day with five hundred dollars cash for her. She'd tried to refuse it, but Luke convinced her to keep it, stating he would figure out what book it was and buy it if he needed to.

Gradually, over the summer, their guard came down. They'd started to show little parts of themselves I'd never seen before. Suddenly, the small crimes William accused them of seemed much easier to understand.

"You are criminals," William growled before heading around the growing pile of foam in front of us.

Presley bounced up and down, and I knew it was only a matter of time before he pulled me headfirst into the foam.

Things were changing, and nothing with The Legion was easy, but Zach and Luke were determined this was where we needed to be. And wherever Kimberly was, I wanted to be there too. But like the weight of Presley on my arm, we were chained to The Legion, and I wondered how long I could stand the pain in my hand as we pulled each other in the opposite direction.

One thing I knew was that if they hated us today, then tomorrow they really wouldn't be happy.

Acknowledgements

Thank you to my mom for being supportive of my publishing journey.

Thank you to my sister for listening to all of my publishing adventure stories.

Thank you to my critique partners. I'm confident the book would have never made it to publishing without you.

A big thank you to my editors and my cover artist for making my dream become a reality.

Follow the Author

Links to my newsletter so you can stay up to date.

Follow me on Amazon so you never miss a release.

Facebook Reader Group

Instagram

Printed in Great Britain
by Amazon